Grasmere, 2011

Selected Papers from the Wordsworth Summer Conference

Grasmere, 2011

SELECTED PAPERS FROM
THE WORDSWORTH SUMMER CONFERENCE

COMPILED BY RICHARD GRAVIL ON BEHALF OF
THE WORDSWORTH CONFERENCE FOUNDATION

𝓗𝓔𝓑 ☼ Humanities-Ebooks, LLP

Cover photograph: Skiddaw from the Solway Coast © Florian Bissig

First published by *Humanities-Ebooks, LLP,*
Tirril Hall, Tirril, Penrith CA10 2JE

The Pdf Ebook is available to individual purchasers exclusively from
http://www.humanities-ebooks.co.uk
and to libraries from EBSCO, Ebrary and MyiLibrary.

The paperback is available exclusively from Lulu.com

ISBN 978-1-84760-191-9 Pdf
ISBN 978-1-84760-192-6 Paperback
ISBN 978-1-84760-193-3 Kindle

Contents

Foreword

This selection of lectures and papers is the fourth such to be published on behalf of the Wordsworth Conference Foundation. All four books are available in pdf form to libraries from MyiLibrary.com, and from EBSCO, and to individuals from Humanities-Ebooks, and from Lulu.com in paperback. This collection will also be available from Amazon in Kindle format, though of course without the same elegant layout that is possible in Pdf and print form, and with endnotes rather than footnotes.

Richard Gravil, *1 December 2011*

Ann Wroe

The Necessity of Atheism: 200 years young[1]

Shelley's *Necessity of Atheism* was the document that got him expelled from Oxford in March 2011. Its genesis was a peculiar mixture of public and private grievance, youthful bravado and a sincere search for truth. Shelley challenged his readers to prove to him that God existed. Their intemperate reaction did much to set him on his path towards becoming, half voluntarily, a social outcast. Yet his atheism is complex, and in the end very different from what the word seems to imply.

In Oxford 200 years ago, towards the end of February, a tall, long-haired, slightly stooped young man came out of University College with a package under his arm. The university authorities were already wary of this 18-year-old first-year student: expensively but untidily dressed, with a proud, wild look, and known as a troublemaker. Percy Bysshe Shelley was the son of a Sussex landowner, but was already driving his father to distraction with his uncontrollable ways; he had been a star pupil at Eton, but had already made several attempts on the place with electrical machines and gunpowder.

He crossed the High, passed the Bodleian, and strode towards Munday & Slatter's printing shop and stationer's on the corner of the Broad. Mr Munday had already published Shelley's violently Republican-flavoured *Posthumous Fragments of Margaret Nicholson*, at his own expense, and in fact Shelley's father had asked him par-ticularly to indulge his son in his 'printing freaks'.[2] By that, poor Timothy Shelley probably meant nothing more ruffling to morality than the eye-rolling, bosom-heaving Gothic romances his son had

---

1 A slightly shorter version of this paper was delivered as the first annual Shelley lecture to the British Humanist Association in March 2011.
2 P. B. Shelley, *The Letters of Percy Bysshe Shelley*, ed. by Frederick. L. Jones, 2 vols (Oxford: Oxford University Press, 1964), I, 26n.

already produced, such as *Zastrozzi* and *St Irvyne*. But Mr Munday's tolerance was about to be much more severely tested. Once inside the door, Shelley put down his package, took out a handful of slim booklets, and scattered them inside the window and over the counter. Thus was published *The Necessity of Atheism*.

This clarion call was not Shelley's unaided work. He was helped with it—at least as far as formulating his thoughts went—by his best friend at University College, Thomas Jefferson Hogg, and together they had been feverishly plotting it by letter all through the Christmas holidays. The usual festivities of the season went on downstairs while, upstairs, blaspheming pens raced swiftly across the paper. At this remove it is impossible to say for certain who was responsible for what; but Shelley seized charge of the final form of it, the printing and the distribution. And the title, for a start, bears his strong mark upon it. He had named his 'little tract', as he fondly called it in the opening Advertisement,[1] to cause maximum offence. Atheism was necessary: necessary for progress, necessary for man's liberation. And it was not only necessary, but fated, inevitable, as mankind and history surged towards enlightenment, if we are to give the word 'Necessity' the full force it carried for Shelley in 1811. Necessity swept God out of the universe; they could not exist together. And Shelley was harnessing this force for his own purposes, dispersing his explosive material in a way that presaged his 'Ode to the West Wind', written eight years later:

> Scatter, as from an unextinguished hearth
> Ashes and sparks, my words among mankind! (ll.66–67)[2]

Indeed his words became ashes very quickly. In about 20 minutes, in fact. A fellow of New College spotted the booklets, had no need to read them, for the title was enough, had the whole lot swept up, and ordered Mr Slatter and Mr Munday to burn them, in his presence, in

---

1   P. B. Shelley, *The Prose Works of Percy Bysshe Shelley*, ed. E. B. Murray, 1 vol. (Oxford: Oxford University Press, 1993), 2.

2   P. B. Shelley, *Percy Bysshe Shelley: The Major Works*, ed. Zachary Leader and Michael O'Neill, Oxford World Classics Series (Oxford: Oxford University Press, 2003), 414.

the back kitchen.[1]

The repercussions were dire. Shelley and Hogg were hauled separately before the Master and Fellows of University College, were plied with questions about the pamphlet, and refused to answer. And so they were expelled. Shelley had been at Oxford for less than two terms. He despised the place for many reasons, not least its narrow-mindedness and pompous religiosity; it was 'insipid' and 'uncongenial', he moaned to William Godwin the next January, and, in short, 'I could not descend to common life' (*Letters*, I, 228). His very expulsion was proof of its intellectual barrenness, since, as he indignantly told his fuming father, 'no argument was publickly brought forward to disprove our reasoning' (56). But all the same, he was shattered to be thrown out. It marked the beginning of his break with his father, and his life as a social outcast. You could argue that both the break and the pariah status were bound to come eventually, as a result of Shelley's refusal to conform with contemporary values on more or less every count. But his sudden ejection from Oxford certainly did not help.

Suppose you had been in Munday & Slatter's on that day, with your 21st century sensibilities unchanged. Suppose you had bought a copy (it cost sixpence, fairly steep for an octavo of 14 pages, some of them blank), or suppose you had had it thrust urgently into your hand by Shelley, for this *was* urgent work, to him. What would you have thought of it? The answer, I think, is that no reasonable person today would be in the least offended by it. You might say it was too rational; you might find its style achingly pompous, especially for an 18-year-old. (Shelley did tell Godwin, though, when he sent him a copy, that he had 'compressed' it 'from much prolix reasoning', and we should be grateful indeed for that.[2]) And you might, just possibly, think it was a prank.

Shelley at the time was a wicked prankster, though not many knew it, and Shelley scholars themselves did not know the extent of it until a batch of unknown letters resurfaced in an attic in 2005. He had

---

1   *Letters*, I, 52n; *The Prose Works*, 320.
2   B. C. Barker-Benfield, 'A Spoof Letter to William Godwin', *Bodleian Library Record*, vol. XXI no. 1 (for April 2008, publ. 2009), 112–115.

started to make a habit of writing atheistical letters to clergy and other gentle, unsuspecting types for a while, under false names, pretending to be a Christian in confusion. Ralph Wedgwood, for example, a cousin of the famous potter Josiah, had been the butt of such missives all through December and January, both from Shelley and 'my learned friend Mr Hogg'[1]. Shelley, while thanking him effusively for his 'well written' and 'elucidating' letters, delighted to tangle him in unanswerable argument, and on the 15th he lowered the boom with typical Shelleyan scorn: 'You will [say that] the assumption of mortality brought Christ nearer to the condition of Man—that is to suppose a mass of electrified clay possessing the power to confine, fetter & deteriorate the omnipresent intelligence of the universe. That is to suppose one of the meanest of the Creator's works as imposing a restraint upon the free agency of the Creator himself;—but these superstitions are almost too monstrous to demand a serious refutation.' (Darwall-Smith, 82). Poor Wedgwood, to be accused of demeaning God—and by a mocking teenager who delighted to demean Him at every opportunity.

No pranksterism, however, colours *The Necessity of Atheism*. The argument is short, serious, focused and sincere. It was, perhaps, the mildest possible expression of Shelley's disbelief; elsewhere he called it a 'metaphysical pamphlet', milder still (*Letters*, I, 88). The epigram comes from Bacon: 'The human mind cannot in any way accept as true that which lacks a clear and obvious demonstration.' So there is the theme laid out: a polite, but vigorous, request for proof of God's existence, and a passionate plea for truth, for 'love of truth' has pushed Shelley to write this, and, as he concludes, 'Truth has always been found to promote the best interests of mankind.'[2]

His arguments are very simple. In essence they are the arguments of Locke and Hume, his favourite philosophers of the moment. Why do we believe in anything? Shelley asks. Because we are convinced by the evidence of our senses, our own experiences, or other people's experiences. Shelley calls these the three 'degrees of excitement', that

---

1   Robin Darwall-Smith, 'The Student Hoaxers: The New Shelley Letters', *University College Record*, vol. XIV, no. 1 (2005), 79.
2   The text of *The Necessity of Atheism* is taken from *The Prose Works*, 1–5.

go to make up the 'passion' of belief: the only time in *The Necessity of Atheism* when he gets at all hot under the collar. (We have to be a bit careful about Shelley when he gets into states of excitement, for as Nora Crook discovered a few years ago, that is his term for an erection; and you can certainly sense an almost sexual charge under this surge of necessary and irresistible reasoning.) In the case of God, however, Shelley's three degrees of excitement prove inadequate. Our senses do not tell us that God exists. Nor does our physical experience. Some say the world must have been created; but it is equally reasonable, indeed easier, to suppose that it has existed for all eternity. The generative power itself, the first cause of life, does indeed seem beyond our understanding. But, says Shelley, to suppose that life is produced by 'an eternal, omniscient, Almighty Being', is no help; in fact, it makes creation even more incomprehensible. As for the testimony of other people, 'it is required', Shelley says sternly, 'that it should not be contrary to reason.' And since such testimony is bound to be of miracles, or other things contrary to reason, it will not do. Though Shelley does not explore the subject here, he writes in his notes to *Queen Mab* that there is no such event as a miracle; only operations of Nature that we do not yet understand.[1] When God is subjected to the full glare of reason, he simply crumbles away.

'From this it is evident', runs the last part of Shelley's argument, 'that having no proofs from any of the three sources of conviction: the mind *cannot* believe the existence of a God. It is also evident that as belief is a passion of the mind, no degree of criminality can be attached to disbelief ... Every reflecting mind must allow that there is no proof of the existence of a Deity.'

To this Shelley adds an unnecessarily cocky flourish: 'Q.E.D.' And he signs his work, rising to a shout, 'Thro deficiency of proof, AN ATHEIST'. Yet apart from these provocations, and that title, there is nothing in *The Necessity of Atheism* that deserves the fire. Shelley keeps off the explosive subject of God made man entirely — though, as Wedgwood had experienced, he had plenty of sanguinary views

---

1   *Queen Mab*, note to VII, ll. 135-136, in *The Complete Poetical Works of Percy Bysshe Shelley*, ed. by Thomas Hutchinson (Oxford: Oxford University Press, 1960), 822–23.

about that. And he silently challenges his readers—in his mind the bishops and heads of the Oxford colleges, to whom he has also sent copies—to answer his arguments: to set him right if he is wrong.

It all seems reasonable enough. We might well sympathise with 'my learned friend Mr Hogg', who wrote ruefully soon afterwards that he and Shelley had simply been 'carrying perhaps a little too far some of the arguments of Locke for the amusement of a rainy morning' (*Letters*, I, 114n). But consider what these two young men had done. Whether or not this was the first atheist pamphlet ever published in England (and it is likely that it was), it was the first explicit salvo not only against the unquestioning Anglicanism that held sway there, but also against the God who legitimised the king. The established Church not only underpinned all authority and morality, but also helped to keep at bay revolutions of the sort that had occurred across the Channel. A mere handful of radical thinkers, notably Godwin and Tom Paine, objected to what Shelley saw as an intolerable establishment of religion: a system of eternal punishments and rewards exacted by a tyrannical God who was a sort of cross, to him, between a bloated Hanoverian oaf, like the Prince Regent, and his own father. (He sent his father a copy of *The Necessity of Atheism* too; Timothy Shelley scrawled 'Impious' on the flyleaf (*Letters*, I, 55n).) Shelley believed that truth would never flood human minds until religion was removed. People had to learn to think for themselves and say what they thought, freely. There was no ostensible political colour to his pamphlet, as far as the text went. But for most of those who heard him this was Jacobinism pure and simple. Sentiments like his led straight to the Terror and the guillotine.

Shelley was well aware of, even revelled in, the risks he was taking. ('I send you a *book*', he wrote to his friend Edward Fergus Graham, in a letter that reads more like a whisper of conspiracy; '…I will write more tomorrow—Now can only say silence and despatch.' (*Letters*, I, 51–52). Though he did not think the Oxford publishers would object to it very much ('Mr Munday's principles are not *very* severe,—he is more a votary to Mammon than God' (*Letters*, I, 27)), the booklet was nonetheless printed not in Oxford or London, but in safer Worthing; and even there the printer, Mr Phillips, was advised by Messrs Slatter and Munday to destroy both the types and the manuscript to avoid prosecution under the Blasphemy Laws. 'No degree of criminality can be attached to disbelief,' Shelley had written; but the authorities did attach it, all the same. 'The book is not, & I fear cannot be published,' Shelley told Godwin as he sent it to him in February or March (Barker-Benfield, 113), though originally, with typical extravagance, he had told Graham to advertise it 'in 8 famous papers & in the Globe', and boasted that it had reached 'all the Bishops' (*Letters*, I, 52). He kept his name off it, too, writing even in that cover-letter to Godwin as 'Jennings Stukeley', 'a common friend to Nature, Justice & Reason'. Shelley knew that men were routinely jailed for radical opinions; he had already helped to raise money for Peter Finnerty, an Irish radical, by getting his *Poetical Essay* printed a month or so before. Merely to be a Deist—to acknowledge a Supreme Being, but not the so-called truths of Scripture—could lead to prison, as happened to Tom Paine's publisher, Daniel Eaton, the next year.

That particular incident encouraged another printed appeal by Shelley, his *Letter to Lord Ellenborough*, the judge in the Eaton case, pleading for freedom of speech and of the press. But in a way *The Necessity of Atheism* went deeper than that. It was a plea for freedom of thought. 'Truth is *my* God' Shelley wrote to Elizabeth Hitchener, his Sussex spinster-correspondent, later that year, '& *say* he is Air Water, Earth or Electricity but I think *your's* is reducible to the same simple Divinityship' (*Letters*, I, 98). In other words, there was no awful being out there; no one to tremble at, no one to fear.

Atheism now, of course, is not what it was then. Then, in the popular view, it encompassed Deism, agnosticism and even tremulous uncertainty. The word atheist, as Shelley himself jotted later in a notebook, still often carried its ancient Greek meaning of one who mocked or opposed the gods, while still implying they were there. He put himself proudly in this company, together with Diogoras, Theodorus and Protagoras.[1] His 'little tract', far from being straightforwardly dismissive, also implied the gods were there—and could be knocked down, with just a little reasonable thought.

---

1   *Bodleian MS Shelley adds e.4: A Facsimile Edition*, ed. by P. M. S. Dawson. *Bodleian Shelley Manuscripts* vol. 3 (London and New York, 1987), f. 85v.

What led him to make this explosive gesture? Many motives: some worthy, some less so, some purely personal. He had denied God first as a schoolboy at Eton, where "Atheist Shelley" enjoyed the horror it caused others, tingling the spine and lifting the hair like his beloved galvanic machine. But atheism began to surface in earnest in his letters in the early autumn of 1810, when his irreligious opinions had put a premature end to his first serious love affair with his pretty young cousin, Harriet Grove. (According to him she thought he was a Deist rather than an atheist, but the miserable effect had been the same [*Letters*, I, 35].) It was not merely God he hated in those letters. It was Christianity: 'Oh! I burn with impatience for the moment of Xtianity's dissolution,' he wrote to Hogg that December, two short months before *The Necessity of Atheism* appeared. 'It has injured me; I swear on the altar of perjured love to revenge myself on the hated cause of the effect which even now I can scarcely help deploring' (*Letters*, I, 27). That 'cause' and 'effect' was perhaps the only time Shelley made God the unquestioned first cause of anything.

He inveighed against Jesus, too, more particularly and personally. Older, calmer Shelley appreciated the Jacobin in Jesus, and went through the New Testament spotting revolutionism in Matthew, Mark, Luke and John.[1] But the Shelley who was planning *The Necessity of Atheism* found him unbearable. A picture of Jesus on the wall of his bedroom at Field Place, possibly placed there deliberately by his parents, looked down on him as he was writing (*Letters*, I, 102), inflaming him all the more perhaps with its gentleness: those 'patient looks', that 'lighted stare' described later in Act 1 of *Prometheus Unbound* (ll. 586, 597).[2] 'Oh how I wish I *were* the Antichrist,' he wrote to Hogg in January 1811, 'that it were *mine* to crush the Demon, to hurl him to his native Hell never to rise again' (*Letters*, I, 35). He saw himself twisting the dagger in Christ's breast, shouting out meanwhile his favourite words of Voltaire (words he used again among his epigrams for *Queen Mab*): *Ecrasez l'infame!* Crush the monster (*Letters*, I, 29).

---

1   *Shelley's 'Devils' Notebook: Bodleian MS Shelley adds e.9*, ed. by P.M.S. Dawson and Timothy Webb. *Bodleian Shelley Manuscripts* vol. 14 (London and New York, 1993), 1–15.
2   In *The Major Works*, 251–52.

If Shelley had not been frustrated in love, perhaps his hatred would have been less keen. But the plain urge to defend free thought led him in the same direction. So did the impulse to defy his parents, both father (who tried to 'save' him, according to Hogg, by reading him, with occasional distracted tears, passages from William Paley's orthodox Christian works[1]) and his soft-hearted, bewildered mother. Sheer intellectual curiosity, his keenness to find a first cause behind the universe, added to Shelley's determination to shift God aside as an obstacle to free inquiry. Simple love of argument kept his defiance burning. ('Xtians will not argue,' he complained to Hogg in December 1810; 'it destroys the very nature of the thing to argue, it is contrary to *faith*' (*Letters*, I, 28).)

But Shelley also embraced the title of atheist for its drama and capacity to outrage, and he clung to it proudly all his life. Over the years his Godwinian rationalism wrestled increasingly with mystical Platonist idealism, but still he proclaimed himself an unbeliever: as fiercely in the visitors' book at Chamonix in 1816 as in the sixth canto of *Queen Mab* three years earlier, when he furiously lambasted man for bringing God into the world:

> The changing seasons, winter's leafless reign,
> The budding of the heaven-breathing trees,
> The eternal orbs that beautify the night,
> The sun-rise, and the setting of the moon,
> Earthquakes and wars, and poisons and disease,
> And all their causes, to an abstract point
> Converging, thou didst bend, and called it GOD!
> The self-sufficing, the omnipotent,
> The merciful, and the avenging God!
> Who, prototype of human misrule, sits
> High in heaven's realm, upon a golden throne,
> Even like an earthly king; and whose dread work,
> Hell, gapes forever for the unhappy slaves
> Of fate, whom he created in his sport,

---

1   Thomas Jefferson Hogg, *The Life of Percy Bysshe Shelley*, 2 vols only published (London: Moxon, 1858), I, 307–309.

> To triumph in their torments when they fell! (ll. 96–110)[1]

What Shelley most loathed about the Judeo-Christian God was that he created man, weak and sinful, and then damned him for being so. And what most irked him about man was that, like a slave, he accepted in devoted submission this appalling state of affairs. Yet it was self-inflicted. Where would God be, Shelley asked at the end of 'Mont Blanc'—the poem he wrote at Chamonix—if man had not inserted him, gratuitously and unnecessarily, into every scene of life?

> And what were thou, and earth, and stars, and sea,
> If to the human mind's imaginings
> Silence and solitude were vacancy? (ll.142–44)[2]

Shelley liked his atheism to shock people, undoubtedly. He loved the dramatic and pathetic irony that he, the ardent benefactor of all mankind as he saw himself, could be labelled as a wretch and a monster just because he refused to believe. His first wife, Harriet Westbrook, an intelligent but impressionable teenager, admitted that he terrified her with his atheism, as he did with his tales of goblins and ghosts[3]. He could scare friends, too. The artist Benjamin Haydon recorded him at a dinner party in 1816, this boyish, sickly-looking creature, carving his vegetarian stalk of broccoli (or cabbage) and remarking, 'As to that detestable religion, the Christian...!'[4] In *Julian and Maddalo* in 1818 Shelley described the character Julian, based on himself, as 'a complete infidel, and a scoffer at all things reputed holy'[5]. 'Infidel' was a word he loved, though Maddalo, or Byron, seemed to see it more as an annoyance, or even as a dangerous pose:

> You were ever still
> Among Christ's flock a perilous infidel,

---

1   *The Major Works*, 47–48.
2   *The Major Works*, 124.
3   Edward Dowden, *The Life of Percy Bysshe Shelley*, 2 vols (London: Lippincott, 1886-7), I, 144.
4   B. R. Haydon, *The Diary of Benjamin Robert Haydon*, ed. Willard Bissell Pope, 5 vols (Cambridge, Massachusetts: Harvard University Press, 1960), II, 298–99.
5   Preface, in *The Major Works*, 212.

A wolf for the meek lambs—if you can't swim
Beware of Providence. (ll.115–18)

Surely some of the most prescient words in poetry. But Shelley, who never feared drowning, also never feared what Providence might have in store for him. As far as he was concerned, there was fun in atheism, just as there might be comedy in sinking, like a stone, along-side chunks of ballast. In the doggedly tragic *Rosalind and Helen* he painted himself as Lionel, the mocker the priests hated, 'and he/ Repaid their hate with cheerful glee' (ll. 689–90)[1]. 'They attack me for my detestable principles I am reckoned an outcast,' he had crowed in a letter eight years earlier, 'yet [I] defy them & laugh at their inefficient efforts' (*Letters*, I, 27). Nothing had changed. If there was damnation in it, he dared to be damned: 'May God (if there be a God) blast me!' he told Hogg, and joyously awaited the lightning strike.

In general, however, he wore the label seriously. His note to *Queen Mab* in 1813, explaining the words 'There is no God!' in the 7th canto, repeated the arguments of *The Necessity of Atheism* almost word for word, just expanding them a little, and putting more Hume in. He had not shifted. When Trelawny asked him near the end of his life why he called himself an atheist ('it destroys you in this world') Shelley fooled around a bit at first. 'It is a word of abuse to stop discussion,' he replied; 'a painted devil to frighten the foolish, a threat to intimi-date the wise and good.' Painted devils were his idea of fun. But then, seriously: 'I used it to express my abhorrence of superstition; I took up the word as a knight took up a gauntlet, in defiance of injustice.' The injustice he meant was that, as he went on, 'The delusions of Christianity are fatal to genius and originality; they limit thought.'[2] Trelawny could invent conversations; this, though, sounds plausible enough. Believers, to Shelley, were forcibly prevented—and pre-vented themselves—from realising their full, unfettered potential as rational human beings. The atheist, by contrast, walked free and stood tall, above all that.

And he was also a political rebel. Bacon had contended, as Shelley

---

1   *The Complete Poetical Works*, 178.
2   Edward John Trelawny, *Records of Shelley, Byron and the author*, 2 vols (London: Basil Montagu Pickering, 1878), I, 92–93.

pointed out in his notes to *Queen Mab*, that atheism 'never disturbs the government' because it made men virtuous and clear-sighted (*The Major Works*, 82). But to Shelley virtue and clear sight worked only in one direction, towards revolution, since government and established religion went hand in glove to tyrannise the country:

> Clothed with the Bible, as with light,
> And the shadows of the night,
> Like Sidmouth, next, Hypocrisy
> On a crocodile rode by.[1]

Sidmouth was not only loathesome to Shelley as the Home Secretary who had congratulated the yeomanry for cutting down peaceful political protestors at Peterloo in 1819; he had also, in 1812, sent agents out to spy on Shelley and the subversive leaflets he was floating out in bottles, hopefully to Ireland, across the Bristol Channel. The crocodile had long been Shelley's symbol of religion: a stiffly grinning totemic beast with torches blazing round it, fed on human fat and attended by wails of human misery.[2] It wept tears, too, but they were tears of hypocrisy: just like the priests, 'God's slaves', lies dripping from their tongues, who

> whilst one hand was red
> With murder, feign to stretch the other out
> For brotherhood and peace. (*Queen Mab*, VII, ll. 239–41)

Against all this apocalyptic horror stood the fearless, struggling figure of the atheist. He had haunted Shelley's verses from the beginning. One of the earliest poems in the Esdaile notebook, dating from 1809, sneered at 'Religion, more keen than the blasts of the North', which 'darts its frost through the self-palsied soul'.[3] But the atheist's first explicit appearance was in *Queen Mab* in 1813, striding manfully towards the pyre to presage, by his death, the end of the

---

1   *The Mask of Anarchy*, ll. 22–25, in *The Major Works*, 400.
2   In 'Falsehood and Vice: A Dialogue.' Note to *Queen Mab* IV, ll. 178–79, in *The Major Works*, 74.
3   'Love and Tyranny' in P. B. Shelley, *The Esdaile Poems: Early Minor Poems from the 'Esdaile Notebook'*, ed. by Neville Rogers (Oxford: Oxford University Press, 1966), no. 42, 76.

morally bankrupt old order. The speaker who describes him here is the Wandering Jew, Ahasuerus, one of Shelley's favourite characters, whom we meet again in *Hellas* in 1821: the philosopher who dares to mock the suffering Christ, and on whom God takes an eternal, terrible revenge.

> I was an infant when my mother went
> To see an atheist burned. She took me there:
> The dark-robed priests were met around the pile;
> The multitude was gazing silently;
> And as the culprit passed with dauntless mien,
> Tempered disdain in his unaltering eye,
> Mixed with a quiet smile, shone calmly forth:
> The thirsty fire crept round his manly limbs;
> His resolute eyes were scorched to blindness soon;
> His death-pang rent my heart! The insensate mob
> Uttered a cry of triumph, and I wept.
> 'Weep not, child!' cried my mother, 'for that man
> Has said, 'There is no God.' (VII, ll. 1–13)

There is no God. Shelley had never dared say as much in *The Necessity of Atheism*. Now, though indirectly, he had dared. We have seen that in his note for *Queen Mab*, carefully explaining that phrase, Shelley repeated *The Necessity* again, almost word for word. But there was one significant difference from the original. His note begins: 'This negation must be understood solely to affect a creative Deity. The hypothesis of a pervading Spirit coeternal with the universe, remains unshaken.'[1]

Possibly Shelley was covering his back here, hoping to protect his printers, or trying not to provoke the thought police. In 1817, when his publishers objected to bits of *Laon and Cythna*, a story both Godless and incestuous, he toned down his atheistic ideas—though with how much wriggling or reluctance, his friends seem to disagree. But that was the only time he ever censored himself. 'Truth is my God', after all: truth, candour and unreserve, the holy trinity of Shelleyan virtues. In any case, *Queen Mab* was privately published,

---

1   *The Major Works*, 79.

as *The Necessity of Atheism* was. He was not bound to put in a caveat of any sort. His amended note seemed simply intended to explain that, though a pantalooned and blood-smeared God might have left his universe, numinous mystery had not. Several years later, in his *Essay on Christianity*, Shelley continued the thought, writing without scorn or cynicism of 'the interfused and overruling Spirit of all the energy and wisdom included within the circle of existing things'.[1] It seems, therefore, that our wolfish atheist may not have been quite as fierce as he appeared.

What he believed comes into sharper focus when we read on in *Queen Mab*. There the atheist's death-cry, 'There is no God!' is taken up by Nature, and by the endless cycles of life, death and rebirth that point, in Shelley's view, to the eternal existence of the universe. Nothing and no one has created it. It has always existed, and the unending vibration of the great chain of being echoes in the smallest things. 'Let every seed that falls', he writes,

> In silent eloquence unfold its store
> Of argument: infinity within,
> Infinity without, belie creation;
> The exterminable spirit it contains
> Is nature's only God … (VII, ll. 19–24)

God the Creator—too limiting, too judgmental, above all too anthropomorphic, the looming shadow of man's worst side—has vanished from the scene. Set against infinity within and without, the established notion of God is simply too small for Shelley. In its place here is the spirit of Nature, the force of life: 'exterminable' perhaps, in the narrow sense that seed and plant will die, but elsewhere in his poem called 'eternal' and 'imperishable', the power that brings to birth, controls, whirls through and scatters all created things (I, ll. 274, 276).

Spirit lives and dwells in Shelley's poetry. He invokes it everywhere, often with a capital letter, and his fascination with it and reverence for it only gets stronger through his life. 'Wild Spirit, which

---

1   *The Prose Works of Percy Bysshe Shelley*, ed. H. Buxton Forman, 4 vols (London: Reeves and Turner, 1880), II, 341.

art moving everywhere; / Destroyer and Preserver; hear, O, hear!'—
as he prays to the West Wind (ll. 13–14). His 'Ode to Liberty' of 1820
invokes 'the Power unknown'—again, capitalised (l. 233)[1]. And in
a lesser-known entry in his notebooks, a fragment of around 1817
apparently meant for *Laon and Cythna*, he includes also, as in 'West
Wind', a strong sense of divine agency; of his own passivity; of veneration; of surrender.

> There is a power whose passive instrument
> Our nature is — a Spirit that with motion
> Invisible & swift, its breath hath sent
> Amongst us,— like the wind on the wide Ocean — …..
> This Spirit, chained by some remote devotion
> Our choice or will demandeth not nor heedeth
> But for its hymns doth touch the human souls it needeth [2]

What is this Spirit? Certainly it is a 'what' and not a 'who', although
often Shelley seems drawn irresistibly to describe dazzling, usually
female, figures of divine light, seen for the briefest time and leaving
both ecstasy and agony behind. Sometimes, too, he calls this spirit
'Thou'—though without any religious baggage, it seems, for God
and superstition have been thrown out so decidedly that he is starting
again, as Harold Bloom notes in 'Shelley's Mythmaking', alone in the
vastness of the universe, with a clean slate. Whatever he addresses—
whatever he kneels to, in his own startling terminology— he both
longs to name it and refuses to; for once named, or described, this
Spirit has gone, as instantly and surely as Beauty disappears from
lake, or moonlight, or interweaving trees.

In his more rational early works Shelley applies the words 'Fate'
and 'Necessity' to the motive force of the universe; in *Queen Mab*,
it seems reducible to life moving through Nature, though also life
enthroned in power. But in those same early writings, indeed in the
January just before *The Necessity of Atheism* appears, he has fixed on
another name for it: 'the Spirit of Love, the harmonised intelligence

---

1   *The Major Works*, 473.
2   *Drafts for Laon and Cythna: Facsimiles of Bodleian MS Shelley adds e.14 and
    e.19*, ed. Tatsuo Tokoo. *Bodleian Shelley Manuscripts* vol. 13 (London and New
    York, 1992), 5–6.

of infinite Creation…Love, love *infinite in extent*, eternal in duration' (*Letters*, I, 35). This letter, sent to Hogg, must have caused those sardonic eyebrows to quiver a little. It may also surprise us. But in 'Love and Tyranny' in 1809 Shelley had already expressed his adoration for Love, for its power 'to create, to eternize, to live' and its capacity to bind even the free (*Esdaile* 42, ll. 14–18). And to the end of his life, in his notebooks and essays—and most explicitly in his poetry—the empowering, inspiring force in his universe is simply the spirit of Love.

The reason he wrestles with it so, and feels he must somehow identify it, is because, as a poet, something regularly comes to take possession of him. Initially he hesitates to name it, but he feels it: 'something mysteriously and illimitably pervading the frame of things.'[1] It moves over him as though body and mind were the tight-stretched strings of a lyre ('Make me thy lyre, even as the forest is!'[2]) and it sometimes seems to him that his only purpose—his poet's purpose—is to wait, silently, for it to come. Its visitations, as he writes in *A Defence of Poetry* in 1821, are like 'the interpenetration of a diviner nature through our own, but its footsteps are like those of a wind over the sea, which the coming calm erases, and whose traces remain only as on the wrinkled sand which paves it.' Yet they also remain, of course, in the poems that come afterwards. Poetry, in fact, 'redeems from decay the visitations of the divinity in man.'[3]

This is a passage that can be read in two ways: that divinity comes into man from beyond him, or that divinity is within man to begin with, waiting only to be discovered and acknowledged. It seems to me that Shelley intends both meanings to be valid. There is, for him, a Spirit beyond man, call it Necessity, or Liberty, or Love, or whatever you will; but that spirit is also within him, co-existing, co-eternal, in every way equal: unenslaved, unenslavable, unbowed and boundless. 'Whatever may be [man's] true and final destination,' he writes in his essay *On Life*, 'there is a spirit within him at enmity with nothingness and dissolution.'[4]

---

1   *Essay on Christianity*, Forman, II, 341.
2   'Ode to the West Wind', I. 57.
3   *The Major Works*, 697, 698.
4   *The Major Works*, 634.

Shelley believes this not only because he has rejected God, though that is certainly important, but because he has experienced directly what seems to be a pure and limitless source of love and liberation within himself. He writes about this all his life; but he first mentions it explicitly, and what he calls its 'temple' within his heart, in 'A Sabbath Walk' in the summer of 1811. He is in Wales, listening to the church bells across the valley, but he will not go; he refuses to 'love by the clock', for to a good man every day is a Sabbath:

> The God he serves requires no cringing creed,
> No idle prayers, no senseless mummeries,
> No gold, no temples, and no hireling priests,—
> The winds, the pine-boughs and the waters make
> Its melody. (*Esdaile* 2, ll. 47–51)

For Shelley there is nothing divine or sacred in religion, or in God. What is sacred lies in Nature and in man. The human mind and imagination, and the human heart—Shelley does not always differentiate between them—are where all the power of the universe, all its motion and potential, come to a still focal point: a stillness before they are worked on and sent out again, into unbounded space. Imagination, for Shelley, bursts from that tiny point, like a glowing coal catching fire in the air, to be strong and dazzling as the sun: it is 'the faculty which contains within itself the seeds at once of its own and of social renovation.'[1] Liberty, too, blazes from human hearts: 'Thine own pure soul,/ Moulding the mighty whole', as he puts it in his 'New National Anthem' in 1819 (ll. 15–16).[2] Infinite, unending Love lives and gathers force there. 'Whoever has maintained with his own heart the strictest correspondence of confidence,'writes Shelley in his *Essay on Christianity*, 'who dares to examine & to estimate every imagination which suggests itself to his mind, who is that which he designs to become, & only aspires to that which the divinity of his own nature shall consider & approve ... he, has already seen God.'[3]

Unfettered, unenslaved, free-thinking man, loving and imagining, therefore has the power of the Universe at his disposal. He can

---

1   *A Defence of Poetry*, in *The Major Works*, 696–97, 687.
2   *The Major Works*, 445.
3   Forman, II, 243.

unleash an almost nuclear potential to make the world anew. 'The lightning is his slave;' cries Shelley, speaking for awakened Earth, in *Prometheus Unbound*:

> heaven's utmost deep
> Gives up her stars, and like a flock of sheep
> They pass before his eye, are numbered, and roll on!
> The tempest is his steed, he strides the air;
> And the abyss shouts from her depth laid bare,
> 'Heaven, hast thou secrets? Man unveils me; I have none.'
>   (IV, ll. 418-23)[1]

Shelley has indeed disposed of God in his universe. And in his place, striding like a colossus, comes man. Shelley's 'divinity' is his own true, inner self: himself as he could be. Man, if he has only the will and the desire, can become God, but not a God who oppresses: a God who, free himself, sets others free. It is all possible, and as possible for us, now, as it was when Shelley first tried, in his 'little tract', to clear the air for freedom of thought and the rebuilding of the world.

> Let every seed that falls
> In silent eloquence unfold its store
> Of argument: infinity within,
> Infinity without...

And that seed, of course, whether seed of the soul, of renovation or of the word, is blown there by the great force of Necessity, which in Shelley morphs gradually into the irresistible power of Love: that wild west wind, the Spirit of unending birth, rebirth and change, the scatterer of sparks and ashes among mankind—which is also, incidentally, the only principle Shelley ever prays to.

---

1   *The Major Works*, 308.

Stephen Gill

'Two Consciousnesses': Wordsworth's Sequels

On 20 June 1845 two of Wordsworth's friends, Isabella Fenwick and Kate Southey, returned to his home, Rydal Mount, after a two-day excursion into the south-western Lake District. The following morning they described their visit to Furness Abbey and the mixture of sensations it had unexpectedly prompted. Mostly there was shock. The sacred ruin was being ravaged by the construction of a railway line, he was told, 'so near to the East window that from it Persons might shake hands with the Passengers!!' (21 June 1845). But their distress at the sight had been tempered by the 'picturesque appearance' of the navvies resting amidst the ruins, as they took their midday meal. Wordsworth was 75 years old and almost at the end of writing, but what he heard over the breakfast table moved him to compose this sonnet before the day was out:

> *At Furness Abbey*
>
> Well have yon Railway Labourers to THIS ground
> Withdrawn for noontide rest. They sit, they walk
> Among the Ruins, but no idle talk
> Is heard; to grave demeanour all are bound;
> And from one voice a Hymn with tuneful sound
> Hallows once more the long deserted Quire
> And thrills the old sepulchral earth, around.
> Others look up, and with fixed eyes admire
> That wide-spanned arch, wondering how it was raised,
> To keep, so high in air, its strength and grace:
> All seem to feel the spirit of the place,
> And by the general reverence God is praised:
> Profane Despoilers, stand ye not reproved,
> While thus these simple-hearted men are moved?
>   June 21st, 1845.

So 1845. But this was not Wordsworth's first utterance about the vandalism at Furness Abbey. Five years earlier he had visited the ruin, when the railway project was first being mooted. As yet it was no more than a possibility and the sonnet that Wordsworth wrote on that occasion was able to dwell on the calm and beauty of the scene:

> *At Furness Abbey*
>
> Here, where of havoc tired and rash undoing,
> Man left this Structure to become Time's prey
> A soothing spirit follows in the way
> That Nature takes, her counter-work pursuing.
> See how her Ivy clasps the sacred Ruin,
> Fall to prevent or beautify decay;
> And, on the mouldered walls, how bright, how gay,
> The flowers in pearly dews their bloom renewing!
> Thanks to the place, blessings upon the hour;
> Even as I speak the rising Sun's first smile
> Gleams on the grass-crowned top of yon tall Tower
> Whose cawing occupants with joy proclaim
> Prescriptive title to the shattered pile,
> Where, Cavendish, *thine* seems nothing but a name![1]

The poem celebrates the healing power of Time and Nature. At the dissolution of the monasteries 'rash undoing' caused 'havoc' at Furness Abbey, but how blessed once more is the spirit of the place now that Nature's 'counter-work' is in command. Having 'left this Structure to become Time's prey', what right to lordship can Man have here? But though the contrast between Nature's 'Prescriptive title' and Cavendish's nominal one makes for a fine conceit with which to end, a fine conceit is all it is. It was William Cavendish, Earl of Burlington and future 7th Duke of Devonshire, who owned the abbey grounds, not the birds, and as a prime mover in the newly formed Furness Railway Company he had authorised a line through his possession. He was even ready, if engineering needs demanded,

---

1   For both sonnets see *Last Poems 1821–1850*, ed. Jared Curtis (Ithaca and London: Cornell University Press, 1999), 350, 397.

to countenance demolition of some of the surviving buildings. The havoc of the past was being perpetrated once more, driven this time, the poet declares, not by religious zeal but by Mammon.

Both sonnets were published in Wordsworth's Collected Poems in 1845. That the poet felt very strongly about Furness Abbey was obvious. But readers in 1845 cannot have known quite how much the place meant to him, nor why. What remained concealed in 1845 was that both sonnets stood in relation to other poetry about Furness Abbey written much earlier and to richly sedimented memories from earlier still.

As he fashioned childhood memories in 1799 into the beginning of his autobiographical life's work, Wordsworth drew on his first visit to the abbey ruins, a 'scheme of holiday delight', that must have taken place in the early 1780s. In the passage on Furness Abbey in *The Two-Part Prelude*, II, 98–139, life and death are in counterpoint. The *memento mori* repose of the cross-legged knight and the stone abbot contrasts with the schoolboys' wanton energy. Living trees and ruined towers stand 'Both silent and both motionless alike', sheltered by their valley setting from the sea-wind passing overhead. And, most vivid memory of all, an invisible bird in the nave banishes the gloom cast by the dripping ivy, singing so sweetly

> that there I could have made
> My dwelling-place, and lived for ever there
> To hear such music.

When he wrote these lines Wordsworth was primarily concerned to chart the stages of the process by which Nature's ministry of joy and fear fashions the human mind. The schoolboy's visit to Furness Abbey is placed on a continuum which, within the opening books of the autobiographical poem, begins with a naked infant standing alone in a thunder-shower and ends with a seventeen-year old joining in the song of the one life.

The significance of Furness for Wordsworth, however, was not limited to this single childhood 'spot of time'. As the poem explored further the stages by which the young adult became assured of his poetic vocation it took in more, and more diverse, autobiographical and historical materials and Furness was, so to speak, revisited. In late summer 1794 Wordsworth had stayed at Rampside, on the south coast of Furness faced by Piel island with its castle, built by the monks of Furness Abbey. On a particularly beautiful day Wordsworth walked east along the coast to Cartmel Priory and there visited the grave of William Taylor, the Headmaster of Hawkshead Grammar School who had encouraged his first attempts at writing verse. Pausing at Chapel Island, on which the monks had erected a chapel 'where in ancient times/Masses were said at the hour which suited those/Who crossed the sands', Wordsworth asked a passing traveller for news and heard the thrilling tidings that '*Robespierre was dead*'. Uttering a 'hymn of triumph', Wordsworth returned home and in the verse that records this event (*1805*, X, 539–566) he repeated, with verbal echoes and one line verbatim, the conclusion to the earlier account of visiting Furness Abbey (*1805*), II, 140ff.:

> I pursued my way
> Along that very shore which I had skimmed
> In former times, when spurring from the Vale
> Of Nightshade, and St Mary's mouldering fane,
> And the stone abbot, after circuit made
> In wantonness of heart, a joyous crew
> Of schoolboys, hastening to their distant home,
> Along the margin of the moonlight sea,
> We beat with thundering hoofs the level sand.

The repetition of the line, 'We beat with thundering hoofs the level sand', is, Howard Erskine-Hill observes, 'Perhaps the most breathtaking poetic *coup* of *The Prelude*.'[1] In a section dealing with the conflicted and confusing experience and emotions of the adult Wordsworth in the 1790s, the recollection of the schoolboys as 'a joyous crew' invites the contrast of their innocent 'wantonness of heart' with the much more complex 'glee of spirit' in which the poet poured out his hymn of triumph. For it was sadly premature. With the fall of Robespierre it was possible for those who had welcomed

---

1   Howard Erskine-Hill, *Poetry of Opposition and Revolution: Dryden to Wordsworth* (Oxford: Clarendon Press, 1996), 250.

the French Revolution to believe that its course would once again be guided by the ideals of liberty and equality and not the politics of terror. The rise of Napoleon ended such hopes—at least in most English breasts—and by the time he was recalling that hymn of triumph on Leven Sands Wordsworth could see how wrong he had been. 'Come ye golden times', he had exclaimed, but they had not come and in 1805 Wordsworth was drilling in uniform once a week, a member of the volunteer militia raised to repel a likely French invasion.

When Wordsworth revisited Furness Abbey in poetry over forty years later yet more painful contrasts were in play. To make their visit to the ruins and the sea the schoolboys had had to dissemble with the innkeeper who let them have their horses, 'for the intended bound/ Of the day's journey was too distant far/For any cautious man'—the abbey is about twenty miles south of Hawkshead. Now the railway system that was on the point of bringing tourists into the heart of the Lake District at Windermere was about to open up once remote Furness. Though primarily intended to transport industrial freight, the Furness Railway line was bound to join up with others to carry tourist passengers. And so it proved.

Wordsworth's grief at the idea may seem unwarranted—even hypocritical, given that many of the tourists had with them the latest edition of his *Guide to the Lakes*—but it is understandable. Wordsworth had only to look at his sonnet written some five years before, 'Here, where of havoc tired', to be reminded of his much earlier attempt to capture in verse his recollection of visiting the 'sequestered ruin' of Furness Abbey when he was still a schoolboy. But though the poetry remained to 'enshrine the spirit of the past', as *The Prelude* put it, the 'holy scene' itself, as Wordsworth has learnt from Isabella Fenwick and Kate Southey, has changed forever.

All of this poetry prompted by the ruins of Furness Abbey serves an an introduction to the topic of this lecture. Wordsworth actually visits a place—in this case, once when he is a schoolboy and once, for the last time, when he is an old man. But he also visits and revisits it through the act of reviewing his own poetry about it and in the act of this artistic revisiting registers his awareness of what Hardy devastatingly calls 'Time's mindless rote'. Such revisitings were a life-long compulsion and they take us to the matrix from which all of his finest poetry emerges. There is, on the one hand, the recognition of the past as other, past. How memorably this almost baffled sense of recognition is expressed in the 1799 *Prelude*:

> So wide appears
> The vacancy between me and those days,
> Which yet have such self-presence in my heart
> That sometimes when I think of them I seem
> Two consciousnesses, conscious of myself
> And of some other being.
> (*1799 Prelude*, II, 26–31)

But on the other hand there is the determination to maintain continuities. One passage that has always seemed quintessential Wordsworth to me is to be found among the material written for *Michael,* but not used in the published poem. The poet-narrator has been speaking of the mountains and the vestiges of human endeavour among them:

> thus it is
> That in such regions, by the sovereignty
> Of forms still paramount to every change
> Which years can bring into the human heart
> Our feelings are indissolubly bound
> Together, and affinities preserv'd
> Between all stages of the life of man.
> Hence with more pleasure far than others feel,
> Led by his son this Shepherd now went back
> Into the years which he himself had lived.[1]

There is a tension here between a sense of the past as so other, so distanced that one can observe a former self as another being and an equally powerful sense of the connections that bind one to the past, connections that don't enslave but actually feed the present—preserving affinities. This tension is felt everywhere in Wordsworth, but it is particularly evident in the Fenwick Notes and here it is really

---

1   *Lyrical Ballads, and Other Poems, 1797–1800*, ed. James Butler and Karen Green (Ithaca and London: Cornell University Press, 1992), 328

very striking—not least because in the notes the73 year old poet is so disarmingly open. He declares of *An Evening Walk*, for example, published exactly fifty years earlier:

> There is not an image in it which I have not observed; and now, in my seventy third year, I recollect the time & place where most of them were noticed. I will confine myself to one instance—

> > Waving his hat, the Shepherd from the vale
> > Directs his winding dog the cliffs to scale.
> > The dog bounds barking mid the glittering rocks
> > Hunts where his master points the intercepted flocks.

> I was an eye-witness of this for the first time while crossing the pass of Dunmail Raise.—Upon second thought, I will mention another image:

> > And fronting the bright west yon oak entwines
> > Its darkening boughs & leaves in stronger lines.

> This is feebly & imperfectly exprest; but I recollect distinctly the very spot where this first struck me. It was in the way between Hawkshead and Ambleside, and gave me extreme pleasure.[1]

I think there is something very winning about the situation of the elderly poet, prosing on to Isabella Fenwick about how sharply he remembers his earlier self and sensations, when it is clear that all the memories are prompted by his own poetry. In fact at one point he seems to recognize this. Commenting on the natural phenomenon celebrated in the sonnet 'November 1, 1815; he said, 'Suggested on the banks of the Brathay, by the sight of Langdale Pikes. It is delightful to remember these moments of far-distant days, which probably would have been forgotten if the impression had not been transferred to verse.'[2]

Exactly! Remembering and Writing: these two have always been integrated acts of mind and heart for Wordsworth. Think of these haunting lines from Book XI of *The Prelude*:

---

1   *An Evening Walk*, ed. James Averill (Ithaca and London: Cornell University Press, 1984), 301.
2   *The Fenwick Notes of* William *Wordsworth*, ed. Jared Curtis (London: Bristol Classical Press, 1993), 23.

> The days gone by
> Come back upon me from the dawn almost
> Of life: the hiding places of my power
> Seem open; I approach, and then they close;
> I see by glimpses now; when age comes on
> May scarcely see at all, and I would give,
> While yet we may, as far as words can give,
> A substance and a life to what I feel:
> I would enshrine the spirit of the past
> For future restoration.
>   (1805 *Prelude*, XI, 334–343)

The days gone by were continually coming back to Wordsworth, or actively being recalled, through the medium of his own poetry. The rest of the lecture is going to explore some examples of this creative interplay between past and present, both in lived experience and in poetic creation.

I want to start with a poem from Wordsworth's 1822 collection *Memorials of a Tour on the Continent, 1820*. It is called 'The Three Cottage Girls', a celebration of the beauty and vigour of an 'Italian Maid' and 'The Helvetian Girl'. There is a third Maid, of course, as the poem's title indicates, but she had not been encountered on the 1820 tour, but in August 1803 during William and Dorothy's tour of Scotland and she had been memorialized in the poem 'To a Highland Girl (At Inversneyde, upon Loch Lomond)', published in 1807. That poem closes with an address to her:

> Nor am I loth, though pleased at heart,
> Sweet Highland Girl! from Thee to part;
> For I, methinks, till I grow old,
> As fair before me shall behold,
> As I do now, the Cabin small,
> The Lake, the Bay, the Waterfall;
> And Thee, the Spirit of them all![1]

---

[1]   *Poems, in Two Volumes, and Other Poems, 1800–1807*, ed. Jared Curtis (Ithaca and London: Cornell University Press, 1983), 194.

Having lived in Wordsworth's memory ever since, she was now summoned again for further poetic life in 'The Three Cottage Girls':

> Sweet Highland Girl! a very shower
> Of beauty was thy earthly dower,'
> When Thou didst pass before my eyes,
> Gay Vision under sullen skies,
> While Hope and Love around thee played
> Near the rough Falls of Inversneyd![1]

While ostensibly recording fresh experience from the recent continental tour, 'The Three Cottage Girls' in fact only becomes really eloquent with the declaration that the much earlier encounter remains vivid to the inward eye:

> Time cannot thin thy flowing hair,
> Nor take one ray of light from Thee;
> For in my Fancy thou dost share
> The gift of Immortality;
> And there shall bloom, with Thee allied,
> The Votaress by Lugano's side;
> And that intrepid Nymph, on Uri's steep, descried!

And when Wordsworth revised the poem fourteen years later for his 1836 collected *Poetical Works*, it was this declaration, and the figure of the Highland Girl that preoccupied him. The stanza quoted a moment ago was expanded to

> rough Falls of Inversneyd!
> Have they, who nursed the blossom, seen
> No breach of promise in the fruit?
> Was joy, in following joy, as keen
> As grief can be in grief's pursuit?
> When youth had flown did hope still bless
> Thy goings—or the cheerfulness
> Of innocence survive to mitigate distress?

---

1   *Sonnet Series and Itinerary Poems, 1820–1845*, ed. Geoffrey Jackson (Ithaca and London: Cornell University Press, 2004), 386.

VI

But from our course why turn—to tread
A way with shadows overspread;
Where what we gladliest would believe
Is feared as what may most deceive?
Bright Spirit, not with amaranth crowned
But heath-bells from thy native ground,
Time cannot thin [1]

To recap: for the comprehensive revision undertaken for his new collected edition in 1836, Wordsworth returns to the poem of 1822 and registers the challenge to him now—1836—of the prophecy about the Highland Girl made then—1822—which was itself a return to the prophetic declaration with which the original poem, 'To a Highland Girl' concluded in 1807. At each stage the affirmation made in the closing lines of the first poem is enlarged, strengthened, and reaffirmed. For readers in Wordsworth's lifetime evidence of this particular process of revisiting ended with 'The Three Cottage Girls'. In fact it did not end until 1843, when the poet returned yet again to the Highland Girl and declared in the privately recorded Fenwick Note: 'The sort of prophecy with which the verses conclude has through God's goodness been realized, and now, approaching the close of my 73rd year I have a most vivid remembrance of her and the beautiful objects with which she was surrounded.'[2]

Only one element is missing in this rich concatenation—the memory of the Highland Girl herself. What Wordsworth is remembering is the girl celebrated in the poem and in his sister's journal. Time cannot thin *her* flowing hair. But by 1843 the real Highland Girl, if still alive, must have been middle-aged. It seems unlikely that she had ever seen a copy of *Poems, in Two Volumes* or heard of its author. What she was in August 1803 Wordsworth, 'through God's goodness' could remember whenever he thought of his poem, but did she, I've often wondered, have any memory at all of the two English travellers, who took refuge in the ferry-house on Loch Lomond?

1   Sonnet Series, p.386.
2   Fenwick *Notes*, ed. Curtis, p.26.

That's perhaps a diversionary thought. Even without her voice, the relation of historical fact, poetic creation, and the exercise of memory in these two poems is sufficiently dynamic to highlight just how important it was to Wordsworth to maintain affinities by going back *as a poet* 'into the years which he himself had lived'.

How did he do it? One way was through sequels. Wordsworth was fond of companion pieces, such as the two sonnets on the Hamilton Hills, published in 1807, and he liked what we might call almost sequels—sequels in all but name—such as the ode 'Composed Upon an Evening of Extraordinary Splendor and Beauty' as almost sequel to the 'Intimations' ode. But in some cases the sequel firmly announces itself as such. The Yarrow poems are the obvious cases in point. Three poems, using the same stanza form, register a non-visit and subsequent visits to the same place, the latter sequels alluding to earlier poems. There is astonishing daring here— a sequel to a sequel. But much has been written about these fine poems, [1] so I thought in this lecture I would focus elsewhere.

I want to look at 'Beggars'. It was written in March 1802 and published in *Poems, in Two Volumes* in 1807. Out on a walk the poet encounters a vagrant woman, who possesses both the beauty of an Amazonian Queen and the stature and mien of a 'ruling Bandit's wife, among the Grecian Isles.' The tale of woe she tells is clearly far-fetched, but the poet gives her some money, touched by her demeanour. I want to quote the rest of the poem to bring out its gaiety and fleetness of movement.

> I left her, and pursued my way;
> And soon before me did espy
> A pair of little Boys at play,
> Chasing a crimson butterfly;
> The Taller follow'd with his hat in hand
> Wreath'd round with yellow flow'rs, the gayest of the land.
>
> The Other wore a rimless crown
> With leaves of laurel stuck about:

---

1   I would mention in particular chapter six of Michael Baron, *Language and Relationship in Wordsworth's Writing* (Harlow: Longman, 1995).

And they both follow'd up and down,
Each whooping with a merry shout;
Two Brothers seem'd they, eight and ten years old;
And like that Woman's face as gold is like to gold.

They bolted on me thus, and lo!
Each ready with a plaintive whine;
Said I, 'Not half an hour ago
Your Mother has had alms of mine.'
'That cannot be,' one answer'd, 'She is dead.'
'Nay but I gave her pence, and she will buy you bread.'

'She has been dead, Sir, many a day.'
'Sweet Boys, you're telling me a lie;
It was your Mother, as I say—'
And in the twinkling of an eye,
'Come, come!' cried one; and, without more ado,
Off to some other play they both together flew.[1]

This is one of the most appealing of Wordsworth's encounter poems. Unlike the little girl of 'We Are Seven' or the Leech Gatherer of 'Resolution and Independence', these 'joyous vagrants', as they are termed in one revision, do not admonish the poet, explicitly or implicitly—they just delight him. This, we are reminded, is the poet whose 'grand study' in educating little Basil Montagu was 'to make him happy',[2] who delighted in Hartley Coleridge, Six Years Old, 'exquisitely wild', and who in lyrics such as the extempore 'Written in March, While resting on the Bridge at the Foot of Brother's Water' exulted in the life of man, beast and plant.

Fifteen years later Wordsworth revisited 'Beggars' and so powerful is the recollection of 'Their daring wiles, their sportive cheer' that it was inevitable the sequel poem should open with the question, 'Where are they now, those wanton Boys?'[3] The poet has no answer,

---

1   *Poems, in Two* Volumes, ed. Curtis, 113–116.
2   'Our grand study has been to make him *happy*'. DW to Mrs John Marshall, 19 March [1797]. *The Letters of William and Dorothy Wordsworth: The Early Years 1787-1805*, ed. Chester L. Shaver (Oxford: Clarendon Press, 1967), 180.
3   *Shorter Poems, 1807–1820*, ed. Carl H. Ketcham (Ithaca and London: Cornell University Press, 1989), 231–233.

but chooses to dwell on the 'genial hour' in which he met them and its significance for him now. It was March, 'When universal nature breathed / As with the breath of one sweet flower ... / Soft clouds, the whitest of the year, / Sailed through the sky—the brooks ran clear'. But 'genial' leads back to the 'genial faith, still rich in genial good' of 'Resolution and Independence' and with it the suggestion that the poet is recalling the spring-time of his creative life. 1802 was a turbulent year in which Coleridge's 'Dejection: An Ode' ('my genial spirits fail / And what can these avail / To lift the smoth'ring weight from off my breast?' was intertwined with Wordsworth's 'Where is it now, the glory and the dream?'. But it was also Wordsworth's second *annus mirablis* as a lyric poet, and it is that which he celebrates in the sequel to 'Beggars'. Whatever was the underpinning of that creative year: 'to my heart is still endeared / The faith with which it then was cheered; / The faith which saw that gladsome pair/Walk through the fire with unsinged hair.'

The allusion here to the book of Daniel and the fiery furnace is to be noted. Unbeknownst to his readers, this revisiting of 'Beggars' also involved reaching back to another earlier poem, for Wordsworth had made this Biblical allusion before in a similar context. In Book Seven of *The Prelude* the memory returns to him of an infant he saw in a London theatre, placed upon a table amidst 'dissolute men/And shameless women' (387-388):

> but I behold
> The lovely Boy as I beheld him then,
> Among the wretched and the falsely gay,
> Like one of those who walk'd with hair unsinged
> Amid the fiery furnace. He hath since
> Appear'd to me ofttimes as if embalm'd
> By Nature; through some special privilege,
> Stopp'd at the growth he had; destined to live,
> To be, to have been, come and go, a Child
> And nothing more, no partner in the years
> That bear us forward to distress and guilt,
> Pain and abasement, beauty in such excess
> Adorn'd him in that miserable place. (VII, 395–407)

In both of these allusions to *Daniel* 3:23-26 similar ideas are in play—the baby and the little boys remain in Wordsworth's memory with their beauty and innocence untouched by the flames—but the tone and emphasis of the two are different. In the *Prelude* it is as if the poet is so burdened by a sense of the inevitability of life's course as 'distress and guilt/Pain and abasement' that he wishes for the child escape, even at the cost of premature death, 'embalmed', or, worse still, a stunted life, 'Stopped at the growth he had …a child/And nothing more.' The 'Sequel' to 'Beggars' is less intense. As in its contemporary, the 'Ode, Composed Upon An Evening of Extraordinary Splendor and Beauty', the tone is melancholy, as if the product of a chastened realism, but also irradiated by a sort of reverent gratitude. The poet delights in the still fresh memory of the 'gladsome pair', and finds strength to affirm the continuing efficacy of the faith that had supported him then. In that poetic faith, he is able to acknowledge that that the little boys cannot have walked unsinged through the fiery furnace, while building his prayer for their 'immortal bloom' on the hope that 'pitying Heaven' will protect them, they were 'so happy and so fair.'

Why did Wordsworth revisit 'Beggars' fifteen years after its composition? No evidence survives to suggest an answer, though the composition in the same year, 1817, of poems such as 'Ode.—1817', 'Ode: The Pass of Kirkstone' and 'Ode. Composed Upon an Evening of Extraordinary Splendor and Beauty', suggests one. These are all poems that in a sense involve retrospection: they definitely mark the emergence of the post *Excursion* lyric Wordsworth. But these poems were all published soon after composition, in the 1820 volume, *The River Duddon.* The sequel to 'Beggars' wasn't. It lay in manuscript for another seven years before being issued in the five volume *Collected Poetical Works* of 1827. It was printed in sequence with 'Beggars' as 'Sequel to the Foregoing. Composed Many Years After.' But the title was untrue. As any punctilious reader checking in their *Poems, in Two Volumes* would have discovered, 'Beggars' had been greatly revised for its appearance in 1827. Revisiting his 'Sequel' ten years after writing it had prompted Wordsworth to revisit its original after twenty-five.

The sequels mentioned so far are all public. The poet invites the reader to perceive the overt relationship between poems, not least by making the invitation unmissable through clear signposting. The 'Ode. Composed Upon an Evening of Extraordinary Splendor and Beauty' when first published in the 1820 *River Duddon* collection, was accompanied by a note, which read: 'The reader, who is acquainted with the Author's Ode, intitled, 'Intimations of Immortality, &c' will recognize the allusion to it that pervades the last stanza of the foregoing Poem.' Yes, indeed! And the clear implication is that those who don't had better look it up. Similarly the Yarrow poems draw attention to their sequentiality, partly (and obviously) in their titles, but also in the headnote to 'Yarrow Revisited': 'The title Yarrow Revisited will stand in no need of explanation, for Readers acquainted with the Author's previous poems suggested by that celebrated Stream.'

Yes, sequel poems were one way of maintaining affinities. But Wordsworth had another way. It is the way of reclaiming poetry from an earlier period for use in new work, not publicly, by way of signaled allusion or quotation marks, but privately, in seamless refashioning.

As a way in let's take the closing line of a sonnet from his middle years, 'Mutability', published in 1822 in *Ecclesiastical Sketches*. Mutability is the universal law for earthly things. 'Truth fails not', but her outward forms

> melt like frosty rime
> That in the morning whitened hill and plain
> And is no more; drop like the tower sublime
> Of yesterday, which royally did wear
> Its crown of weeds, but could not even sustain
> Some casual shout that broke the silent air,
> Or the unimaginable touch of Time.[1]

It's a wonderful close, a thrilling line, but it was already 25 years old when Wordsworth used it here. It had been written in 1796 for what editors have since called 'A Gothic Tale', a sequence of Spenserian stanzas connected in some ways to his current enterprises, the narrative 'Adventures on Salisbury Plain' and the dramatic 'The Borderers'.

---

1   *Sonnet Series*, ed. Jackson, 197.

All three pieces of work remained unpublished. One stanza describes a ruin:

> Whose walls had scattered many a stony heap.
> The unimaginable touch of time,
> Or shouldering winds, had split with ruin deep
> The towers that stately stood as in their prime,
> Though shattered ...[1]

'The unimaginable touch of Time'. Wordsworth recalled the one wonderful line, rescued it from a discarded notebook, and by placing it so that the whole sonnet seems keyed together by its sonority, gave it, paradoxically in a poem about mutability, the strength to outface time.

In this act of poetic recycling I don't think very complex forces were in play. Wordsworth remembered a fine line and salvaged it. And of course this was a not uncommon practice of his. In some cases, though, the incorporation of earlier work in later spans such a large gap in time that it seems to me to point to hugely complex emotional activity in the poet as past and present are bound together in the act of writing. It certainly produces fascinating poems.

The richest example is perhaps 'Musings Near Aquapendente', published in 1842. At one point in this poem, a memorial of the Italian tour of 1837, Wordsworth presents himself as musing while journeying through the Appenines. His thoughts go back to his own dear mountains and as they do the years drop away and he starts to think about the time he climbed Helvellyn with Sir Walter Scott. What happens now poetically is astonishing. Lines written 37 years ago but never published are spliced into the verse, enacting in themselves the bridge across time that the poem it speaking of. But I have written about this poem elsewhere and spoke about it here two years ago in a different context, so I won't say anything more about it now. Another example, though, seems to me of comparable interest and it is with it that I shall draw to a close.

In 1817 Wordsworth wrote two odes 'To Lycoris'. Odd title, one

---

1   *The Borderers*, ed. Robert Osborn (Ithaca and London: Cornell University Press, 1982), 752.

might think, but as Wordsworth tells us in a Fenwick, he found the name in Virgil and Ovid. 'Lycoris' was the name given to the beloved of the Latin poet Gallus; it is being used here, Carl Ketcham suggests, because 'it was well established as a pseudonym.' The second ode ('Enough of climbing toil! ...') concludes with an address to an unnamed companion, who is urged, as they rest on their mountain walk, to lapse into contentment by

> shutting up thyself within thyself
> There let me see thee sink into a mood
> Of gentler thought, protracted till thine eye
> Be calm as water when the winds are gone,
> And no one can tell whither. Dearest Friend!
> We two have known such happy hours together.[1]

What is remarkable here is the appearance of these lines in a poem otherwise belonging to 1817-1818, for they were composed in 1799 during one of the many draftings for 'Nutting' but remained unused in the version of the poem published in *Lyrical Ballads* (1800). Tidied up, the lines took on a discrete identity as a short poem called 'Travelling' and Wordsworth thought well enough of it to include it in the manuscript collection of as yet unpublished verse prepared for Coleridge to take with him on his Mediterranean travels in 1804. But though other lyrics in this manuscript, such as the 'Ode (There was a time)" and the 'Ode to Duty', were published in Wordsworth's next collection, *Poems, in Two Volumes*, in 1807, 'Travelling' was not published then, nor later. So what led Wordsworth to revisit it in 1817?

The two odes to Lycoris belong to a period when Wordsworth was taking stock. Poetically he had arrived at the staging post, Maturity, with the publication in 1815 of his first Collected Poems. The appearance of *The Excursion* the year before had announced his intention to complete an ambitious philosophical work of which this was only a part. He had, at last, an income just sufficient to support his family. But there was the other side of the ledger. In 1816 Wordsworth's brother Richard had died, aged only 48. Before that in 1812 two of

---

1   *Shorter Poems*, ed. Ketcham, 254.

Wordsworth's children had died within months of each other. And before that his beloved sailor brother, John, had died in shipwreck.

John's death was a violent penetration into the domestic security Wordsworth had been so carefully nurturing ever since his return to Grasmere and the pain of it was sharpened by the fact that they had not seen John in a long time. In September 1800 Wordsworth and Dorothy had accompanied him up the track from Grasmere to the point where it descends to Patterdale and there they had 'stood till [they] could see him no longer, watching him as he *hurried* down the stony mountain.'[1] This place of farewell became a sacred spot to Wordsworth—aged 73 he could still describe exactly where he and his sister had stood. And in 1817 they passed it once again. Wordsworth and Dorothy were returning from Ullswater and they took the route over Helvellyn which meets the Patterdale track at Grisedale Tarn.

As products of a chastened temperament the odes to Lycoris reflect not only Wordsworth's ever-present sense of the possible irruption of the calamitous unforeseen, but also the awareness of his own approach at age 57 to 'life's dark goal'. What is striking, though, is that both poems in different ways honour youth. The 'Ode to Lycoris' does it directly, welcoming youth's smiles—'May pensive Autumn ne'er present/A claim to her disparagement'—but in the second ode the honouring is more complicated. The poem concludes with a refusal to mourn the passing of the years, as it celebrates the life-giving reciprocity inherent in memories of such tenderness that age can recall them without repining. But these concluding lines also privately enact what they publicly declare. To end the ode Wordsworth returned to 'Travelling', a poem which carried a particular charge for brother and sister. In May 1802 Dorothy had 'soothed' William by repeating '"This is the spot" over and over again' (journal entry 4 May 1802). Now the lines took up a new place in a poem which celebrated their togetherness once more. The last lines of the second Lycoris ode fuse the Wordsworths of 1799 and 1817, binding days each to each, as it were, by poetry. The last lines are also a gesture to Dorothy Wordsworth, the significance of which no-one but she and her brother could gauge.

---

1   Dorothy Wordsworth to Lady Beaumont, 11 June 1805. *Letters*, ed. Shaver, 598.

I have been exploring so far ways in which Wordsworth went back into the years he himself had lived *through poetry*. We have seen him reclaiming old, unused materials for new purposes; examining past creation and assessing it in the light of the passing of time. We have seen Wordsworth alive to the fact of two consciousnesses—of himself and of some other being, yet at the same time determined to assert affinities between all the stages of his life. And all of this has been a creative process that issued in poems that took their place in the evolving whole of Wordsworth's poetic corpus.

And the endeavour continued to the very end of the poet's life. I want to close by considering one of the very last poems he wrote. The 1849-50 collected edition of his work included 'I know an aged Man', a short poem, written in 1846, about the isolation felt by an old man forced at last to enter a workhouse. While he could still manage to survive in his own cottage, the old man—wife, children and kindred all dead—had formed a bond with a robin he fed daily,

> in love that failed not to fulfil,
> In spite of season's change, its own demand,
> By fluttering pinions here and busy bill;
> There by caresses from a tremulous hand.[1]

Incarceration in the workhouse—he is termed a 'captive'—keeps the old man alive, but it severs him from relationship and love.

Could there be a better example of affinities preserved? 'I know an aged Man' is a Victorian poem—as he tremulously reaches out to the bird, the old man could be a figure in a painting by such a master of sentiment as Robert Martineau—and it appeared in a Victorian collection, Wordsworth's final edition of 1849–50. But Victorian though it is, this vignette on the pathos of old age also looks back half a century, to the first important collection that carried Wordsworth's name on its title-page, the 1800 *Lyrical Ballads*. In this collection 'The Old Cumberland Beggar' had contributed to the contemporary debate about vagrancy at a moment when, as Wordsworth later described it, 'The political economists were …beginning their war upon mendicity in all its forms, & by implication, if not directly, on Alms-giving

---

1   *Last* Poems, ed. Curtis, 399.

also.'[1] Acknowledging that the beggar will suffer if left to wander in the 'eye of Nature', the poem declares it better that he should live and die within a community that knows and succours him, rather than survive on loveless charity within a workhouse, and exhorts law-givers, 'ye/Who have a broom still ready in your hands/To rid the world of nuisances', to listen. But History, Economics and Politics, heard other voices. In 1834 the Poor Law Amendment Act regularised the provision of in-door relief through a revised workhouse system and all Wordsworth could do—in which he was joined by Carlyle and Dickens from the younger generation—was to condemn those elements of the new dispensation that violated the 'most sacred claims of civilised humanity.' (Postscript to *Yarrow Revisited*, 1835). When 'I know an aged Man' was written the new-style workhouse system was a reality, which was not going to be altered by poetical protest. But though the tone of 'I know an aged Man' is muted compared with 'The Old Cumberland Beggar', the poem remains faithful to the kinds of affirmation that have characterised Wordsworth's poetry from *Lyrical Ballads* on.

And 'The Old Cumberland Beggar' and 'I know an aged man' link us also to the Furness Abbey sonnets with which we began. For the sonnet beginning 'Well have yon Railway labourers' resonates with all the other poems of his, from *Lyrical Ballads* onwards, in which Wordsworth has insisted on the 'world of ready wealth' open to the 'heart that watches and receives' ('The Tables Turned', 1798). The navvies are responding to something that cannot be measured or valued in cash terms—a sense, as Wordsworth had struggled to define it 45 years earlier,

> Of majesty, and beauty, and repose,
> A blended holiness of earth and sky.[2]

All his writing life he had insisted on the 'profit' of listening to the 'sounds that are / The ghostly language of the ancient earth' (1805 *Prelude*, II, 327–28). But now? The whistle of the train is not just

---

1   *Fenwick Notes*, ed. Curtis, 56.
2   *Home at* Grasmere, ed. Beth Darlington (Ithaca, New York: Cornell University Press, 1977), 46.

a threat to the beauty of a particular spot, nor even harbinger of the world that Hopkins was to lament in 'God's Grandeur' as being 'seared with trade; bleared, smeared with toil'. It is the signal of the triumph of a particular cast of mind, one that thinks 'profit' means cash and does not care to see 'Proteus coming from the sea;/Or hear old Triton blow his wreathed horn'.

Mark J. Bruhn

An Independent Mind? Wordsworth's Dualism

In their introduction to *The Languages of the Psyche: Mind and Body in Enlightenment Thought*, G. S. Rousseau and Roy Porter summarize the history of psychophysiological investigation from Plato and Aristotle through Hegel and Bergson, and then pause to ruminate on the consequence of this well-conserved and widely disseminated inheritance:

> Given this philosophical paean down the millennia affirming the majesty of mind, it is little wonder that so many of the issues that modern philosophy inherited hinged upon mapping out the relationships between thinking and being, mind and brain, will and desire, or (on the one hand) inner motive, intention, and impulse, and (on the other) physical action .... Not only that, but the kinds of words, categories, and exempla to resolve such issues have continued—for better or worse—to be the ones familiarized by Plato, Locke, and Dewey.[1]

Whatever he may imply to the contrary, Wordsworth makes no exception to the institutional rule, especially when it comes to his powers (and thus to his poetics) of introspection. 'And *now* it was', Wordsworth writes early in book 3 of *The Prelude*, 'Residence at Cambridge',

> ... that through such change entire,
> And this first absence from those shapes sublime
> Wherewith I had been conversant, *my mind*
> *Seemed busier in itself than heretofore—*

1   Rousseau and Porter, eds. *The Languages of the Psyche: Mind and Body in Enlightenment Thought* (Berkeley and Los Angeles: University of California Press, 1990), 10.

At least I more directly recognized
My powers and habits. Let me dare to speak
A higher language, say that *now I felt*
The strength and consolation that were mine.
As if awakened, summoned, rouzed, constrained,
I looked for universal things, perused
The common countenance of earth and heaven,
And, *turning the mind in upon itself,*
Pored, watched, expected, listened, spread my thoughts,
And spread them with a wider creeping, felt
Incumbences more awful, visitings
Of the upholder, of the tranquil soul,
Which underneath all passion lives secure
A steadfast life. But peace, it is enough
To notice that *I was ascending now*
To such community with highest truth.
        (1805 3.101–120; emphasis added).[1]

This is a remarkable if seldom noticed passage, the associative logic
of which at once conceals and communicates Wordsworth's univer-
sity-mediated awakening to the interior life of the mind. As always
in Wordsworth, the repeated terms tell the tale: conflating those
I've italicized, we learn that 'now it was' that Wordsworth 'felt the
strength and consolation that were his in 'awful' or awe–inspiring
'Incumbences' that came when he 'turn[ed] the mind in upon itself'
and 'pored [over], watched, expected, [and] listened [to] … [his]
thoughts', which accordingly 'spread' and 'spread … wider' until
they encompassed 'highest truth'. The *Oxford English Dictionary*
cites Wordsworth's use of the rare 'incumbences' here to illustrate
an obsolete but eminently Wordsworthian definition of 'incumbency' (sense 1.a): 'The condition of lying or pressing upon something; brooding; a spiritual brooding or over–shadowing'. This sense
of spiritual insight or visitation is reinforced by the parallelism that
equates 'the upholder' with the 'tranquil soul that underneath all pas-

---

1   All quotations of *The Prelude* are from William Wordsworth, *The Prelude 1799,*
     1805, 1850, ed. Jonathan Wordsworth, M. H. Abrams, and Stephen Gill (New
     York: W. W. Norton, 1979). Unless otherwise noted, quotations are from the
     1805 version of the poem.

sion lives secure', a somewhat murky idea Wordsworth renders in a still 'higher' (if not especially clearer) language in the revisions leading to 1850's 'visitings / Of the Upholder, of the tranquil soul, / That tolerates the indignities of Time, / And, from the centre of Eternity / All finite motions overruling, lives / In glory immutable' (3.119–124).

Of whose 'tranquil' and 'immutable' 'soul', 'secure' from 'passion' and 'tolerantly' immune to 'the indignities of Time', does Wordsworth speak, his own or, as the high-flown language might suggest, God's? What exactly is the source and content of this awful incumbency to which Wordsworth is at once 'awakened' and '[a]roused', but also 'summoned', as to an ecclesial office, and 'constrained', as with a solemn obligation (both 'office' and 'obligation' being later senses of 'incumbency')? And in which 'such community' precisely does he 'ascend' to this 'highest truth'?

These are critical questions, both for internal, compositional reasons and for external, interpretative ones. For these are the verses with which Wordsworth recommences work on *The Prelude*, and they put him on the track of the unprecedented epic theme he'd elsewhere identified as the 'fear and awe / [That] fall upon us often when we look / Into our Minds, into the Mind of Man— / My haunt, and the main region of my song' ('Prospectus' to *The Recluse*, 38–41). In early 1804, however, Wordsworth recounts his awakening to this uniquely introspective theme in terms that express his residual uncertainties about the scope of his subject and his ability to address it. Within 25 lines of the passage we've been analysing, we find Wordsworth reflecting that, though 'Unknown' and 'unthought of' at the time, 'yet I was most rich, / I had a world about me—'twas my own, / I made it; for it only lived to me, / And to the God who looked into my mind' (3.141–144). We might pause here to wonder which 'God' is this—the one who only a paragraph earlier was said to 'turn the mind in upon itself' and 'pore' upon and 'watch' what there transpires? However that may be, the sequence proceeds and within thirty lines Wordsworth achieves an obviously tentative formulation of his 'heroic argument' about the mind's as-yet 'incommunicable powers':

> . . . Of genius, power,
> Creation, and divinity itelf,
> I have been speaking, for my theme has been
> What passed within me. Not of outward things
> Done visibly for other minds—words, signs,
> Symbols or actions—but of my own heart
> Have I been speaking, and my youthful mind.
> O heavens, how awful is the might of souls,
> And what they do within themselves while yet
> The yoke of earth is new to them, the world
> Nothing but a wild field where they were sown.
> This is in truth heroic argument,
> And genuine prowess—which I wished to touch,
> With hand however weak—but in the main
> It lies far hidden from the reach of words.
> Points have we all of us within our souls
> Where all stand single; this I feel, and make
> Breathings for incommunicable powers. (3.172–188)

Ten books and many months later, Wordsworth will reiterate this theme of the singular experience of interiority, only now in prophetic terms and tones that convey a retrospective awareness of his actual achievement:

> Imagination having been our theme,
> So also hath that intellectual love,
> For they are each in each, and cannot stand
> Dividually. Here must thou be, O man,
> Strength to thyself—no helper hast thou here—
> Here keepest thou thy individual state:
> No other can divide with thee this work,
> No secondary hand can intervene
> To fashion this ability.'Tis thine,
> The prime and vital principle is thine
> In the recesses of thy nature, far
> From any reach of outward fellowship,
> Else 'tis not thine at all. (13.185–196)

For all his self-assurance in proclaiming this constitutive independence of mind, Wordsworth is rather disingenuous here in insisting that no 'helper' or 'outward fellowship' contributed to the development of this allegedly self-sufficient 'intellectual love', that 'no secondary hand … intervene[d]' in his particular case 'To fashion this ability'. What's become of that celebrated *'community'* of 'highest truth' with which the Cambridge books began?

It is worth remarking that that beginning was toward an envisioned five-book version of the autobiography, which would have more exactly corresponded to the characterization Wordsworth gave of his unpublished poem in the 1814 Preface to *The Excursion*: he intended, he wrote, to 'take a review of his own mind, and examine how far Nature and Education had qualified him' 'to construct a literary Work that might live'.[1] The doublet 'Nature and Education' captures precisely the scope of the five-book Prelude, which would have devoted two books to 'Childhood and Schooltime', and three books to the Cambridge years of 1787–1791, including 'Residence at Cambridge', the elliptical ruminations on 'Books', and the mountain-top epiphanies of the Alps and Snowdon.[2] Wordsworth had this original double emphasis on the formative influence of nature and education squarely in mind when he wrote in March 1804 to De Quincey with advice upon the latter's matriculation at Oxford: 'love Nature and Books; seek these and you will be happy'.[3] This same sentiment inspires his wishful prescription in Book 5 for the education of 'real children': 'May books and Nature be their early joy' (5.447). Wordsworth's counsel in both cases is doubtlessly generalized from his own collegiate experience, with which he had been preoccupied for the past eight weeks in expanding his autobiography from his 17th to his 21st year. He writes regretfully of his first vacation from Cambridge, for example, that summertime's

> vague heartless chace
> Of trivial pleasures was a poor exchange
> For books and Nature at that early age.

---

1   William Wordsworth, *The Excursion*, ed. Sally Bushell, James A. Butler, and Michael C. Jaye (Ithaca and London: Cornell University Press, 2007), 38.
2   See William Wordsworth, *The Thirteen–Book Prelude*, vol. 1, ed. Mark L. Reed (Ithaca and London: Cornell University Press, 1991), 19ff.
3   Ibid.: 38.

[....] Far better had it been to exalt the mind
In solitary study, to uphold
Intense desire by thought and quietness.
   (4.304–306, 311–313)

A few lines earlier, Wordsworth specifies these 'trivial' summertime 'pleasures' as 'gawds / And feasts and dance and public revelry
/ And sports and games' that 'Seduce[d] me from the firm habitual
quest / Of feeding pleasures, from that eager zeal, / Those yearn-
ings which had every day been mine, / A wild, unworldly–minded
youth, given up / To Nature and to books . . .' (4.273–275, 278–282).
Presumably the count of 'every day' includes the many passed during
Wordsworth's just completed first year at Cambridge, but notably any
trace of this institutional experience is expunged by 1850, which now
depicts the derelict scholar more simply perhaps, but less account-
ably, as 'A wild, unworldly-minded youth, given up / *To his own
eager thoughts*' (4.490–491, emphasis added). The elision of 'Nature
and books' as the sources and sustenance of his 'feeding pleasures'
is striking, and its purpose isn't far to seek: by replacing 'books'
in particular with 'his own eager thoughts' (the epithets 'wild' and
'unworldly' conserving a sense of the natural), Wordsworth contrives
to assert the independent development of his introspective mind.

   This brings me to what I called the external, interpretative reasons
for revisiting Wordsworth's institutional formation. When it comes to
the Cambridge years, at least, criticism tends to take Wordsworth at
his final word rather than his first, reproducing Book 3's sound-bite
that 'Imagination slept' without its qualification 'and yet not utterly'
(3.260) and characterizing all four years in terms that strictly apply
only to the first. Wordsworth does admit about that first year that 'In
… mixed sort / The months passed on, remissly, … in vague / And
loose indifference, easy likings, aims / Of a low pitch—duty and zeal
dismissed . . .' (3.328–333). But the same paragraph makes a crucial
exception to the general rule of laxity—'Not that I slighted books—
that were to lack / All sense' (3.371–372)—and book 6 opens by sum-
marizing his second and third years at Cambridge, in which 'I lived
… / More to myself, read more, reflected more, / Felt more, and settled daily into habits / More promising. Two winters may be passed

/ Without a separate notice; many books / Were read in process of this time—devoured, / Tasted or skimmed, or studiously perused— / Yet with no settled plan' (6.22–29). The question of Wordsworth's philosophical formation has long exercised criticism, but definite answers have been notoriously hard to come by, mostly because, as critics from Woodring to Richardson have argued, Wordsworth suppresses his intellectual sources. Yet criticism has largely disregarded the evidence that at least some of these sources—and in terms of Wordsworth's introspective capacities and claims, perhaps the most important—may be those encountered by the 'wild, unworldly youth' when he went up in mathematics at St. John's College of Cambridge University.

Attention to these institutionally-mediated sources illuminates a central tenet of Wordsworth's psychological thought that likewise too frequently escapes critical notice or, if noted, emphasis: his mind-body dualism. Especially at a time when criticism, following larger trends in the human sciences, is prone to emphasize Wordsworth's materially embodied and environmentally situated mind, it's vital to remind ourselves of his philosophical and psychological dualism, and to pose anew the questions of its sources and significance. As an early but representative instance of the now-prevailing critical attitude, I cite the late Jonathan Wordsworth from an article of 1981, remarking the 'curious and characteristic physical emphasis' in Wordsworth's thought and verse:

> Lacking Wordsworth's 'more than usual organic sensibility,' at times we probably read more abstractly than he expected. The 'high objects' with which the child's emotions are intertwined in *The Prelude* (1799, i.136) are not exalted aims, but chunks of the countryside—probably in fact mountains, with an unconscious pun on 'high.' 'Things', too, tend to have a very concrete thingness: who else would call man a 'thinking thing'?[1]

Unfortunately, this is just the wrong passage to make the point about Wordsworth's peculiarly 'material' and 'embodied' poetics (Jonathan

---

1   Jonathan Wordsworth, 'As with the Silence of the Thought', in *High Romantic Argument: Essays for M. H. Abrams* (Ithaca and London: Cornell University Press, 1981), 41–76

Wordsworth's words), for the immediate answer to the critic's question is René Descartes, the father of modern philosophical dualism,
who famously defined the mind as an immaterial 'thinking thing' (*res
cogitans*) as contradistinguished from the objective world of material or 'extended things' (*res extensa*). The line quoted from 'Tintern
Abbey'— 'All thinking things, all objects of thought'—would thus
have been immediately recognized in Wordsworth's day as expressly
Cartesian and explicitly dualistic.

Of course, the poem makes no bones (if you'll pardon the expression) about its introspectively validated dualism—the inward-look-
ing poet meditates on the 'picture of the mind' 'Until, the breath of
[his] corporeal frame / And even the motion of [his] human blood /
Almost suspended, [he is] laid asleep / In body and becomes a living
soul' (61, 43–48). Conducting to this paradoxically 'sublime' yet
'serene and blessed mood', the same paragraph of 'Tintern Abbey'
earlier explains, are introspectively generated feelings that communi-
cate with some 'purer' faculty of 'mind': 'sensations sweet, / Felt in
the blood, and felt along the heart; / And passing even into my purer
mind, / With tranquil restoration' (27-30, 37, 41). As the words 'felt'
and 'tranquil' in particular signal, here is a first, verse formulation of
the famous definition of poetry subsequently advanced in the Preface
to *Lyrical Ballads* (1800): 'I have said that poetry is the spontaneous
overflow of powerful feelings; it takes its origin from emotion recol-
lected in tranquillity; the emotion is contemplated till, by a species of
re-action, the tranquillity gradually disappears, and an emotion, kindred to that which before was the subject of contemplation, is gradually produced, and does itself actually exist in the mind' (740).[1] As
in *The Prelude* passage that posits a 'tranquil soul' 'underneath' and
'secure' from 'all passion', but with a good deal more psychological subtlety, this definition systematically distinguishes (even as it
coordinates) emotional and tranquilly contemplative modes of mind:
as the one 'is gradually produced', the other 'gradually disappears'.
Thus, in the lines from 'Tintern Abbey', the 'tranquil restoration' per-

---

1   Quotations of 'Tintern Abbey' and the Preface to *Lyrical Ballads* are from
Poetical Works of William Wordsworth, ed. Thomas Hutchinson and Ernest de
Selincourt (London: Oxford UP, 1936, rpt. 1960).

tains to 'my purer mind', and *not* to the 'sensations sweet, / Felt in the blood, and felt along the heart'. As they 'pass' into 'purer mind', these 'motion[s] of our human blood' are almost completely 'suspended'— only then do we become a tranquil and a living soul that can see into the life of things (including its own sensations and feelings). These verses and the poetic theory that echoes them embody what Simon Jarvis has recently characterized as Wordsworth's 'common–sense ... Cartesianism', a dualistic perspective that 'Wordsworth often, ... like most other writers of the period, takes as exhaustively dividing the possible ontological [and therefore psychological] options, "sensuous or intellectual", "discursive or intuitive"'.[1]

The question is thus not whether Wordsworth was exposed to this Cartesian tradition but only when, and while Jarvis argues for 1801 and accepts Duncan Wu's suggestion that Coleridge was the conduit, I think there can be little doubt that his first and most sustained exposure was during his Cambridge years. We know, for example, that Wordsworth owned both Descartes' *Geometry*, originally published with *The Discourse on the Method* in illustration thereof, and his *Principles of Philosophy*, works which, according to Christopher Wordsworth's 1877 *Account of the Studies at the English Universities in the Eighteenth Century*, remained as canonical texts at Cambridge and elsewhere. Other texts commonly in use at Cambridge through the eighteenth century gave rather fulsome recapitualtions of the 'new method' of Cartesian introspection, including Jacques Rohault's *Physics*, a text which Wordsworth also owned and which opens with a glowing précis of the Cartesian system. We know moreover, thanks to the scholarly recoveries of Jane Worthington Smyser and Theresa Kelley in particular,[2] that in working up the Dream of the Arab for the five-book *Prelude* of 1804, Wordsworth adapts materials that he probably first encountered at Cambridge: namely, Descartes dream of philosophical election, as reported in Adrien Baillet's *Life of*

---

1   Simon Jarvis, *Wordsworth's Philosophic Song* (Cambridge: Cambridge University Press, 2007), 171 (quoting *The Prelude*).
2   Jane Worthington Smyser, 'Wordsworth's Dream of Poetry and Science: The Prelude, V', *PMLA* 71 (1956): 269-275; Theresa M. Kelley, 'Spirit and Geometric Form: The Stone and the Shell in Wordsworth's Arab Dream', *SEL* 22 (1982): 563-582.

Descartes, and Flavius Josephus's story of the flood, as recounted in the Tacquet/Whiston edition of Euclid's *Elements*. To this list should be added *Don Quixote*, which Wordsworth very likely read in Spanish under the Cambridge modern language tutor Agostino Isola. Of course, given his intention when he returned to *The Prelude* in early 1804—to give his 'Education' in general and 'Books' in particular their due place in the history of his own philosophical and poetic development—the creative confluence of Cambridge-era reading in Spanish literature, Euclidean geometry, and philosophical biography in the Dream of the Arab seems probable both circumstantially and psychologically.

A further consideration that increases the probability of Wordsworth's Cambridge-era exposure to these and related works is a textual one: the dualistic psychology expressed in the Dream of the Arab conforms closely to the pattern of thought and diction with which Wordsworth consistently characterizes the intellectual substance and introspective consequence of his studies in geometry at Cambridge. For example, the dream sequence condenses the universe of human knowledge into shell and stone, 'poetry and geometric science', the one 'in passion uttered' and therefore 'sensuous', the other 'By reason built' and therefore 'intellectual' (5.39, 42). The latter kind of knowledge, epitomized by Euclid's *Elements*, 'h[o]ld[s] acquaintance with the stars, / And wed[s] man to man by purest bond / Of nature, undisturbed by space or time' (5.104–106). This language of a 'pure' and communally held intelligence transcending time and space is echoed in those early lines of book 3, 'Residence in Cambridge', where Wordsworth writes of his introspective discernment of 'the tranquil soul, / Which underneath all passion lives secure'. If this 'tranquil soul' doesn't yet sound especially Euclidean, consider Wordsworth's development of the thought by 1850: 'let me dare to speak / A higher language, say that now I felt / What independent solaces were mine, / To mitigate the injurious sway of place / Or circumstance [...] felt / ... visitings / Of the Upholder, of the tranquil soul, / That tolerates the indignities of Time, / And, from the centre of Eternity / All finite motions overruling, lives / In glory immutable' (3.99–103, 118–123). Wordsworth had evidently discovered at this time a dispassionate, abstract, time- and space-transcending 'soul', 'intelligence', or 'thinking substance' (*res cogitans*), but it would be hard to believe that the 17-year old could have conceived of its 'independent solaces' quite independently.

Nor did he of course. When Wordsworth in late March or early April of 1804 scuttled the five-book arrangement he'd largely achieved, he began anew by rearranging and expanding the Cambridge materials into a four-book sequence, including what is now presented as Book 6. He now resumes, with less prolixity and slightly greater candor, the topic of the 'many books / ... read in the process of this time—devoured, / Tasted or skimmed, or studiously perused ...' Though Wordsworth essential evades the subject again, as he had in the symbolic displacements of the Dream of the Arab, he is nevertheless conscious that his very language will record debts left otherwise unacknowledged: 'T'would be a waste of labour to detail / The rambling studies of a truant youth', he writes, for they 'may be easily divined, / What, and what kind they were' (6.110–112). Still, the most profound and influential of these studies demands franker and fuller consideration, and in giving it, Wordsworth effectively discloses the institutional underpinnings of his introspective claims:

> Yet must I not entirely overlook
> The pleasure gathered from the elements
> Of geometric science. I had stepped
> In these inquiries but a little way,
> No farther than the threshold—with regret
> Sincere I mention this—but there I found
> Enough to exalt, to chear me and compose. (6.135–141)

This passage is effectively a reprise of the one early in book 3 announcing Wordsworth's introspective awakening, only now the 'strength and consolations' that come from 'turning the mind in upon itself' are given their mathematical pedigree:

> Yet from this source [geometry] more frequently I drew
> A pleasure calm and deeper, a still sense
> Of permanent and universal sway
> And paramount endowment in the mind,

> An image not unworthy of the one
> Surpassing life, which—out of space and time,
> Not touched by welterings of passion—is,
> And hath the name of, God. Transcendent peace
> And silence did await upon these thoughts
> That were the frequent comfort of my youth. (6.150–159)

Here, geometric reasoning is the acknowledged source of Wordsworth's introspective and dualistic insight concerning 'the tranquil soul / That underneath all passion lives secure'. And this too is the dualistic psychological point illustrated by the ensuing narrative of John Newton: shipwrecked and despairing of survival, Newton 'beguile[s] his sorrow, and almost / Forget[s] his feeling' by tracing out 'diagrams' from 'A treatise of geometry' (6.165, 171–174). Wordsworth offers this 'self-taught' geometer as the image of his former and sometime 'studious' self:

> even so—if things
> Producing like effect from outward cause
> So different may rightly be compared—
> So it was with me then, and so it will be
> With poets ever. Mighty is the charm
> Of those abstractions to a mind beset
> With images, and haunted by itself,
> And specially delightful unto me
> Was that clear synthesis built up aloft
> So gracefully, even then when it appeared
> No more than as a plaything, or a toy
> Embodied to the sense—not what it is
> In verity, an independent world
> Created out of pure intelligence. (6.165, 169, 173–187)

The dualism of this transcendental mathematics is explicit: 'abstractions', 'clear synthesis', and 'pure intelligence' are systematically ranged over against 'images', 'embodi[ment]', and 'sense'.

One doesn't have to read far in the mathematical literature of the day to find precedents for Wordsworth's notions here and indeed for the very forms of his speech. I'll let one example stand for the many

I have in store to offer. The first number of the London–based periodical *The Mathematician* (1745–1750, a 1751 compilation of which
was held by St. John's during Wordsworth's time there) commences
with a 'curious dissertation on the rise, progress, and improvement
of geometry', a survey which concludes by asserting that 'the next
improvement must be the science of pure Intelligences'.[1] This geometric science of pure intelligence is evidently an example of what
Thomas De Quincey, reflecting on Wordsworth's years and studies
at St. John's College, characterizes as 'the sublimer mathematics'
or 'the higher geometry'. Though the phrases 'sublimer mathematics' and 'higher geometry' may be strange and unrevealing to our
ears, De Quincey's short-hand use of them denotes an established
tradition whose contents and advocates were well-known through at
least the 1830s, at least to University men. To illustrate the impact
of Wordsworth's student 'admiration' of the 'higher geometry', 'the
secret' of which 'lay in the antagonism between this world of bodi-
less abstraction and the world of passion', De Quincey cites from
memory passages of Wordsworth's Dream of the Arab, which he
introduces as follows:

> And here I may mention appropriately, and I hope without breach
> of confidence, that, in a great philosophic poem of Wordsworth's,
> which is still in MS., and will remain in MS. until after his death,
> there is, at the opening of one of the books, a dream, which reaches
> the very *ne plus ultra* of sublimity in my opinion, expressly framed
> to illustrate the eternity and the independence of all social modes
> and fashions of existence, conceded to these two hemispheres,
> as it were, that compose the total world of human power—math-
> ematics on the one hand, poetry on the other.[2]

De Quincey's reminiscence is telling in so many respects, from the
construction that suggests an 'appropriate' mention of the poem may
nevertheless be a 'breach of confidence' (perhaps because it indicates
the institutional mediation of ideas that Wordsworth preferred to rep-

---

1   *The Mathematician: Containing Many Curious Dissertations on the Rise,
     Progress, and Improvement of Geometry*, London: John Wilcox, 1751
2   Thomas De Quincey, *Literary Reminiscences*, vol. 1 (Boston: Ticknor, Reed,
     and Fields, 1981), 319.

resent as his own), to the disclosure of authorial intention implied by 'expressly framed', suggesting that the notion of 'independence of all social modes and fashions' belongs not just to Wordsworth but to the 'sublimer mathematics' of which he was a student. Evidently, Wordsworth's ontologically independent mind is not his alone, but the full story of its institutional dependence remains to be told.

Research for this paper was supported by a Regis University
SPARC Faculty Fund grant

Madeleine Callaghan

Shelley and the Ambivalence of Idealism

When writing this paper, I was struck by Carlos Baker's belief that Shelley 'would never for more than a moment have agreed with Auden's dictum that "poetry makes nothing happen."'[1] Despite my agreement, I found myself hesitating over the idea of the length and the importance of 'a moment' in the poetry, and over what exactly poetry can make happen. The potential that burns with 'electric life' in Shelley's poetry seems propelled by uncertainty and indefinability. From moment to moment, from word to word, from interpretative possibility to interpretative possibility, the poetry shapes for itself an artistic freedom defined by a resistance to closed interpretative circles. *Alastor* and *The Triumph of Life* share a particular kind of strangeness; each poem explores the limitations and opportunities of embodiment, straining the boundaries of narrative poetry to create and question the Shelleyan vision. In this paper I shall examine the similarities between Shelley's early *Alastor* and his final *terza rima* in *The Triumph of Life* to suggest that exploration of idealism as a deeply fraught yet compelling concept was there from the first to the last in his tough minded though sensitively wrought poetry. Shelley's idealism was always veined with a steely–eyed awareness that heaven remained, and maybe would always stay, 'unascended'.

F. R. Leavis, despite his overt revulsion from Shelley's brand of poetic intelligence, provided some thoughtful ways to approach poetry. His criticism that 'The effect of Shelley's eloquence is to hand poetry over to a sensibility that has no more dealings with the intelligence than it can help' goes some way to suggesting Shelley's

---

1   Carlos Baker, *The Echoing Green: Romanticism, Modernism, and the Phenomena of Transference in Poetry* (Princeton N.J.: Princeton University Press, 1984), 108.

evasion of systematic and totalising thought.[1] In particular, it helps to elucidate the ways in which Shelley refuses to offer a didactic pattern, throwing open the poetry to wave upon wave of ambiguous inferences that deliberately fail to develop a patterned form of certainty. Yet, as Michael O'Neill argues, this lack of certainty does not seem in either *Alastor* or *The Triumph of Life* to elicit a 'mandarin, self–delighting scepticism'.[2] Rather, the lack of certainty forms the ground of Shelley's poetic imaginings, as he reaches toward the possibilities of certainty even as he weaves doubt into his lines. The moment of what ought to be vision, pivotal in *Alastor* and *The Triumph of Life*, forms the centre of both poems. United by the spectral female, in *Alastor*, the ideal figured as 'the veilèd maid', and in *The Triumph of Life*, as a female Shape all Light, Shelley presents the encounter with vision as created by or represented as a woman. The episodes are as teasingly like as they are patently unlike, Shelley's narrator in *Alastor* offering information to the reader that is spurned by *The Triumph of Life*'s inclusion of Rousseau's first–person narration of his experience. In *Alastor*, the presence of the female figure is called into question by the narrator, who suggests the dream–like nature of her being:

> A vision on his sleep
> There came, a dream of hopes that never yet
> Had flushed his cheek. He dreamed a veilèd maid
> Sate near him, talking in low solemn tones.[3] (149–54)

Though vision comes, we are no closer to knowing whether the Poet has passed through the gates of horn or of ivory – there is no pat answer to the reality of visionary power in the Poet, or the extent of empathic qualities in the narrator. Shelley attempts to locate the reader in an immersed state, where the experience of vision matters

1   F. R. Leavis, *Revaluation: Tradition & Development in English Poetry* (Harmondsworth: Penguin, 1964), 175.

2   Michael O'Neill, *The Human Mind's Imaginings: Conflict and Achievement in Shelley's Poetry* (Oxford: Clarendon Press, 1989), 180.

3   Percy Bysshe Shelley, *Alastor, Percy Bysshe Shelley: The Major Works*, ed. Zachary Leader and Michael O'Neill, Oxford World's Classics (Oxford: Oxford University Press, 2003). All quotations from the poetry and prose of Shelley will be taken from this edition.

more than our own sense of what is real or unreal. Shelley suggests the sexuality of the dream through the Poet's flushed cheek, and the veilèd maiden's status as a poet implies that she may figure as a fantasy of what *On Love* describes as 'a miniature as it were of our entire self' (632). The possibility that the veilèd maiden functions as a projection of the self throws the Poet's quest into doubt, but this possibility does not decode the episode's full meaning because such decoding will fail to respond to its effect. The encounter between the Poet and the 'veilèd maiden' loses none of its power by its deliberately shaky grasp on the actual:

> His strong heart sunk and sickened with excess
> Of love. He reared his shuddering limbs and quelled
> His gasping breath, and spread his arms to meet
> Her panting bosom: . . . she drew back a while,
> Then, yielding to the irresistible joy,
> With frantic gesture and short breathless cry
> Folded his frame in her dissolving arms.
> Now blackness veiled his dizzy eyes, and night
> Involved and swallowed up the vision; sleep,
> Like a dark flood suspended in its course,
> Rolled back its impulse on his vacant brain. (181–91)

This undulating passage shows Shelley paradoxically accessing the most control over his orgasmic subject matter. The 's' sounds of the first line, with 'strong', 'sunk', 'sickened', and 'excess' whisper into the reader's ear, as Shelley seduces the reader into melting into the description, mirroring the Poet folding himself into the arms of the veilèd maiden. Though Shelley's narrator transports his reader, the mastery with which he does so leaves no room to suggest a loss of control on his part. Danger tinges the lines as the Poet seems to yield his strength to his vision; her withdrawal signals some self–autonomy over her movements, while his shuddering limbs and breathlessness suggest his weakness in relation to her strength. Though Shelley's syntax does not clarify anything, the 'irresistible joy' seems hers, not his. As he folds himself into her already dissolving arms, the narrator cannot resist uniting them by sound; her 'dissolving arms' mirror his 'dizzy eyes' – if she is in the process of vanishing, then he has been blinded by their psychosexual encounter. The uncertainty surrounding her existence, her meaning, and her effect on the poet lends an enigmatic splendour to the lines which refuse to be corralled into fact. The veilèd maid elides ossifying into a symbol of the ideal by Shelley making her seem neither a self–contained emblem nor an inadvertently confused and confusing figure. Rather, she is more expressive of the ambivalence and ineffability that came to distinguish Shelley's poetry. Like the self–divided Preface to *Alastor*, Shelley renders the text in such a way that it can be interpreted cleanly by the reader, but only at the expense of losing part of the experience of reading the poem. Any interpretative certainty becomes a kind of death in Shelley's living poetry even as, paradoxically, this resistance to final meaning becomes a closed form in and of itself.

The Triumph of Life shows Rousseau encounter another visionary figure, the Shape all Light. A similar kind of overpowering by the spectral female occurs, yet like in *Alastor*, Shelley renders the scene as a complex tissue of co–existing interpretative possibilities as he replicates in the mind of the reader the shifting sands of consciousness undergone by Rousseau. Rousseau attempts to command the Shape all Light, demanding of her an understanding of how, where, and why he has come to this particular place:

> ... If, as it doth seem,
> Thou comest from the realm without a name
>
> 'Into this valley of perpetual dream,
> Show whence I came, and where I am, and why—
> Pass not away upon the passing stream.
>
> 'Arise and quench thy thirst, was her reply.
> And as a shut lily stricken by the wand
> Of dewy morning's vital alchemy,
>   (*The Triumph of Life* 395–401)

Though seeming to come from an authoritative standpoint, Rousseau's questioning contains an affecting poignancy as he asks that she not 'Pass not away upon the passing stream' while knowing that his plea

will avail him nothing. By attempting to impose certain limits upon
his experience, he seeks to escape the 'perpetual dream'. Paul de Man
claims that here 'Rousseau is not given a satisfactory answer, for the
ensuing vision is a vision of continued delusion that includes him'.[1]
Yet to make this argument, there would have to be a clear line between
that which is delusion, and that which is truth. Shelley makes no such
cleavage between the two as instead experience comes to the fore;
just as in *Alastor* the 'truth' of the Poet's experience becomes secondary to the fact of the experience itself. Perhaps sensing Rousseau's
de Man–like urge to identify the difference between truth and delusion, the Shape all Light eludes Rousseau's attempt to define, stat-
ing blandly: 'Arise and quench thy thirst'. Her command, stripped of
self–assertion, compels Rousseau, and his image of the lily responding to nature's imperative suggests her power over his state. Yet, his
metaphor suggests less her tyrannical power over his thought than
a beautifully natural response to an external stimulus. The loss of
Rousseau's self–autonomy seems not a grievous matter, and more a
necessary surrender:

> 'I rose; and, bending at her sweet command,
> Touched with faint lips the cup she raised,
> And suddenly my brain became as sand
>
> 'Where the first wave had more than half erased
> The track of deer on desert Labrador;
> Whilst the wolf, from which they fled amazed,
>
> 'Leaves his stamp visibly upon the shore,
> Until the second bursts; — so on my sight
> Burst a new vision, never seen before,
>   (*The Triumph of Life* 396–411)

The self–description of the enchanted Rousseau begins with his following of her 'sweet command', and his lingering over the description
creates a disorienting effect on the reader. The reader experiences a
half–identification and a half–disengagement from the description as

---

1   Paul de Man, 'Shelley Disfigured', *Deconstruction and Criticism*, Harold Bloom
     et al (New York: Seabury Press, 1979), 45.

Shelley replicates in the mind of the reader the shifting sands of consciousness undergone by Rousseau in the poem. The mind becoming a desert allows the motion of the waves to take over, as the series of semi–effacements and the wolf's 'stamp' overpowers the reader's imagination.

These bursting visions crowd into *The Triumph of Life* as Shelley places no certain footholds for the reader to cling to in the description. The reader's mind attempts to follow and enter into the description as the *terza rima* lines twist and weave themselves around one another, but Shelley prevents interpretative finality by the constant shifts which propel the poetry. The idealism inherent in the concept of the vision is half–undercut, yet Shelley refuses nihilism so as to prevent the reader from retreating into the certainty of clarity. Unlike Paul de Man, I cannot claim that 'We now understand the shape to be the figure for the figurality of all signification'.[1] To circumscribe the lines would be to attempt to impose a structure that Shelley evades by raising his Shape all Light to the status of an uninterpretable figure, and reduce Rousseau's experience to a comprehensible encounter between two definite symbols. Idealism and scepticism are lost in the face of untranslatable experience.

Despite the openness of *The Triumph of Life* to many interpretative possibilities, to assign certain kinds of ethical interpretations to this episode runs the risk of making the text into a didactic upbraiding of Rousseau's despair. To describe Rousseau's experience as positive or see its function as a salutary warning to the Shelleyan narrator or reader would be to misrepresent Rousseau's loss of self–autonomy. When Hugh Roberts argues that 'Rousseau and the narrator are looking at life through the wrong end of the telescope, and are therefore unable to see the beauty that rises out of its constant figurations',[2] the critique overlooks the at best ambiguous presentation of the mass of humanity who dance 'tortured by the agonizing pleasure' (141) that leaves them 'senseless' (160) and desolate. Rousseau, like the narrator observes the scene, 'Struck to the heart by this sad pageantry'

---

1   de Man, 62.
2   Hugh Roberts, 'Spectators Turned Actors: *The Triumph of Life*', in *Shelley's Poetry and Prose*, selected and ed. Donald H. Reiman and Neil Fraistat, A Norton Critical Edition, 2nd ed. (New York: Norton, 2002), 766.

(176). To remain aloof seems the preferable option than melting into
the senseless mass. Previously, Rousseau had declared his quasi
Byronic self–mastery and self–destruction.

> I was overcome
> By my own heart alone, which neither age,
> 'Nor tears, nor infamy, nor now the tomb
> Could temper to its object.'—
>   (*The Triumph of Life* 240–43)

As O'Neill writes, 'Entangling as they clarify, these lines fascinate;
they have the thrust of a verdict and the strut of a boast'.[1] This kind of
embattled individualism seems less Shelleyan and more Byronic, or,
as a responsive reader of the Romantic poets, Yeatsian. Shelley and the
reader cannot not offer unqualified assent to this kind of self–assertion,
yet Shelley embeds in the lines sympathy with and an attraction to this
type of self–mastery even as he registers his recoil from the degenera-
tion suffered by Rousseau. Like Keats's *Hyperion* poems, the reader
responds to the fallen Titan-like Rousseau. But this sympathy is often
suspended by critics who view Rousseau as representing a set of negative values. Jerrold Hogle refers to *The Triumph of Life* as holding
within it 'a moment of choice, hints at the better choice, and laments
the effects of the wrong choice so often made throughout Western history'.[2] Roberts too argues for the idea of a choice, writing that: 'If we
return to *The Triumph of Life* and, turning actor not spectator, avoid
Rousseau's mistake of demanding a value that is not at risk in the flux
of process, then we find the apparent nightmare of life's dance is a
product of incorrect seeing, or choosing an inappropriate scale'.[3] Yet
the idea of 'incorrect seeing' or perceiving the poem as advocating
'the right choice' suggests a right course, or a correct mode of seeing,
yet Shelley avoids presenting this kind of clarity throughout his poem.
The overlap between the narrator's perception and Rousseau's suggests a similar, yet not identical outlook, and to condemn their sight
would involve us in making the kind of moral decision that Shelley

---

1   O'Neill, 185.
2   Jerrold E. Hogle, *Shelley's Process: Radical Transference and the Development
     of His Major Works* (New York; Oxford: Oxford University Press, 1988), 335.
3   Roberts, 766.

recoiled from when he wrote that 'Didactic poetry is my abhorrence' (Preface to *Prometheus Unbound*, 232).

However, the importance of sight resounds through the poem, and *Alastor* offers a similar type of ambiguity. As Carlos Baker writes, *The Triumph of Life* 'is rather a reaffirmation than a palinode',[1] and these similar preoccupations show the intellectual stability of Shelley's poetic career. By remaining:

> Obedient to the light
> That shone within his soul, he went, pursuing
> The windings of the dell.—
> (*Alastor* 492–94)

the Poet follows his own perceived path, seeing a Spirit that beckons him into the 'abode where the Eternal are' (*Adonais* 55: 495). The passage immediately preceding this assertion of 'the light / That shone within his soul' repeatedly uses the word 'seem' to define the unique kind of vision possessed by the Poet. By pursuing his own path, the Poet is brought to his demise, a demise that leaves the narrator in 'pale despair and cold tranquillity' (*Alastor* 718). Like in *The Triumph of Life*, the perceptions of both Poet and narrator are left open to dispute and made vulnerable to moral censure. Our individual responses are 'all like bubbles on an eddying flood' (*The Triumph of Life* 458) of Shelley's poetic endeavour.

Shelley's tough–minded brand of poetry refuses to offer interpretative certainty as he insists on the importance of poetic experience and the shades of meaning that refine and nuance every reader's separate understanding of his poetry. To paraphrase Yeats, in Shelley's *Alastor* and *The Triumph of Life*, the reader 'no longer knows / Is from the Ought' ('A Dialogue of Self and Soul', 36–37) as Shelley refuses a simplistic form of idealism and beats no retreat into the relative comfort of radical scepticism. Shelley's poetry exists in the moment of its own making. Revealing in each line that he writes that 'deep truth is imageless' (*Prometheus Unbound* 2. 4. 116), Shelley offers poetry replete with images that alter, refresh, and deepen potential meanings that make ambiguity the most moving form of poetic truth.

---

1   Baker, 121

Jacob Risinger

Wordsworth's Commanding Eminence: Self-Government and Stoic Outlook in *The Excursion*

I want to start by doing precisely what Matthew Arnold says one shouldn't do in exploring what he called the 'illusion' of Wordsworth's 'formal philosophy.'[1] In this paper, I examine what I will perversely call the Godwinian subtext of *The Excursion*, but only as part of a larger attempt to rethink the continuity and complex trajectory of Wordsworth's stoicism—his long-standing and perennial desire for a tranquillity that does not negate but stands at a distance from the play of passion. My goal is to say something provocative or at least unusual about both Wordsworth's philosophy and the 'radical roots' of *The Excursion*, but I'll start by pitting one early and eminent Wordsworthian against another, both of whom insinuate in their own way that the poet who equated poetry with 'passion' and 'the history or science of feelings' was marked by a curiously stoic tendency.[2]

At the beginning of the twentieth-century, A.C. Bradley acknowledged the justice and insight of Matthew Arnold's Wordsworthian commentary. But he also augmented Arnold's fixation on Wordsworth's universally accessible and 'unfailing' joy with a reminder that in reading Wordsworth, one frequently finds oneself 'in the presence of poverty, crime, insanity, ruined innocence, torturing hopes doomed to extinction, solitary anguish, [and] even despair.'[3] Arnold had celebrated Wordsworth's poetry as, 'at bottom a criticism of life', but

---

1   Matthew Arnold, 'Wordsworth', *English Literature and Irish Politics*, ed. R. H. Super (Ann Arbor: The University of Michigan Press, 1973), 48.
2   William Wordsworth, 'Note to *The Thorn*', *Lyrical Ballads and Other Poems, 1797-1800*, ed. James Butler and Karen Green (Ithaca: Cornell University Press, 1992), 351.
3   Arnold, 'Wordsworth', 51; A. C. Bradley, 'Wordsworth', *Oxford Lectures on Poetry* (Bloomington: Indiana University Press, 1961), 123–4.

Bradley quite reasonably asks how incisive Arnold allows that criticism to be if his version of Wordsworth elides the 'dark foundations' of life itself. Bradley proposes that Wordsworth's encounters with a 'dark' and 'unintelligible world' reveal by their contrast the poet's philosophic mind, and he concludes that Wordsworth 'unquestionably' saw 'the cloud of human destiny, and [that] he did not avert his eyes from it.'[1] Bradley attributes this unswerving attention and correspondingly sublime detachment to Wordsworth's temperamental 'severity'—to an 'austere passion' and a 'Stoical cast.'[2]

Bradley's formulations strike me as particularly compelling, for they juxtapose a rhetoric of regulation against the 'spontaneous overflow' of powerful emotion without negating either. Like Coleridge's imagination, the idea of an 'austere passion' blurs the distinction between active and passive experience while forcing the question of how 'influxes of feeling' or any overpowering fit of passion can be simultaneously fully experienced and severely restrained.[3] Keep in mind the shared etymology of 'passion' and 'passive,' both of which stem—as Wordsworth notes in the "Essay, Supplementary to the Preface of 1815'—from the Latin *patior*, a verb that connotes a central lack of will in the face of something that must be suffered or endured.[4] Here it is important to recognize the paradoxical logic of stoicism itself: the severe and self-restraining tendency of emotional austerity both works against and enforces passive receptivity, to the point that a willed transcendence of passion becomes none other than a surrender to circumstance itself. The stoic, like Wordsworth's Happy Warrior, transcends 'Pain' and 'Fear' as he '[t]urns his necessity to glorious gain'.[5] For all the attention directed towards the Wordsworthian poet and his infant precursor as an 'inmate of this active universe', there is something central to Lionel Trilling's

1   Arnold, 'Wordsworth', 46; Bradley, 'Wordsworth', 124–5.
2   Bradley, 'Wordsworth', 119, 118.
3   Wordsworth, 'Preface to *Lyrical Ballads*', *The Prose Works of William Wordsworth*, 3 vols., ed. W. J. B. Owen and Jane Worthington Smyser (Oxford: Clarendon Press, 1974), I. 126.
4   Cf. Wordsworth, *Prose Works*, III. 81.
5   Wordsworth, 'Character of the Happy Warrior', *Poems, in Two Volumes, and Other Poems, 1800-1807*, ed. Jared Curtis (Ithaca: Cornell University Press, 1983), 84–86, lines 12–14.

recognition that, in Wordsworth's poetry, 'the element of quietude approaches passivity, even insentience'.[1]

I find Bradley's emphasis of Wordsworth's 'stoical cast' particularly striking, for it evokes the idea of a philosophy so entrenched or diffuse that it has become itself a habit or disposition. To borrow a phrase from Ralph Waldo Emerson, Bradley insinuates that Wordsworth's was 'a Stoicism not of the schools, but of the blood'.[2] In his essay on Wordsworth, Arnold, too, concedes that poetry which asks the question 'how to live' might exceed the boundaries of a 'narrow' philosophical field. As he puts it, moral ideas need not be 'bound up with systems of thought and belief which have had their day' and are 'fallen into the hands of pedants and professional dealers'. For Arnold, one could be stoical without being precisely a Stoic—an insight he affirms by linking Wordsworth to Epictetus, quoting with approval the ancient Stoic's conviction that the end of life is 'to do your duty... to attain inward freedom, serenity, happiness, [and] contentment.'[3]

At surface level, Bradley and Arnold do no more than acknowledge the reality of what Willard Spiegelman has uncontroversially described as Wordsworth's 'middle period of fortitude and mature, even preacherly, stoicism.'[4] But Wordsworth's 'stoical cast' has deeper roots that prompt more troubling reconfigurations; indeed, his continual and evolving fascination with dispassionate modes of knowing and judging should decisively complicate straightforward accounts of his poetic development. Critics have long credited Jane Worthington Smyser's observation that *The Excursion* is 'everywhere bulwarked with the ethics of Stoicism', but I want to suggest that Wordsworth's fascination with a disinterested ethical scheme that abjures passion in favour of self-emancipation and communal good precedes the publication of *The Excursion* by twenty years.[5]

---

1   Lionel Trilling, 'Wordsworth and the Rabbis', *The Opposing Self: Nine Essays in Criticism* (New York: The Viking Press, 1955), 130.

2   Ralph Waldo Emerson, 'Heroism', *Emerson: Essays & Poems* (New York: Library of America, 1983), 373.

3   Arnold, 'Wordsworth', 46–47.

4   Willard Spiegelman, *Wordsworth's Heroes* (Berkeley: University of California Press, 1985), 173.

5   Jane Worthington, *Wordsworth's Reading of Roman Prose* (New Haven: Yale

If we are to credit Arnold's sense that Wordsworth tended to extract and retain 'moral ideas' from more recondite schemes, we have to do what other commentators have not and acknowledge the strange proximity of Wordsworth's mature stoic stance to his erstwhile interest in the rational philosophy of William Godwin.[1]

In recalling his Godwinian fervor in Book X of *The Prelude*, Wordsworth has scant praise for what he calls

> the Philosophy
> That promised to abstract the hopes of man
> Out of his feelings, to be fix'd thenceforth
> For ever in a purer element.[2]

But Wordsworth's mischievous assertion that Godwin's 'tempting' scheme made space for the passions 'to work / And never hear the sound of their own names' repeats a critique of stoicism that Dr. Johnson had perfected in the eighteenth-century, one that negates the stoic enterprise by emphasizing the contradictions that accompany almost any attempt to live up to the ideal of its detachment (*Prelude* X. 812–13). It was a charge Hazlitt also echoed in contending that Godwin's almost inhuman morality directed 'virtue to the most airy and romantic heights, [and] made her path dangerous, solitary, and impracticable.'[3] Nevertheless, the heights of wisdom that Johnson and Hazlitt claimed were impossible to attain hold a sublime appeal that cuts through Wordsworth's retrospective irony:

> what delight!
> How glorious! in self-knowledge and self-rule
> To look through all the frailties of the world
> And, with a resolute mastery shaking off
> The accidents of nature, time, and place
> That make up the weak being of the past,

University Press, 1946), 67.

1   Arnold, 'Wordsworth', 46.
2   Wordsworth, *The Thirteen-Book Prelude*, ed. Mark L. Reed (Ithaca: Cornell University Press, 1991), X. 806–9. All subsequent citations from *The Prelude* will be noted parenthetically.
3   William Hazlitt, 'William Godwin', *The Spirit of the Age*, *The Selected Writings of William Hazlitt*, ed. Duncan Wu (London: Pickering & Chatto, 1998), VII. 89.

> Build social freedom on its only basis,
> The freedom of the individual mind.
>   (*Prelude* X. 818–825)

Coleridge entertained no illusions about what he described as the 'Stoical Morality which disclaims all the duties of Gratitude and domestic Affection', and by almost all accounts Wordsworth, reunited with Dorothy and entrenched in nature, had thrown off Godwin and his hyper-rational benevolence by 1796.[1] Nevertheless, Godwin's advocacy of an 'independent intellect' impervious to circumstance and accident casts a long shadow over Wordsworth's career, one that belies the simplicity of his ironized dismissals. Though its significance alters substantially, the uncanny persistence of the individual mind's freedom is evident at the end of *The Prelude* in the rhapsodic celebration of the 'genuine Liberty' of a mind that, exalted by the vastness of its own being, has 'sovereignty within and peace at will' (*Prelude* X. 829, XIII. 122, 114). While Wordsworth's abbreviated 'Essay on Morals' rejects outright any unfeeling morality that places 'an undue value...upon that faculty which we call reason', the dispassionate and disinterested undercurrent of Godwin's ethical thought persists in Wordsworth's later work.[2]

I do not mean to imply that Wordsworth remained a covert, Grasmere–based Godwinian throughout the Napoleonic Wars, nor do I emphasize his 'stoicism' to deny that Wordsworth found his peculiar genius in squaring his profound thought with deep and powerful feeling.[3] Indeed, it is precisely the centrality of Wordsworth's obedience to what he called 'the strong creative power / Of human passion' that makes his recurrent invocation of the steadfast law of reason or an immutable duty that remains unshaken 'by the storms of circumstance' so compelling.[4] While much has been said about *The*

---

1   S. T. Coleridge, *Lectures 1795 on Politics and Religion*, ed. Lewis Patton and Peter Mann (Princeton: Princeton University Press, 1971), 164.

2   Wordsworth, *Prose Works*, I. 103.

3   Cf. Coleridge, *Biographia Literaria*, ed. James Engell and W. Jackson Bate (Princeton: Princeton University Press, 1983), 80.

4   William Wordsworth, *The Excursion*, ed. Sally Bushell, James A. Butler, and Michael C. Jaye (Ithaca and London: Cornell University Press, 2007), 1: 512–513, 4: 71. All subsequent citations from *The Excursion* will be noted parenthetically.

Borderers as a text that comes to terms with and subsequently exor-
cises Wordsworth's own Godwinian enchantment, the debate surrounding the transcendent freedom that stands as supplement to stoic
detachment returns with a vengeance to make up a central portion of
the philosophical dialogue in *The Excursion*. To a certain extent, this
should not be surprising; as Nicholas Roe has persuasively observed,
The Recluse is not divorced from Wordsworth's radical years but ultimately 'finds its fullest significance in the integration of this background with the more immediate influence of Coleridge's thought.'[1]
What, then, are we to make of the proximity of radical disinterest-
edness and what some have seen as Wordsworth's conservatively
indifferent apologetics all in a single dialogic work? The return of a
Godwinian repressed in *The Excursion* unearths not only a strange
and often unacknowledged sympathy between Wordsworth and
Godwin's respective trajectories, but it also offers an object lesson on
how Wordsworth extracts philosophical tropes from formal systems.

The first intimation of a Godwinian subtext in *The Excursion*
materializes in a complicated example of its autobiographical mediation. On the course of their journey, the Wanderer forewarns his
companion poet of a solitary hermit who once shook off his grief
and 'uncomplaining apathy' by investing his confidence in the 'false
philosophy' of a revolutionary era (*Excursion* 2: 218, 275). For the
Wanderer, this philosophy is the substantiation of 'a proud and most
presumptuous confidence / In the transcendent wisdom of the age,'
one that attempted to 'cast out' fear, circumvent 'restraints', and abjure
'natural passion' (*Excursion* 2: 250–1, 257, 273, 3: 745). To put it
reductively, the Wanderer paints the Solitary as a grieving stoic who
becomes a revolutionary stoic and ultimately an eloquent defender of
stoic ethics—a sage who lives 'at safe distance' from the world in a
tranquil Vale, impervious to the intrusion of 'sickness, or accident, or
grief, or pain' (*Excursion* 2: 331, 389). The interpretative challenge
this malleable apathetic example poses to the celebration of common
life and domestic affections in *The Excursion* can be quickly resolved
by linking it to a despondency that must be corrected. But, as Kevis

---

1   Nicholas Roe, *Wordsworth and Coleridge: The Radical Years* (Oxford:
Clarendon Press, 1988), 34.

Goodman has argued, the Wanderer's own palpable design is itself predicated on a corrective virtue that rises above 'Ill-governed passions, ranklings of despite / Immoderate wishes, pining discontent, / Distress and care' (*Excursion* 4: 213–215).[1] The Wanderer, purposefully detached from the 'groaning nations' and their political upheavals, follows a path blazed by the Solitary and even Godwin himself in commending self-government over and above overt political action (*Excursion* 4: 299). As he puts it, 'the Wise / Have still the keeping of their proper peace; / Are guardians of their own tranquillity' (*Excursion* 3: 321–323).

In *The Spirit of the Age*, Hazlitt had declared that 'Mr. Godwin [was] a mixture of the Stoic and of the Christian philosopher', a characterization that could judiciously be extended to the Wanderer and the later Wordsworth equally as well.[2] Both Godwin and the Wanderer had Calvinist tenets 'deeply wrought in [their minds] in early life', but this background is replaced for both by a self-achieved belief structure that Wordsworth describes as 'dictated' by 'human reason' (*Excursion* 1: 443). For the Wanderer, this transposition unsurprisingly occurs over the course of his 'habitual wanderings out of doors,' and his life follows a path that he later describes as 'parallel to nature's course' (*Excursion* 1: 434, 4: 490). But while classical stoicism holds that the exercise of reason will lead men to a life lived according to nature, the Wanderer describes an opposite tendency, one in which wisdom begins not in the rational understanding of 'human nature only' but by exploring 'All Natures,—to the end that [one] may find / The law that governs each'. Attuned to the 'mighty commonwealth of things' that springs from 'creeping plants to sovereign man', one might gradually scale the 'heights of speculation' as natural knowledge breeds delight, and delight breeds a love suited to 'thought and to the climbing intellect' (*Excurrsion* 4: 336-338, 345–346, 358-9, 351). Strangely, then, the Wanderer ends in possession of the Reason and 'independent intellect' from which the Godwinian begins, with the crucial distinction that his disinterested

---

1   Cf. Kevis Goodman, *Georgic Modernity and British Romanticism: Poetry and the Mediation of History* (Cambridge: Cambridge University Press, 2004), 123.
2   Hazlitt, *The Spirit of the Age*, VII. 90.

and reasonable benevolence remains compatible with human feeling and affection (*Prelude* X. 829).

This reconciliation of stoic rationality with a passionate sensibility—one of the central cruxes of *The Excursion*—need not be seen as simply another retelling of Wordsworth's preferred and providential biographical narrative. In John Thelwall's *The Peripatetic*—a text that Henry Crabb Robinson and others have compared to *The Excursion*—Thelwall imagines a similar transposition of values in his short compendium of "Hints for the Stoics," confessing:

> I cannot see why the finest susceptibilities of nature should be considered as unworthy of those who boast the highest order of natural intellect—or why *Reason*, which is only the aggregate of sensation, collected and exhibited in one lucid focus, should think she shews her own strength and dignity by degrading the feelings, without which she never could have existed, or by stifling them when they presume to rise.[1]

Wordsworth's romantic rediscovery of this insight, famously expressed by Hume, is generally thought to signal his rejection of Godwin's frozen regions, 'where the understanding [is not] warmed by the affections'.[2] But the narrative becomes more complex with the recognition that Godwin himself was not statically and inflexibly linked to an arctic circle of apathy. It's impossible to say whether Wordsworth, safe at Racedown Lodge, ever made it past the "Preface" to Godwin's revised edition of *Political Justice* in 1796. Despite his professed ambivalence, Wordsworth, like Godwin, was tempering and revising an earlier, abstract rationality. In an unpublished account from 1796, Godwin himself acknowledged that he held the first version of *Political Justice* to be "blemished" by three principal errors:

> 1) Stoicism, or an inattention to the principle that pleasure and pain are the only bases upon which morality can rest; 2) Sandemanianism, or an inattention to the principle that feeling,

---

1   John Thelwall, *The Peripatetic*, ed. Judith Thompson (Detroit: Wayne State University Press, 2001), 255–256.

2   Hazlitt, 'Mr Godwin', *The Spirit of the Age*, VII. 93. Cf. David Hume, *A Treatise of Human Nature*, ed. David Fate Norton and Mary J. Norton (Oxford: Oxford University Press, 2000), 266.

and not judgement is the cause of human actions; 3) the unqualified condemnation of the private affections.[1]

While Wordsworth's poetic passions pulled him away from radical
politics and new iterations of *Political Justice*, his fascination with
the power of a place beyond feeling outlasted even Godwin's stoicism. This fortitude appears predictably in pieces such as 'The Ode
to Duty' and 'The White Doe of Rylstone,' and it unexpectedly com-
plements and qualifies sensibility in 'Resolution and Independence'
and the 'Intimations Ode'. In this sense, *The Excursion* exhaustively
explores a foundational romantic question. Its most succinct formulation occurs in a rare instance of rhetorical humility, one in which the
Wanderer ponders the transposition of 'naked reason' in a question
that even he, for once, hesitates to answer. As he puts it, how can one
reconcile:

>   the passive will
> Meek to admit; [with] the active energy,
> Strong and unbounded to embrace, and firm
> To keep and cherish? How shall Man unite
> A self-forgetting tenderness of heart
> And earth-despising dignity of soul?
> Wise in that union, and without it blind!
>   (*Excursion* 5: 574–580)

The Excursion, of course, yields no conclusive answer, but I'd like
to construct one possibility by linking Geoffrey Hartman's insight
that the poem has deep roots 'in the topographical and contemplative poetry of the eighteenth century' with the philosopher Charles
Taylor's notion that modern selfhood involves inhabiting a 'moral
topography'—'of being able to find one's standpoint' in a moral
landscape and become 'a perspective in it.'[2]

In his account of his early misfortunes, the Solitary calmly

---

1   Cited in Mark Philp, *Godwin's Political Justice* (Ithaca: Cornell University Press,
      1986), 142.
2   Geoffrey Hartman, *Wordsworth's Poetry 1797–1814* (New Haven and London:
      Yale University Press, 1964), 296; Charles Taylor, *Sources of the Self: The
      Making of Modern Identity* (Cambridge: Harvard University Press, 1989),
      111–112.

describes the stroke of 'fatal Power' that shattered his early and uninterrupted happiness. When both of his children are suddenly caught in the 'gripe of Death,' he is aggrieved and all the more so when he discovers that traumatic loss has left his wife 'incalculably distant': as he puts it, she was 'Calm as a frozen Lake when ruthless Winds / Blow fiercely, agitating earth and sky" (*Excursion* 3: 646, 648, 672, 659–660). While his wife passively submits to 'Heaven's determinations,' the Solitary himself admits that 'the eminence on which her spirit stood, / Mine was unable to attain' (*Excursion* 3: 667–669). Here is another image of a 'mighty Mind', an eminence unperturbed by passion and passing necessity (*Prelude* XIII. 69). The concise topographical formation harks back not only to the prospect poems of the eighteenth century but to Book Eleven of *Paradise Lost*, where the obscure trajectory of divine Providence becomes legible to Adam from atop the mountain. But given the trajectory of the Solitary's political future and the drift of Wordsworth's political past, we might gloss his wife's composure with Godwin's insight, in *Political Justice*, that a 'consequence of the doctrine of necessity is its tendency to make us survey all events with a tranquil and placid temper, and approve or disapprove without impeachment of our self possession.' For Godwin, the heights of what he calls a 'comprehensive view' render one 'superior to the tumult of passion'.[1]

Even the Wanderer inclines toward such a view, dreaming of the 'awful sovereignty' and 'final EMINENCE of Age': a 'superior height' and 'disencumbered' solitude in which one might obtain 'fresh power to commune with the invisible world, / And hear the mighty stream of tendency" (*Excursion* 9: 53, 70, 71, 87–88).

In closing, I want to pause over one last eminence in *The Excursion*. In attempting to escape the melancholy that follows in the wake of the French Revolution, the Solitary travels to North America to 'roam at large,' 'to observe, and not to feel'. Temperamentally adverse to the 'Big Passions' on display in American cities, he becomes a 'detached Spectator' who seeks in the wild 'a composing distance from the

---

1   William Godwin, *An Enquiry Concerning Political Justice, Political and Philosophical Writings of William Godwin*, ed. Mark Philp (London: William Pickering, 1993), III. 173.

haunts / Of strife and folly' (*Excursion* 3: 899–900, 908–909, 913–914). In this venture, he imagines himself as not unlike an independent and particularly contemplative noble savage who,

> having gained the top
> Of some commanding Eminence, which yet
> Intruder ne'er beheld, he thence surveys
> Regions of wood and wide Savannah, vast
> Expanse of unappropriated earth,
> With mind that sheds a light on what he sees.
> (*Excursion* 3: 944–952)

Of course the ideal of a noble savage turns out to be as true to life as the ideal of unmitigated stoicism or pure and benevolent rationality, but the Solitary consistently demonstrates a desire to achieve precisely the 'contemplative position' that Coleridge, in the *Table Talk*, tied to the genius of Wordsworth's philosophical poetry: 'His proper title is *Spectator ab extra*.'[1]

Arnold would probably quibble with an attempt to assign Wordsworth's spectatorship to any particular person or school, but Godwin led Wordsworth to speculative heights he was loath to abandon, even after Godwin's scheme itself seemed bankrupt. Hazlitt claimed that Godwin placed 'the human mind on an elevation, from which it [could command] a view of the whole line of moral consequences'—a moral and poetic position parallel to that of what John Barrell has described as the prospect poem's 'disinterested man of comprehensive vision'.[2] Wordsworth scaled these stoic and disinterested heights again and again. In the 1970s, Michael Cooke claimed that stoicism 'posed a threat to romantic poetry, to the romantic spirit itself.'[3] But it was stoicism—planted by Godwin, confirmed by the classics, nurtured by nature, and upheld by temperament—that gave Wordsworth a commanding view of his own poetic vocation. As he

---

1   Samuel Taylor Coleridge, *Specimens of the Table Talk of Samuel Taylor Coleridge*, ed. Henry Nelson Coleridge (London: John Murry, 1851), 186.

2   Hazlitt, *The Spirit of the Age*, VII. 89; John Barrell, *English Literature in History, 1730-80: An Equal, Wide Survey* (London: Hutchinson & Company, 1983), 61.

3   Michael Cooke, *The Romantic Will* (New Haven and London: Yale University Press, 1976), 216.

put it in *The Prelude*:

> Oft in those moments such a holy calm
> Did overspread my soul, that I forgot
> That I had bodily eyes, and what I saw
> Appear'd like something in myself, a dream,
> A prospect in my mind (*Prelude* 2: 367–71).

Jessica Fay

Wordsworth's Poetic Cells: Hermits, Silence, and Language

The Recluse's Cell

From the 1790s onwards William Wordsworth's poetry features numerous hermits, anchorites, nuns, monks, solitaries, wanderers, and recluses. Early examples include the forest hermit in 'Tintern Abbey' and the *Lyrical Ballad* on 'St Herbert's hermitage, Derwent Island'. Wordsworth and Coleridge are both associated with the authorship of 'The Mad Monk', which was published in the *Morning Post* on 13th October 1800 under the pseudonym 'Cassiani jun': Cassianus (or St John Cassian) was a fifth–century theologian and monk who lived as a hermit in Egypt.[1] There are various further examples of nuns and hermits in Wordsworth's *Poems, in Two Volumes*, particularly 'Nuns fret not', and an anchorite features in the sonnet 'To the River Duddon'. In 1808 the poet incorporated the story of St Basil, a fourth–century founder of western monasticism, into 'The Tuft of Primroses' and there are several parallels between Basil's life and Wordsworth's.[2] Further examples include five 'Inscriptions supposed to be found in and near a Hermit's cell', which Wordsworth composed in 1818. The 1835 *Yarrow* sequence includes a poem on the anchoress 'St Catherine of Ledbury', and examples from *Ecclesiastical Sketches*

---

1 Stephen Parrish argues that 'The Mad Monk' was written by Wordsworth; David Erdman claims it is by Coleridge. For details of the authorship debate see *Lyrical Ballads, and Other Poems*, ed. by James Butler and Karen Green (Ithaca: Cornell University Press, 1992), Appendix V, 802–4 and Carol Landon, 'Wordsworth, Coleridge, and the Morning Post: An Early Version of 'The Seven Sisters'', *The Review of English Studies*, New Series, 11 (1960), 392–402, 397.

2 See Simon Jarvis, *Wordsworth's Philosophic Song* (Cambridge: Cambridge University Press, 2007), 111–32.

include the sonnets entitled 'Cistertian Monastery' and 'Monks, and Schoolmen'. A significant number of Wordsworth's 'Memorials of a Tour in Italy, 1837' focus on his visits to the monasteries of Laverna, Vallambrosa, and Camaldoli. Wordsworth's travelling companion, Henry Crabb Robinson, records their encounters with Franciscan and Benedictine monks and explains how the poet was so taken by the idea of the twelfth-century life of St Francis that he frantically sought a text on the monk's life. The travellers were welcomed by these monks and at Camaldoli Wordsworth sought out and entered an hermitage where a few monks resided with particular severity and discipline.[1] Wordsworth's fascination with inscriptions, epitaphs, graveyards, and, more pertinently, ruined monasteries can also be read as part of this discourse: the Grande Chartreuse, Bolton Abbey, and Furness Abbey are leading examples.

Wordsworth's responses to hermits and their places of retreat are ambiguous. In some cases he is envious of the hermit's life; in others he is disapproving of severe asceticism and highlights the potential dangers of solitude. In *The Prelude* Wordsworth laments the time when like a cowled monk 'who hath forsworn the world', he was 'zealously' disconnected from his heart (1805. XI. 76f).[2]

Furthermore, Wordsworth's poetry contains numerous secular spaces of stillness and quietness; examples include 'Glen Almain', which depicts a 'still place, remote from men', that has a deeper silence than 'A Convent or a hermit's Cell' (23f) and the 'Westminster Bridge' sonnet, in which Wordsworth throws a quilt of majestic stillness and quietness over the vast city of London. Non–religious characters in Wordsworth's poetry also often inhabit places of or crave solitude, tranquillity, and silence; for instance the titular 'Old Man

---

1   *Diary, reminiscences and correspondence of Henry Crabb Robinson*, ed. by Thomas Sadler, 3 vols. (London: Macmillan, 1869), III, 127f.

2   Samuel Johnson's *Rasselas*, which Wordsworth owned a copy of, contains a variety of responses to enclosure, contemplation, and hermitic solitude. Female characters are attracted to the enclosed life but their male companions warn these women away from the 'danger of the cloister' on account of the joys of love and marriage. Solitary retirement is associated with a 'rejection of pleasure'. See *The History of Rasselas: Prince of Abyssinia*, ed. by Thomas Keymer (Oxford: Oxford University Press, 2009) and Chester L. Shaver, *Wordsworth's Library: A Catalogue* (New York: Garland, 1979), 141.

Travelling' and 'The Solitary Reaper'. But solitude is also sometimes dangerous and debilitating as in 'Lines left upon a seat in a
yew tree'.

Although hermits had become fashionable additions to eighteenth–century landscape gardens, the examples above indicate that
Wordsworth was probably more interested in the lives of hermits
who dwelt in the Middle Ages.[1] The poet had access to texts on
church history and asceticism from an early age: Duncan Wu notes
that Edward Gibbon's *History of the Decline and Fall of the Roman
Empire* was a standard text at Hawkshead.[2] Pierre Bayle's *General
Dictionary, Historical and Critical* also included church history and
was an important source for Wordsworth and Coleridge in 1798
(Wordsworth's Reading, 10). Another important source of information on French and Italian monasteries is Joshua Lucock Wilkinson's
The Wanderer (published 1798), which recounts Wilkinson's tour of
the continent and which Wordsworth probably read in manuscript
(Wordsworth's Reading, 148).[3] On 28th December 1809 Dorothy
Wordsworth wrote to Lady Beaumont to thank her for sending them
'the most interesting narrative of the life of "an English Hermit".
Dorothy continues: 'I ought to have said more of the pleasure we
received from the interesting history of the Hermit, but I have not
room for it. Coleridge wishes it could be published in The Friend, but
perhaps this cannot be allowed.'[4]

During the Middle Ages there were two distinct types of Christian
solitaries; hermits (from the Greek *eremia* meaning desert) and
anchorites (from *anachorein*, meaning to withdraw).[5] Between 1100

---

1   See William Gilpin, *Observations, relative chiefly to picturesque beauty, made
in the year 1772, on several parts of England; particularly the mountains, and
lakes of Cumberland, and Westmoreland*, 2 vols. (London, 1792), vol. II, 44–6
on the picturesque effect of vagrant figures.
2   *Wordsworth's Reading 1770–1799* (Cambridge: Cambridge University Press,
1993), 158.
3   Jarvis has noted that at the end of the eighteenth century discussion of asceticism was coloured by the Revolutionary assault on French monasteries: see
Wordsworth's Philosophic Song, 112.
4   *The Letters of William and Dorothy Wordsworth: The Middle Years*, ed. by
Ernest de Selincourt (Oxford: Oxford University Press, 1937), vol I, 350f.
5   For an introduction to hermits and anchorites see Rotha Mary Clay, *The Hermits
and Anchorites of England* (Detroit: Singing Tree Press, 1968). Throughout this

and 1300 AD hermits began to separate themselves from monasteries which were becoming increasingly ritualistic, avaricious, and political. Radical reform took the shape of a retreat into forests and wildernesses. In England during the eleventh and twelfth centuries the term 'anchorite' came to describe a solitary who lived an enclosed life. The anchoritic dwelling was often painfully small, sometimes no more than 2.4 metres square with a window sometimes no more than 53 centimetres square.[1] This extreme enclosure signalled the anchorite's irreversible separation from the material world and his or her faithful anticipation of the afterlife. The last rites were administered before the reclusory door was walled up and in many cases the anchorite's cell was prepared in advance to serve as his tomb. The reclusory was therefore, like the tomb or graveyard, the space in which the physical and the transcendent, the present and the absent, intersect. The anchorite gave him or herself entirely to prayer and meditation spending large parts of the day in silence. Before the widespread dissolution of religious houses that took place in the sixteenth century there is evidence of at least 750 cells in England scattered throughout every county; there were even cells in the city of London.[2] Wordsworth witnessed at first hand a re–enactment of this dissolution during the French Revolution.

As an extensive traveller, a fervent walker, and head of a hospitable family Wordsworth was hardly a secluded hermit or contained anchorite.[3] But in the Preface to *The Excursion* Wordsworth casts himself as a recluse in retirement, and compares the relationships between his poems to the structure of a medieval church:

> the two Works [*The Prelude* and *The Recluse*] have the same kind of relation to each other, if he may so express himself, as

---

paper I use the adjective 'hermitic' to refer to hermits, anchorites, and enclosed monks of various orders.

1   Christopher Cannon, 'Enclosure', in *The Cambridge Companion to Medieval Women's Writing*, ed. by Carolyn Dinshaw and David Wallace (Cambridge: Cambridge University Press, 2003), 109–23, 109.

2   For a comprehensive survey of the daily lives of anchorites see Ann K. Warren, *Anchorites and Their Patrons in Medieval England* (Berkeley: University of California Press, 1985).

3   See MS page 159 on *The Excursion* in *The Fenwick Notes of William Wordsworth*. ed. Jared Curtis (Humanities-Ebooks, 2007), 195..

the Anti-chapel has to the body of a gothic Church. Continuing this allusion, he may be permitted to add, that his minor Pieces, which have been long before the Public, when they shall be properly arranged, will be found by the attentive Reader to have such a connection with the main Work as may give them claim to be likened to the little Cells, Oratories, and sepulchral Recesses, ordinarily included in those Edifices.[1]

In forming an analogy between his smaller poems and the little cells, oratories, and sepulchral recesses of a gothic church, Wordsworth conceptualises these poems as contained spaces of quietness and reverence. This architectural metaphor draws together the physical places in which hermits reside and the imagined poetic spaces that Wordsworth constructs. A poem itself becomes a metaphorical cell or hermitage; a contained space which is separate from the material world and in which a solitary figure, such as the reader, might contemplate. As the hermit retreats from the fever of the world into his cell, so the reader might enter the separate world of a poem.

There are of course important arguments concerning Wordsworth's Christian or, in some cases, 'semi–atheistic' tendencies and their development.[2] In attending to Wordsworth's poetic appropriation of hermits and their cells, however, I do not wish to offer any argument for or against Wordsworth's religious or denominational allegiances. Rather I seek to demonstrate an interesting resonance between Wordsworth's sustained yet ambiguous interest in hermitic figures and his conception of what constitutes the most appropriate type of poetry and poetic language. I will briefly consider three things: first I question how Wordsworth's presentation of hermits reflects certain characteristics of language and silence; secondly I consider the hermit's contemplation and containment as conditions in which Wordsworth suggests poetry and poetic language might be fruitfully cultivated; finally I offer a reading of Wordsworth's 'Inscription for the spot where a hermitage stood on St Herbert's Island, Derwent-Water' as a poetic cell or oratory into which the poet invites the reader.

---

1   *The Excursion*, ed. by Sally Bushell, James A Butler and Michael C Jaye (Ithaca: Cornell University Press, 2007), 38.

2   See for example William Ulmer, *The Christian Wordsworth 1798–1805* (Albany: State University of New York, 2001).

Silence, Containment, and the Preface to *Lyrical Ballads*

Lane Cooper notes that Wordsworth and Coleridge had a particular interest in hermits during their Quantockian days.[1] Cooper provides a series of examples and puts this interest down to the influence of Spenser, Milton, and Parnell. But he does not offer a specific argument as to why hermits might have intrigued Wordsworth (and Coleridge) as anything more than stock literary characters and an element of revived medievalism. On the premise that they are stereotyped and artificial, Cooper is not able to establish any relation between examples of hermits in the poet's work.

Cooper's conclusion that Wordsworth's interest in hermits is generic and derivative is, at least in part, a result of the methods Wordsworth uses to present them. Particularly in his early poetry, Wordsworth often hides the hermit from the reader's view, signifies him indirectly, or pictures him from a distance; and the poet rarely gives the hermit a voice. Thus the hermit remains liminal. In 'Tintern Abbey' Wordsworth indicates the potential presence of a hermit by the smoke of an unseen fire:

> wreathes of smoke
> Sent up, in silence, from among the trees,
> With some uncertain notice, as might seem,
> Of vagrant dwellers in the houseless woods,
> Or of some hermit's cave, where by his fire
> The hermit sits alone. (18–23)[2]

Wordsworth's use of the passive voice and the mounting up of indeterminate semblances such as 'might seem' and 'uncertain notice' contribute to the effect of distance. The sibilance of these lines acoustically reflects the hushed, hidden, and silent nature of the hermit's life.[3] The hermit in 'Tintern Abbey' is of course marginal and the

---

1 'The "Forest Hermit" in Coleridge and Wordsworth', *MLA*, 24 (1909), 33–6.

2 All quotation of *Lyrical Ballads* and 'The Mad Monk' is taken from *Lyrical Ballads and Other Poems* ed. by Butler and Green. References appear parenthetically in the text.

3 James Heffernan has noted that vagrants hover on the edge of the poet's consciousness particularly in 1798 since he and Dorothy had themselves been displaced when they were unable to renew the lease on Alfoxden House:

ruined abbey itself is absent from the poem, but even where a hermit is the main subject of the poem he is presented indirectly. This is the case in 'The Mad Monk' where the poet signifies the indeterminate presence of the hermit–monk by the sound of a singing voice heard from beyond Mount Etna: 'A Hermit, or a Monk, the man might be, | But him I could not see' (5f). Moreover, from records of their tour of Italy we see that Wordsworth and Crabb Robinson diverted their journey to include the monastery of Camaldoli in the hope of speaking to a Benedictine monk that Robinson had met six years previously. The monk was present but the visitors could not see or speak to him because, they presumed, he was engaged in one of his silent days. This biographical incident thus reflects the absent-presence of hermits in Wordsworth's poetry. It is difficult therefore to discern any particular characteristics of Wordsworth's hermits because the poet's presentation of them is oblique. But *oblique* is precisely the interesting factor: I suggest that Wordsworth's obfuscated presentation of hermits highlights an element of their significance rather than their insignificance. Despite the fact that hermits seek out and inhabit the margins of society, Wordsworth persists in noticing and representing them. He thus encourages the reader to recognize their contemplative demeanour and their quiet place in the world.[1]

Wordsworth's interest in reclusive figures underlines the value he attaches to silence. The poet perceived a connection between poetry and silence particularly in relation to his brother John. In 'When to the Attractions of the Busy World' (published 1815) Wordsworth describes John as a 'silent Poet' (88) and, after his death in 1805, Wordsworth described him to George Beaumont as 'meek, affectionate, silently enthusiastic, loving all quiet things, and a Poet in every thing but words'.[2] For Wordsworth, quietude and silence were important qualities pertaining to poetic spirit. The hermit or anchorite that chose to live in silence thus shares habits with the 'silent Poet' that

---

'Wordsworth's "Leveling" Muse in 1798', in *1798: The Year of the Lyrical Ballads*, ed. by Richard Cronin (Basingstoke: Macmillan, 1998), 231–53.

1   See Jonathan Wordsworth, *The Borders of Vision* (Oxford: Clarendon, 1982) for a discussion of Wordsworth's marginal figures.

2   *The Early Letters of William and Dorothy Wordsworth*, ed. by Ernest de Selincourt (Oxford: Clarendon, 1935), 447.

Wordsworth so admires.

Silence is the absence of sound; hence the recognition of silence is recognition of an absent-presence. Language itself operates in a similar way; that is, words represent absent objects or ideas. And yet when Wordsworth constructs quiet spots or moments of silence in his poetry — when he writes about silence — this process of signification is iterated. Linguistically–constructed spots of silence are no longer strictly silent. The poet must deploy language, which is itself a present–absence, in order to signify silence. Wordsworth's indirect presentation of hermits, who chose to hide themselves from the community, echoes a process whereby a present sign indicates a distant or absent object. Wordsworth's indirect presentation reflects reclusive habits of silence, and indicates a connection between hermits and semiotics. It becomes relevant therefore that the hermit remains hidden or, as Cooper concluded, indeterminate and artificial.

A connection between hermitic habits and language is further developed in Wordsworth's prose. In the Preface to *Lyrical Ballads* we learn that Wordsworth is anxious about language because of its multiplicity and ambiguity. On the other hand he admires language that is characterised by repetition, containment, and stability. Wordsworth values 'rustic language' because it has been cultivated within an enclosed community where 'our elementary feelings exist in a state of greater simplicity and consequently may be more accurately contemplated and more forcibly communicated' (*Lyrical Ballads, and Other Poems,* 743). Situated contemplation and simplicity facilitate powerful communication as they subdue and purify the associative capacity of the mind. Wordsworth continues: 'such a language arising out of repeated experience and regular feelings is a more permanent and a far more philosophical language than that which is frequently substituted for it by poets' (744). Wordsworth repudiates poets who substitute genuine local attachments and repetition for 'arbitrary and capricious habits of expression' (744). The type of poetic language that Wordsworth advocates is therefore cultivated under conditions that the hermit values.

Wordsworth goes on to describe his own 'habits of meditation' (744), and in the 1802 revisions to the Preface he states that a poet is a man equipped with a 'disposition to be affected more than other men by absent things as if they were present' (751). The poet has 'an ability of conjuring up in himself passions, which are indeed far from being the same as those produced by real events' (751). Wordsworth thus defines the poet in terms of his separation from the material world and he uses a vocabulary of contemplation to do so. The poems of *Lyrical Ballads* are the tools with which Wordsworth proposes to cultivate the reader's propensity to become excited without recourse to 'gross and violent stimulants' (746). Wordsworth argues that 'frantic novels, sickly and stupid German tragedies, and deluges of idle and extravagant stories in verse' (747) have given men a 'craving for extraordinary incident' (746): 'When I think upon this degrading thirst after outrageous stimulation I am almost ashamed to have spoken of the feeble effort with which I have endeavoured to counteract it' (747). Therefore he wants his poetic 'experiments' to quietly improve the reader's capacity to be stimulated without recourse to 'immediate external excitement' (751). Repetition and simplicity, which cultivate the best type of language, are also the poetic mechanisms Wordsworth uses to cultivate thoughtful, attentive readers.

Wordsworth continues to advocate situated language in the *Essays upon Epitaphs* where the language of epitaphs is appropriate because it is intimately connected with its material environment. The epitaph is inscribed and read beside the remains of the deceased within the churchyard, and in the second essay Wordsworth describes the graveyard as an 'enclosure'. We thus recall the anchorite's perpetual proximity to his tomb. Wordsworth's prose documents therefore indicate a relationship between situated contemplation and the most appropriate, permanent means of poetic expression. Wordsworth's admiration for language that is characterised by containment, habituation, and permanence resonates with the circumstances of the hermit's life. The hermit is attached to a particular spot and thrives on contemplation. This locality and stability counters the multiplicity of language and the mind's over-active associative capacity.

Poetic Space

I will conclude by briefly looking at Wordsworth's 'Inscription: For the Spot where the Hermitage stood on St Herbert's Island, Derwent-Water'.

> If thou in the dear love of some one friend
> Hast been so happy that thou know'st what thoughts
> Will, sometimes, in the happiness of love
> Make the heart sink, then wilt thou reverence
> This quiet spot — St. Herbert hither came   5
> And here for many seasons, from the world
> Remov'd, and the affections of the world,
> He dwelt in solitude. He living here,
> The island's sole inhabitant! had left
> A Fellow-labourer, whom the good Man lov'd   10
> As his own soul; and, when within his cave
> Alone he knelt before the crucifix,
> While o'er the lake the cataract of Lodore
> Peal'd to his orisons, and when he pac'd
> Along the beach of this small isle and thought   15
> Of his Companion, he had pray'd that both
> Might die in the same moment. Nor in vain
> So pray'd he: — as our Chronicles report,
> Though here the Hermit number'd his last day
> Far from St. Cuthbert his beloved friend,   20
> Those holy Men both died in the same hour.

An inscription is permanently, physically attached to a particular place. The specificity of Wordsworth's title identifies this poem with a particular locality or 'spot'.[1] Like a situated epitaph it therefore has an implied, fixed place of reading. Wordsworth addresses the reader directly and asserts the reader's proximity to the hermitage via deixis. He thus conflates the location of the inscription (Derwent Island) and the subject of the inscription (the hermitage) with the space of the poem.[2]

---

1   Wordsworth's sustained interest in this hermitage is evident in that he published significantly different versions of it in 1800, 1815, and 1827. See *Lyrical Ballads, and Other Poems*, 179–81.

2   Herbert Lindenberger notes Wordsworth's repeated use of island imagery in rela-

Wordsworth does not describe the hermitage or the island, but his repetition of 'here' points to the text itself as a quiet spot or cell. Thus the poet invites the reader to dwell quietly within the space of the text and glimpse therein the qualities of Herbert's life. Wordsworth presents the word 'removed' almost before the reader expects it (we might expect it at the beginning of line eight), and the half–rhyme between 'remov'd' and 'solitude' highlights Herbert's isolation. The parataxis of the clauses 'from the world' and 'the affections of the world' enacts this disconnection between the hermit and the community. The island, the hermitage, and the inscription are delimited spaces, as is the poem. Herbert prayed that he and St Cuthbert 'Might die in the same moment' (17): with the emphasis on 'removed' the reader imagines the hermitage from the outside, and yet Wordsworth's use of the preposition 'in' on line seventeen turns the reader's attention towards the internal space of the enclosure. Furthermore the preposition turns a moment of time into a spatial location. The spatially and temporally separate histories of Herbert and Cuthbert coincide at the hour of their death; the present and the absent intersect; the tangible world meets the intangible world. The text itself makes similar intersections possible.

In the Preface to *Lyrical Ballads* Wordsworth frames his ideas about language in terms of contemplation, repetition, and stability. The hermit's habitat echoes the containment and repetition that Wordsworth argues will cultivate the most genuine type of poetic language. The 'Inscription for St Herbert's Island' encapsulates the space in which the hermit chose to be confined and is an enactment of Wordsworth's later conceptualisation of his smaller poems as 'little Cells, Oratories, and sepulchral Recesses' of a gothic church. Wordsworth wants the reader to experience the excitement of the passions through containment and habit, without recourse to 'gross and violent stimulants'; he points to his texts as spaces in which the reader, like the hermit, might cultivate this capacity. Wordsworth's poetry is scattered throughout with hermitic figures, but rather than regard these quietly present fig-

---

tion to solitude and contemplation in *The Prelude*. See 'Images of Interaction in The Prelude', in *The Prelude: 1799, 1805, 1850*, ed. by Jonathan Wordsworth, M.H. Abrams and Stephen Gill (New York: Norton, 1979), 642–663, 649–54.

ures as if they were absent, I have attempted in this paper to use them as a means of thinking about how the poet conceives of poetic space and poetic language.

Matthew Rowney

Where the Wheel Isn't: the Peripatetic in 'The Old Cumberland Beggar' and 'The Solitary Reaper'

Balzac wrote: 'Walking is vegetating; strolling is life.' A 'walk' is programmatic, passive, and a means to an end, while to "stroll" is 'to admire grand pictures of misery, love, joy, graceful or grotesque portraits; to look into the depths of thousands of lives.'[1] Similarly, in early medieval England prayer was a means to an end, each Latin syllable read aloud, with little attention to meaning, while by the late medieval period, silent prayer, or what was sometimes called 'prayer of the heart' was a growing practice.[2] While Romantic pedestrianism is not neatly aligned with either of these formulae, we might say that for many Romantics, Wordsworth in particular, to walk is to assume a mind set in order to invoke a prayer of the heart, that is, a profound internal meditation. Walking provides a coherent structure connecting physical and mental activity to social experience and poetic composition, offering a unique vantage point from which to interrogate received notions of culture, subjectivity, social hierarchy and historical change. Yet at the same time the walker (and the coherent structure of peripatetics) is vulnerable, not only to the unpredictability of the road, but to his or her own affective emergencies, experiences that resist interpretation and escape this model of walking as a solely unifying and regenerative experience. These moments where control is lost and meaning slips complicate and in their turn interrogate any straightforward understanding of poetic activity provided by the structure of pedestrian practice.

---

1   Honore De Balzac, *The Physiology of Marriage* (Baltimore: John Hopkins University Press, 1997), 48.
2   Paul Saenger, "Books of Hours and the Reading Habits of the Later Middle Ages." In *The Culture of Print*, ed. Roger Chartier (Princeton, NJ: Princeton University Press, 1989).

Within this peripatetic framework I will examine images of the pedestrian and circulation within Wordsworth's 'The Old Cumberland Beggar' and 'The Solitary Reaper', poems which negotiate a paradox of simultaneous absence and presence by affective engagement with marginal social figures in the landscape. I will explore ways in which repetitive motion within the landscape communicates with that of the pedestrian and with the cultivating labour of poetic composition, or in other words, how steps become meter and strides become morphemes, and how these group together into the strolling meditation that is the walk and the poem.

In the *Tao Te Ching* we find the lines:

> Thirty spokes
> meet in the hub.
> Where the wheel isn't
> is where it's useful.[1]

Put another way, being achieves its significance through non-being, function is wedded to form is wedded to formlessness as a space inside a wheel within a wheel. In 'The Old Cumberland Beggar', it is the beggar's uselessness, his absence from society, his invisibility, which constitute the radical importance of his value, his presence and his purpose.

What the beggar has come from and returns to, 'the eye of Nature', is also that of which he is a part. This is illustrated when his eyes, 'they', stare upon the ground from which he is made, and to which he will return, the dust to dust. This formation is paralleled in 'Tintern Abbey', where the way of seeing of the poet's youth is described as 'an appetite, a feeling, and a love' (81) in contrast to the mature poet's vision of 'A presence ... /... a sense sublime / Of something far more deeply interfused' (94–96).[2] The diversity of sensual phenomena is refined into a presence and the mortal eyes of the individual partake of the transcendent Eye of the imagination.

From its first two words 'I saw' to the two transcendent Eyes at its

---

1   Lao Tzu, *Tao Te Ching*, trans. Ursula K. Le Guin (Boston: Shambhala Publications, 1997), 11.
2   Sytephen Gill, ed., *William Wordsworth: The Major Works* (Oxford: Oxford University Press, 1984).

close, the poem structures itself as a commentary on the movement of the ocular towards the oracular. The spatial configurations of the poem place the beggar as the central ocular object within a vast natural space, the object of the narrator's vision, but also a representative of vision itself, a kind of pupil in the eye. We first find him sitting 'on a low structure... /...at the foot of a huge hill' (3–4). Later we are given a dilating picture of the expanse the beggar cannot see, culminating in the line: 'And the blue sky, one little span of earth' (50), again contracting and pinpointing the field of vision against an exterior hugeness. Ground is reiterated as the beggar's field of vision: 'On the ground (45) ... along the ground (47) ... one little span of earth (50) ... for ever on the ground' (52). This concentration of vision on one spot over a period reminds us of our own position as readers. Our eyes follow the metered feet of the poem, 'in the same line, / At distance still the same' (57–58), like the beggar's eyes follow the marks left in the road by the carts that have passed, his vision unvarying in its direction or distance from its object. Our reading takes up the recuperative effect of the narrator and his subject's walking, our eye encompassing his 'stated round', the beggar reflected, as it were, at the centre.

Wordsworth's shift from the underlying georgic to the overtly political with his address to the 'Statesman' creates a contrast between social positions, which again pinpoints the beggar, now within the orb of the State. As 'value' itself came to be defined in increasingly utilitarian terms, the questionable value of the beggar also implied the questionable value of the poet. If the beggar's steady downward gaze resembles the reader's, we can see the project of the poem and its poet as anti-utilitarian, as aligned with the supposedly useless circulation of the beggar. The marks 'in one track' (55) describe the steps of the walk, our action of seeing and what it is we see. We track the poem's metrical feet and find our own sense of regeneration from this circulation. The marks, 'Impressed on the white road' (57) are also the words impressed on the page of the poem, which 'Must needs impress a transitory thought' (116) on the mind of the reader.

We might read something of the nature of this thought within the poetic tradition evoked by the comparison of people in the landscape to fruit:

The easy man
Who sits at his own door, and like the pear
Which overhangs his head from the green wall,
Feeds in the sunshine; the robust and young,
The prosperous and unthinking, they who live
Sheltered, and flourish in a little grove
Of their own kindred... (108–14)

This passage, with its door, garden, pear, prosperity, and flourishing grove recalls another described in Homer:

> And without the courtyard by the door is a great garden, of four plough-gates, and a hedge runs round on either side. And there grow tall trees blossoming, pear-trees and pomegranates, and apple-trees with bright fruits, and sweet figs, and olives in their bloom. .... Pear upon pear waxes old, and apple on apple, yea, and cluster ripens upon cluster of the grape, and fig upon fig.[1]

The fruitful and bounteous pastoral world is evoked to represent the sheltered and vegetative existence of the unthinkingly healthy and prospering populace. The poet, like Milton in 'Lycidas', must open up and delve within this pastoral garden to reveal the tragic residing there:

And with forced fingers rude,
Shatter your leaves before the mellowing year
Bitter constraint and sad occasion dear,
Compels me to disturb your season due: (4–7) [2]

The leaves, in this sense, are human ones, the 'robust and young' (before the mellowing year) who 'flourish in a little grove', whose sense of sheltered complacency must be shattered by the figure of the beggar. The bitter constraint of the beggar's existence reminds us of dearth, want, debilitation, and death, compelling a deeper contemplation of the bounty of nature ('Et in Arcadia Ego') and a more profound understanding of our relation to each other and ourselves.

---

1   Homer, *The Odyssey*, trans. S.H. Richards and Andrew Lang (New York: Macmillan, 1883), VII.113-14.
2   John Milton, *The Complete Poems* (London: Penguin, 1998).

As the beggar represents the pupil in the eye, he also represents the space 'where the wheel isn't' which is also the space of the walk: in the central stanza of the poem, he binds together the spokes of the poem and of his social milieu:

> the Villagers in him
> Behold a record which together binds
> Past deeds and offices of charity
> Else unremembered, and so keeps alive
> The kindly mood in hearts which lapse of years,
> And that half-wisdom half-experienced gives
> Make slow to feel, and by sure steps resign
> To selfishness and cold oblivious cares. (80–87)

A society without charity, an ungiving humanity, is a vexed form, a paradox of 'oblivious cares' which align it with, on line 37, the 'rattling wheels' of the mundane, 'The dreary intercourse of daily life' in 'Tintern Abbey' (132), a course which, though circular, moves in extremity towards the type of pointlessly repetitive suffering witnessed within the infernal circles of Dante. What such a society, divorced from the bonds of sympathy would resemble is something akin to Wordsworth's description of St. Bartholomew's fair: 'what anarchy and din / Barbarian and infernal!' (660–1). The 'record which together binds' (81) in 'The Old Cumberland Beggar', is 'jumbled up' (691) and disjointed in the passage from *The Prelude*. The project of pedestrianism, the steps that recover and reintegrate, is interrupted, and instead of uniting into a coherent whole, "by sure steps" becomes resigned to a society whose fragmentation is represented as a space filled with disembodied heads. The implosion of our vision onto the figure of the beggar is here exploded into a thousand 'grimacing, writhing, screaming' (673) shards. The walker and the reader who accompanies him realize that these sights all have potential value that will not (within the mind and the poetry, but also implicitly in social terms) be fully realized. The justice one can reasonably request from those in power (as in the address to the statesman) becomes a mockery when faced with a 'Parliament of Monsters' (692).

In contrast to the frenetic motion described in the St Bartholomew's

Fair passage, the beggar is nearly motionless. From lines 53 to 60 the word 'still' is repeated three times, in both the sense of 'continuing' and 'unmoving'. The close placement invites conflation of meaning: though it would appear that the world continues to move in its habitual way, oblivious of his stillness, it is perhaps also true that the 'stillness' of his enduring presence places him at the centre of activity. In *Home at Grasmere* a similar type of stillness is achieved. According to Anne Wallace:

> 'All things' round back towards the walkers, as if they were a still centre, and yet they move along a path that leads through the vale...the passage places the pedestrians at the moving centre of circles, holding the circling as Grasmere does, but also moves them through and into the vale.[1]

The beggar is also at the moving centre of circles, in his circulation through the landscape and among the society within it. Yet the beggar, to accomplish his purpose in the poem, must provide a diminutive presence, a near invisibility, to illustrate his overlooked importance. This identity is partially constructed through negative definition. The beggar is 'not older now' (23), the horseman 'does not throw ... his alms upon the ground' (26), 'nor quits him so' (29), the postboy passes 'without a curse ... or anger in his heart' (42–3). 'His age has no companion' (45) ... never knowing what he sees' (54), he does 'no vulgar service' (124), is 'unblamed, uninjured' (159) and his eyes 'no more behold the horizontal sun' (181). Lamb similarly evokes the beggar with a flurry of negatives:

> No rascally comparative insults a beggar...He is not in the scale of comparison. He is not under the measure of property...No one twitteth him with ostentation...No one accuses him of pride... None jostle with him...No wealthy neighbour seeketh to eject him...No man sues him. No man goes to law with him.[2]

Lamb uses the beggar's absence and aloofness from polite urbanity to illustrate its flaws. Wordsworth instead stresses the good that the

---

1   Anne Wallace, *Walking, Literature, and English Culture* (Oxford: Oxford University Press, 1993), 124.
2   Charles Lamb, *The Works Of Charles and Mary Lamb*, Vol. 2 (Minneapolis: Filiquarian Publishing, 2010), 110.

beggar's frailty and want bring out in others. Both writers, in weigh-
ing their descriptions negatively, indicate something they are writing
against as much as for. Yet this distinction is complicated if we consider certain other abject figures within Wordsworth's poetry, revealing the type of affective emergency mentioned earlier.

The old Cumberland beggar's interactive and repeated circulation
culminates in: 'all behold in him / A silent monitor' (114–5). The use
of 'behold' here adds emphasis to its earlier use in line 81, and, as J.
H. Prynne writes in his meticulous book-length discussion of 'The
Solitary Reaper': 'There is … a biblical flavour to the usage, that if
we look comprehendingly at what we see we shall recognize evidence
or proof of what has been claimed or predicted, a confirmation of
God's manifest providence'.[1] That the beggar, a marginal and practi-
cally invisible figure, should become the subject and example of profound meditation is a theme in the Gospels as well as in Wordsworth,
who reminds us through his gesture towards biblical language that
providence often works in mysterious ways. We 'behold' both the
beggar and the reaper, conspicuous through the subtlety and unexpected nature of their meanings, their ocular and oracular roles. Yet
the poems vary substantially in terms of peripatetics. While 'The Old
Cumberland Beggar' fulfils a unifying and sublimating role, 'The
Solitary Reaper' is full of unresolved affect amidst a disjointed soci-
etal background. We walk along with the beggar as part of a successful project of peripatetics, returning to a society refreshed and rein-
vigorated by this circulation. We walk past the solitary reaper real-
izing that the society represented in her song is no longer; the poet is
set apart by a labour and a song that is foreign. Our walk is not excur-
sive but itinerant, not a circle but a line; we must travel on, conflicted
and restless, along the seemingly endless public road. Prynne writes:
'Birdsong, too, has no ending in this sense, as also certain kinds of
human feeling and memory that will not come to closure' (87). The
poem, placid on its surface, labours unceasingly beneath.

In the headnote to 'The Old Cumberland Beggar', Wordsworth
predicts that the beggar is of a class that "will probably soon be

---

1   J. H. Prynne, *The Solitary Reaper and Others* (Cambridge: Cambridge Printers
     Ltd., 2007), 20.

extinct". This is also true of the reaper and her culture: her method of reaping, her songs, and (almost) the language in which she sings were being overtaken by a culture of utilitarian progress, which was, according to Prynne,

> disbanding the oldest kinds of human connection and rhythm in favour of modern impersonal methods…that will improve crop yields…and put an end to singing like this. (77–8)

'The Solitary Reaper' presents a kind of breaking of the social circle, which the stated round of 'The Old Cumberland Beggar' had inscribed. Both poems deal with the unrelenting machinery of improvement: the figure of the beggar invoking a trumping humanism, the reaper a foreign history and a song we cannot understand. The absence which gives 'The Old Cumberland Beggar' such metaphorical significance does not disturb the equanimity of the narrator in the way that it does in 'The Solitary Reaper', where the sense of absence is given both in the solitude of the reaper herself and the questioning voice at the centre of the poem: "Will no one tell me what she sings?" His lack of comprehension reflects an unresolved affective disturbance echoed within the landscape and the singer's social difference. The narrator's distance, physically, socially, linguistically, romantically, from his subject is in direct contrast to the sound of her song, which surrounds the listener and overflows the landscape that contains it, creating an impossible distance within an inescapable closeness.

The structure of 'The Solitary Reaper' everywhere signifies absence. The four stanzas of the poem are each composed of two four-line groups. The fourth line of the first stanza interrupts the iambic pattern with the spondee 'Stop here', which also indicates a potential disruption of the walk. Each line has four beats except for the fourth line of the last three stanzas, which has three. This slight rhythmic variation contributes to a sense of forward propulsion by creating a psychological demand for a return to the set rhythmic pattern. The insistence on a fourth and its absence has further implications. As Derek Attridge points out: '… the four-beat rhythm has been a recurrent feature in the rhythmic arts of Western Europe; and it seems likely that this is a reflection of something fundamental in the fac-

ulty of rhythmic production and perception itself.'[1] The meter inten-
sifies the sense that there is something fundamentally missing from
the poet's experience that threatens to disrupt not only the peripatetic
project, but also the vision, as expressed in 'The Old Cumberland
Beggar', of an integrated society.

Disturbance is also reflected by the poem's rhyme scheme. While
the majority of the lines appear in alternate rhyming pairs and cou-
plets, there are two places, in the first and last stanza, where the lines
do not rhyme. Lines one and three, ending in "field" and "herself",
and lines 25 and 27, ending in "sang" and "work." In part, these lines
serve to break up the monotony of the rhyme, as singing breaks up
the monotony of work, or the figure breaks up the monotony of the
landscape. But they also signify the greater lack of integrated experience the poem describes. This lack is discernible in the unrhymed
words: both in what she sang and in the depopulated field in which
she does her work.

The sympathy of the poetic labour with the reaper's labour and with
the narrator's walking is reiterated in the lines: "And, as I mounted
up the hill, / The music in my heart I bore" (30–31) and points to
walking as a type of composing, where steps become meter, strides
become morphemes that group together excursions into poems. Yet
as with other blocks to the recovery of meaning here, assimilation
is disrupted when the speaker claims ignorance of the subject of the
song, wondering if its matter is of 'far-off things, / And battles long
ago,' (19–20) or 'Some natural sorrow, loss, or pain' (23). To the
modern reader, the far-off and long ago is always already 'the history
of the present', implicated to some degree in any naturalized sorrow.
The reaper's solitary condition reflects a fractured society and recalls
the troubled history of the highlands, including the Jacobite rebellion of 1745, its subsequent defeat, and the repressive measures the
Tory government took to pacify the region. In combination with
industrialization, enclosure and war, the countryside became increasingly deserted and its population impoverished. As Dorothy records
being told by a local inhabitant: 'the glens were much more popu-

---

1   Derek Attridge, *The Rhythms of English Poetry* (London: Longman, 1982), 82.

lous than now'.[1] If we remember that the first line, which ends in 'field', is unrhymed, we can see a landscape marked by an absence and threaded with a despair both 'far-off' and immediate, 'long ago' and contemporary.

Rebecca Solnit writes: 'A solitary walker ... is unsettled ... drawn forth into action by desire or lack.'[2] Absence or lack haunts both 'The Solitary Reaper' and 'The Old Cumberland Beggar' in disrupting and unifying ways, motivating a desire for integration and intelligibility that is fulfilled by the beggar and frustrated by the reaper. Both describe something 'That has been and may be again!' (24), the unifying experience of the recognition of the value of marginality, and the disruptive recognition of the powerlessness of the individual in the experience of forces beyond his control.

By the end of the poem, the presence of the old Cumberland beggar has become increasingly rarefied; he silently fades into the poem's cyclical movements. This sense of diminishment is especially clear in the lines: 'The vacant and the busy, maids and youths, / And urchins newly breeched all pass him by' (64–5). From maid to youth to urchins newly breeched, we witness a retrogression, a journey into a place where action is no longer relevant, a foreshadowing of the beggar's final walk into the eye of creation. Finally, his existence itself evaporates; he becomes, like his class, gradually extinct, yet continuing still to fulfil his purpose as an example to his time and our own.

While the circular path of the old Cumberland beggar is denied to the pedestrian of 'The Solitary Reaper,' perhaps another type of circulation offers itself. If *Home at Grasmere* can be read as the poet's 'journey of ever-decreasing circles into the geographical and human heart of his adoptive home',[3] then we can think of the song that the poet hears as repeated within the poet's mind long after he has left the scene of its performance, circulating, however problematically, 'Long after it was heard no more' (32). The conditions of poverty and

---

1   Dorothy Wordsworth, *Journals of Dorothy Wordsworth* Vol. 2. (New York: Macmillan, 1897), 186.
2   Rebecca Solnit, *Wanderlust: a History of Walking* (New York: Penguin, 2001), 26.
3   Robin Jarvis, *Romantic Writing and Pedestrian Travel* (New York: St. Martin's Press, 1997), 114.

indigence the poems describe have yet to be resolved, and continue to echo through our consciousness. Freud, in describing a complication that sometimes occurs within psychoanalysis, also describes this social problem when he writes: 'He is obliged to repeat the repressed material as a contemporary experience instead of, as the physician would prefer to see, remembering it as something belonging to the past.'[1] Perhaps we can see Wordsworth's poems, in their continuing reverberation, as an aid in recovering memory, with the hope that in exposing this knowledge, we will no longer be doomed to walk continually the same path without knowing what we see.

---

1   Sigmund Freud, *Beyond the Pleasure Principle* (London: The Hogarth Press, 1961), 12.

Gregory Leadbetter

Wordsworth's 'Untrodden Ways': Death, Absence and the Space of Writing

In this essay I revisit the enduring enigma of the 'Lucy' poems—those tiny fragments of Wordsworth's vast output, which neverthe-less loom large among his achievements. So much so, that they read as the products of a distinctive voice, or poetic technique—funda-mentally related to some of the most powerful elements of his other work, but essentially discrete in character and effect. Even within the familiar grouping, there are poems where this voice, or technique, is more pronounced: 'She dwelt among the untrodden ways', 'Three years she grew in sun and shower', and the shortest and most ellipti-cal of them, 'A slumber did my spirit seal'.

I want to consider here the distinctive *imaginative manoeuvre* of that technique, in which Wordsworth seals a beloved, singular and beautiful being—notably, a child—in the earth, and in her death, lures the mind over the horizon of human knowledge: performatively enacting a process of grief that might evanesce the psychological boundary that divides the human mind from the greater life of the '*active* universe' (*Prelude* (1805) II. 266) in which it participates.[1] That manoeuvre in turn constitutes the poems' *imaginative function*, as poems—not the function they served for Wordsworth, necessarily, which we can only speculatively infer (though I will touch on that too)—but the function that derives from the qualities and virtues of their particular verbal architecture.

There are, I should say, other of Wordsworth's poems where this

---

1 For a rich reading of the 'Lucy' poems with similar themes in mind, see Richard Gravil, *Wordsworth's Bardic Vocation, 1787–1842* (Basingstoke: Palgrave Macmillan, 2003), 156–74.

technique is operative, most of which were written around the same time: in 'There was a Boy', for example, where the silence of death and absence carries the charge of living forms; in 'The Danish Boy', a ghost in the noon-day shadow of a dell where the animals don't go, who 'Yet seems a form of flesh and blood'—a literary brother to Lucy Gray; and the 'Matthew' poems, where the character Matthew blends with figures of lost children, and the effect of their death— the paradoxical presence of their absence—alters the experience of seeing and feeling the familiar landscape he inhabits. But the 'Lucy' poems are the most concentrated examples of how death and absence become an imaginative space in Wordsworth, a space of writing conducive to 'unknown modes of being' (*Prelude* (1805) I. 420). They are, in Geoffrey Hartman's sensitive commentary, 'lyrics of passage', where the poem itself becomes a 'ritual', invoking 'transition between states of consciousness'.[1]

I want to start with a poem not normally grouped with the 'Lucy cycle', ironically—namely, 'Lucy Gray'. There are certain stylistic, biographical and textual reasons for its isolation, historically,[2] but the poem is clearly related to the rest of the group. It ends in a fairly conventional folk-ghost-story style—

> —Yet some maintain that to this day
> She is a living child;
> That you may see sweet Lucy Gray
> Upon the lonesome wild.

Nonetheless, the poem does more than this. It identifies the dead girl

---

1   Geoffrey Hartman, *Wordsworth's Poetry, 1787–1814*, 2nd edn. (New Haven: Yale University Press, 1971), 157, 380 n 35.

2   See Mark Jones, *The 'Lucy Poems': A Case Study in Literary Knowledge* (Toronto: University of Toronto Press, 1995), 11. In Wordsworth's final, rather arbitrary arrangement, 'Lucy Gray' is placed under 'Poems referring to the Period of Childhood'; 'Strange fits of passion have I known', 'She dwelt among the untrodden ways' and 'I travelled among unknown men' under 'Poems founded on the Affections'; and 'Three years she grew in sun and shower' and 'A slumber did my spirit seal' under 'Poems of the Imagination'. This might say more about the inefficacy of Wordsworth's thematic divisions than anything else. I proceed here that on the basis of their thematic, verbal and technical similarities, their proximity in composition and, however idiosyncratically, in publication, it is valid to discuss the poems as a group.

with the life of the natural world: her 'solitary song' 'whistles in the wind'. And there are other connections. The second stanza runs:

> No mate, no comrade Lucy knew;
> She dwelt on a wide moor,
> —The sweetest thing that ever grew
> Beside a human door!

Her solitariness, her singleness, as a flower-like growing 'thing', echoes 'She dwelt among the untrodden ways', 'Three years she grew' and 'A slumber did my spirit seal'.

Moreover, and most relevant to the present paper, the poem foreshadows the double-tongued technique, common to the 'Lucy' cycle, by which our imaginative reception of the fact her death is cheated by the poet's sleight of hand, which identifies her death and absence with a living presence. The double tongue conjures a double vision. The third stanza continues: 'You yet might see the fawn at play, / The hare upon the green', but not the 'sweet face of Lucy Gray'. In that simple juxtaposition, implicitly *identifying* Lucy with those animals, the poem keeps her there, at play, on the green, in the persistence of *their* presence; Lucy has, as it were, 'gone into the hare'. In that crucial manoeuvre, the poem shares DNA with those customarily grouped together as the 'Lucy' cycle.

One major reason for its differentiation from those poems, however, is of course that Wordsworth traces its tale to 'a circumstance told me by my Sister, of a little girl, who not far from Halifax in Yorkshire was bewildered in a snow-storm'.[1] On the other 'Lucy' poems, he is notoriously silent—and in those poems, perhaps on the track of the deceptively simple technique he has stumbled upon, moves beyond pure narrative into the *sui generis* mode that characterises their peculiar authority.

From its first word, 'Strange fits of passion have I known' alienates its speaker from a putative psychological norm—and indeed, we have Wordsworth's own witness to the strange state he was in when he was writing these poems. In a letter to Coleridge from Goslar in

---

1   *The Fenwick Notes of William Wordsworth*, ed. Jared Curtis, revised and corrected (Humanities-Ebooks, 2007), 38.

December 1798, he says: 'When I do not read I am absolutely consumed by thinking and feeling and bodily exertions of voice or of
limbs, the consequence of those feelings'.[1] It conjures a peculiar picture of Wordsworth's nervous agitation, familiar to poets as a sign that
something wants to be said. The speaker of the poem says 'I will dare
to tell', and it was (and is) an act of daring, on Wordsworth's part, to
tell that potent thinking and feeling, those 'fits of passion'—however
obliquely. Here, the poem's speaker allows himself to be hypnotised
by the moon, and his journey becomes linked with its descent. 'In
one of those sweet dreams I slept, / Kind Nature's gentlest boon!',
he recalls—but this is the balladeer's technique, so brilliantly used
by Coleridge in 'Christabel', of stoking tension by innocent assur-
ances, no sooner uttered than undercut. For the poet/speaker turns
out not to be 'sleeping' in a sweet dream, but riding entranced into
the underworld—where the moon, the focus of his passion and his
vision, leaves him in darkness: 'the bright moon dropped'. The poem
has reached its destination, as the poet wakes up to see his beloved
in the underworld: '"Oh mercy!" to myself I cried, / "If Lucy should
be dead!"'.[2] That word, *if*, makes Lucy's death a portal onto another
order of thought, unspoken but active, freshly if disturbingly alert
to life, that continues beyond the edge of the poem—continues, of
course, into the other poems in the cycle.

From their first publication onwards, 'She dwelt among the untrodden ways' came immediately after that dark awakening—following
the thought of Lucy's death with a line that opens onto her *dwelling*
among 'untrodden ways'. Encoded in that wonderful, paradoxical
phrase, where there are 'ways' that are 'untrodden', Lucy occupies an
impossible space, beyond the reach of logic and the norms of human
understanding. Her life, in this double-tongued sense, already inhabits the chthonic realm, before we learn of her death. She is a 'Maid',
we are told, but she is also 'A violet by a mossy stone / Half-hidden
from the eye!'—and the metaphor is so *solid* here, in the best ballad

---

1   *The Letters of William and Dorothy Wordsworth, The Early Years, 1787–1805*,
    ed. E. de Selincourt, 2nd edn., rev. Chester L. Shaver (Oxford: Clarendon Press,
    1967), 236.
2   Wordsworth's changes to the early draft, deleting the original final stanza to end
    the poem here, accentuate that destination.

style, that 'Lucy' could be the flower, and the Maid and her grave the metaphor. Again, this doubles Lucy—the maid and the violet—and invests those simple images with multi-planar meaning, so that the poem, like its sisters, becomes an exemplary text of the effect Coleridge describes, where the imagination, 'hovering between two images', produces 'a strong working of the mind', which substitutes 'a grand feeling of the unimaginable for a mere image'.[1]

Lucy's half-hiddenness, distributed between these images, is the poem's active ingredient. Her life *and* her death are 'Half-hidden from the eye' in the poem's construction, which mixes each with the other—coaxing the mind to splice them together, in the very consciousness of her death. The final stanza enacts the grief that jolts the poet/speaker into the hypersensitized order of apprehension that the poem invokes—'she is in her grave, and, oh, / The difference to me!'—and makes the reader intimate with that act of grief, letting them in on the secret of her life in the speaker's love for her. 'She lived *unknown*, and *few could know* / When Lucy ceased to be' (my emphasis), brings the reader in to a space of knowing that is also the space of her death: her 'untrodden ways' are, tantalisingly, at once open and closed.

'I travelled among unknown men', placed immediately after 'She dwelt among the untrodden ways', in the later collections, was written after the other 'Lucy' poems, and feels a little remote from them in the explicitly patriotic message in the foreground. Nevertheless, its first line connects and contrasts with the first line of the previous poem: here the speaker travels among unknown men, while the object of his thoughts, Lucy, dwells among untrodden ways. The poet is a voyager in the unknown, where he finds, in that mental space, the dead Lucy, sealed in the body of England, which in turn is sealed within the mind of the poet. England's fields, and the mountains where he felt the joy of his desire, are made precious by the thought of Lucy's play, and made vivid by Lucy's absent gaze:

> Thy mornings showed, thy nights concealed
> The bowers where Lucy played;

1   *Lectures 1808–1819: On Literature*, ed. R. A. Foakes, 2 vols (Princeton, NJ, and London: Princeton University Press and Routledge, 1987), I 311.

> And thine too is the last green field
>   That Lucy's eyes surveyed.

The poet sees with the eyes of the dead—and this is the order of vision to which the poem leads: back to the mode of those earlier 'Lucy' poems.

'Three years she grew in sun and shower' stands out in the group for several reasons—not least its personification of 'Nature', and Lucy's relationship to her. Here, Lucy is a flower again, figuratively speaking, before she is human. And after those three years of growth, 'Then'—notice the strong intervention of that word—she is claimed by 'Nature': 'She shall be mine, and I will make / A Lady of my own'. Not quite human at the start of the poem, Lucy is never quite human throughout. For 'Nature', here, equates with death—a Hades, snatching an infant Persephone—and all her life as Nature's own, after those three years in sun and shower, is a phantom: the speech marks around Nature's words are an underworld.[1] Again, with the tact of the poet's double tongue, Wordsworth gives this darker Nature a language as light as a breeze on a sunny day: a stream of stunning blessings. But, with frightening irony, these are the blessings of being 'taken' by Nature to 'live / Here in this happy dell': 'Thus Nature spake—The work was done— / How soon my Lucy's race was run! / She died'. That 'work' takes us back to that moment, 'Then', at the beginning of the poem, at which Nature intervenes to claim her. 'How soon my Lucy's race was run' implies that three years was all she had in 'sun and shower'—and her consummation as Nature's own is in death: the paradox of a death that carries human consciousness into hidden life. Nature's speech—her act of possession—sows its own clues: 'hers shall be the breathing balm, / And hers the silence and the calm / Of mute insensate things'; her form will be moulded by the 'silent sympathy' of the storm's grace; 'beauty born of murmuring sound / Shall pass into her face': she is being absorbed, as she

---

1   It is highly unusual for Wordsworth to play with the idea of 'Nature' in this way: in 1799, it was fast settling into a term meant at once to satisfy, harmonise and discipline the poet's 'Unmanageable thoughts' (*Prelude* (1805) I. 149). 'See Gregory Leadbetter, *Coleridge and the Daemonic Imagination* (New York: Palgrave Macmillan, 2011), 58–60

swells into her absent maturity.

The unsettling apprehension of that absence is received as a legacy by the poem's speaker, in verse of awesome poetic control: she 'left to me / This heath, this calm, and quiet scene'. The framing theatre of grief, 'The memory of what has been, / And never more will be', invests the speaker—and hence the heath, that calm, and quiet scene—with the ecstasy of her being *in* Nature, carrying the mind into the earth, to see and feel through the poem's 'darling', sacrificial Persephone, Lucy—whose death has opened that ground.

'A slumber did my spirit seal', the most condensed of the 'Lucy' cycle in its mastery of productive ellipsis, famously does not name its mysterious female as 'Lucy', but even if its publication history did not link it as a complementary piece to other 'Lucy' poems (which it does), its imaginative occupation of death—an essay into the order beyond the human order—certainly does:

> A slumber did my spirit seal;
>   I had no human fears:
> She seemed a thing that could not feel
>   The touch of earthly years.
>
> No motion has she now, no force;
>   She neither hears nor sees;
> Rolled round in earth's diurnal course,
>   With rocks, and stones, and trees.

That first line announces the poem's oddity. Its trance-like 'slumber' echoes the speaker's 'sleep' in 'Strange fits of passion have I known', which follows the 'sinking moon to Lucy's cot'. Here, the poet approaches her again. The plural syntax of that first line blurs agency: did a slumber seal his spirit, as we tend to read it, or did his spirit seal that slumber—implicating him in laying the girl in the ground? That tinge of transgression hints at the psychic crossing the poem makes between the human and the *in*human: an imagined sacrifice to sound the life beyond human existence. 'I had no human fears' is, once again, beautifully double-tongued, evoking both a calm in the face of an inhuman presence, and the possibility that the speaker experiences *inhuman* fears. After two short lines, we're already outside the usual mental habitat. And then, as if out of nowhere, 'she' appears, and 'seemed a thing': she is at once the inhuman presence he calmly faces, and the focus of his inhuman fears—once more, in that 'seeming', hovering between states, 'The touch of earthly years' and their absence, an imaginative manoeuvre that summons 'a strong working of the mind'. The shift into the present tense in the second stanza brings her closer in the very moment she is interred. 'We see into the life of things' through a 'presence that disturbs'. Fittingly, the poem does not explicitly declare her death: she has no motion, force, 'neither hears nor sees', but she is *there*—'in earth's diurnal course, / With rocks, and stones, and trees'.

'A slumber did my spirit seal' crowns a cycle in which this complex dispersal of Lucy's life, effected by the double-tongued technique I have described, opens up 'untrodden ways' where the mind—unhelped by the ritual act at the heart of this poetry—could not otherwise go.

If that technique is essential to their imaginative function as poems, what then—to conclude—of their function for Wordsworth? The clues, as we have them, lie not in prose comment, but in his poetry. In their 'undetermined sense / Of unknown modes of being', the 'Lucy' poems share kinship with the peculiar order of panic central to the narrative of his life and mind, taking shape in Goslar at the same time. Here, the space of writing becomes an invocation to 'Forms that do not live / Like living men'; a space to listen for 'The ghostly language of the ancient earth' (*Prelude* (1805) I. 419–20, 425–26; II. 328); an opening onto 'inaccessible worlds, to regions / Where height, and depth, admits not the approach / Of living man, though longing to pursue' (*Excursion* III. 642–44). For Wordsworth, perhaps, the poems summoned the silence in which Lucy might sing in his ear.

Daniel Robinson

Wordsworth's Sonnets, Newspaper Verse, and the 'Moving Accident'

The moving accident is not my trade,
To curl the blood I have no ready arts;
'Tis my delight, alone in summer shade,
To pipe a simple song to thinking hearts.

These lines come not from a sonnet but from Wordsworth's 'Hart-Leap Well', the poem that opens the second volume of the 1800 *Lyrical Ballads*.[1] I open with them because they express Wordsworth's general ambivalence toward and even his discomfort with narrative poetry, storytelling, or poetry that requires for its successful reception the relation of an exciting tale. Personally, I like this aspect of Wordsworth because I believe plot is often the enemy of art. Indeed, I take this stanza as something of a motto for Wordsworth's *Lyrical Ballads*: here, in 1800, he tells us what he shows us to great effect in 'Simon Lee', for example, from the 1798 volume.

My comments here will consider the beginning of Wordsworth's serious work as a sonneteer. I begin with 'Hart-Leap Well' because I am trying to understand why, shortly thereafter, Wordsworth begins writing sonnets in earnest, a mode that is contrapuntal to both the narrative poetry he had written and would continue to write, as well as to the philosophical epic with which he would struggle throughout his career. I don't think Wordsworth liked having to organize his moments of lyrical insight around a series of 'moving accidents' and, after the 'Salisbury Plain' poems, I don't think he has any ambition to write a long narrative poem in lyrical stanzas such as, say, *The Faerie Queene.*

---

1   *Lyrical Ballads, with Other Poems*, 2 vols (London: T. N. Longman and O. Rees, 1800), 2: 8.

I want to suggest that we think of *Lyrical Ballads* and its preface as part of the context for Wordsworth's serious adoption of the sonnet in 1802, even though there are no sonnets to be found there; furthermore, another important part of that context is newspaper verse. This shift in Wordsworth's career involves a turn towards lyric and the placing of short lyrics, specifically sonnets, in the public space of the newspaper, where a sonnet becomes immersed in a hodgepodge of popular culture, presented among the more-or-less 'moving accidents' of the daily news.

We might begin with Wordsworth's canny allusion to *Othello*, which illuminates the issue of narrative. Desdemona falls in love with Othello while hearing him relate to her father his tales 'of most disastrous chances, / Of moving accidents by flood and field'. In 'Hart-Leap Well', the poet-narrator admits that his approach may not seduce any young women, but he does hope it will appeal to 'thinking hearts'. The New Cambridge Shakespeare edition glosses the phrase 'moving accidents' as 'stirring adventures', which is obviously the primary sense Wordsworth means to convey;[1] the phrase, moreover, suggests to me the sequencing of episodes in order to tell a story, one narrative element moving to the next—plotting as plodding, if you will, from the perspective of the inventor of the tale. These are incidents—a potential synonym for 'accidents'—not only emotionally moving, but moving forward in terms of plot. I'd also like to think of 'accident' in the Aristotelian sense that would inform textual editing—as a non-essential property of a thing or event. At least Wordsworth would like to think of plot as non-essential in order to distinguish his poetry from the 'deluges of idle and extravagant stories in verse' that, not being an avid novel-reader, he would have read in various periodicals, including the daily newspapers.

Wordsworth recalled later that he wrote 'Hart-Leap Well' while struggling with 'The Brothers', which is ostensibly a dramatic and narrative poem, itself a formal concept with which he struggles in the expanded preface of 1802 as he continues to justify writing 'the language of real men' in verse. He remarks that this poem came easy

---

1   *Othello*, ed. Norman Sanders, 2nd edn (Cambridge: Cambridge University Press, 2003), 84.

to him, completing it in 'a day or two' before returning to work on 'The Brothers'.[1] I wonder if the stanza above, coming as it does at the opening of part two of the poem, functioned as something of a writing prompt that self-reflexively liberated him from the confines of narrative verse. It seems to me that the paragraphs added to the preface in 1802 almost exclusively pertain to the subjective quality of lyric verse—even though for several paragraphs the topic seems to be dramatic poetry—'where the Poet speaks through the mouths of his characters'—but really isn't.[2] Wordsworth tells us at the end of the inserted section that everything he has said also holds true 'where the Poet speaks to us in his own person and character' (*ibid.* 404). This section includes the famous 'What is a Poet?' / 'a man speaking to men' passage, another piece which pertains directly to the subjective feelings and experiences and the imaginative creations and recreations of the lyric poet. His 'practice' as a poet has given him 'a greater readiness and power in expressing what he thinks and feels, and especially those thoughts and feelings which, by his own choice, or from the structure of his own mind, arise in him without immediate external excitement' (*ibid.* 400). He restates this idea many more times, adding that the poet's subject is truth and his purpose is the giving of pleasure, until finally this draft resumes with material from the 1800 preface that contains Wordsworth's important distinction between the artifice of meter and that of 'what is usually called poetic diction', the latter being 'arbitrary, and subject to infinite caprices upon which no calculation whatever can be made'. Meter stands because it

> obeys certain laws, to which the Poet and Reader both willingly submit because they are certain, and because no interference is made by them with the passion but such as the concurring testimony of ages has shewn to heighten and improve the pleasure which co-exists with it. (*ibid.* 404)

Indeed, these are the terms of the 'formal engagement' he asserts that a poet makes 'by the act of writing in verse' (*ibid.* 391). There is no

---

1   *The Fenwick Notes of William Wordsworth*, 2nd edn, revised and corrected, ed. Jared Curtis (Penrith: Humanities-Ebooks, 2007), 65.
2   *Lyrical Ballads and Related Writings*, ed. William Richey and Daniel Robinson (Boston: Houghton Mifflin, 2002), 399.

more binding formal engagement between a poet, his reader, and a formal poetic tradition than the sonnet—with the notable exception, particularly for Wordsworth, of the epic. Indeed, the early drafts of *The Prelude* offer a clearer picture of Wordsworth becoming or aspiring to become an epic poet around this time, more so than a picture of what he indeed became—a bona fide sonneteer.

The 1800 *Lyrical Ballads* was an ending to a kind of poetry, to a kind of book, that Wordsworth would produce; but it, especially its preface, also was a beginning for what we might call Wordsworth's solo career—one that would become dominated, at least publicly, by well over 500 sonnets. The poems from *Lyrical Ballads* would eventually be subsumed in a largely lyric canon as established by Wordsworth himself—with only *The Excursion* and, later, *The Prelude* standing apart as counterpoints to the hundreds of short poems Wordsworth wrote. So, *Lyrical Ballads* is part of the context for Wordsworth as sonneteer, even though there are no sonnets to be found there. Obviously, the 1800 edition shows Wordsworth experimenting greatly with lyric—the Lucy and Matthew poems being well-known examples. Wordsworth's first experiment in sequencing lyric is the series 'Poems upon the Naming of Places', in which Wordsworth adapts blank verse to approximate the proportions of lyric poetry. This approach is obviously informed by the success of 'Tintern Abbey', which Wordsworth considered a kind of blank verse ode; this sequence or series develops similarly but in shorter segments that may function as strophes. Only the fourth in the sequence, 'There is an Eminence', approaches the compactness of a sonnet.

As I have written in an article on Charlotte Smith, her *Elegiac Sonnets* involve a conception of what I call 'formal paradoxy' that may have influenced *Lyrical Ballads* in the yoking of disparate forms to create a kind of nonce form.[1] The formal paradoxy suggested in the phrase 'Lyrical Ballads' indicates a preference for the lyric over the narrative. Wordsworth obviously never abandoned narrative but it is clear that lyric poetry came more naturally to him. Wordsworth knew what he was doing by invoking the pastoral tradition in the 1800

---

1   '*Elegiac Sonnets*: Charlotte Smith's Formal Paradoxy', *Papers on Language and Literature*, 39 (2003), 185–220.

Lyrical Ballads, well aware of the way in which that tradition combines narrative with lyric. And, as he explains in the preface, the term *lyric* connotes to him a more sophisticated approach to meter and form than is typical in traditional ballads. His example is 'Goody Blake and Harry Gill', but other poems such as 'Simon Lee', 'The Last of the Flock', and 'The Thorn' also demonstrate a kind of experimentation with meter and stanza that looks forward to the shapes of poems by Tennyson and Poe. The shaping of unusual stanzas in *Lyrical Ballads* is similar to Southey's approach to his 'Metrical Tales' and to Mary Robinson's approach to her *Lyrical Tales*—and even, I would add, to M. G. Lewis's ballad 'Alonzo the Brave', from his novel *The Monk*, which inspired both Southey and Robinson to use Lewis's 'Alonzo' meter and which is no doubt haunting Wordsworth's consciousness when writes about his not having 'ready arts' 'to curl the blood'.

Such innovations notwithstanding, building off of the longstanding perception of the sonnet as a formal contest of skill, Wordsworth comes to the sonnet with notions of the form as a metonymy for poetic rigor and of the sonneteer as a poetic identity for himself, alternatives to the rustic balladeer and the epic poet. Sonnets are a major facet of his career-long rumination on how poetic form contains, tempers, and restrains 'powerful feeling' in order to facilitate profound thinking—by piping 'a [not-so-]simple song to thinking hearts'. But, considering the issue of lyric and narrative in Wordsworth's poetry that it raises, is it possible to argue that the sonnet is the epitomic Wordsworthian form?

This is too large of a question for me to answer here, but I think we can begin to think about it by going back to the beginning of Wordsworth's career as a sonneteer. Naturally, this narrative involves Milton, although I do believe Milton's influence, or the effect of that influence, has been overstated, especially by Wordsworth himself. But allow me to recap: although he later claimed that he already was familiar with them, Wordsworth apparently rediscovered Milton's sonnets when Dorothy read them to him—as he would later acknowledge. This is a watershed moment in the lore of Romantic sonneteering. On Friday, May 21, 1802, Dorothy notes simply, 'William wrote two sonnets on Buonaparte, after I had read Milton's sonnets to him'.[1] A fairly bland description of what Wordsworth recalls to Isabella Fenwick as his 'taking fire' and writing three sonnets in one afternoon. Dorothy, moreover, registers no amazement at her brother's taking up this form which, as he later recalled to Walter Savage Landor, he previously had considered to be 'egregiously absurd'. The birth of her brother's sonneteering alter-ego at this moment, a creature who would go on to spawn so prolifically, seems to have made little impression on her. Maybe this is because sonnets were already a part of the plan for her brother's career.

If he was modeling that career on Milton's, this aspiration arrives after, or, rather, out of, the *Lyrical Ballads*, which reveal little that is Miltonic. And it coincides generally with Wordsworth's resumption of *The Prelude* and with Coleridge's continued exhortations to produce the great epic. Echoing Johnson's definition of a sonnet, Coleridge, meanwhile, was chagrined, even hurt, to learn that Wordsworth had been 'writing such a multitude of small Poems' instead of moving forward with *The Recluse*.[2] Wordsworth claimed that he viewed sonneteering as a kind of procrastination: perhaps alluding to his incomplete epic project, he wrote to Landor, 'I have filled up many a moment in writing Sonnets, which, if I had never fallen into the practice, might easily have been better employed'.[3] It is almost as if he displaced one type of Miltonic activity for another. But I'm wary of treading down the familiar path of attributing displaced anxiety and insecurity in one area where there is manifest proficiency and confidence in another.

Simply put, Wordsworth realized he was good at writing sonnets, so why does there need to be anxiety? Wordsworth still, many years later, felt compelled to exhort a phantom critic to 'scorn not the sonnet'. So, what about Milton's sonnets—there are only a modest 23 of them, 18 of which in English—appealed to Wordsworth? We only have testimony from decades later. Furthermore, he tells Landor

1   *The Grasmere and Alfoxden Journals*, ed. Pamela Woof (Oxford: Oxford University Press, 2001), 101.

2   *Letters of Samuel Taylor Coleridge*, ed. Earl Leslie Griggs, 6 vols (Oxford: Clarendon Press, 1956–71), ii, 1013. See also i, 527.

3   *The Letters of William and Dorothy Wordsworth: The Later Years*, ed. Ernest de Selincourt, 2 vols (Oxford: Clarendon Press, 1939), i, 70–71.

in 1822, 'I was singularly struck with the style and harmony, and the gravity, and republican austerity of those compositions' (*ibid.* 70). One of the things that so appealed to him about Milton's sonnets was what he described to his brother John as the 'energetic and varied flow of sound crowding into narrow room' with 'the combined effect of rhyme and blank verse'. He also names his favorite of Milton's sonnets, including the sonnet to Cromwell but adding 'except [the] last two lines'.[1] This happens to be the only one of Milton's English sonnets to end with a couplet—a practice he does not like and thus rarely follows. While he praises (faintly) Shakespeare's sonnets, he rarely imitates them: in fact, his first published sonnet, written when he was 17, on Helen Maria Williams, is the only one of his several hundred to follow the pattern of a Shakespearean sonnet. What Wordsworth most appreciates about Milton's sonnets is his characteristic ejambing of the octave and sestet, creating what Wordsworth refers to as the 'intense Unity' of 'the image of an orbicular body,—a sphere—or a dew drop' (*Later Years* II, 653). This is in contrast to the impression of several movable parts in the English sonnet's construction—three quatrains and a couplet.

Wordsworth liked to give the seemingly contradictory but ultimately complementary impressions that the sonnet was a limiting and demanding form and that writing one was an easy enough feat for him to do. In the postscript to *The River Duddon*, Wordsworth discusses the constraints of the sonnet form, justifying his borrowing of Coleridge's idea on the grounds that Coleridge may feel free to go ahead with his own poem due to 'the restriction which the frame of the Sonnet' has imposed upon him, 'narrowing unavoidably the range of thought, and precluding, though not without its advantages, many graces to which a freer movement of verse would naturally have led'.[2] The image of the narrow room is one Wordsworth frequently associates with the sonnet, and he shows that he is comfortable within its bounds. In the 'Prefatory Sonnet' that leads his series of sonnets in 1807—now referred to by its first line, 'Nuns Fret Not

---

1   *The Early Letters of William and Dorothy Wordsworth*, ed. Ernest de Selincourt (Oxford: Clarendon Press, 1935), 312.
2   *The River Duddon, A Series of Sonnets: Vaudracour and Julia: And Other Poems*. London: Longman, 1820, 38.

at Their Convent's Narrow Room'—Wordsworth asserts that he can move about freely within the confines of the sonnet:

> In sundry moods, 'twas pastime to be bound
> Within the Sonnet's scanty plot of ground;
> Pleas'd if some Souls (for such there needs must be)
> Who have felt the weight of too much liberty,
> Should find short solace there, as I have found.[1]

So, this narrow room is also a kind of arena where Wordsworth may distinguish himself as a sonneteer. Even the adjective in line 14, 'short' modifying 'solace', tropes the form itself more explicitly than the later-revised line's 'brief solace', which draws attention away from the form's compactness. Another regrettable revision, perhaps.[2]

So, who is Wordsworth the sonneteer? He is a poet who, like Anna Seward, Mary Robinson, and Milton, viewed the writing of a sonnet a formal contest of skill. Wordsworth also found the sonnet to be a kind of crucible for thinking about feeling, of imparting poetic pleasure, and of communicating his peculiar insights. But Wordsworth also used the sonnet to respond to contemporary events and to express concerns he may or may not have shared with his public—and this is the second thread I consider connected, and worth exploring: Wordsworth as newspaper poet. Wordsworth comes to this cumulatively, through a process of contributing political sonnets to the newspaper. He begins writing sonnets as a newspaper poet; and throughout his career, the poems of his that most often appeared in the periodical press were sonnets. The periodical context of Wordsworth's sonnets has been greatly underappreciated, because in the textual, contextual, and paratextual space of the newspaper the poetic is literally marginal and the medium itself is literally disposable. In late Georgian newspapers, poetry served a purpose much in the way the comics section does in today's papers; it filled space when needed and provided diversion for readers—just as the gossipy, snarky paragraphs that usually

---

1 *Poems, In Two Volumes*, 2 vols (London: Longman, Hurst, Rees, and Orme, 1807), i, 101.

2 See Frederick Burwick, '"Narrow Rooms" or "Wide Expanse": The Construction of Space in the Romantic Sonnet', *Re-Mapping Romanticism: Gender, Texts, Contexts*, ed. Fritz-Wilhelm Neumann (Essen: Blaue Eule, 2001), 49–64.

follow the poems did. Aside from comic epigrams, short lyrics are the most common type of poem in the newspaper—although occasionally longer odes and ballads appear too. Sonnets are just the right size to ensure publication when space is available. The terms of the 'formal engagement' to which the poet and reader submit are altered when made in the space of a daily newspaper: they are less weighty, less binding, more generally ludic, obviously ephemeral. Indeed, one of the reasons Southey collected poems for his two volumes of *The Annual Anthology* was to rescue poems he considered 'too good to perish with the newspapers in which they are printed'.[1] This means of course that most newspaper poetry did perish, so to speak, and there was no guarantee of reprinting.

This is certainly the risk of publishing poems in newspapers that address contemporary topics like most of Wordsworth's newspaper sonnets did. Most of the sonnets Wordsworth wrote before the 1807 *Poems, In Two Volumes* appeared in periodicals. Wordsworth's first published poem, signed 'Axiologus', was his sonnet to Helen Maria Williams in the *European Magazine* in 1787.[2] He never collected this poem for preservation. For the most part, he considered the Napoleon sonnet to be the start of his sonneteering—although other sonnets appeared more recently in Stuart's papers than the 'Axiologus' sonnet of 1787. When Wordsworth rediscovered the sonnet in 1802, he shortly thereafter sent at least seven of the 'Sonnets Dedicated to Liberty', as they were called in 1807, to Daniel Stuart for publication in *The Morning Post*. Thus, Wordsworth began a practice of contributing sonnets to newspapers that would continue throughout his career. The next 11 sonnets that Wordsworth published before the appearance of the 1807 *Poems, in Two Volumes* were in daily newspapers, 10 in *The Morning Post* and one in *The Courier*, both owned

---

1   *A Memoir of the Life and Writings of the Late William Taylor of Norwich*, ed. J. W. Robberds, 2 vols (London: John Murray, 1843), i, 239.

2   For more on this sonnet and Wordsworth's engagement of the sonnet of sensibility, see Richard Gravil, *Wordsworth and Helen Maria Williams; Or, the Perils of Sensibility* (Penrith: Humanities-Ebooks, 2010); Daniel Robinson, '"Still Glides the Stream": Form and Function in Wordsworth's River Duddon Sonnets,' *European Romantic Review*, 13 (2002), 449–64; and Peter Spratley, 'Wordsworth's Sensibility Inheritance: the Evening Sonnets and the "Miscellaneous Sonnets"', *European Romantic Review*, 20 (2009), 95–115.

and edited by Stuart. Wordsworth's newspaper sonnets over the next 15 years or so complete an entire sequence on the Napoleonic conflict that can stand entirely separate from the book publications. He published in *The Friend* a group of seven sonnets on the Tyrolese peasant resistance to Napoleon. In January of 1814 Wordsworth published in *The Courier* a sonnet celebrating Napoleon's defeat at Leipzig. And then there are the Waterloo sonnets that Leigh Hunt so deplored and that appeared in *The Champion* in January and February of 1816. Indeed, the 1845 sonnet on Furness Abbey that Stephen Gill discusses on page 25–27 above is one of three sonnets Wordsworth wrote about the Windermere railway. The other two appeared in *The Morning Post* (then under new ownership).

We know Dorothy's reading Milton's sonnets to him prompted Wordsworth's serious engagement with the form—but what prompted Dorothy's reading of them? I believe Wordsworth turned to Milton's sonnets, perhaps requested that she read them, because he already was flirting with the idea of being a more publicly engaged poet by writing sonnets for *The Morning Post*. Given the political nature of several of Milton's sonnets, it seems natural that Wordsworth would use them as a model for newspaper verse. And, given the ephemeral nature of most newspaper poetry, Wordsworth's stance in most of these sonnets does seem to be a reversal of the script established by the Romantic-period sonnet revival: Wordsworth takes the obvious applicability of the sonnet as an inward lyric form to the age of sensibility and adapts the form as a means of crafting a poetic persona of public engagement. The 'republican austerity' of Milton's sonnets might make them seem like an appropriate model for writing sonnets on political subjects for a wider audience. (Hunt and Hazlitt both noted the irony here.) Dorothy notes in her journal of 24 December 1802 that her brother was again reading Charlotte Smith's sonnets as well (*Grasmere Journal* 186). Wordsworth was drawn to Smith as soon as he had claimed the sonnet for himself, but it was her approach to the sonnet that had become so prolifically imitated in the periodical press—as his first sonnet demonstrates. It is almost as if Wordsworth re-read Smith to exorcise her influence.

So, thanks to Robert Woof's scholarship on Wordsworth's and

Coleridge's poetry in Stuart's papers, we know that Wordsworth already was involved with Stuart and the paper when he 'took fire' and wrote the Napoleon sonnet.[1] Several poems of his had appeared first in the *Post* and others from *Lyrical Ballads* had been reprinted by Stuart to help boost sales of that volume. In fact, Wordsworth's only translation of one of Petrarch's sonnets appeared in *The Morning Post* twice. Stuart printed the sonnet beginning 'If grief dismiss me not to them that rest' in February of 1798. Coleridge no doubt gave this poem to Stuart as he did other of Wordsworth's poems—but, even so, it is Wordsworth's first published sonnet since the 'Axiologus' one of 1787. This one appeared with the initials 'W. W.'; but Wordsworth was uncomfortable with the notion of contributing poetry to newspapers as a hired gun. So, although he later denied having worked for Stuart, Wordsworth did contribute poems to the paper and looked to Milton for inspiration to do so.[2] Perhaps he did so because so much newspaper poetry is disposable and he had his eye on longevity, which the sonnet since Petrarch promises to the poet.

And here's where Mary Robinson comes into the story. In 1799, she had succeeded Southey as Stuart's 'laureate', a term Southey used to describe the position of regular poetic correspondent. She contributed more than 100 poems to *The Morning Post* during the last year of her life. But Stuart apparently had become frustrated with Robinson's and Coleridge's debilitations and tried to enlist Wordsworth as a regular contributor in July of 1800. In a letter of July 24th, 1800, Robinson

---

1   R. S. Woof, 'Wordsworth's Poetry and Stuart's Newspapers: 1797–1803', *Studies in Bibliography* 15 (1962), 149–89.

2   In 1838 Stuart was prompted to refute Gillman's portrayal of his professional relationship with Coleridge, writing to the *Gentleman's Magazine*, Stuart happened to mention Wordsworth, who took umbrage at the implication that he, like Coleridge and Lamb, was a salaried employee. Wordsworth complained to Stuart that his reference 'would lead any one to infer that I was a paid Writer of that paper. . . . I am quite certain that nothing of mine ever appeared in the Morng[sic] Post, except a very, very, few sonnets upon political subjects, and one poem called "The Farmer of Tillsbury Vale", but whether this appeared in the Morng[sic] Post or The Courier, I do not remember' (*Letters of William and Dorothy Wordsworth: The Later Years*, Part III, 2nd ed., ed. Ernest de Selincourt and Alan G. Hill [Oxford: Clarendon Press, 1982] 589). He goes on to detail every periodical publication he can think of in support of his assertion that 'the last thing that could have found its way into my thoughts would have been to enter into an engagement to write for any newspaper—and that I never did so' (*ibid.* 590).

complains to an unknown correspondent that Stuart has withheld her weekly wage because of her persistent illnesses;[1] at just about the same time, on July 11th, Coleridge informs Stuart that 'Wordsworth's state of health at this present time is such as to preclude all possibility of writing for a Paper' (*Letters* II, 8). This, incidentally, is the same letter in which Coleridge passes along Wordsworth's thanks to Stuart for reprinting poems from *Lyrical Ballads* in the *Post* and in the *Courier*, adding that 'we are convinced you have been of great service to the sale' (*ibid.* 9). In October, Robinson writes that Stuart has requested a termination of their business arrangement. Two months later she was dead, and Stuart was for several months without a laureate.

Robinson's absence does show in the paper. I have spent some time at the Newberry Library in Chicago where a number of 'lost' issues of *The Morning Post* are neatly bound, including many days and years missing from the Burney collection. We have a good record of what Wordsworth and Coleridge published in the paper, but that picture is incomplete without having a view of the other poems printed there. I noticed a significant decline in the amount of poetry published in the *Post* for several months after Robinson's death at the end of 1800. Even with a war on, Stuart liked for there to be a significant amount of entertainment in the paper—gossip, fashion, sport, and poetry, much of which is downright goofy, including some comic poems by Coleridge. And although he reprinted poetry from other sources, his preference was for 'Original Poetry' as the column was designated in its heading.

Stuart turned to the Dove Cottage circle. They were reading *The Morning Post*, and Coleridge was writing prose and poetry for it from Keswick. On September 19, 1801 perhaps again responding to Stuart's interest in Wordsworth, Coleridge writes to him asking him to send a free paper to Sarah Hutchinson in Durham, promising that this gesture will prompt Wordsworth to contribute 'as a sort of acknowledgment for this new Debt' (*Letters* II, 760). Two months later, Wordsworth writes to Stuart asking to borrow £10 promising that Coleridge will repay it or, as must have seemed more likely to

---

1   See Sharon M. Setzer, '"Original Letters of the Celebrated Mrs. Mary Robinson"', *Philological Quarterly* 88 (2009), 305–35.

everyone, that Wordsworth himself will provide 'articles for your Paper, in value to that amount' (*Early Letters* 329–30). Wordsworth closes by thanking Stuart 'for the entertainment your excellent Paper affords me' (*ibid.* 330). Entertainment is actually a big part of the exchange economy between editor, writer, and reader at work in newspaper verse. Shortly thereafter, on January 27, 1802, Dorothy notes that William is writing to Stuart and that she 'copied sonnets for him', for Wordsworth or for Stuart, or both (*Grasmere* 58). These would be the translation of Petrarch again, which appeared two weeks later in the *Post*, and, on the day after, the Cambridge sonnet, greatly revised, 'Calm is all Nature as a resting wheel', later called 'Written in very early youth', in 1807. And possibly these include a sonnet-like 15-line poem called 'Written in a Grotto' that E. H. Coleridge attributed to Wordsworth, an attribution accepted by editors Knight and Hutchinson but rejected by De Selincourt and Woof.[1] These appeared unsigned. Perhaps Wordsworth had forgotten or did not even know that the Petrarch sonnet had appeared with his initials four years earlier.

Presumably, these poems fulfilled Wordsworth's debt to Stuart. Nonetheless, Wordsworth went on to publish in the *Post* the seven sonnets Stuart calls 'little Political essays' signed 'W. L. D'.[2] These sonnets show him engaging his public in a direct but politically mediated way. The newspapers were just as blatantly ideological and biased as the news media today. So, our perception of the political nature of a sonnet changes when we read it among other discourse expressing similar political views as opposed to reading a book where one sonnet sits alone on the page—as Wordsworth preferred for his sonnets to do. As newspaper verse, the sonnets are disposable newspaper amusements—appearing among poems by such figures as Bardd Cloff, Hafiz, F., T. S., and V. R. G. Alan Liu's treatment of *The Morning Post* sonnets deliberately excludes non-political ones, giving the impression that Wordsworth was focused only on seriously engaging Coleridge's political writing. But dozens of

---

1   See Woof 183.
2   Wordsworth's editor Thomas Hutchinson long ago interpreted these initials to mean *Wordsworth Libertati Dedicavit* (see Woof 159).

other Napoleon poems appeared in *The Morning Post* before and after Wordsworth's sonnet. Isn't it likely that Wordsworth's sonnets engage these other poems? Certainly Stuart's readers would have read them in the context of entertainment and information. But what we find is that the political voice of Wordsworth's 'political sonnets'—of what Liu calls the 'political advocacy' of them—becomes somewhat muted when there are dozens of other poems expressing similar views though often in much broader strokes.[1] Political poetry is rather run-of-the-mill in a newspaper—and the particular political perspective Wordsworth imparts in *The Morning Post* seems rather tame, or at least subtle, compared with the other poems appearing therein. But then, if the sonnets are not polemical necessarily, the writing of sonnets for the *Post* becomes what it has always been—a demonstration of poetic skill and lyric insight. The poet is a sonneteer more than an advocate.

So, what about the other sonnets in *The Morning Post*? Surely the presence of other sonneteers in the *Post* ought to be as much a part of the story as is Dorothy's reading of Milton to Wordsworth. My work next will have to examine Wordsworth's sonnets in relation to these mighty competitors—particularly the formidable figures of Thomas Stott (T. S., Hafiz) and Sarah Elizabeth Villa-Real Gooch (V. R. G.), who were the most prolific sonneteers in the *Post* at this time. And these poets show that the sonnet of sensibility is alive and kicking. Moreover, around the same time that Wordsworth was contributing his political sonnets, Stuart was also printing Wordsworth's translations of Metastasio, who was an icon of the Della Cruscans early in the 1790s. We should not forget that, in many ways, publishing poems in the newspaper for mass consumption in a disposable format remained for some time a vestige of the legacy left by Della Crusca and publisher John Bell. Stuart clearly employed Southey and Robinson to rekindle something of a similarly sensational fire.

---

1   Alan Liu, *Wordsworth: The Sense of History* (Stanford: Stanford University Press, 1989); see 426–42. For more on the contexts of these early sonnets, see Stephen C. Behrendt, 'Placing the Places in Wordsworth's 1802 Sonnets', *Studies in English Literature, 1500–1900* 35 (1995); 641–67; and Peter Spratley, 'Annette, Caroline and Reclaiming Liberty: Wordsworth in Calais', *Romanticism* 16 (2010), 293–304.

Wordsworth was not only being Miltonic: could there be a touch of Della Crusca on the origins of Wordsworth the sonneteer?

Appendix:
Wordsworth's Sonnets Published Prior to
Poems, In Two Volumes (1807)

[Composition dates from relevant Cornell Wordsworth volumes]

1. Sonnet, on Seeing Miss Helen Maria Williams Weep at a Tale of Distress [She wept.—Life's purple tide began to flow] pub. *European Magazine* 1787 [Wordsworth's only Shakespearean sonnet]

2. [If grief dismiss me not to them that rest] translation from Petrarch, in Racedown Notebook, transcribed late 1795 or early 1796; printed as 'Sonnet' (W. W.) in *MP* 13 Feb. 1798 beneath 'Translation of a Celebrated Greek Song' (Publicola); reprinted as 'From Petrarch' (unsigned) *MP* 2 Feb. 1802; first sonnet published in the *MP*; this and 'Written at Evening' copied by DW on 27 Jan. to send to Stuart

3. Sonnet. Written at Evening [Calm is all Nature as a resting wheel] / [Evening Sonnets III: 'On the village Silence sets her seal'] comp. circa 1789; revised as 'Written at Evening' for *MP* 13 Feb. 1802; 'Written in very early Youth' *1807*

[ ]. Written in a Grotto *MP* 9 Mar. 1802; attributed to Wordsworth by E. H. Coleridge; attribution accepted by Knight and Hutchinson, rejected by De Selincourt and R. Woof

4. Sonnet. [I griev'd for Bonaparte—with a vain] (W. L. D.) *MP* 16 Sept. 1802; reprinted 29 Jan. 1803 as 'Sonnet. No. I'. above 'Sonnet. No. II' (Is it a reed that's shaken by the wind) with the following headnote:

> We have been favoured with a dozen Sonnets of a Political nature, which are not only written by one of the first Poets of the age, but are among his best productions. Each forms a little Political Essay, on some recent proceeding. As we wish to publish them in connection with each other, we now Reprint No. I. and No. II. the first from our Paper of September last; the second from our

Paper of the present month. The other Numbers shall follow in succession. (headnote, 29 Jan. 1802)

comp. 21 May 1802; reprinted untitled *1807* as number 4 of 'Part the Second. Sonnets Dedicated to Liberty'

5. [untitled; Is it a reed that's shaken by the wind] (W. L. D.) *MP* 13 Jan. 1803; reprinted *MP* 29 Jan. 1803 as 'Sonnet. No. II. August, 1802' beneath 'Sonnet. No. I' (above)

The following beautiful lines, never before published, were written by one of the first poets of the present day; and we call attention tot them the more particularly, as the sentiments they express so closely agree with those of this Paper (headnote, 13 Jan. 1802)

comp. August 1802; reprinted 'Calais, August, 1802', number 2 of 'Part the Second. Sonnets Dedicated to Liberty'

6. Sonnet. No. III. To Toussaint L'Ouverture [Toussaint! the most unhappy man of men] (W. L. D.); *MP* 2 Feb. 1803; comp. August 1802; reprinted *1807* as 'To Toussaint L'Ouverture', number 8 of 'Part the Second. Sonnets Dedicated to Liberty'

7. Sonnet. No. IV. The Banished Negroes (W. L. D.) [We had a fellow-passenger that came] *MP* 11 Feb. 1803; comp. late Aug-early Sept. 1802; reprinted *1807* as 'September 1st, 1802', number 9 of 'Part the Second. Sonnets Dedicated to Liberty'

8. Sonnet. No. V. August 15, 1802. (W. L. D.) [Festivals have I seen that were not names] *MP* 26 Feb. 1803, printed beneath 'Half an Ode. On the Ode for the New Year' by Fingal; comp. 15 Aug. 1802; reprinted *1807* as 'Calais, August 15th, 1802' number 5 of 'Part the Second. Sonnets Dedicated to Liberty'

9. Sonnet. No. VI. (W. L. D.) [It is not to be thought of, that the flood] *MP* 6 Apr. 1803; comp. second half of 1802; reprinted *1807* untitled as number 16 of 'Part the Second. Sonnets Dedicated to Liberty'

10. Sonnet. No. VII. England (W. L. D.) [When I have borne in memory what has tam'd] *MP* 17 Sept. 1803; comp. second half of 1802; reprinted *1807* untitled as number 17 of 'Part the Second. Sonnets Dedicated to Liberty'

11. Sonnet. Translated from the Italian of Milton. Written during his Travels. [A plain Youth, Lady, and a simple Lover] translated from Milton's Sonnet 6 ('Giovane piano, e semplicetto amante') printed in *MP* 5 Oct. 1803; final sonnet to appear in the *MP* under Stuart's editorship; comp. Nov. 1802–early Jan. 1804; reprinted in the *Poetical Register* for 1803 (1805, unsigned); never reprinted by WW

12. Sonnet (unsigned) [I find it written of Simonides] *MP* 10 Oct. 1803; comp. between 21 May 1802 and 7 Oct. 1803; never reprinted by WW; but see *Essay on Epitaphs* I

13. Sonnet. Anticipation. By Wm. Wordsworth, Esq. [Shout, for a mighty Victory is won!] *Courier* 28 Oct. 1803; comp. Oct 1803; in letter to George Beaumont of 14 Oct. 1803; reprinted in *The Anti-Gallican; or Standard of Loyalty, Religion and Liberty* (1804), *The Poetical Register* for 1803 (1805), and in *1807* as 'Anticipation. October, 1803', number 25 of 'Part the Second. Sonnets Dedicated to Liberty'

Mary A. Favret

The General Fast and Humiliation

> In this world, only those people who have fallen to the lowest degree of humiliation, far below beggary ... —only those people, in fact, are capable of telling the truth. All the others lie.
> —Simone Weil

Beginning with the reign of Elizabeth I, the Protestant monarch of Great Britain did occasionally proclaim a General Fast and Humiliation for the kingdom. The wording varied little over the centuries. Here is typical language, from 1795: '[A] Proclamation for a General FAST and Humiliation before Almighty God, to be observed in the most Devout and Solemn Manner, by sending up our Prayers and Supplications to the Divine Majesty: For obtaining Pardon of our Sins, and for averting those heavy Judgments which our manifold Provocations have most justly deserved, and imploring His Blessing and Assistance on the Arms of His Majesty by Sea and Land, and for restoring and perpetuating Peace, Safety, and Prosperity to Himself, and to His Kingdom.' Royal subjects were required 'reverently and devoutly' to observe the public fast on a specified day to avoid the 'wrath and punishments' of His Divine Majesty, and to do so 'upon pain of such punishment as [His British Majesty] may justly inflict on all such as contemn and neglect the performance of so religious and necessary a duty.'[1]

A General Fast could be called in the wake of a great disaster, as when a terrible hurricane flooded half of London, destroying thousands of homes and buildings during the reign of Queen Anne. The most common catalyst for the proclamation of fast and

---

1   Great Britain. *By the King, A proclamation, for a general fast* (London: George Eyre and Andrew Strahane, 1795), 1.

humiliation however was war, and especially military defeat —also called 'humiliation'—on the battlefield or at sea. Such proclamations appeared sporadically in the seventeenth century, every several decades or so. Their frequency increased in the eighteenth century, as the wars in North America especially entailed bruising defeats. The last decade of that and the first fifteen years of the next century, however, brought an unprecedented acceleration. For every single year of the Revolutionary and Napoleonic wars, sometimes even twice a year, the crown called for a day of fasting and humiliation. In 1811, for instance, the new Regent's very first public action was to issue 'A General Fast on account of the War.' On the appointed day, shops, banks, courts and the stock market all closed; no mail was delivered. 'The whole nation, in the midst of its business, its pleasures, and its pursuits,' Anna Barbauld explains, 'makes a sudden stop and wears the semblance, at least, of seriousness and concern.'[1] Collections were taken up—sometimes for local charities, sometimes for British soldiers and sailors imprisoned in France. As ordained by the proclamation, the Church of England devised a special liturgy for the day, with selected readings from scripture and prayers that were published and distributed throughout the kingdom. Thousands of subjects assembled in their local churches to participate in that liturgy and hear the Fast Day sermon preached. Prominent churchmen then published their sermons, which subsequently glutted the marketplace (titles such as 'Food for a Fast-Day' (1795) or 'Food for National Penitence' (1793) were not uncommon). The day of fasting and humiliation was proclaimed, sustained, extended and preserved through the medium of print; a flood of words swirled into the void produced—or at least imagined by—collective abstinence and humiliation.

I. General Questions

This recurrent practice poses a set of questions, not least of which is the question of its significance: how seriously should we take this 'semblance at least of seriousness and concern' and its special inten-

---

1   Anna Leticia Barbauld, *Selected Poetry and Prose*, eds. William McCarthy and Elizabeth Kraft (Peterborough, Canada: Broadview, 2002), 298.

sity in the Romantic period? It might easily be dismissed as the tool of cynical politicians and 'hypocritical zeal,' as dissenting preacher John Aikin proposed; but it might nevertheless prove substantial and instructive, bearing a truth about the wartime culture of Romantic Britain.[1] This paper will obviously follow the latter path. It proposes that the General Fast and Humiliation in time of war generates what psychologist Sylvan Tomkins calls an 'affect theory': and by 'theory' he means something quite specific, similar to strategy or protocol. In response to the unsorted stimuli of on-going war, this practice helped to organize disparate, present as well as more archaic feelings into a 'conscious report' and called it General Humiliation.[2] Humiliation serves here as 'a simplified and powerful' interpretation of an otherwise overwhelming set of forces (Tomkins 165). The theory or protocol generated aims then to foresee, evaluate and control the affective impact of a distant war: to foresee that we could suffer humiliation (thus narrowing our fears to this particular threat); to evaluate the force and extent of such humiliation; and to control its impact by, in a sense, absorbing its emotional force before it hits. With Tomkins, we might understand affect theory as 'affect acting at a distance,' so that 'the affect [in this case humiliation] need never be [immediately] activated or [immediately] experienced' (167). Yet Tomkins also argues that in the case of a negative affect such as humiliation, its theory can be remarkably potent and self-reflexive, so that even as it works to ward off it may sometimes activate and amplify; the distance may disappear, the feeling may be actualized (165). The emotional impact of distant war may be structured and routed through narrow channels, but nevertheless—or all the more—brought home.

As a governing affect of wartime, humiliation proves complex and interesting for at least two reasons: first because of its peculiar semantic fluidity in the Romantic period; and second because even before it presents itself as a generalizing theory, humiliation is consti-

---

1   John Aikin, *Food for national penitence; or, a discourse intended for the approaching fast day* (London: J. Johnson, 1793), 14.

2   Sylvan Tomkins, *Shame and its Sisters: A Sylvan Tomkins Reader*, ed. Eve Sedgwick and Adam Frank (Durham: Duke UP, 1995), 164. In explaining Tomkins' idea of affect theory, Sedgwick and Frank use the term 'everyday theories,' to emphasize the heterogeneity, adaptability and contingency of the idea (23).

tutively implicated in questions of the individual and the general. You may notice that I've borrowed from Tomkins a model designed for individual psychological experience and applied it to a 'general' and indeed official practice: and yet the dynamics of humiliation warrant and indeed promote this translation. As a theory (in Tomkins's sense) of wartime affect, General Humiliation in the Romantic period allows precisely for movement or translation among general states—indeed sovereign States—and individual feelings and, as various writers demonstrate, between the state of war and everyday emotions. This paper will consider along its way works by Coleridge, Wordsworth, Austen and Byron, and will end by devoting some attention to Kant's essay *Towards a Perpetual Peace* and Anna Barbauld's extraordinary pamphlet, *Sins of Government, Sins of the Nation, or a Discourse for the Fast Appointed April 19, 1793*, where such translation between individuals and general states produces one of the period's greatest pieces of anti-war writing. Before thinking through humiliation and engaging Barbauld's or Kant's interpretation, though, I will lay out some of the quandaries raised in thinking seriously about this practice, and the very notion of General Humiliation.

To begin perhaps with the most obvious difficulty: A Day of General Fast and Humiliation was to be observed generally by all subjects of the throne. Those who 'contemned or neglected' the practice would 'suffer severe punishment.' If one did not suffer generally, that is, one would suffer individually. Members of Dissenting churches, not to mention non-Christians, understandably found this condition of the proclamation hard to bear. The blanket demand that all participate in a state religious practice and, in most instances, offer up prayers for military victory, threatened certain subjects more than others. Yet as Joseph Priestley points out in the preface to his 1793 Fast Day sermon, the proclamation was not deemed to carry 'the force of law,' so that 'Quakers and many Dissenters [were] known to disobey the requisition with impunity.'[1] With each new proclamation, Dissenters would debate their obligation to participate and their

---

1   Joseph Priestley, *A Sermon preached…April 19ᵗʰ, 1793, being the day appointed for a general fast* (London: J. Johnson, 1793), iv.

preachers—like Aikin and Priestley, and in her own way, Barbauld—
would publish their own Fast Day sermons, marking the event as a
matter of public discourse. Evidence shows that the lower classes
were not necessarily expected to participate in the proclaimed abstinence and prostration. Given extra alms, the poor were in fact thought
to feast on fast days.[1] Occasionally, in latter years, factory owners
paid their employees to attend church services on a Day of Fasting
and Humiliation.

How general then were the fasting and the feeling, and who really
participated? A scholar might scroll through databases of diaries and
journals, hoping to find accounts of individual fasting Britons: I've
done this and found only scant mention of General Fast Days, and
even fewer details of actual abstinence or humiliation. Anna Seward
in her letters snipes at those who blandly apologize for 'lying abed
the morning, drinking creamed tea on a fast-day'); Miss Mary Berry,
obviously a very well-connected young woman, joked in her diary in
1811 that 'Lord Hartington begged me to give him a little party on
Wednesday next, the fast day.' Other than these indications that the
Fast was casually breached and the breaches casually noted, references
to Fast Days in letters and journals surface rarely. Among women of
an evangelical bent, they appear as prompts to reflection on the local
minister's sermon; otherwise, they serve simply as a mode of dating.
It's difficult to know, then, what counted as fasting, let alone humiliation. The Countess of Hardwicke explains that her household turned
off the kitchen fires for the fast day and she set the tone by eating
only bread and water. 'Many no doubt will abstain from all food,' she
adds, 'but I know that would make me ill, and unfit me for the duties
of the day' (234).[2] There was no uniformity. Total abstinence from

---

1   See the entry for 28 February 1810 in *Extracts of the Journals and
     Correspondence of Miss Berry from the Year 1783–1852*, vol. 2, ed. Lady
     Theresa Lewis (London: Longmans, Green, & Co., 1866): 'Finest spring day
     that ever was felt, which was lucky, for it was the fast day appointed, and con-
     sequently a day of feasting and rejoicing to all the lower orders of people. After
     church, Agnes and I walked in Hyde Park. In my life I never saw it so full of walk-
     ers' (412).

2   Anna Seward, Letter to Humphrey Repton, February 23, 1786, *Letters of
     Anna Seward: Written Between the Years 1784 and 1807*, vol. 1. (Edinburgh:
     Archibald Constable, 1811), 399; Berry 457; and Susan Liddell Yorke, Countess

food and drink, a diet of bread and water, no meat (or cream), simply meager servings or no eating before sunset: whether the reigning rationale was to abstain from the pleasures of this world, or simply to limit what the body took in, these were all possible options for the body that fasted, if it fasted.[1] Perhaps, though, this desire for individual testimony is misguided: the phenomenon of the General Fast and Humiliation may not have lived in individual practices or indeed private feeling. Such individualism runs exactly counter to the practice, where ascesis operates less as self-denial (with all the signs of spiritual distinction such denial might allow) than as collective withholding, where the individual surrenders to the general and the general itself is formed in and by surrender.

The archive of references to the General Fast and Humiliation, then, assembles itself not in diaries and letters but elsewhere: in the posted proclamations and liturgies; in Fast Day sermons, of course, and periodical reviews of those sermons; in newspaper reports; and, to a surprising degree, in poetry published in the period. Cowper, Coleridge and Wordsworth all invoke fasting and public humiliation in works of a decidedly prophetic strain. Though he does not name the Fast and Humiliation specifically, the outcry of the generic 'humble man' in Coleridge's 'Fears in Solitude' (1798) mimics the rhetorical structure of many Fast Day sermons: 'We have offended, Oh! my countrymen! / We have offended very grievously.'[2] The poem proceeds to give long list of 'our' sins, culminating in a condemnation of the general lust for war: 'We, this whole people, have been clamorous/ For war and bloodshed' (ll. 14, 41–42; 100–101).[3] Though a

---

of Hardwicke, Letter of April, 1847, *Extracts of letters from Maria, Marchioness of Normanby et al.*, ed. by Georgina Bloomfield (Hertfordshire, England: Simson & Co., 192), 424.

1   William Combe's poem, *The Fast-Day* (London: J. Bow 1780) has this Illuminating footnote: 'It is, I believe, a general matter of faith among devout Christians, that, on days of public fasting and humiliation, no one should eat meat till after the services of the day, which are generally completed at four in the afternoon. In this particular, all persons of Fashion give a very striking example of attention to the duties of such public solemnities' (20, fn.2).

2   Samuel Taylor Coleridge, 'Fears In Solitude', in *The Complete Poems*, ed. William Keach (London: Penguin, 2003), 239.

3   Like the Fast Day discourses of Aikin or his sister, Anna Barbauld, Coleridge's poem wrests the general 'we' away from the Established Church's Fast Day

lyric 'I' does emerge in the last section of the poem, it depends upon and claims communion with the 'we' that dominates the first 175 lines, and it folds back into 'thoughts that yearn for human kind'— the feelingly impersonal words that close the poem.

Another problem, concerning fasting itself. The General Fast and Humiliation was not precisely an act of self-discipline, but a performance ordained by and for the state. This type of fasting does not immediately fit our given scholarly models: state-sponsored fasting does not lead to the individual mystical experience so vividly explored in the work of Caroline Walker Bynum and others; nor does it conjure the contemporary anorexic, who 'starves at large, deliriously,' 'pursuing hunger for its own sake.'[1] Nor does such fasting evoke the hunger strikes of political prisoners, suffragettes and other desperate protesters against the State; the General Fast stands, perhaps, as the direct opposite of such protests. The proper analog seems closer to examples in the Hebrew Scriptures, notably the passage in the book of Joel where the prophet, envisioning an army swarming upon the Israelites, calls for communal fasting in 'solemn assembly,' with public weeping, and repentance by 'the people'—all this understood as a powerful alternative to military response.[2] Bynum tells of a slightly different practice in the early Christian Church; their 'corporate practices' of fasting functioned in part to restore the economy of the whole congregation.[3] Members of means would fast and dis-

---

toward a more general criticism of the war.

1   Maud Ellman, *The Hunger Artists: Starving, Writing and Imprisonment* (Cambridge: Harvard UP, 1993), 7. Ellman cites historians who argue that religious abstinence and 'a civil practice of fasting with a hostile purpose against an enemy' were once conjoined. In this instance, God would be considered the enemy and fasting the form of violence most effective in subduing him: 'what appears to the modern Christian as sacrifice and humiliation may once have been in some of its aspects, a way of taking the kingdom of heaven by storm' (12–13).

2   'Blow the trumpet in Zion, sanctify a fast, call a solemn assembly: Gather the people, sanctify the congregation, assemble the elders, gather the children, and those that suck the breasts: let the bridegroom go forth of his chamber, and the bride out of her closet. Let the priests, the ministers of the LORD, weep between the porch and the altar, and let them say, Spare thy people, O LORD, and give not thine heritage to reproach, that the heathen should rule over them' (*King James Bible*, Joel 2, 15–17).

3   Caroline Walker Bynum, *Holy Feast, Holy Fast: The Religious Significance of*

tribute the food they would have consumed to the very poor, the alimentary benefits circulating not simply within individuals but now between bodies in the community. All members would pray for healing. Though the British fasts were similarly understood to be communal and included an element of alms-giving by the well-to-do, they emphasized the work of humiliation and repentance rather than a redistribution of goods. If these wartime Fast Days aimed to restore or repair the communal body, they had to compass not only the living bodies of those in need at home, but those injured, imprisoned, starving, diseased and dead members of the community elsewhere: those bodies brought low by war.

This image allows the possibility of coordinating the devastation of war with the state of being-brought-low that is General Humiliation. Current accounts of humiliation tend to identify it as a remarkably inward and idiosyncratic, even individuating emotion. Tomkins— perhaps the most cited writer on the topic—begins by pairing humiliation with shame; he calls the affect 'shame-humiliation' and offers a vivid portrait of its internal, private workings: 'While terror and distress hurt, they are wounds inflicted from the outside which penetrate the smooth surface of the ego; but shame is felt as an inner torment, a sickness of the soul …. [T]he humiliated one …feels himself naked, defeated, alienated, lacking in dignity or worth' (Tomkins, *Shame and its Sisters*, 133). Could such a feeling be experienced generally, as the sickness of a collective soul? The proclaimed form of humiliation is not individual—something uniquely familiar to each of us—but general, suffered commonly and in common. It confesses what the king's proclamation understood as 'our manifold sins and provocations,' with some ambivalence sounding in that possessive pronoun. The more democratically inclined Barbauld would translate this phrase into 'sins of the nation.' In either case, these were faults and failings held in common. It seems important even in this communal mode to recognize the nearly existential depth plumbed by humiliation, separating it, as Tomkins suggests, from the more punctual feelings of terror or distress. Unlike Tomkins' shame-humilia-

Food to Medieval Women (Berkeley, CA: University of California Press, 1987), 38–9.

tion, though, General Humiliation is curiously initiated from outside and on high (that is, by royal decree) and also, like all humiliation, generated from within. General Humiliation admits that 'we'—sovereign and subjects—have all already been brought low by 'our' failings and wrong-doings. Both anterior to and resultant from the King's words, humiliation hovers outside any one person. Its temporal vectors were similarly unstable. Announced for its curative effects, the General Humiliation seems designed at once to explain the present situation and ward off future humiliations and yet to organize the world in a simple, eternal and impersonal structure of dominance and submission.

By projecting this simple power structure, allied with seemingly magical thinking, the intensification of proclamations for a General Fast and Humiliation during the Romantic period may strike us as regressive, decidedly irrational and resistant to concurrent secularizing impulses. It aligns with a reactionary sacralization of the British monarchy in a time of war with republican France, a nation that had initially severed its ties to Christianity. Early in the Revolution, the French Convention debated the idea of a national fast but rejected it, deciding it smacked too much of superstition and tyranny. Perhaps, in a revolution sparked by the shortage of bread, it would also be deemed impolitic. This sort of rational calculation was not yet afloat in Britain, though it would surface later, notably in 1832.[1] On the one hand we find this curious holdover from Elizabethan times, from a threatened Protestantism, professing a sacred, cosmic understanding of the collective body and moral feeling. On the other hand, as the newspapers all indicate—the newspaper, hardly a sacralizing medium—the practice was thoroughly routine. With the exception of 1803, when hostilities with France were resumed after a brief period of peace, by the second decade of the war most newspapers reported on the General Fast and Humiliation with a canned sentence or two. The same obligatory adjectives parade in the press—'suitable,' 'appropriate,' 'fitting,' 'solemn'—each betraying not simply the for-

---

1   See for example "M.", 'The General Fast: An Ode to the Right Honourable, the Ultra-Tory Saints ... -- a screed on their hypocrisy; the fast was called in response to the Cholera epidemic', *The Metropolitan*, March 1832, 318–19.

malization of the practice, but also its apparent lack of a transcendent aim, of anything beyond the proper social order. The General Fast and Humiliation operated, in other words, as both a sacred, searching duty in response to global warfare and as a thoroughly socialized and customary practice in a modern, media culture.

We might then discount these Fast Days as acts of historical desperation, all the more intense in the face of their obsolescence. By the mid-nineteenth century the practice did wither away. Why it withered is as complicated a question as why it flourished in Romantic wartime. One might assume that a sense of its inefficacy grew: it was no longer perceived to have actual power. Yet the Fast and Humiliation had been deployed several times during the war with the American colonies with no military benefit, and that result did not deter its use during the wars with France. More to the point perhaps, its non-military benefits became harder to discern. One might assume, similarly, that charges of hypocrisy in 1832 rendered Fast Days rhetorically and politically implausible—though such charges had circulated in the discourse of the 1790s without slowing the proclamations. Coleridge's 'Fears in Solitude' is again a good example, for it condemns the hypocrisy of the Fast Day's solemn bellicosity without abandoning the call for general humiliation:

> (Stuffed out[1] with big preamble, holy names,
> And adjurations of the God in Heaven,)
> We send our mandates for the certain death
> Of thousands and ten thousands! (ll. 101–04) [2]

Constitutional restrictions to the Anglican Church in the 1820s and repeal of the Corporation and Test Acts certainly compromised the authority of the practice. In addition, the onset in the 1830s and 40s of

---

1   Coleridge's backhand mention of the Fast.
2   William Cowper is even more vociferous in his 'Expostulation,' nailing both the inefficacy and the hypocrisy of the Fast: 'Thy fastings, when calamity at last / Suggests the expedient of a yearly fast, / What mean they? Canst thou dream there is a power / In lighter diet at a later hour, / To charm to sleep the threatenings of the skies, / And hide past folly from all-seeing eyes? / The fast that wins deliverance, and suspends / The stroke that a vindictive God intends, / Is to renounce hypocrisy (ll. 200-08).' *The Poems of William Cowper,* ed. by John D. Baird and Charles Ryskamp, Vol. 1 of 3 (Oxford: Clarendon Press, 1995), 298.

a bio-political regime organized not by warfare but by epidemics and famine probably made rituals of withholding and prostration unconscionable. The call in 1832 for a General Fast and Humiliation on behalf of the cholera epidemic and again in 1847 for the Irish Famine met resistance so vociferous it nearly annihilated the practice. The last official Fast and Humiliation in Britain came in response to the Indian Rebellion in 1857.[1]

We could spend even more time teasing out these knotted problems. In what follows I want rather to accept these difficulties as the necessary backdrop to this question: how might the intensive and extensive practice of a General Fast and Humiliation in the Romantic period have been suited to and indeed revelatory of the modern experience of warfare? Even while recognizing the oppressiveness that takes concentrated form whenever state decrees mix with religious observance, can we find a conceptual apparatus that nevertheless reckons the nearly existential and still pressing force of general fasting and general humiliation?

For the impact of its timeliness as well as its difference, I'll drag in the example of Texas Governor Rick Perry's recent declaration that August 6, 2011 be a 'Day of Prayer and Fasting for Our Nation in Texas,' with its accompanying event, known simply as 'The Response,' where citizens were invited to gather in solemn assembly in Houston's enormous Reliant Park, 'the world's first retractable roof, air-conditioned, natural grass football stadium,' to have their prayer and abstinence from worldly pleasures televised nationally.[2] Perry's smug call to 'Americans of faith to pray on that day for the healing of our country, the rebuilding of our communities and the res-

---

1   Paul Williamson, 'State Prayers, Fasts and Thanksgivings: Public Worship in Britain 1830–1897', *Past and Present* 200.1 (2008), 121–74 (123).

2   The proclamation was subsequently echoed by Paul LePage, Republican governor of the state of Maine. On the 71,00-seat Reliant Stadium, see http://www.reliantpark.com/about. A copy of Perry's proclamation is available at http://governor.state.tx.us/news/press-release/16246/. The bilingual video produced to advertise the event can be found at http://vimeo.com/user7327338 (accessed July 12, 2011). For news reports see for example: http://www.nytimes.com/2011/06/12/us/politics/12prayer.html; http://blogs.dallasobserver.com/unfairpark/2011/06/as_the_governor_declares_august_6_day_of_prayer_one_response_to_rick_perrys_the_response.php.

toration of enduring values as our guiding force' cites as precedent President Abraham Lincoln's 1861 Fast Day Proclamation. It ignores, however, Lincoln's pained plea for 'public humiliation.' Lincoln hoped the nation would 'bow in humble submission to [God's] chastisements; to confess and deplore their sins and transgressions ...; and to pray, with all fervency and contrition, for the pardon of their past offences.'[1] Perry's call rejects as well the penitential weight of George III's proclamations: 'those heavy judgments which our manifold sins and provocations have most justly deserved.' Perry fails, in other words, to give the event its gravity: the lowering gestures customarily required before praying for blessing or assistance. That the Governor's Day of Prayer and Fasting for a Nation in Crisis was a highly scripted media event makes it no more modern than the Fast Days of the Romantic period. Its distance from, if not negation of, those earlier days lies precisely in its failure to engage fully the emotional—and indeed political—value of humiliation, general or otherwise.[2]

II. Humiliation Theories

The political operations of humiliation may elude us because the meaning and value of the term humiliation shifted during the eighteenth century from an impersonal state or activity to an intimate feeling. From its earliest appearance in English, humiliation was paired semantically with humility, a virtue, and attached itself especially to redemptive acts of religious devotion. For Christians, acts of humiliation had special warrant: Jesus Christ himself had chosen humiliation, that is, the lowering of his divine nature into mortal flesh.[3]

---

1 Lincoln's proclamation, the constitutionality of which is still debated, can be found here: http://www.presidency.ucsb.edu/ws/index.php?pid=69891#axzz1T9bspNi2

2 Less than a week after 'The Response,' Perry announced his candidacy in the Republican primary for President of the United States. Perry's proclamation does admit that 'even those who have been granted power by the people must turn to God in humility,' and it recognizes the language of humiliation in earlier proclamations, but his does not pick up or promote that affective stance.

3 See for example, the short poem by John Wesley, 'In His humiliation His judgment was taken, &c.' *The Poetical Works of John and Charles Wesley*, ed. G. Osborn, vol. 8 (London: Wesleyan-Methodist Conference Office, 1868): '**Justice** He could not obtain / In His humble state beneath, / No humanity from

Humiliation thus designated an 'action' or 'condition' rather than a feeling. It had a physical, nearly gravitational force. As condition, it functioned not subjectively but quite objectively: to humiliate was to bring low, down to earth, down to the very ground (as the root word, humus, reveals). Prior to the mid-eighteenth century, the usual sense of humiliation referred to 'the physical act of bowing, of prostrating oneself' (Miller 175). In this sense, humiliation was a grave and frequently ritualized gesture of submission to a higher authority. It also testified to the common ground of human mortality—the 'human kind' that concludes Coleridge's 'Fears in Solitude.'[1] In spring, during the season of Lent, Christians repeatedly heard this reminder: 'Remember Man that you are dust and unto dust you shall return'; not coincidentally, Lent offered the season for most Fast Days. Humiliation designated the pull of earth on all human kind.

When Wordsworth in an 1832 sonnet defended the proclamation of a General Fast and Humiliation, he invoked this older conception of humiliation. Lashing out at critics of the Fast, the poet claimed they had 'doffed/ The last of their humanity'—as if their resistance to collective humiliation served as denial and betrayal of the human condition.[2] Wordsworth complicates his case, however, making the General Humiliation less an avowal of shared humanity (and its shared vulnerability, in this instance, to disease) than a tool against political reform, using general submission to block the general will. 'Chastised by self-abasement' (in his words), 'the people' in the reform year of 1832 ought to ask God to ward off not only cholera but also, Wordsworth prays, the 'pestilence of revolution' (ll. 9, 14). But this is only to admit that revolution, like cholera, might remind 'the people'—but not 'us' and certainly not 'me'—of their shared humanity.

---

man, / No relief---but pain and death. / Took from earth, He of our sins / Doth the chastisement receive, / Endless life's immortal Prince / Dies, that all mankind may live' (33).

1   Thus Robert Bloomfield in his poem, *The Banks of Wye* (London; Vernor et al., 1811) contemplates a tombstone and blandly observes, 'Humiliation bids you sigh, / And think of poor mortality' (Bk. 1, 265–66)

2   William Wordsworth, 'Upon the Late General Fast, March 1832,' *Poetical Works*, ed. Thomas Hutchinson, rev.ed., Ernest de Selincourt (Oxford: Oxford University Press, 1981), 402.

We have already seen that the royal proclamations were more hotly contested in 1832 than in prior years, in part because the political rhetoric on both sides understood humiliation as a lowering of 'the people.' But this was not the only possible reading of the politics of General Humiliation. In religious custom, humiliation could wield a leveling force, marking out and demonstrating a general, that is to say human, condition shared by sovereign and subjects, allies and enemies alike. It was essential that the King and his ministers participate in the public rituals associated with the Fast Day. This understanding of humiliation practiced humility, yet there was nothing necessarily humiliating about it. Indeed the adjective 'humiliating,' in its role of carrying the emotional price of humiliation, was scarcely in use even in the early decades of the nineteenth century.[1] Rather, the general, leveling and impersonal aspect of humiliation still governed meaning. It was this aspect of humiliation that fascinated Byron more than any of the other major poets of the period, and he extracted its political value in ways quite different from Wordsworth's sonnet. Byron enlists the term in scene 4 of Act 2 of *Manfred*, when Manfred is advised to bow down to Arimanes, 'Sovereign of sovereigns.'[2] Manfred refuses, in these words:

> ... —many a night on the earth,
> On the bare ground, have I bowed down my face,
> And strewed my head with ashes; I have known
> The fulness of humiliation—for
> I sunk before my vain despair, and knelt
> To my own desolation. (Byron 176; II. iv. 37–42)

Manfred will not bow to Arimanes because he knows himself to be already fully, that is positively, humiliated. Which is to say that Manfred has already encountered and acknowledged the limits of his mortal condition. In a move that outrages the king's spirit servants,

---

1   William Ian Miller, *Humiliation: And Other Essays* (Ithaca; Cornell UP, 1993) cites the OED's use 'humiliating' in Adam Smith's *Wealth of Nations* (1776) where Smith refers to bankruptcy as a 'humiliating calamity' (176). A search of the English poetry database shows only 8 uses of the term in poetry published between 1780 and 1835.
2   George Gordon, Lord Byron, *Byron's Works* (London: John Murray, 1846), 175.

Manfred invites the 'Sovereign of sovereigns' to share this humiliation: 'Bid *him* bow down to that which is above him,/ The overruling Infinite (176; II. iv. 46–47). The political valence turns sharper in
Canto IV of *Childe Harold's Pilgrimage*, where the poet records the
humiliation of specific nations and emperors. A long historical note
details with admiration the 'ceremony of humiliation' performed twice
by Fredric Barbarossa to Pope Alexander III: after publicly prostrating himself at the pope's feet, the emperor withdrew his armies from
Italy (Byron 771; n4). A subsequent long note on the political demise
of Venice takes up the new word 'humiliating,' as Byron imagines
the 'humiliating spectacle of a whole nation loaded with chains'. He
has not left behind humiliation's physical ground: 'humiliating' here
charts the nearly gravitational decline of the 'degraded capital' and
its republican virtues: Venice 'must fall to pieces …and sink more
rapidly than it rose,' lowering 'into the slime of her choked canals.'
Venice, according to the poet, 'may be said …'to die daily'.' For
Byron, humiliation reveals the mortal limits of the political and economic systems of Venice. 'The present race cannot be thought to
regret the loss of their aristocratical forms, and too despotic government; they think only on their vanished independence.' The 'general
decay' and lowering suffered by Venice may be inevitable 'in the due
course of mortality,' Byron explains, but he cannot talk of its humiliation without layering it with the degradation of its nobility and the
crushing effects of a wealth dependent upon slavery (772–73; n7).

As the example of Venice reminds us, humiliation in its general
form moved not just in the religious but also the geopolitical sphere.
There humiliation indicated not a *feeling* of abasement so much
as actual military defeat and subjugation: historians might analyze
the humiliation of Carthage by the Romans, as Venice had suffered
humiliation before the Turks; the humiliations of the Seven Years'
War were known to have crippled France; Tom Paine, in *The Crisis*,
could imagine Britain reducing its American colonies 'to a state of
perfect humiliation' through taxation; later the British themselves
suffered humiliation in North America. In all these instances, humiliation designated a political and often economic state of affairs, felt—
though felt hardly seems the right word for such systemic overpower-

ing—let's say borne quite generally by a population.

All this suggests that in its earlier dispensation, and indeed lasting into the nineteenth century, humiliation was inherently general. It referred either to the common condition of being human, and therefore a fallen nature shared with other members of a species; or it referred to a political and economic order, where one set of humans fell beneath the power of another. Either way, as a condition humiliation was suffered by humans by virtue of their humanity; it rehearsed their limitations and vulnerabilities and imagined a world organized according to a single vertical distinction: up or down. Regarded as an action, humiliation dramatized that pre-existing or structural condition, giving it concrete form either as literal prostration, prayerful supplications, imposed taxes or tribute, or, in the case of war, the fallen bodies that measure defeat.

Yet only part of the story resides here, since we know humiliation underwent a transformation in the latter decades of the eighteenth century from an 'action or condition' to its modern dispensation as an 'an experience of the self by the self,' to borrow Tomkins' words (136). Humiliation once had required a full body display, a falling to the ground, but in its migration in the direction of shame and embarrassment, its modern companions, such display declined to a dropping of the eyes, a bowing of the head. Its verbal expression is now less supplication than apology, 'the most frequent ritual of humiliation' we now practice (Miller, *Humiliation,* 163). Working hard to distinguish humiliation from shame and embarrassment, William Ian Miller pares it down to a linked action and feeling: humiliation is 'a piercing of vanity and deflating of pretensions' together with the felt experience of such deflation (240, n4; also 137). He calls upon Jane Austen to ferry humiliation to its more modern usage:

> 'How despicably I have acted,' [Elizabeth Bennett] cried. 'I who have prided myself on my discernment! I who have valued myself on my abilities! ...How humiliating is this discovery! Yet how just a humiliation.'[1]

For Miller, as for Austen, humiliation in its modern manifestation

---

1   Jane Austen, *Pride and Prejudice*, ed. by Vivien Jones (London and New York: Penguin Books, 2003), 202.

plays a fundamentally comic role: it serves to 'puncture pretensions' and thereby regulate identity (Elizabeth says, 'Till this moment I did not know myself!' [202]). Its force derives from a finely calibrated social order. Miller proposes that the feeling of humiliation affects those who dread being found to have violated not 'serious moral and legal norms' but only social norms, such as 'norms of bodily control or decorousness' (Miller 138). Social norms and one's acquiescence to those norms secure this understanding of humiliation.

In a more ethically charged analysis, Frances Ferguson situates humiliation in a distinctly modern social order, organized not vertically but horizontally. She treats humiliation alongside envy: both emotions, she claims,

> accompany democracy and identify the possibilities and the limits of political justice. As the emotions that register the injustices of social regard and the inequalities in the distribution of public endorsement of individuals, envy and humiliation are almost by definition the emotions that would interest political theorists who debate the advantages and disadvantages of democracy …[;] they are emotions that are resolutely extra-individual emotions.[1]

A democratic emotion, this humiliation is not quite Byron's levelling form of lowering. Ferguson has something less direct in mind: by democratic and extra-individual, she means primarily two things. First, this pair of emotions depends upon a certain abstracting principle that allows comparisons between individuals of the same kind or species (replacing the cosmological difference between god and man). Without this recognition of comparable others, and without a system of coordinating norms or expectations, the modern feeling of neither envy nor humiliation would work. Here the common ground of an older humiliation, which is to say the earth-bound ground of the human, has been translated and abstracted into a system of comparisons and finely articulated gradations, such that Ferguson discerns the emergence of a 'fully rationalized and rational emotion' (903). No longer a shared mortality vertically contrasted to the immortal,

---

1   Frances Ferguson, 'Envy Rising,' *English Literary History* 69.4 (2002), 889-905 (889).

now an elaborate set of mundane distinctions governs humiliation—comically or not. Second, and as an extension of the first, these extra-individual emotions are 'detached from [actual] objects that would enable us to explain them' (as in, say, the case of greed); they are tethered not to the ground and the grave but rather to a network of 'social relation' (889). Both envy and humiliation help maintain, albeit negatively, 'the general' as a social and political reality. Because we imagine ourselves as democratic equals, 'members...of the same general political species,' we feel distinctions intensely; honing our sense of justice requires us to register acutely inequalities and deviations. Humiliation is one of the ways 'quantitative differences become qualitative ones' in this system, and it operates primarily by noting social failure or error.[1] Central in producing and organizing a self—indeed in binding together the self's emotional world—humiliation nevertheless requires the background of an abstracted, impersonal world.

Though her essay goes on to analyse envy exclusively, Ferguson invites a re-consideration of humiliation. 'Envy,' she proposes in her reading of Coleridge, Bentham and Dickens, 'becomes an attitude towards the structures of [society] rather than an attitude towards a specific person'; more pointedly, it functions as 'protest ...against a state of affairs' (903). Is humiliation then envy's compliant twin, surrendering to a dense and un-masterable state of affairs? Not necessarily: already in Byron's 'humiliating spectacle' of Venice, we glimpse another possibility, where humiliation marks out or punctuates a failed state of affairs that critically highlights a republican ideal. Byron's point is less that Venice has surrendered to the Turks than that it now recognizes its political and ethical failures. Applied to one state among other states, humiliation in Byron's hands exhibits a melding of old and new forms: sunk low, the Venetians learn to value neither wealth nor power but 'only their [lost] independence.' In the prophetic tones adopted by the poet in this section of *Childe Harold's Pilgrimage*, general humiliation becomes the condition for a future freedom.

Taken together, Byron's ruminations on Venice, Wordsworth's sonnet, and Elizabeth Bennett's outburst remind us that the meaning

---

1   Sedgwick and Frank, Introduction to Tomkins, *Shame and its Sisters*, 13.

of humiliation was in agitation this period. The term moved between external condition and inner feeling, between political and emotional states, and between impersonal and personal perspectives. For this very reason, it was precisely suited to express both the condition of a nation at war and the response to that condition. The frequent, even annual call for a General Fast and Humiliation, an organized response to distant war, sounded amidst this agitation, with its swirl of residual theological and political as well as emergent psychological meanings. Its very mobility allowed humiliation to translate and coordinate several levels of wartime experience: condition, action and, newly, inner feeling in response to an abstracted state of affairs. Bodies—simply human bodies—were indeed falling to the ground, displaying their mortality. Human failure, error and wrong-doing pushed their way insistently to public notice. This humiliation could be read both as the reminder of common humanity before heaven and as the mark that distinguishes losers from winners; it could be read too as the small failure that upholds a larger political ideal. It could signal both the unique fall of individuals and the collective 'sins of the nation.' It was the occasion for general abasement and a reason to lower one's head and avert one's eyes.

III Romantic Humiliation

If for Ferguson the exemplary site for envy is the classroom, the site of humiliation may well be the battlefield. Perhaps it's more exact to say that in current psychological accounts of the emotion, there persists an older understanding of humiliation as suffered by armies and nations. Tomkins, for instance, in his presentation of shame-humiliation, sends the term back to the battlefield, so that his humiliated individual is theorized according to the general form of military defeat. The word 'defeat' or 'defeated' appears so often in Tomkins' analysis of humiliation that its metaphoric quality dissolves into commonplace. Recall the portrait he draws: '[T]he humiliated one ... feels himself naked, defeated, alienated, lacking in dignity or worth' (133; see e.g. 137, 138, 150, 172). At least four times in a 20-page stretch, military defeat serves additionally as his clinching analogy, culminating in this passage: '[H]umiliation and defeat ...can be in the life of a child what the loss of a great war can be for a nation—the beginning of an unceasing preoccupation with an intolerable threat' (177; see also 157, 161, 175). Tomkins' use of 'defeat' demonstrates the translation humiliation performs between person and nation—as if since childhood we might all have been living in the shadow—cast forward or backward —of military defeat. In such a way, humiliation mediates between warfare and the everyday. Tomkins' analysis brings humiliation more or less into its current accepted form, in which we take on defeat and humiliation unceremoniously, as part of the normal, everyday course of individual development.

It seems to me at this moment, while acknowledging the fluidity that permits modern humiliation to migrate from the general to the individual, or from the political state of things to the emotions that flare up and mark its edges, that we might want to hold on to the ceremonial, impersonal form of General Humiliation. For this formal version of humiliation, I have tried to show, not only bears the weight of actual bodies fallen in war; it licenses a profound acknowledgement of alongside a shared responsibility for the fallen state of things. This balance is indeed what some Romantic writers took away from the practice of the General Fast and Humiliation.

Anna Barbauld's 'Sins of Government, Sins of the Nation', like other dissenting fast day sermons, exploits the critical political potential of General Humiliation. Like her brother John Aikin and her mentor, Joseph Priestley, Barbauld in 1793 bows to the king's proclamation, fully accepting the call to fasting and humiliation as a national examination of conscience. At the heart of her excoriating anti-war sermon she emphasizes the two-way translation between individual and national that humiliation allows. 'Every individual, my brethren, who has a sense of religion and a desire of conforming his conduct to his precepts, will frequently retire into himself to discover his faults ...' she offers. 'Nations have likewise *their* faults to repent of, *their* conduct to examine ..., they should engage in the same duty' (299). This moral equation then opens a political vision where responsibility for the nation's sinful acts—but also sovereignty itself—rests not in the monarch but his subjects. Built into the proclamation of General Humiliation Barbauld finds a logic that makes each individual responsible for those national sins and offenses: why else, she insists, would King and Parliament ask us to repent? It would be 'presumption' or 'absurd mockery' to repent of sins that were not of our own making (300). 'By thus calling us together on every public emergency, [government powers] remind us that these [sins and crimes] are all our own acts; and that for every violation of integrity, justice or humanity in public affairs, it is incumbent on every one of us to humble himself personally before the tribunal of Almighty God' (299). By shifting from the discourse of power to that of penitence and humiliation, Barbauld enacts a political shift as well, building her horizontal, democratic vision.[1] From the egalitarian vantage underwritten by humiliation, she unleashes her searing critique of war.

> War ... is a state in which it becomes our business to hurt and annoy our neighbor by every possible means; instead of cultivating, to destroy; instead of building to pull down; instead of peopling, to depopulate; a state in which we drink the tears and feed upon the misery of our fellow-creatures. (312)

If, as Barbauld sets it up, the very structure of fasting and humiliation depends upon the moral code of persons, and shores up our common humanity, then war makes a 'total and strange inversion' of that structure (311). War is the state of affairs Barbauld most pointedly condemns—'it ought to make a large part of our humiliation this day'—and that condemnation rises in crescendo from the collective humiliation ordained by the crown itself (312).

In a different context, but only two years later, Immanuel Kant also calls upon this critical force. Looking with disquiet at the triumphal celebrations of the Prussians after the Treaty of Basle in 1795, Kant offers a critical response to the recent end of warfare. Refusing partisanship, his analysis of the situation insists, even more than Barbauld's, upon situating war on the level of the human race.

---

1   In a remarkable passage, Barbauld offers her 'translation' of the Proclamation, ventriloquizng the 'governors' who issued it. At the end of this revised proclamation, 'the 'governors' (cynically?) offer this: 'the guilt be upon your [the people's] heads; we disclaim the awful responsibility' (300-301).

> At the end of a war, when peace is concluded, [Kant writes,] it would not be unfitting for a nation to proclaim, after the festival of thanksgiving, a day of atonement [*Busstag*], calling upon heaven, in the name of the state, to forgive the great sin of which the human race continues to be guilty, that of being unwilling to acquiesce in any lawful constitution in relation to other nations but, proud of its independence, preferring instead to use the barbarous means of war.... Festivals of thanksgiving during war for a victory won ... introduce [*hirieinbringen*] a joy [*Freude*] at having annihilated a great many human beings or their happiness [*Glück*].[1]

The sin is general (it belongs to the human race) and on-going (Kant will not place it in the past tense). The response to sin, moreover, is tracked via emotional states: Kant's Day of Atonement, his equivalent to the British General Humiliation, folds a massive loss of life together with a massive loss of happiness. As David Clark notes in his superb analysis of Kant's essay, this passage is 'one of several sober reminders' in *Perpetual Peace* that the defeated in general 'are not mere abstractions but precious, singular creatures).'[2] Clark goes on to suggest that 'the [Prussian] 'festivals of thanksgiving' ...[may] seem consolatory, pacific, and felicitous but in Kant's hands they are described as harbouring an aggression and a murderous nonchalance about lost lives' (62). In other words, Kant suggests, without general humiliation and atonement, without recognition of and responsibility for fallen lives, the violence of war lives on.

We might think of the General Fast and Humiliation, then, as a mechanism for producing something more than bankrupt feeling or political consensus. We might consider the way it unearths strategies and language for, as well as responsiveness to, an undifferentiated and overwhelming experience: the distant slaughter of thousands of fellow humans. It provides, in however compromised a fashion, a flexible instance of an 'affect theory' for wartime. As a theory it

---

1   Immanuel Kant, *Toward Perpetual Peace: A Philosophical Project*, Cambridge Edition of the Works of Practical Philosophy, trans, and ed. by Mary Gregor (Cambridge: Cambridge UP, 1996), 357, 328.

2   Clark's 'Unnsocial Kant: The Philosopher and the Un-regarded War Dead,' *The Wordsworth Circle* 41.1 (2010), 60-69 (62).

builds from specific historical instances to a general thought: recall how the wording of the proclamations vary minimally from year to year, century to century. As a theory, too, its generalizations can be applied to an immediate, present need. We have followed how, in the history of its usage, humiliation underwent translation from general to particular, from an overarching condition to an individuating feeling that nonetheless rebounds against the backboard of an abstracted norm. But humiliation's ancient, common ground—the body fallen to earth—continues to echo, and echo loudly in wartime.

Monika Class

Coleridge and Phrenology

In his preface to *Reminiscences of Dr. Spurzheim and George Combe*, Nahum Capen, an American publisher and supporter of phrenology, lamented in 1880 that 'Coleridge got [only] a glimpse of the great discovery'.[1] Convinced of the scientific value of phrenology, Capen speculated that 'whether from being too old [...] or whether, though having an intellect apt for philosophic search, he yet lacked the warm hospitality to new truths' (vi–vii). For Capen, who compared the merits of phrenologists to those of Newton, Coleridge had dismissed phrenology much too easily. The publisher's assumptions indicate that he did not know that Coleridge had engaged with phrenology thoroughly and critically. The poet's perusal of Spurzheim's work was part of his interest in German physiology, which became increasingly popular in Britain at the time.

In 1807, Coleridge's future friend, Henry Crabb Robinson published a pamphlet entitled *Some Account of Dr. Gall's New Theory of Physiognomy*. It summarized the brain-based psychology by the Vienesse physician Franz Josef Gall and Johann Gaspar Spurzheim.[2] Robinson's translation was not the first account of Gall's theory. *The Monthly Review, The Edinburgh Review, The Medical and Physical Journal,* and *The Gentleman's Magazine* had published on the topic in 1802, 1803, 1805 and 1806 respectively.[3] Robinson initially regarded Gall's work as a potentially lucrative translation project: 'It

---

1 Nahum Capen, *Reminiscences of Dr. Spurzheim and George Combe* (Boston: Fowler and Wells, 1881), vi–vii.

2 Henry Crabb Robinson, *Diary, Reminiscences, and Correspondence of Henry Crabb Robinson*, ed. Thomas Sandler. 3 vols. Vol. 1 (London Macmillan & Co., 1869) 219. Hereafter called '*Diary*' followed by the volume number.

3 Roger Cooter, *The Cultural Meaning of Popular Science: Phrenology and the Organization of Consent in Nineteenth-Century Britain* (Cambridge: Cambridge University Press, 1984) 22.

occurred to me that I might make this new science known in England, and accordingly I purchased of Spurzheim, for two Friedrichs d'or, a skull marked with the organs. I bought also two pamphlets, one by Hufeland, and the other by Bischoff, explanatory of the system.' (*Diary*, I 219). Robinson had returned from Germany recently after having spent a large part of his five-year stay at Jena.[1] There he met Dr Gall and dined with him on several occasions in the company of other guests of the duchess.[2] Robinson disapproved of Gall's manners, 'utterly wanting in tact', because the doctor dared to challenge a noblewoman by questioning: 'What's the name of the organ, your highness?' (*Diary*, I 219). Robinson, an expert in Kantian and post-Kantian philosophy,[3] took issue with Gall's rejection of metaphysics. The rational dissenter agreed with Bischoff's assessment that 'no one suffered more than [Gall] himself from this narrowness of mind; for [...] he finds himself within the territory of metaphysics before he is aware of it'.[4] Robinson apparently thought little of Gall's theory and of his own translation: 'The work itself excited hardly any public interest, but just at the time a new and enlarged edition of Rees's *Cyclopaedia* was coming out, and the whole substance of the article on Craniology was copied from my work, the source being suitably acknowledged' (*Diary*, I 219).

Seven years later, and one year before the battle of Waterloo, a more successful attempt of introducing Gall's theory in Britain took place. After separating from Gall,[5] Spurzheim 'arrived in London in

1   James Vigus, 'Henry Crabb Robinson's Initiation into the "Mysteries of the New School"', in *Romantic Localities: Europe Writes Place*, ed. Christoph Bode and Jacqueline Labbe (London, Vermot: Pickering & Chatto, 2010), 145–56, 145.

2   Eugene Stelzig, *Henry Crabb Robinson in Germany: A Study in Nineteenth-Century Life Writing* (Lewisburg: Bucknell University Press, 2010) 111.

3   James Vigus, 'Introduction', in *Henry Crabb Robinson: Essays on Kant, Schelling, and German Aesthetics*, ed. by James Vigus (London: Modern Humanities Research Association, 2010), 1–25.

4   Christian Heinrich Ernst Bischoff, *Some Account of Dr. Gall's New Theory of Physiognomy Founded Upon the Anatomy and Physiology of the Brain and the Form of the Skull with the Critical Strictures of C.W. Hufeland*, M. D., transl. by Henry Crabb Robinson (London: Longman, 1807) 58.

5   Trevor Levere, 'Coleridge and the Human Sciences: Anthropology, Phrenology and Mesmerism', in *Science, Pseudoscience and Society*, ed. M. Hanen et al. (Waterloo, Ont.: Wilfried Laurier University Press, 1980), 171–92, 181.

March 1814 to begin his three-year lecturing tour through Britain and Ireland'.[1] While his audience in London included artists like Benjamin Haydon,[2] Spurzheim's first English publication *Physiognomical System of Doctors Gall and Spurzheim* received widespread public attention (Cooter, 25). Spurzheim thus initiated a process of British reception of German medical theory that would eventually develop into a hugely popular movement under the name of 'phrenology'. The theory assumed, according to Fernando Vidal, (1) that the brain is the organ of the mind, (2) that the mind is composed of innate faculties, which develop further until man reaches adulthood, (3) that each faculty has its own brain organ (ranging between 27 and 36 faculties), (4) that the size of the organ is proportional to the strength of the corresponding faculty, and that the brain is shaped by their differential growth, (5) that since the skull is shaped by the underlying brain, its bumps reveal psychological aptitudes and tendencies.[3] The name of the theory was coined by Thomas I. M. Forster and published in the *Philosophical Magazine* in 1815 (Cooter, 60). From 1823 onwards, phrenological societies and journals were founded all over Britain. Although phrenology was seen as highly controversial from the start, George Combe's *The Constitution of Man* (1828) sold a thousand copies a year until 1834; in 1855, the book ranked fourth in all-time readership behind only the *Bible, Pilgrim's Progress* and *Robinson Crusoe*.[4] Phrenology gradually lost its claims to be scientific from the late 1830s onwards, but, as Roger Cooter notes, 'there is little evidence before mid-century that phrenology actually did come to be identified wholly as "pseudoscience"' (98).

1   Eric C. Walker, 'Reading Proof, Aids to Reflection, and Phrenology', *European Romantic Review*, 8 (1997), 323–40, 330.
2   Penelope Hughes-Hallett, *The Immortal Dinner: A Famous Evening of Genius & Laughter in Literary London, 1817* (London, New York: Viking, Penguin Group, 2000) 255.
3   Fernando Vidal, 'Brainhood, Anthropological Figure of Modernity', *History of the Human Sciences*, 22 (2009), 5–36, 15.
4   T. M. Parissinen, 'Popular Science and Society: The Phrenology Movement in Early Victorian Britain', *Journal of Social History*, 8 (1974), 1–20, 9.

Coleridge's criticism of phrenology

Coleridge belonged to the group of British readers who first read Spurzheim's work. His perusal of Spurzheim's *Physiognomical System of Doctors Gall and Spurzheim* (published in the second edition in 1815) preceded his interest in animal magnetism (Levere, 186). It is known from Coleridge's letter to the surgeon R. H. Brabant that the poet read the *Physiognomical System* between November and December 1815 at a time when he was recovering from the strenuous completion of chapters five to thirteen of *Biographia Literaria* (Levere, 182).[1] His immediate reaction to Spurzheim was disparaging; indeed Coleridge thought that it was 'below criticism' (*Letters* IV 613).

The negative response at this moment in Coleridge's life does not come as surprise considering that Coleridge was working on his refutation of Hartley's materialism in Chapter VI of *Biographia Literaria*. Coleridge's critique of Hartley could also be applied to Gall's theory, for both profess the central role of the nervous system for the human mind.[2] However, later on, in the 1820s, Coleridge became interested in the contemporary debate about mankind in zoological terms (Levere 1980, 178). Coleridge followed the progress of phrenology in Britain, and in 1830, Coleridge spelt out his criticism in some more detail: 'It is just quackery committed by Spurzheim, to say that he has actually discovered a different material in the different parts of organs of the brain, so that he can tell a piece of Benevolence from a bit of Destructiveness &c.' (24 July 1830).[3] Here, Coleridge did not reject brain-based psychology per se, but criticized Gall's and Spurzheim's compartmentalization of the brain.

For Coleridge, 'the notion of distinct organs [...] in the brain itself [was] absurd' (*Table Talk* I 183). He insisted that 'every act, however

---

1   Samuel Taylor Coleridge, *Collected Letters of Samuel Taylor Coleridge*, ed. Earl Leslie Griggs. 6 vols. Vol. 4 (Oxford: Oxford University Press, 1971) 613. Hereafter called '*Letters*' followed by the volume number.

2   Alan Richardson, *British Romanticism and the Science of Mind* (Cambridge: Cambridge University Press, 2002) 48.

3   Samuel Taylor Coleridge, *Table Talk: Recorded by Henry Nelson Coleridge*, ed. by Carl Woodring. 2 vols. Vol. 1 (London: Routledge, 1990) 183–84. Hereafter called '*Table Talk*' followed by the volume number.

you may distinguish it by name, is truly the act of the entire man' (*Table Talk,* I 183). The fragmentation of the human mind into '36 Double Organs' was incompatible with the poet's life-long quest for metaphysical oneness.[1] Coleridge summed up his views in 1828 as follows: 'the Ground of Man's nature is the Will in a form of Reason. It is this which gives the Totality, One-ness, and it is the various metamorphoses, degradations, and varying relations of the Will, which determine the particular energies, functions & acts of his existence'.[2] It is telling that Coleridge rejected phrenology partly on the grounds of the very concept through which Spurzheim tried to distinguish his craniology from its influential precursor: Johann Caspar Lavater's *Physiognomical Fragments* (*Physiognomische Fragmente* 1775-78). Spurzheim emphasized that 'according to him [Lavater] the form of every part, separated from the rest, indicates the form of all other parts, and even of the whole body. [...] Our observations do not agree with this proposition'.[3] For Coleridge, Spurzheim committed a crucial mistake by deviating from the reciprocal relationship between part and whole (Richardson, 48).

The essay 'On Reason and Understanding' in *The Friend* of 1818 contains a further, hitherto unnoticed, explanation for Coleridge's rejection of Gall's and Spurzheim's theory.[4] It is bound up with Coleridge's early interest in German physiology: during the spring of 1799, Coleridge studied under Blumenbach physiology and natural history at the Georg August University of Göttingen. He found the lectures 'delightful' (*Letters,* I 494), writing home: 'I have attended lectures of physiology, anatomy, & natural history with regularity and have endeavoured to understand these subjects' (*Letters,* I 519).

---

1   Samuel Taylor Coleridge, *The Notebooks of Samuel Taylor Coleridge I-III,* ed. Kathleen Coburn. Vol. 3 (Princeton: Princeton University Press, 1957–73) §4355. Hereafter called '*Notebooks*' followed by the volume number.

2   Samuel Taylor Coleridge, *Shorter Works and Fragments,* ed. H. J. Jackson and J. R. de J. Jackson. 2 vols. Vol. 2 (Princeton: University of Princeton Press, 1995) 1384. Hereafter called '*Shorter Works*' followed by the volume number.

3   Johann Gaspar Spurzheim, *The Physiognomical System of Drs Gall and Spurzheim.* 2nd edn (London: Baldwin, Cradock and Joy, 1815) 253–54.

4   Samuel Taylor Coleridge, *The Friend,* ed. Barbara E. Rooke. 2 vols. Vol. 1 (Princeton: Routledge & Kegan Paul, 1969) 154–55. Hereafter called '*The Friend*' followed by the volume number.

Coleridge had the opportunity to meet Professor Blumenbach in private, to lead engaging conversations with him, become friends with his son and to see the professor's large collection of skulls, which Blumenbach's family teasingly called 'Golgotha' (*Notebooks,* III §4047). Blumenbach's studies were so interesting for Coleridge that he considered translating Blumenbach's *Manual on Natural History* (*Handbuch der Naturgeschichte*) after this return to England (*Letters,* I 590). Coleridge never realized this plan, but he kept perusing Blumenbach's works: references and allusions to the manual of natural history occur in his notebooks from 1803 to 1811; in 1828 he wrote annotations on the margins of his copy of *On the Natural Diversity of the Human Species* (*Über die natürliche Verschiedenheit des Menschengeschlechts).*

In 1815, Dr John Elliotson accomplished what Coleridge had failed to do. The physician, future mesmerist and president of Phrenological Society of London published the first English translation of Blumenbach's *Institutions of Physiology* (Latin original). It was a success, sold out in 1816,[1] and the second edition appeared in 1817.[2] Coleridge censured the second edition in 'On Reason and Understanding'. He specifically opposed the notion that man and animals share the faculty of reason. For Coleridge animals only partake in the lower nature of human life (*Shorter Works,* II 1386): all that animals possess is 'instinct' and 'appetites' (*Shorter Works,* II 1390–91). In a note to the main text that addresses this issue, Coleridge accused Elliotson of distorting Blumenbach's work: 'I know that the good and great man [Blumenbach] would start back with surprise and indignation at the gross materialism [...]: the more so because during the whole period, in which the identification of Man with the Brute in *kind* was the *fashion* of Naturalists, Blumenbach remained *ardent* and *instant* in controverting the opinion, and exposing its fallacy and falsehood, both as a man of sense and as a Naturalist.' (*The*

---

1   John Elliotson, *The Institutions of Physiology by J. Fred Blumenbach, Professor of Medicine in the University of Gottingen [sic], translated from the Latin of the Third and Last Edition, and supplied with numerous and extensive notes,* 2ⁿᵈ edn (London: Bensley and son, 1817), ii, iii. The first edition is not available. Hereafter called '*Institutions*'.

2   Elliotson, *Human Physiology,* 5ᵗʰ edn (London, 1840) 344–415. It contains a detailed account of Gall's theory under the heading 'the nervous system'.

Friend, I 155). Coleridge's criticism referred to a particular passage in Elliotson's translation: his so-called 'independent addition' to Blumenbach's work.

This section in the second edition of Elliotson's translation consisted of a short treatise 'upon the characteristics and varieties of mankind' (*Institutions,* ii; see also 376 ff.). It compared human and animal psychology zoologically on the basis of physiological similarities. 'I cannot conceive an animal without perception and volition', Elliotson wrote, 'nor can I conceive these in an animal without a brain, any more than the secretion of bile without a liver or something analogous' (*Institutions,* 378). Provided that the brain was the organ of the mind, animals shared, according to Elliotson, some mental faculties with humans. This conception agreed with Gall's view of animal psychology. For Gall, 'the real detractors of the human species are those, who think they must deny the intelligence of animals, to maintain the dignity of man'.[1] It is generally assumed that Elliotson became interested in phrenology in the early 1820s (Cooter, 52).[2] However, the treatise 'upon the characteristics and varieties of mankind' in the second edition of *Institutions of Physiology* discloses that Elliotson drew on Spurzheim's work by 1817. Footnotes in Elliotson's translation refer to the *Physiognomical System* (*Institutions,* 383, 386). It is true, however, that Spurzheim's views on animal intelligence were less radical than those of Gall. In contrast to the latter, Spurzheim highlighted the distinction between those faculties shared by man and animals, such as 'Destructiveness', 'Benevolence', and 'Love of Approbation', and those that belong to man alone, such as 'Veneration', 'Hope', and 'Ideality', which signified the propensity to write poetry (Parissen, 5). Nevertheless, Spurzheim made it clear that 'intellectual faculties [...] are common to animals and man' (*Physiognomical System,* 339). Although Coleridge ascribed sensibility and 'Understanding' to higher brutes, he took issue with 'the identification of man with

---

1   Francois [sic] Joseph Gall, *On the Function of the Brain and of Each of Its Parts,* trans. Winslow Lewis. 6 vols. Vol. 1 (Boston: Marsh, Capen & Lyon, 1835) 94.

2   According to Cooter, Elliotson 'turned to phrenology around 1822' (1984, 52). Elliotson met Gall for the first time in London, at James Deville's phrenology shop, and later, in the company of Sir Ashley Cooper, at St. Thomas Hospital; he subsequently visited him in Paris in 1826 and 1827 (Cooter 1984, 319).

the brute' (*Friend,* I 155 n). Coleridge felt more favourably inclined towards phrenology when it came to the dimension that dealt with human crania as an index of character.

Coleridge's tentative approval of phrenology

Coleridge owned a copy of John Abernethy's *Reflection on Drs. Gall and Spurzheim's Physiognomy* (published in 1821). Abernethy observed that although physicians, poets, and philosophers had studied physiognomy before, phrenology presented the most systematic study of the human head as an index for character at the time: 'As many learned men who have published on the same subject, have not represented it in the same manner; [...] I feel warranted in ascribing the phrenology [...] to these ingenious and scientific men [Gall and Spurzheim]'.[1] Similarly, Coleridge appreciated above all, the physiognomical dimension of Spurzheim's work. Coleridge's notebook entry dated to August 1817 states that Spurzheim was 'beyond all comparison the greatest Physiognomist that has ever appeared' (*Notebooks,* III §4355).

Coleridge had been interested in physiognomy for at least two decades. In 1796, he described his facial features to John Thelwall in revealing detail: 'As to me, my face, unless when animated by immediate eloquence, expresses great Sloth, & great, indeed almost idiotic, good nature. 'Tis a mere carcase of a face: fat, flabby, & expressive chiefly of inexpression.-Yet, I am told that my eyes, eyebrows, & forehead are physiognomically good-; but of this the Deponent knoweth not. [...] I cannot breathe through the nose- so my mouth, with sensual thick lips, is almost always open' (*Letters,* I 259–60). Reading Spurzheim in late 1815 appears to have rekindled Coleridge's interest as an observer of human character. The poet jotted down the words in the same months: 'the Eye is a Window not only which the Soul sees, but thro' which it may be seen! Closed Shutters & locked Doors are but Transparencies, I find, to an Observer, whose penetration has been perfected by much experience.' (*Notebooks,* III §4273). Here Coleridge saw the human eye not only as the agent of the soul

---

1   John Abernethy, *Reflections on Gall and Spurzheim's System of Physiognomy and Phrenology* (London: Longman, 1821) 12.

but also as an index to the soul. It is this dimension of phrenology, the minute observation of human character and the acceptance of contradictory nature of man, which appears to have won Coleridge's approval ten years later.

The phrenological readings of the head of a notorious murderer elicited a positive response from Coleridge. Phrenologists had detected a large development of the bump of Benevolence on the cranium of the late John Thurtell. Numerous critics saw the phrenological readings of Thurtells head as a proof for the failure of the theory because they thought that Benevolence was incompatible with the actions of the 'archetypal cold-blooded murderer' (Cowling, 123): 'The very marked, *positive* as well as comparative, magnitude and prominence of the Bump, entitled BENEVOLENCE (see Spurzheim's Map of the Human Skull) on the head of the late Mr. John Thurtel [sic], has woefully unsettled the faith of many ardent Phrenologists, and strengthened the previous doubts of a still greater number into utter disbelief'.[1] In 1825, however, Coleridge embraced the reading of Thurtell's head publically in *Aids to Reflection*: he noted 'On MY mind this fact (for *fact* it is) produced the directly contrary effect; and inclined me to suspect, for the first time, that there may be some truth in the Spurzheimian Scheme' (*Aids* 151 n). Coleridge even applied phrenological terms to account for and defend the reading of Thurtell's cranium: 'Mr Thurtel's Benevolence was insufficiently modified by the unprotrusive and unindicated Convolutes of the Brain, that secrete honesty and common-sense. The organ of Destructiveness was indirectly *potentiated* by the absence or imperfect development of the Glands of Reason and Conscience, in this "*unfortunate Gentleman!*"' Coleridge's explanation is not free from mockery, for in Spurzheim's *Physiognomical System* (1815) organ names such as 'honesty', 'common-sense', 'Reason', 'Conscience' cannot be found in the list given (579–81). Some phrenological designations bothered Coleridge: 'Craniologists may not see cause to *new-name* this' (*Aids* 151 n). Nevertheless Coleridge's defence seems to draw on an important aspect of phrenological theory: the significance of brain organs

---

1   Samuel Taylor Coleridge, *Aids to Reflections*, ed. John Beer (Princeton: Princeton University Press, 1993) 150–51. Hereafter called '*Aids*'.

is not always positive, that is, one bump does not always correspond exactly to one psychological propensity only. Spurzheim described the organ of Firmness for instance as 'situated in the midst of these feelings, in order to strengthen their ability' (353). His English mediator George Combe would elaborate this in the *System of Phrenology:* 'the organs of Self-esteem, Concentrativeness, and Firmness, form a group which has no relation to external objects; their influence terminates on the mind itself; and they add only a quality to the manifestations of the other powers'.[1] Coleridge embraced this interdependence of mental powers in *Aids to Reflections*: Thurtell's 'Benevolence was insufficiently modified' by the proportions of other brain organs. For Coleridge the inconclusive development of Benevolence in Thurtell's brain could be explained through the impact of other brain organs; indeed Spurzheim's theory could make sense for Coleridge as long as the respective brain organs were not seen as distinct or independent developments.

Coleridge's comment on Thurtell's remarkable phrenological development coincided roughly with the time when Spurzheim came to take Coleridge's life mask and to phrenologize his head. As Morton Paley has pointed out,[2] various dates for Coleridge's first meeting with Spurzheim have been suggested, but whenever that may have been, it is clear from a letter first published by Eric Walker in the *European Romantic Review* that the life-mask was not made until May 1825 (Walker, 325). On this occasion or another meeting, Spurzheim phrenologized Coleridge's head detecting an unusual development of the organ of Locality – the sense of orientation – and his want of the organ of Ideality. All that Coleridge had to say about his skill to find his way was, 'if there were two roads to a place, tho' I have been twenty times to it, it is pure Luck if I don't take the wrong one' (Coleridge cited in Walker, 325). Henry Nelson Coleridge believed 'the beginning of Mr. C.'s liking for Dr. Spurzheim was the hearty good humour with which the doctor bore the laughter of a party, in the presence of which he, unknowing of his man, denied any

---

1   George Combe, *A System of Phrenology* (Edinburgh, London: John Anderson, Longman, 1830), 286.

2   Morton D. Paley, *Portaits of Coleridge* (Oxford: Oxford University Press, 1999), 80–81.

Ideality, and awarded an unusual share of Locality, to the majestic silver-haired head of my dear uncle and father-in-law.' (*Table Talk* II 64 n. [24 June 1827]; Paley, 81). Despite this friendly encounter, Coleridge later described Spurzheim as 'the most ignorant German I ever knew' (*Table Talk,* I 183).

To come back to the beginning of this essay, old age did not prevent Coleridge from following the latest contemporary debates on science, including that on phrenology, closely: a year before he died, a sick man, he attended one of the public meetings of the British Association for the Advancement of Science, founded in 1831 by a group of radical young men around John Herschel and Charles Babbage, who were frustrated by the elitism and fustiness of the Royal Society.[1] Though no extant evidence exists to indicate Coleridge's opinion about the event, it is likely that he witnessed the heated debates on the scientific status of phrenology (Cooter, 90–93): Coleridge got more than just a glimpse of the new German brain-physiology and knew that its scientific value was hotly debated in his country.[2]

---

1   Richard Holmes, *The Age of Wonder: How the Romantic Generation Discovered the Beauty and Terror of Science* (London: Harper Press, 2008) 448.

2   I'd like to thank the organizers and participants of the Wordsworth Summer Conference, my colleagues at the Centre for the Humanities and Health at King's College London, Neil Vickers, and Brian Hurwitz, for their respective suggestions for this paper and the European Union for their research funding.

Stacey McDowell

The Playwright Keats Might Have Been

During the summer months of 1819 John Keats and his friend Charles Brown were busily engaged in a joint venture: the writing of the play *Otho the Great*. The pair worked diligently. 'Brown and I are well harnessed again to our dog-cart, the tragedy', Keats wrote in late July.[1] And they had much to discuss: whether or not to include an elephant in the plot, for example, (though there was some dispute over historical accuracy), or whether the tenth-century Roman emperor would be the type to go in for practical jokes (should he threaten to 'cold pig' a newly-married couple on their wedding night—that is, throw a bucket of cold water over them while the pair were in bed?). Brown recorded his attempts to dissuade Keats from this 'obstinately monstrous' proposal, and, in a more serious vein, he related quite precisely the collaborative efforts that went into the play's composition:

> I engaged to furnish him with the fable, the characters, and dramatic conduct of a tragedy, and he was to embody it into poetry. The progress of this work was curious; for, while I sat opposite him, he caught my description of each scene, entered into the characters to be brought forward, the events, everything connected with it. Thus he went on, scene after scene.[2]

From these inauspicious beginnings—what Charles Rzepka calls the 'pot-boiler' approach—it was perhaps inevitable that Keats and Brown's hopes that the play would achieve commercial success were destined to come to nothing.[3] The play was never staged

---

1   *The Letters of John Keats*, ed. Hyder Edward Rollins 2 vols (Cambridge, Ma.: Harvard University Press, 1958), II. 135.
2   *The Keats Circle: Letters and Papers 1816–1879*, ed. Hyder Edward Rollins 2 vols (Cambridge, Ma.: Harvard University Press, 1965), II. 66–7.
3   Charles Rzepka, '*Theatrum Mundi* and Keats's *Otho the Great*: The Self in "Saciety"', in *Romanticism Past and Present*, 8:1 (1984), 35–50.

during Keats's lifetime. Subsequent critics have continued to regard it as a bit of a flop. In 1848 Francis Jeffrey concluded, 'the tragedy is a great failure', and, more recently, Thomas McFarland has condemned 'the giant nullity of *Otho the Great*'.[1] Measured praise has come from Bernice Slote, while Charles Rzepka and Philip Cox have commended the drama, if not for its stylistic achievement, at least for its psychological complexity.[2] For the majority of critics of Keats's works, however, their silence on the subject proves its most damning dismissal. And yet, most would agree that some of Keats's most famous pronouncements on poetic composition reveal him thinking about the role of the poet in distinctly theatrical terms. This paper considers how Keats's sense of the dramatic aspect of writing poetry is developed when it comes to the writing of a play.

Keats and Theatricality

If the narrative of Keats's literary afterlife has tried conveniently to overlook *Otho*, the unfortunate glitch in the summer that saw the composition of his great odes, Keats himself, at least, had had high hopes for his success as a playwright. As the play neared completion he wrote to his friend Bailey, 'one of my Ambitions is to make as great a revolution in modern dramatic writing as Kean has done in acting' (*Letters*, I. 139). The 'revolution' Keats refers to is the innovation in so-called 'natural acting' popularised by Edmund Kean. Kean had caused a sensation when his passionate, seemingly unrestrained performances overturned the formal gestures and dignified, measured expression of the classical style favoured by the likes of John Philip Kemble, and Keats had written the leading role in *Otho* specifically with Kean in mind.[3] Kean is a 'wonder', Lord Byron

---

1   *Keats Circle*, ii. 249; Thomas McFarland, *The Masks of Keats: The Endeavour of a Poet* (Oxford: Oxford University Press, 2000), 179.
2   See Bernice Slote, *Keats and the Dramatic Principle* (Lincoln, Ne.: University of Nebraska Press, 1958), 104–20; Rzepka, '*Theatrum Mundi* and Keats's *Otho the Great*', 35–50; Philip Cox, *Gender, Genre and the Romantic Poets: An Introduction* (Manchester: Manchester University Press, 1996), 94–103.
3   For an excellent account of Keats's attitude towards Kean and theatricality see Jonathan Mulrooney, 'Keats in the Company of Kean', *Studies in Romanticism*, 42:2 (2003), 227–250.

had enthused, 'his style is quite new—or rather natural—being that of Nature'.[1] This paradoxical notion of a highly stylised naturalism formed one of the central tenets of nineteenth-century performance theory. Yet Kean had complained bitterly about the fact that his carefully studied and meticulously rehearsed performances were praised for the ease of their impulsiveness. William Hazlitt, for example, in a theatre review of December 1816 contrasts the apparent naturalness of Kean to the 'deliberate intention on the part of Mr Kemble to act the part finely'. 'He [Kemble] did not enter into the nature of the part', Hazlitt continues, 'He did not seem to feel the part itself as it was set down for him, but to be considering how he ought to feel it.'[2] In contrast, Kean's power as an actor can be traced in his ability to disguise such apparent self-consciousness through what was, in fact, a highly conscious and stylised artistic performance.

What can it mean, then, for Keats to connect the revolution that Kean was making in acting with what he himself sought to achieve in writing? I'd like to suggest that Keats seizes upon the paradox of natural acting to explore the tensions he encounters in what he sees as his role as a poet. And, without making too much of the overlaps, I wish to draw attention to the shared language employed by Hazlitt, Brown and Keats in describing the process of dramatic self-projection in order to see how this theatrical mode informs Keats's conception of his own writing practice. As Hazlitt had outlined the need to 'enter into the nature of the part', Brown describes the manner in which Keats was to 'enter into the characters' in the writing of *Otho*. These are phrases familiarly associated with the sympathetic imagination, but slightly less familiar is Brown's sense that while he provided the cues, the 'dramatic conduct' of a tragedy, Keats was to 'embody it into poetry'. How exactly is one to body forth poetry in this manner? Well, for Keats, the power to give tangible form to an artistic ideal, to blend impulsive feeling with poetic craft, had been realised in Kean's acting. Reviewing a performance of Kean as Richard III, Keats was particularly alert to the way in which the actor deployed rhetorical

---

1   Quoted in Jane Moody, *Illegitimate Theatre in London, 1770–1840* (Cambridge: Cambridge University Press, 2000), 230.
2   William Hazlitt, *The Complete Works*, ed. P. P. Howe, 21 vols (London: Dent, 1930), V. 346.

skill to create the impression of spontaneity: 'There is an indescriba-
ble gusto in his voice', Keats writes (invoking Hazlitt's famous term),
'Kean delivers himself up to the instant feeling, without a shadow of
a thought about any thing else'.[1] Yet Keats is careful to stress that
this effect is achieved through careful analysis: Kean has the 'intense
power of anatomizing the passion of every syllable'. The vocabulary
of anatomy and embodiment employed in these accounts is pertinent
to the appearance of a body on stage, but it is an aspect of charac-
terisation which Keats would relate to the manner in which he wrote
poetry, too.

In his famous account of the 'poetical character' written in October
1818, Keats runs together the terms character, body, identity and self.
'As to the poetical Character itself', he writes, 'it has no self—it is
everything and nothing—it has no character', moreover, the poet 'has
no identity—he is continually in for and filling some other body'
(*Letters*, I. 387). The impression that the poetic character, by inhabiting another body, is somehow left with no character of its own
reflects what Jonas Barish terms the 'antitheatrical prejudice' of the
nineteenth century, the anxiety about imitation which could be traced
back to Plato's warning that assuming another's character risked
supplanting one's own 'true' character.[2] But Keats makes a radical
departure in suggesting that this might be no bad thing, that the dis-
placement of self might be desirable, delightful even, for the kind of
poet, who, in Keats's words 'has as much delight in conceiving an
Iago as an Imogen. What shocks the virtuous philosop[h]er, delights
the camelion Poet' (*Letters*, I. 387). The poet's imaginative ability to
enter into another's role circumvents moral consciousness, as Keats
seizes on the Shakespearean characters whose performances, perhaps
more so than any others, unsettle the audience's ability to distinguish
between the true and the false self. And in a still more radical departure from the expectations of character integrity, Keats implies that
there is no such thing as a 'true' or 'essential' self.

---

1   Keats's review was printed in *The Champion*, 21 December 1817. It is reprinted
     in *The Poetical Works & Other Writings of John Keats,* ed. H. B. Forman, rev.
     M. B. Forman, 8 vols (New York: Phaeton Press, 1970), V. 229.
2   Jonas Barish, *The Antitheatrical Prejudice* (Berkeley: University of California
     Press: 1981), 295–349.

As the letter progresses, Keats envisions the artistic process of entering into another as opening up a gap between the self that performs—the 'I' that speaks or writes at any given moment—and the self that observes. Rather than an anguished sense of dissolution, this leads to an amused self-questioning:

> But even now I am perhaps not speaking from myself; but from some character in whose soul I now live. I am sure however that this next sentence is from myself. (*Letters*, I. 388)

While the introduction of the word 'soul' here seems to invoke a more traditional, Cartesian model of self, Keats's account is set within the context of what seems to anticipate a modern, Butlerian notion of performativity, as he goes on to suggest that there is no essential self which pre-exists language or performance. In the same letter he teasingly relates:

> It is a wretched thing to confess; but is a very fact that not one word I ever utter can be taken for granted as an opinion growing out of my identical nature—how can it, when I have no nature? (*Letters*, I. 387)

At once confiding and undermining the very notion of a confiding voice, the words Keats utters playfully give voice to what J. L. Austin would come to theorize as 'performative utterances', the words Keats utters do not arise organically out of his pre-existing nature, but form the very means by which his self is brought into being. As Angela Esterhammer outlines in *The Romantic Performative*, such verbal action brings into existence the very conditions which constitute the validity of the utterance itself.[1] While Keats's ironic self-dramatising warns the reader or listener not to take his words for granted, his confession nevertheless lays claim to its own paradoxical truth. The Romantic Performative, Esterhammer explains, 'grows out of a theorization of the I in its relation to being, objective reality, and other human subjects. It therefore focuses on utterances that not only [...] alter the circumstances in which they are spoken, but also react back on the speaker, altering the I itself and its relation to hearer and con-

---

1   Angela Esterhammer, *The Romantic Performative* (Stanford: Stanford University Press, 2000).

text' (Esterhammer, 99–100). The self, then, is not somehow invalidated by performance; rather, the performance is the means by which the self is constituted in the world.

Otho the Great

At this stage I wish to turn to *Otho the Great*. The play reveals a metatheatrical fascination in its own staging of 'honest' versus 'dishonest' performances; its central tension revolves around instances of deception and disguise, and the disjuncture between the audience's insight versus a character's misreading of another individual or scene. Set in tenth-century Germany during a campaign by the Roman Emperor Otho to suppress Hungarian uprisings, the plot focuses initially on the intrigues of the Duke Conrad. Having been previously opposed to Otho, Conrad has since performed a volte-face, winning Otho's favour and securing his consent for the marriage between Otho's son, Ludolph and Conrad's sister, Auranthe. As soon as the arranged marriage has taken place, however, it is revealed that Auranthe has a lover. The discovery of his new wife's falseness sends Ludolph mad and the tragedy ends with a near-farcical marriage feast, staged as a kind of play within a play as the members of the court are obliged to act as though they haven't noticed anything awry.

At the beginning of the play, Conrad is about to reveal to Auranthe her coming marriage:

> CONRAD   before
>   I utter even the shadow of a hint
>   Concerning what will make that sin-worn cheek
>   Blush joyous blood through every lineament,
>   You must make here a solemn vow to me.
> AURANTHE I prithee, Conrad, do not overact
>   The hypocrite. What vow would you impose?[1]

The vow that Conrad would impose, it turns out, requires Auranthe herself to act the hypocrite. Conrad asks her to swear to conceal her sexual past in order to secure her marriage to Ludolph. But the vow

---

1   John Keats, *Otho the Great*, in *The Poems of John Keats* ed. Miriam Allott (London: Longman, 1970), I.i. 23-29.

she will make to Conrad must perforce invalidate her wedding vows. By asking her to *vow* to deceive, Conrad undermines the validity of the very verbal contract upon which he is depending.

These circumstances provide an analogue to the baffling line: 'do not overact / The hypocrite'. How, exactly, might hypocrisy be overplayed in this manner?[1] First, the remark serves as a warning: don't exaggerate your performance or you risk exposing its artificiality. Act naturally. Yet Auranthe's line implicitly suggests that there might be a way of genuinely acting the hypocrite in opposition to a more overt theatricality. But what is the actor playing the part of Conrad to do with this line? If, as Frederick Burwick conjectures, 'all stage gestures are essentially false, and the players are merely feigning emotions, how might a player then proceed to play a character who is feigning an emotion? It is one thing to feign an emotion, another to feign the feigning of an emotion'.[2] The character Conrad must play, 'the hypocrite', derives from the Greek for an actor on the stage, a pretender, a dissembler.[3] But perhaps deception, in this instance, becomes an avenue to truth; or rather, it threatens to reveal the untruth of all performance.

Whether Keats attached such import to the line is uncertain, but the metatheatrical concern it introduces so early in the play provides a starting point from which to consider Keats's questioning of where the performance of self risks becoming over-contrived and posturing. Later in Act One, Otho denies over-acting the role of emperor. In an attempt to convince the defeated King of Hungary to take him at his word, Otho asserts:

> I do not personate
> The stage-play emperor to entrap applause,

---

1   Rzepka also singles out the line in his fine discussion of the play. See Rzepka, '*Theatrum Mundi* and Keats's *Otho the Great*', 40–45.

2   Frederick Burwick, 'Telling Lies with Body Language', in *Spheres of Action: Speech and Performance in Romantic Culture*, eds. Alexander Dick and Angela Esterhammer (Toronto: University of Toronto Press, 2009), 151. See also Frederick Burwick, *Illusion and the Drama: Critical Theory of the Enlightenment and Romantic Era* (University Park, Pa.: Pennsylvania State University Press, 1991).

3   *OED.*, s.v. 'hypocrite'.

To set the silly sort o' the world agape,
And make the politic smile. (I.ii. 140–146)

But Otho *is* an emperor; he does impersonate this role. He seeks
to convince that his performance of the public role is genuine, that
his is a style of acting set off against a more hypocritical one that
works by deception, tricking its audience to 'entrap applause'. Again,
the distinction between an act and an overacted act uses theatrical
illusion to distinguish a more authentic theatricality. Thirty lines
later Otho declares that truth in fact relies upon a certain degree of
theatricality:

> Not to thine ear alone I make confession,
> But to all here, as, by experience,
> I know how the great basement of all power
> Is frankness, and a true tongue to the world;
> And how intriguing secrecy is proof
> Of fear and weakness, and a hollow state. (I.ii. 175–8)

Keats raises intriguing questions here concerning speech as public
action versus private experience, the linguistic conventions governing the individual and the state, as well as conceptual notions of truth
and sincerity. Otho's suggestion that deception leads to a 'hollow
state' has personal as well as political resonance: it correlates to the
antitheatrical assumption that acting or dissembling leads to a lack of
interiority, or a true 'inner self'. But at the same time Otho suggests
that one's truth is something that can only be known through performance and utterance ('a true tongue to the world'), and paradoxically unveils that there is no truth lying outside of the performance.

By playing off acting with overacting Keats registers the element
of performance composite in all experience. Such awareness would
exculpate him from Gide's famous charge that 'the true hypocrite is
the one who ceases to perceive his deception'.[1] Instead, Keats questions whether a certain degree of hypocrisy is perhaps necessary for
the poet or actor who seeks to disguise the self-consciousness of his

---

1   Andrew Gide, *The Counterfeiters; With Journal of the Counterfeiters* (Second
     Notebook), in *The Counterfeiters*, tr. Dorothy Bussy (novel) and Justin O'Brien
     (journal) (New York: Modern Library, 1955), 187.

or her artistic performance. In stressing the importance of theatricality to Keats, I'd like to develop the line of thinking usefully put forward by Charles Rzepka, who argues that Keats in his poetry comes to occupy an equivalent potion to that of the playwright within a play, transforming himself 'from a character or a persona represented in the theatre of his own work' into a more self-conscious 'stager' of his poetic vision. Rzepka intuits in Keats's work 'an essentially theatrical, which is to say self-distancing, point of view.'[1] But by acting as both playwright and player at once, Keats is able to bring together the 'self-distancing' perspective with the self-reflexive; he comes to embody individual subjectivity as a process of self-exploration brought about by a mobility between the natural and the theatrical. Seeking to turn in on itself the paradox of natural acting, then, Keats finds a means by which the self-conscious performer might move beyond the suspicions or ironies called forth by a subjectivity that continually seeks to catch itself in the act.

---

1   Charles Rzepka, *The Self as Mind: Vision and Identity in Wordsworth, Coleridge and Keats* (Cambridge, Ma.: Harvard University Press, 1986), 168.

Richard Gravil

Mr Thelwall's Ear; or, hearing *The Excursion*[1]

♩♪ | ♩♩ | ♩ | ♪ | ♪♩♪ | ♩ | ♪ ♩ | ♩ |

> Some who the streams of lofty song
> With native force can pour along, /.../
> Will yet from mountain highth descend,
> In puerile rhyme with these to blend;
> With nursery babes to pule & whine,
> Or in an idiot's slaver shine; ...
> ——Thelwall, 'Musalogia', Canto 1 (1827)[2]

If Thelwall could on occasion collude with Byronic Bards and Scotch Reviewers in denigrating Wordsworth's demotic poetry in such fashion, what motivates this literary apostasy is in part a sense of rejection. In 1798 he was notoriously repulsed from Somerset by Coleridge, and in 1804, having chosen Kendal as a base for his lecture tours in the north and in Scotland, felt repulsed again in his desire to join Coleridge, Wordsworth and Southey in their Lakeland fraternity. Understandable resentment suffuses two poems of Thelwall's Kendal period, brought into focus recently by Judith Thompson. One is an

1   This lecture would have been impossible without generous assistance from Paul Betz, in making available to me photocopies of Wordsworth's annotated *Excursion* and it seems appropriate to dedicate this much cut (but still lengthy) version to him, with gratitude. I am also deeply indebted to Judith Thompson for providing copies of published and unpublished work and responding generously to my importunate requests for all kinds of information, and to Ruth Abbott's richly informed discussion of 18th century prosody in her doctoral dissertation, *Wordsworth's Blank Verses: From The Ruined Cottage to The Recluse, 1796–1806*.
2   Cited from the Derby Local Studies Library manuscript of Thelwall's 'Poems.

overt expulsion poem, *On Leaving the Dale of the Kent*, 1804, whose lament at being unable to find a settled home 'Where'er the heart invites' contains a wry allusion (here italicised) to *Frost at Midnight*:

> *I must seek*
> *Far other scenes*; where chance or duty lead;
> And meet the face of strangeness: changing oft
> The half-affianc'd friend;—lost ere well found.
>   And so, farewell! sweet hospitable Dale
> Of wandering Kent

In the other, bitterness is heard even more sharply in this wry address to his first grey hair:

> And thou hast chang'd thy hue, companïon staid
> Of forty varying years; thy darkest brown
> Shifting to silvery whiteness. Be it so:
> It is not the first time that I have met
> An old acquaintance with an alter'd face....
>   (*The first Grey Hair*, Carlisle 1804)[1]

Whether this 'half-affianc'd friend;—lost ere well found' or that 'old acquaintance with an altered face' should be identified as Wordsworth, Coleridge, Southey, all three, or none, is a moot point: the trope of 'greetings where no kindness is' ('The Poem upon the Wye', 131) is common enough in the conversation poem.

In fact, though, the only concrete evidence of Wordsworth–Thelwall relations at this time is a cordial letter of January 1804, much discussed in recent years. In it Wordsworth looks back on having advised Thelwall to approach his Scottish Lectures with circumspection; applauds his pamphlet '*A Letter to Francis Jeffray, Esq., on Certain Calumnies and Misrepresentations in the Edinburgh Review*' (Edinburgh, December 1803), but declines to comment on it in any detail (he is, to do him justice, somewhat preoccupied with

---

1   For the full text of the first of these poems and other MS. poems see Judith Thompson, 'A Shadow in Profile: John Thelwall in the Lake District', *Grasmere 2008: Selected Papers from the Wordsworth Summer Conference* (Tirril: Humanities-Ebooks, 2009, 175–212), 204–5. Note the caret above 'companion' in 'The first Gray Hair' indicating Thelwall's insistence, in the printed *Vestibule of Eloquence* version of this poem (1810), on pronouncing all four syllables.

the ever-expanding *Prelude*); and seems warmly to anticipate further conversation on the business of prosody. The letter contains what is, astonishingly, the poet's lengthiest discussion of the craft of verse.

The key passage in Wordsworth's letter (*EY*, 434–5) is this:

> [Y]our general rule is just that the art of verse should not com-pell you to read in [tone? some?] emphasis etc that violates the nature of Prose. But this rule should be taken with limitations for not to speak of other reasons as long as verse shall have the marked termination that rhyme gives it, and as long as blank verse shall be printed in lines, it will be Physically impossible to pronounce the last words or syllables of the lines with the same indifference, as the others, i.e. not to give them an intonation of one kind or an other, or to follow them with a pause, not called out for by the passion of the subject, but by the passion of metre merely. This might be demonstrated. As to my own system of metre it is very simple, 1st and 2nd syllables long or short indif-ferently except where the Passion of the sense cries out for one in preference 3d 5th 7th 9th short etc according to the regular laws of the Iambic. This the general rule. But I can scarcely say that I admit any limits to the dislocation of the verse, that is I know none that may not be justified by some passion or other. I speak in general terms. The most dislocated line I know in my writing, is this in the Cumberland Beggar. "Impressed on the white road in the same line" which taken by itself has not the sound of a verse ... The words to which the passion is att[ached?] are white road same line and the verse dislocates [for the] sake of these. This will please or displ[ease by th]e quantity of feeling excited by the image, to those in whom it excites [such? much?] feeling, as in one it will be musical to others not. Adieu.

And the letter ends cordially enough:

> Thank you again for your Letter and Pamphlet I shall be glad to see your remarks next summer, and to converse with you on metre. Best remembrances from my sister and wife.
> Yours sincere[ly]
>
> >   WW
>
> I give you joy of your reception at Glasgow ...

Sadly, there is no evidence that the promised conversation ever took place; sadder still, the pamphlet referred to is Thelwall's assault on Jeffrey rather than the 'Introductory Essay on Poetic Rhythmus' which made its first appearance in 1805.

The 'dislocated' line in context, with its stresses italicised, is:

> He plies his weary journey, (x) seeing still, (x)
> And never knowing that he sees, (x) some straw, (x)
> Some scatter'd leaf, or marks which, in one track, (x)
> The nails of cart or chariot wheel (x) have left (/)
> **Im***press***'d on the** *white road*, **(x) in the** *same line*, **(x)**
> At distance still the same. ('Old Cumberland Beggar', 53 ff)

Now line 57 may not look *especially* Jacobinical, and we may all be able to suggest much more dislocated lines in Wordsworth's poetry before or after 1804, but a pentameter made up conspicuously of one iamb, two pyrrhics and two spondees—i.e. having only one iambic 'foot'—does indeed offend the Augustan rule book quite grossly. My 'x's mark where Thelwall certainly, and Wordsworth probably, would have expected a pause of minimal duration, which pauses (as we shall see later) Thelwall and his mentor Joshua Steele would have counted in the scansion while others would not. My terminal *forward slash* on the line preceding the 'dislocated' one indicates what Wordsworth and almost all competent prosodists of the era would have heard as either a suspended tone or a rising tone, anticipating the completion of the syntax: i.e. signalling that there will be an answer to the question that the line leaves hanging, 'have left what?'.[1]

Wordsworth's letter, one should note, changes its focus mid-paragraph from *reading*, which is Thelwall's concern, to *writing*, and one can entertain the possibility that as he does so, Wordsworth quite consciously departs from ground where he might agree with such elocu-

---

1   That this is always the case when a line ending does not coincide with a line break makes Christopher Ricks's treatment of such lines, as if there were an implied close (here, for instance, on 'have left') largely fallacious. See 'A Pure Organic Pleasure from the Lines', in *The Force of Poetry*, Oxford University Press 1984, 89–116) in which Ricks's discussion of such characteristic lines as 'Deem that our puny boundaries are things', 'But in the very world which is the world', and 'My own voice cheer'd me, and, far more, the mind's' does violence to their auditory qualities.

tionists as Sheridan, Burgh and Enfield, about how poetry should be spoken, reverting to a more abstract sense of metre to which, in composition, he adheres. Writing and performance are different arts and there is a considerable gulf in the late eighteenth century between those whose systems of metre include, and those which exclude, grammatical and rhetorical pauses. A line may well have a technical base of regularity (for the benefit of one's fingers as it were) while the ear responds at another level altogether. Wordsworth elsewhere assumes that the 'system of metre' to which he writes will be suspended by the reader in favour of 'the passion of verse' and much of his argument about metre is that the co-presence of regular metre and irregular emotion necessarily involves an 'intertexture' of two 'tunes'. One of the ways in which his poems are designed to 'call forth and bestow power' is the invitation *or even obligation* they confer on the reader 'to modulate, in subordination to the sense, the music of the poem;—in the same manner as his mind is left at liberty, and even summoned, to act upon its thoughts and images' (from the *Preface*, 1815)—an obligation Thelwall fulfils very thoroughly when he reads *The Excursion*.

Brennan O'Donnell, in his wonderfully assiduous study called *The Passion of Metre*, concludes problematically from this letter and other evidence, that:

> 'Wordsworth's verse, in these matters, as in so many others, is indebted primarily to the mainstream tradition of Chaucer, Spenser, Shakespeare, and Milton. That is, he describes and writes perfectly traditional accentual-syllabic English verse, not different in the essentials of its laws and practice from the verse of the poets in whose company he wished to be placed by posterity.'[1]

One could argue, contrariwise, that while Wordsworth indeed sees

---

1 Brennan O'Donnell, *The Passion of Metre: A Study of Wordsworth's Metrical Art* (Kent, OH: Kent State University Press, 1995) 36. I quarrel with this work several times in this essay but it is a book that every student of Wordsworth should read, chew and inwardly digest. O'Donnell, incidentally, reads this line via Derek Attridge's 'rules', whereby double offbeats on *adjacent* syllables have to be balanced by implied offbeats *between* stressed syllables. Set out as o B ŏ B ŏ B ŏ B ŏ B the line looks remarkably *undislocated*. See Derek Attridge, *The Rhythms of English Poetry* (London & NY: Longman, 1982) 175 ff., 357 ff.

himself in the line of Chaucer, Spenser, Shakespeare, and Milton, that selection of poets, along with James Beattie, provides the more conservative proponents of accentual-syllabic verse with most of their examples of how such verse should *not* be written.

Why this should be, may appear in two Miltonic lines which according to Crabb Robinson Wordsworth especially admired (see Henry Crabb Robinson, *On Books and their Writers*, II, 479). Among the consequences of the fall, in Adam's vision of man's future, are

> MaRASmus, (x) and WIDE-WASTing PESTilence,
> DROPsies and ASTHmas, (x) and JOINT-WRACKing RHEUMS

Each of these lines offers two pairs of adjacent offbeats, one of each pair interrupted by a rest, each followed by adjacent beats. There may be some doubt whether WRACK requires weight, because if it does we have three barely separated and highly percussive beats; but if so, it is merely amplifying a similar concatenation a few lines earlier: 'a place … appeared, (x) sad, noisome, dark'). Consider also Milton's description of monsters 'huge of bulk'

> Wallowing | unwieldy | (x) | enor | mous in | their gait

which 'TEMpest the ocean'. Thomas Sheridan, the 18th century's subtlest analyst of prosody, marks the first hemistich as made up of a dactyl and an amphibrach.[1] The line may end with three iambs (Sheridan doesn't say), in which case it makes a passable pentameter, though it could *also* end in a corresponding amphibrach and anapaest, making a rhythmic chiasmus. In strict accentual-syllabic tradition the line's twelve syllables have to be reduced to ten by hearing 'wallowing' as 'wall'wing', and (presumably) eliding 'unwieldy' and 'enormous' into something like 'unwieldy'normous'—or simply turning a blind eye (a frequent recourse when Augustan critics applied their dead rules to living verse) to one of those adjacent vowels. The only difference Thelwall would make to Sheridan's scansion of this twelve syllable pentameter is in the marking of cadences, which, following Joshua Steele, Thelwall insists always begin 'heavy', and in making the caesura a full rest:

---

1   *Lectures on the Art of Reading* (1775), 2: 227–8.

| Wallowing un| wieldy | — | ⁊ e| normous in their | gait |

This is my application of Thelwall's system, not his, but it has, one might feel, a wholly appropriate rolling quality.

Before I leave Wordsworth's 1804 Letter to Thelwall let me enumerate its key points. First, he evidently subscribes to an emergent consensus that artificially regular speaking of blank verse is an abomination. Secondly, he insists that while line endings must be marked, such marking is as least as likely to involve intonation as interruption— a major element in the prosody of Hugh Blair and others (and indeed Thelwall). Thirdly, he seems disconcertingly naïve in his employment of the terms 'long or short' to describe English syllables. This inexact usage, though supported by such authorities as Isaac Watts, *may* in fact support one key feature in Thelwall's complex prosody: in Wordsworth's 'blank verse', whatever 'long' syllables there may be in a line (and length, if we take him literally, is all he commits himself to) there are frequently fewer than five *accents*. Thelwall occasionally scans for all three facets of what is loosely called stress—quantity (length), 'poise' (relative weight, with or without added 'percussion'), both of which must always be present, and accent (significant changes of pitch) which many commentators (including Lord Kames) agreed could occur as infrequently as sense dictates. Fourthly, while Wordsworth acknowledges the 'general rule' of metrical alternation, he overtly dismisses *any limit*, in practice, to the range of justifiable dislocations of such alternation—a dismissal that makes it highly unlikely that he would have subscribed to Derek Attridge's elaborate system of compensations with its finicky 'conditions'.

Rival Methodologies

Brennan O'Donnell concludes from Wordsworth's letter that he had a highly developed theory of metre which was more sophisticated than anything Thelwall would have understood or subscribed to. David Perkins concludes from it in a pioneering but sometimes misleading essay, that Wordsworth, far from being a master of prosody, was even unsure how one should voice a line ending.[1] Neither of these

---

1   David Perkins, 'How the Romantics Recited Poetry', *SEL* 31 (1991) 655–71, 664.

interpretations convinces me; nor indeed does the prevailing suppo-
sition that Wordsworth and Thelwall are necessarily at loggerheads
in this letter. O'Donnell is right, of course, that there were many in
the 18th century who believed with Edward Bysshe, Milton's editor
Bentley, Lord Monboddo and William Mason, that the metrical set
must always rule and that as Mason (the only poet in this quartet but
a truly dreadful one) puts it: 'the first syllable [in an English line]
whether long or short in actual quantity is always pronounced short,
and the next long, and so alternately to the end of every line' (Mason,
Works, 3: 389). But by the time of Wordsworth's schooling it is fair
to say that the weight of opinion had swung behind the contrary position of Lord Kames and Isaac Watts that in reading verse one should
observe the modes of pronunciation, and accentuation and phras-
ing, that are appropriate to prose—i.e. read 'with a prose mouth' in
Southey's phrase—and that if the verse does not sound harmonious
when one does this, that is because the poet does not know his craft.

    None of these advocates of rival systems had the pleasure of read-
ing Wordsworth's Skating spot with its metrically demanding manip-
ulation of 'games / Confederate, imitative of the chase/ And woodland
pleasures' in which the mimetic 'imitative' (think of a skater's rapid
leg action in an accelerating curve) allows me to introduce some varieties of 18th century scansion in a relatively painless fashion. Edward
Bysshe (*The Art of English Poetry*, 1718) would apply his inflexible
system as follows, with the principle accent on 'FED' and secondary
ones upon TA, OF and CHASE:[1]

        x   //   x ∧ / x / x   / x /
        Confed'rate , imitative of the chase

Lord Kames (*Elements of Criticism*, 1762), following his own rule
that a polysyllabic word can only have one accent, might have to scan
it, uneasily, as:

        x   / x ∧ / x x x   x x /
        Confed'rate , imitative of the chase

---

1   In Bysshe's system each line has one principle accent, properly associated with
     the caesura (which, in this case, it clearly isn't).

Samuel Say (*Poems on Several Occasions*, 1745), with his refusal of elisions, and his *brilliant* recognition that in English poetry what we crudely call 'stress' is made up of both quantity and accent would scan it as follows, marking the longer *quantities* with an en-rule and the *accents* with a slash:

    x   / x − ʌ / x − x   x x   −
    Confederate , imitative of the chase

Thomas Sheridan (*Lectures on the Art of Reading*, 1775) would concur I think but he would probably construe the second hemistich as made up of an amphimacer, a pyrrhic and an iamb (so the line begins and ends on an iambic foot):

    x / x x ʌ / x/ x x   x   /
    Confederate, imita tive of the chase

Joshua Steele (in *Prosodia Rationalis*, 1779) and John Thelwall would each offer a dual scansion. Steele would have used musical notation, and Thelwall classical notation to indicate quantity (I illustrate only the latter); and both would have used traditional thesis and arsis marks to indicate 'poise', or pulsation and remission, or 'weight'. I suspect Thelwall would have used his rather rare solid pyramid for the percussive 'heavy poise' on the first syllable of imitative.

    u   − u u   u u − u   u u   −
    Con | federate |— | imitative | ⁊ of the | chase
    ∴ | ∆ ∴∴ |— | ▲ ∴∴ ∴∴ | ∴∴ | ∆

My point is that even Lord Kames, cited as the epitome of correctness, would not insist on five 'beats'. Kames concedes that in blank verse (II, 420–21) considerable variety is possible and desirable: 'the accents are not, like the syllables, confined to a certain number. Some lines have no fewer than five, and there are lines that admit not above one.' 'In a blank verse', Tennyson will insist, 'you can have from three up to eight beats', because 'varying of the beats, of the construction of the feet, of the emphasis, of the extra-metrical syllables and of the pauses, helps to make the greatness of blank verse' (*Alfred

Lord Tennyson: A Memoir by his Son, II, 14)[1].

As a pupil of Hawkshead Grammar, Wordsworth may well have been taught classical prosody in a very strict form. But he was also familiar with one or both of the most famous primers of the age, William Enfield's *The Speaker* (with which Dorothy was familiar), and James Burgh's *The Art of Speaking*. Burgh is famous primarily as a great Whig advocate of liberty, free speech, and universal suffrage and as such was *persona* exceedingly *grata* in the early years of the American Republic. A friend of Franklin, Price and Priestley, and admired by Jefferson, his *Political Disquisitions* (1774) was required reading for republicans in Congress as his *The Art of Speaking* (1761) was at Hawkshead Grammar School. From it, Hawkshead's young classical scholars would have learned that regular as their prosodical compositions might be, their reading of those compositions should not be controlled by the metronome. Burgh's precepts include the advice (derided by Coleridge in *Biographia Literaria* and the *Lectures on Literature*) that 'no person reads well, till he comes to speak what he sees in the book before him in the same natural manner as he speaks the thoughts, which arise in his own mind'—that is, till he gets out of reading in a disengaged fashion, as if the words in the poem are prefaced by 'it says here that'. And this is how Burgh suggests the young scholar should 'speak' Edward Young's *Night Thoughts*:

THE *clock* strikes *one*. We take *no note* of
           time,
But by its *loss*. To give it then a *tongue*
Is *wise* in *man*. As if an *angel* spoke,
I *feel* the *solemn sound*. If heard *aright*,
It is the *knell* of my *departed hours*.
Where are they ?—With the *years* beyond the
           flood.
It is the *signal* that demands *dispatch*.

The stressed syllables in the first few lines number 5, 2, 3, 4, 3, 5 and 2. Burgh's treatment of Spenser is similarly dramatic. In four lines of *The Faerie Queene* he finds 1, 5, 5 and 2 accents respectively: 'At length they chaunst to *meet* upon the way / An *aged sire* (2) in *long black weeds* (3) yclad, / His *feete* all *bare*, his *beard* all *hoarie grey*,

---

1   Cited gratefully from Ruth Abbott, 'Wordsworth's Blank Verses', 18.

/ And by his *belt* his *booke* he hanging had' (the numerals indicating adjacent beats are Burgh's).[1]

Speaking 'in a natural manner', as one would expect of 'a man speaking to men' (especially a man who repudiated the notion that the reader of poetry should have 'his common judgement and under-standing … laid asleep' and enjoy finding himself in a 'perturbed and dizzy state of mind' [Appendix 1802]) also precludes adoption of what Thelwall calls 'a verse mouth'—a supposedly poetical tone quite distinct from the articulation of prose. This is how, in 1805, Thelwall explains the point in his 'Introductory Essay on the Study of English Rhythmus':

> … from my system of reading verse, I preclude all peculiarities of tone, all arbitrary accents, … I know of no such distinction as a verse mouth and a prose mouth: I want only a distinct, a sono-rous, an articulative mouth—a mouth that is 'parcel of the mind,' and a mind that can identify with its author. (xvi)[2]

Thelwall's very confident tone 'I know of no such distinction' may have been encouraged by Wordsworth's recent prosody letter which begins its discussion of poetry by repudiating the phrases 'verse mouth and prose mouth': 'I never used [such] phrases in my life, and hold no such opinions'—which, rightly or wrongly, I take to imply a repudiation also, of 'chaunt'. A fuller and classic formulation of good speaking—whether speaking one's own thoughts or 'reciting' those of others—appears in his companion '*Introductory Discourse on Elocution*' and its conclusion is immensely persuasive:

> *Elocution is the Art, or the Act of so delivering our own thoughts and sentiments, or the thoughts and sentiments of others, as not only to convey to those around us (with precision, force and harmony) the full purport and meaning of the words and sentences in which those thoughts are cloathed; but also, to excite and impress upon their minds—the feelings, the imag-*

---

1   James Burgh, *The Art of Speaking*, 106, 107
2   Thelwall, 'Introductory Essay on Poetic Rhythmus' (1805), cited from *Selections* (London 1812), xvi. The phrase may originate with Southey, whose preface to *Thalaba* claims that it reads itself and cannot be distorted into 'discord': 'a reader 'may read it with a prose mouth, but its flow and fall will still be perceptible'.

inations and the passions by which those thoughts are dictated, or with which they should naturally be accompanied...

Elocution, therefore ... embraces the whole Theory and Practice of the exterior demonstration of the inward workings of the mind.[1]

That Thelwall was a capable and ground-breaking speech therapist there is no doubt. As a phonetician, also, he takes the study and classification of speech sounds and their production far beyond any of his predecessors, aided perhaps by Richard Roe whose work also occupied the first two decades of the 19th century. His contributions to prosody, however, are relatively few, since many of his ideas and most of illustrative anecdotes can be traced to profitable reading in the precursors he acknowledges, such as Joshua Steele (1779), James Odell (1805) and Richard Roe (1801/1820), and indeed, through them, to precursors of theirs he may not to have known.[2]

Thelwall enchaired himself 'Professor of Elocution' in Sheffield in November 1801, and turned seriously peripatetic early in 1802. At the time of his inaugural lecture, I would surmise, his reading in specialised *prosody* was fairly limited. The points he argues with Coleridge (and no doubt) Wordsworth in 1797–98 have largely to do with diction rather than prosody, and the evidence of his interest in rhythm lies in his poetic practice rather than in his epistolary advice to Coleridge at that time.

The 'Advertisement' for Thelwall's twelve Wakefield lectures of 1803 was penned in Rotherham in September 1802 and attached to a

---

1   Quoted from the Bodleian copy of *The Trident of Albion, an epic effusion; and an oration on the influence of elocution on martial enthusiasm; with an address to the shade of Nelson: delivered at the Lyceum, Liverpool, on occasion of the late naval victory. To which is prefixed an Introductory Discourse on the Nature and Objects of Elocutionary Science*, By John Thelwall, Professor of the Science and Practice of Elocution (Liverpool, 1805), 5.

2   Viz.: Joshua Steele, *Prosodia Rationalis* (1779); Richard Roe, *The Elements of English Metre* (London 1801) and *Principles of Rhythm, Both in Speech and Music Especially as Exhibited in the Mechanism of English Verse*, Dublin 1823; J. Odell, *An Essay on the Elements, Accents and Prosody of the English Language* (1806). Whether Thelwall ever came across the true origin of his own analogy between feet and musical bars, and his use of the Greek terms thesis and arsis, in Samuel Say's *Poems on Several Occasions* (1745) or in John Mason's *Two Essays on the Power of Numbers* (1749) I do not know.

prospectus printed in Birmingham in December. In his 1810 *Letter to Henry Cline* (a biographical treatise combining clinical speech therapy with some outline of his poetical ideas) Thelwall records being approached after one of his early lectures (in Hull, early in 1802) by a clergyman who opined that the lecturer seemed 'to have adopted the opinion of Mr Joshua Steele', to which Thelwall replied that 'I had not until that moment ever heard his name'. Yet by December 1802 his prospectus promises to touch (briefly at least) upon Steele's *Prosodia Rationalis* and from 1805 onwards much of 'his' system is simply a simplification of Steele's. To judge from the Wakefield Prospectus, what Thelwall has to say on prosody, in late 1802, can still be compassed in parts of one lecture, Lecture 8, where he treats such 'barbarisms' as elision or 'syncope' of the vowels and dipthongs, along with the structure of English verse and conversational delivery before devoting most of his lecture to standard critiques of the elocution movement's favourite subject, a 'Critical Examination of the Elocution of the Pulpit'. Lecture 9, however does return briefly to definitions of Accent and Emphasis, also very traditional territory, which he illustrates from Dryden and Milton, as Thomas Sheridan mostly did.

Between 1805 (Pontefract) and 1812 (London), however, all his printed *Selections*, for his increasingly elaborate lecture courses, include either his 'Introductory Discourse on the Nature and objects of Elocutionary Science', or his 'Introductory Essay on English Rhythmus'. Both treatises borrow Steele's anecdotal critique of errors in elocution, and his adaptation of musical notation to prosody. Thelwall, most often, uses just 4 of Steele's range of 8 quantities and equivalent pauses. Steele's system, it has to be said, is hopelessly complex, though he presents it with an admirable lightness of touch which the dogmatic Thelwall rarely approaches. Overleaf, for example (in *Prosodia Rationalis,* 167) Steele tries to persuade Lord Monboddo that the first line of *Paradise Lost* really can*not* be read

Of *man*'s first *dis-o-bed-*ience *and* the *fruit.*

Monboddo took the view that the line would break down entirely if one were to stress 'first' and de-stress 'and'.

I thought fo great a poet as Milton would not have put an

unmeaning expletive in the | firſt | line of his | poem; | but that,

on the contrary, he meant to point out *emphatically (not loudly)*

what particular aᶜt of | man's difo | bedience | it was, which had

drawn on him and his race fo | heavy a | puniſhment, | and there-

fore I marked it, of | man's | firſt difo | bedience ; | neither do I

fee any reafon for bringing the accidents attending the fyllables
in the firſt line of a diſtich to tally numerically with thofe of the
fecond: for in that cafe, the cæfure muſt always be in the fame
periods of both lines, which your l—p juſtly remarks as a
great fault in French and Engliſh poetry; though, I think, it

And in the illustration on the next page Steele explains, very amus-
ingly, the concept of 'accentuation' as applied to English and French
pronunciation of the word 'pensioner / pensionaire' (150)

One can trace with some exactness the birth in Thelwall's poetical practice of some aspects of the opinions he voices from 1805
onwards as his own prosodic theory. An easily demonstrable instance
is his rather reluctant abandonment of elision and 'syncope of the
vowels' on which he expatiates in Wakefield as a barbarism, but
which was a regular occurrence in *The Peripatetic* (1793). Indeed his
volume of *Poems Chiefly Written in Retirement* (1801) is still breach-
ing what would soon become a cardinal rule. Its extract from *Albion*
has 'Northumbria' and 'sufferance' in one twelve-syllable line (with
neither appoggiaturae nor elisions marked, so one can only guess
how he would have read these words), but a contracted monosyllabic
'Pow'r' further down on the same page. Effusion VIII of June 1800

To fhew the poffibility of a fimilar inftance in our language,
let us fuppofe a patriot, in a popular affembly, faying, " Sir, I
" would afk, whether we ought to look upon this peace-making
" minifter as the difinterefted friend of mankind, or the

" *penfionaire* of our rivals?" To which the fhouts of the affembly

would probably anfwer *rapidly* in plain Englifh pronunciation,

" *Penfioner, penfioner*." From which, I think, no other gram-

matical or critical confequence could be juftly drawn, except that
the patriot had flily affected a Gallicifm in the pronunciation of a
word, which, independent of * accentuation, was the fame in
both languages.

* Here, for want of a better word, I put ACCENTUATION, as a general term to include
accent, quantity, and *poife.*

has (very oddly) a monosyllabic and barely sayable 'seem'd'st' and
a disyllabic 'turned'st' within four lines of each other, in June 1800.
The frontispiece of the volume is captioned 'Why on the mould'ring
tomb of other times'—with a clear elision in the conventional position—whereas the text of *Cerrig-Enion*, the poem it illustrates, spells
out 'mouldering' and may intend it to be sounded as a three-syllable
word. By the time the volume is put together Thelwall may be *on the
cusp* of challenging the extraordinary brutality 18th century poets routinely displayed towards all those innocent little vowels, but is not yet
making this a principle of 'his' system.

Elision is undoubtedly an eighteenth-century practice, and in
some circumstances (as the manuscript orthography sometimes
shows) Wordsworth himself practised it, but it is already a practice
more honoured, some elocutionists would say, in the breach than
in th'observance. Take *Yew-Trees*. Brennan O'Donnell seems very
exercised by one line in this poem, making three attempts to scan it

Attridge fashion, of which this is the second:

> Huge trunks!— and each particular trunk a growth
> B   ô   B   o   B   oB ŏ   B   o   B

It worries O'Donnell that this option introduces six beats in the line, and that what he calls 'syntactical stress hierarchies' *ought* to subordinate the adjective 'huge' to the noun 'trunks' (could *anyone* really say 'huge TRUNKS' in that line position?), but he also has a problem with 'particular'. He concludes that this word is 'for metrical purposes, a three-syllable word' (as, more easily, he has decided that 'capacious' and 'invet'rately' are also elided), but he makes this very odd proviso: 'this does not mean that the reader must actually pronounce the elision (*or that the poet himself would have done so, or even that it is physically possible to do so*)' (216). So here we have a sort of *beau ideal* of metre in which the mind merely *pretends* to hear only ten syllables, while the ear recognises eleven or even twelve. Thelwall would have none of this (after 1801 at any rate) and would not only regard the 'appoggiatura' syllable in 'particular' as one of the beauties of the line,[1] but insist, somewhat extremely, that 'capacious' also has four syllables (Thelwall took exception to 'capashus' as a barbarism). Standing out against linguistic ebb and flow is always dangerous and always unpredictable: Thelwall's unhappiest elocutionary Canuteism is that 'Henry' is an illegitimate contraction of the more elegant 'Henery'; his happiest is that 'India' is a trisyllabic name, and not as in the shires, 'Ind-ya'.

We can reasonably nominate 1802 as the epoch of Thelwall's rebirth as a prosodist, quite possibly as a result of reading Sheridan or Steele on the aesthetic value of Milton's 'supernumerary' syllables. It is all established by the time of the aggressive marking of 'appoggiatura' in the earliest poems of the Derby MS, *circa* 1805, when Thelwall is putting together his unpublished manuscript collection of *Poems, Chiefly Suggested by the Scenery of Nature*. In its 'Proem' he insists on 'gorgĕous' as trisyllabic (by placing a caret over the 'e'), just as

---

1   Compare Shenstone's widely misunderstood remark that 'wat'ry' in Pope's *Windsor Forest* is 'a great beauty': his point that the word is 'virtually a dactyl' makes clear that it is not the elision but the *resistance* of the supernumerary syllable to elision that distinguishes the line (*The Works in Verse and Prose of William Shenstone*, 3 vols (London, 1764), II, 180. Cf O'Donnell, 83.

eve̋ry, in 'The first gray Hair' is emphatically trisyllabic.

So, by 1804 most of what Thelwall's new prosody may have been in his head (and have been there for a year or two) but Wordsworth could not have had a printed synopsis available to him at the time of the letter discussed earlier. He may, however, have had reports from Keswick of Thelwall's new ideas. In November 1803, certainly, Thelwall boasted to his wife of having enrolled Coleridge, Southey and even Hazlitt 'among the number of my disciples'.[1]

I shall introduce some features of Thelwall's theory while looking at *The Excursion*, but a few points are best illustrated from the Derby ms. Here in the manuscript of the poem 'Jasamin' (MS, 719)

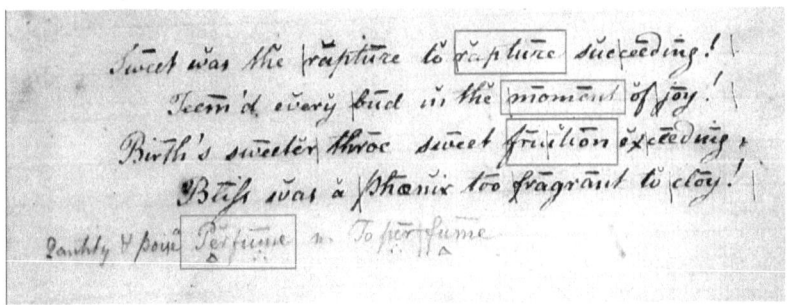

he is distinguishing—whether for his own benefit or to fix in mind a future demonstration from the podium—between quantity and poise. Thelwall knows, full well, that 'rapture' in the top line is pronounced RAPture not rapTURE. If scanning for 'poise' he would illustrate this with a poise symbol on the first syllable and an arsis symbol on the second, as in the word 'perfume' (n) marked ∆ ∴ in pencil at the bottom. But quantitatively he insists that even in the noun the second (unstressed) syllable is actually longer, just as the emphatic syllable in fruition is the shortest (*quantitatively*, fruition is an amphimacer; *accentually* it is an amphibrach—a very good reason, perhaps, for using these terms with circumspection!). The thesis and arsis symbols pencilled here on perfume and perfume, and borrowed from Samuel

1   Damian Walford Davies, *Presences that Disturb: Models of Romantic Identity in the Literature and Culture of the 1790s* (Cardiff: University of Wales Press, 2002) 318.

Say, Joshua Steele and others, are used wherever Thelwall wishes to indicate relative weight in what he calls a *cadence* as defined below in a quotation from the 'Introductory Essay on Poetic Rhythmus':

> A cadence is a portion of tunable sound (or of organic aspiration), beginning heavy and ending light | Δ ∴ |. A foot is a syllable, or number of syllables, occupying the space or duration of such a cadence |fancy Δ ∴ | revelry Δ ∴ ∴| | beautifully Δ ∴ ∴ ∴|. But part of such interval may pass in hiatus or pause .... In which case the cadence will be occupied by an imperfect foot.

An example of his rare employment of musical notation occurs in a redrafting of a 'Sonnet to Stella in the style of Ossian', composed while travelling to Edinburgh for his ill-fated lecture in December 1803 (revised in *The Vestibule of Eloquence* under the title 'Ode from the Land of Mountains').

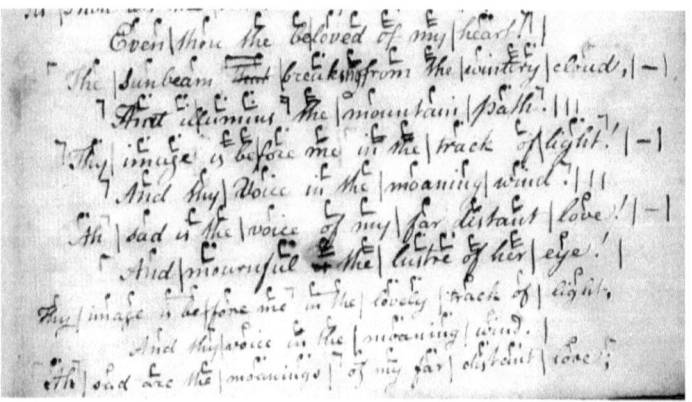

The bottom three lines—rather faint, beginning 'Thy image is before me in the lovely track of light', with minims on 'track' and light'— are an attempted revision of three of the four lines above (MS 727). Extending the first of the repeated lines by insertion of 'lovely', presumably to gain a mirror effect in the second hemistich, Thelwall also slows the passage by promoting such throwaway syllables as 'is be' (in 'is before me') and 'in the' from semi-quavers to quavers, and distinguishing his key terms 'track' and 'light', 'voice' and 'wind', 'sad and love' (not simply the last, as in draft) by minims. Such the precision with which Thelwall's ear was accustomed to work.

Reading *The Excursion*

Henry Crabb Robinson's Diary for 12 February 1815 records Thelwall having 'talked of The Excursion as containing finer verses than there are in Milton and as being in versification most admirable; but then Wordsworth borrows without acknowledgement from Thelwall himself!!'.[1] The two exclamation marks show the diarist unaware how much of *The Excursion* is indeed borrowed from Thelwall—its plot, its title, and much of the poem's psychological interest in blasted hopes and disappointed expectations, and some at least of the Wanderer's more democratic utterance. Both Thelwall and Robinson were among the poem's most assiduous readers. Robinson, Sally Bushell has told us,[2] not only read the poem repeatedly, but read Books 1 & 2 aloud to a none-too-receptive neighbour Mrs Pattison. Thelwall went one better; he read it through it, pencil in hand, marking the 'cadences' of all 9,068 lines (roughly 55,408 cadences!), then (I suspect) went through it again, indicating rhetorical pauses he may have missed the first time through, assessing the requirement for an additional silent cadence or two at the close of particular paragraphs, marking here and there the 'thesis and arsis' of pulsation and remission, once in a while noting where a line has unusually few cadences (and thus either dramatic pauses or what Thelwall calls 'an accelerated rhythmus'), and in general, attempting to unravel what John Taylor Coleridge's review called the poem's 'abstruser harmonies'.

The title page of Thelwall's copy of *The Excursion*, to which we are all indebted to Paul Betz for safeguarding, is inscribed 'scanned throughout in metrical cadences and rhythmical clauses' and in the 'Introductory Essay' Thelwall's brief exposition of 'clauses' makes two points: that 'a line may consist of one, two or three clauses' (lvi) and that clauses are divided (from each other, presumably) by percussion or caesura (lvii). He counts the clauses (or the cadences making

1   *Diary, Reminiscences and Correspondence of Henry Crabb Robinson*, 3 vols, London 1869. 1, 473.
2   *Re-Reading 'The Excursion': Narrative, response and the Wordsworthian dramatic voice* (Aldershot: Ashgate, 2002), 124.

up such clauses) in one poem in the Derby manuscript in this fashion ('Rondeau', MS 721), though the result is not greatly illuminating.
But Richard Roe's first book *The Elements of English Metre* 1801)
coins the term 'rhythmical clause' to describe groups of lines constituting what Kames called a 'cadence', and what Wordsworth, in conversation with Klopstock, called a 'period'—namely *whatever length of
continuous syntax precedes a full stop*. One of the striking things about
Thelwall's copy of *The Excursion* is the extent of what appears to be
simply sidelining: I would hypothesise that rather than merely expressing interest ('this is a good bit!') Thelwall may sometimes be marvel-
ling at the extraordinary length, some of them running for a page or
more, of uninterrupted 'rhythmic clauses' in Roe's sense of the term.

When a friend of Catherine Clarkson in January 1815 complained
of monotony in *The Excursion*, Wordsworth replied immodestly:

> Unitarian hymns must by their dispassionate *monotony* have
> deprived your Friend's ear of all *compass*, which implies of all
> discrimination. To you I will whisper, that *The Excursion* has
> one merit, if it has no other, a versification to which for *variety*
> of musical effect no Poem in the language furnishes a parallel.
> Tell Patty Smith ... to study with her fingers till she has learned
> to confess it'.[1]

If we count only those effects unambiguously supplied by the author
rather than the reader, what Wordsworth means by 'variety of musical effect' might include irregularity of 'beats'; variation of syllabic
quantity; the handling of single and multiple caesurae; the deployment
of line breaks in positions deplored or outlawed by such as Bysshe
and Kames; metrical substitutions, as allowed for in the blank verse
prosody of Sheridan and Beattie as well as by Thelwall; accelera-
tions; surprising enjambments, as exemplified at large by Sheridan's
treatment of *Paradise Lost*; and of course assonance and alliteration
and other aspects of phonetic texture (from hissed along the polished
ice to the murmuring of innumerable bees). Some tonal effects—i.e.

---

1   To Catherine Clarkson, January 1815. What Wordsworth meant by 'compass' I
do not know, but Thelwall defined it in his 1806 *Selections* as covering loud and
soft in volume, high and low in the musical scale and 'Flexure of Tone' in the
sense of 'acerbic', 'warm', 'tender' and so forth.

those of suspension and close, declaration and interrogation, must also arise out of the syntax *if* one is attending to what Wordsworth calls, simply, 'the passion of the verse'. What 'variety of musical effect' does *not* mean is simply a rollicking mix of duple and triple metres as in such popular poetry as Thomas Campbell's 'The Exile of Erin': lively it may sound, but such stuff was offered to beginners in Mr Thelwall's academy as, in practice, highly predictable and child's play to scan.

Thelwall would have anticipated considerable variety in *The Excursion*, from his friendship with Wordsworth in the year of *Lyrical Ballads*, when such poems as Thelwall's *To the Infant Hampden*, Coleridge's *Frost at Midnight* and Wordsworth's *Poem upon the Wye* constituted an ongoing conversation.[1] The first lines of blank verse in *Lyrical Ballads*—lines singled out by Charles Lamb as a revelation of a new sound in poetry—announce the rejection of all that Bysshe and Kames wrote about the proper balance of a pentameter line, with an obligatory caesura after the 4th 5th or 6th syllable and a neat phrasal division either side of it:

Nay, (x) Traveller! (x) rest. (xx) This lonely yew-tree stands	1, 4, 5
Far from all human dwelling: (x) what if here	7
No sparkling rivulet spread the verdant herb;	0
What if these barren boughs the bee not loves;	0
Yet, (x) if the wind breathe soft, (x) the curling waves,	1, 6

Within these provocative lines, with break positions indicated at the right by syllable count, only the third and fourth, with their spoof of conventional diction and music, approach the caesural norm and—rather mischievously—in neither case is a caesura indicated in punctuation, though a reader might reasonably supply one after rivulet (this line has the added piquancy of letting the reader decide whether rivulets or riv'lets are more poetical) and boughs.

For the most part, Thelwall's analysis of *The Excursion* looks disappointingly minimal, but from his simple procedure one can infer a good deal about how Mr Thelwall's Ear exercised itself on Mr

---

1   See Judith Thompson's 'An Autumnal Blast, A Killing Frost: Coleridge's Poetic Conversation with John Thelwall', *SiR* 36 (1997) 427–456 and the coda to my "The Somerset Sound; or, the Darling Child of Speech'.

Wordsworth's Poem.[1] And this, on the next page, is how he begins (the boxes, here and elsewhere, are mine):

Most of the marks here (and throughout) are simply cadential bars. Thus, in the first line, eight slashes mark eight cadences, two of which are silent. Four slashes indicate, predictably enough, that

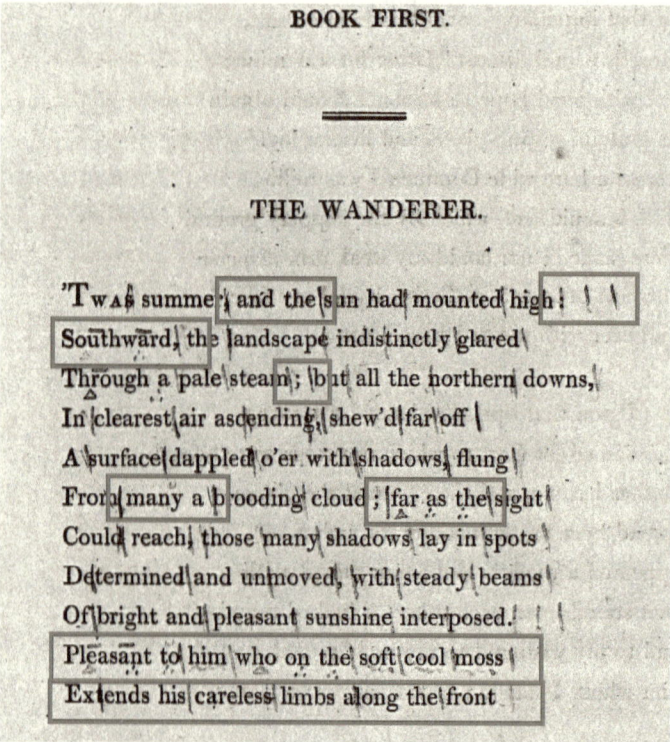

'sum-', 'sun', 'mount' and 'high' carry 'heavy poise' and account for four beats, since each cadence 'begins heavy and ends light'. The second bar does *not* indicate a beat on 'and' but an *implied* beat after summer, amplifying the comma. The dramatic pause at the end of the first line leads into what is quantitatively a spondee though in poise a trochee—followed by a pencilled rest sign which initiates

---

1   *The Excursion*, London 1814, 3. For these facsimile reproductions from John Thelwall's copy of the first edition I am indebted to Paul Betz.

the cadence ending 'the', after which the line is quietly iambic to the close. What one might loosely call a trochee and a spondee initiate the next hemistich, before the strong caesura in line three where Wordsworth's semi-colon is accorded a cadence. In line six Thelwall finds two instances of triple measure—a definite anapaest in 'far as the' but also a secondary one in 'many a' where the caret over the 'y' denies elision. Line 9 ends with another two-bar rest, before the musical intensification of the line beginning 'Pleasant to him...'. This dramatic line is made up of two anapaests and four monosyllabic feet, except that each of these syllables has a wavy underline indicating that each is an expressive cadence—in effect a kind of trochee, ending light in the sustaining of the nasal and fricative and liquid sounds of 'm', ft', 'l' and 'ss'. The final line on this page looks straightforwardly iambic (though it has, of course, six cadences) and it ends with a tone of suspension on 'front' (the faint acute accent here may be intentional), because the next page begins 'Of sOme hUge cAve, whose rOcky cEIling cAsts / A twilight of its own....' which first line has its own drama with three adjacent stresses (or syllables 'in heavy poise') in each half of the line.

These six stresses, incidentally, illustrate Thelwall's principle that the time occupied by the monosyllables 'some', 'huge' and 'cave', will be *exactly* the same as the disyllables 'rocky' and 'ceiling'. The next three lines, following this beautifully balanced six-stress line, are each divided into two-stress halves, with the caesura moving gently forward from line to line, from sixth, to fifth, to third position: 'A twilight of its own, ⋎ an ample shade / Where the wren warbles ; ⋎ while the dreaming man / Half conscious ⋎ of the soothing melody, …'. The poet, however is not dreaming but struggling with the heat. As he confesses 'nor could |my |weak |arm |dis|perse / The |host of |insects |gathering |round my |face / And |ever |with me |as I |paced a|long' Thelwall marks 'dis|perse' as two whole cadences, with what may be additional percussion on 'dis' and a *rising* wavy line above 'perse' registering extreme agitation, before the final lines in the passage assume a very regular iambic. What is happening, it seems to me is that Wordsworth's evident subscription to the eighteenth century aesthetic of similitude in dissimilitude, or variety in uniformity (a principle discovered and promoted prosodically by Samuel Say and others) is being recognised. Without *dissimilitude*, Wordsworth would agree with Say, there can be no art. When similitude takes over, say in an unusually regular iambic line ('The host of insects gathering round my face') there has to be a point to it and we have to be in a position to relish it.[1]

The first utterance of the Wanderer, on page 5, is, as one might expect, distinguished by marked deliberateness:

> Thus did he | speak|. | "I |see around me |here
> Things which you |cannot |see |: |we |die, my |Friend,

Both the period and the colon are amplified into full cadences; the syllables 'I', 'see' and 'here', 'we', 'die' and 'Friend' carry the heavy poise of their cadences, or rather, they *are* cadences. A similarly intense reading is applied to an point in the Wanderer's introduction of Margaret to the poet, a line or two after his famous espial of 'the useless fragment of a wooden bowl'. A simple double sidelining picks out the exclamation of the Wanderer, that 'O Sir the good die

---

1   See Samuel Say, *Poems on Several Occasions* (1745) 101–2, and Thomas Sheridan whose fundamental (and equally Wordsworthian) thesis is that poetic numbers keep the mind in a *constant* state of gentle agitation (my emphasis).

first': but the cadential bars indicate very clearly the value of silence, and the powerful rhythm established by passion:

> But |She
> Who |lived | ⊤within these |walls, | ⊤ at my ap|proach
> A |daughter's |welcome |gave me |; ⊤ and I | loved her|
> As my |own |child|.⊤| O | Sir! | ⊤ the | good | die | first
> And |they | ⊤ whose |hearts | ⊤ are |dry as |summer |dust
> Burn to the socket …

The central lines are given eight cadences apiece. I have interpolated rest marks where Thelwall's bars *cannot* mean a stress on the following syllable (because the syllable in question will not take it), and therefore *must* mean a silent beat (the full-foot rest between 'child' and 'O' is his). What can be heard, however minimal the marking up, is the concentrated 'passion' (Wordsworth's term seems appropriate) upon all of the following terms: own, child, O, Sir, good, die, first; and on they, hearts, dry, summer, dust; and the considerable power that derives from the dual line break in 'And |they | ⊤ whose |hearts | ⊤ ….' —the two lines being given a firm double sideline. Such moments perhaps make Thelwall's engagement with this poem amply evident—indeed his evident commitment to reading it as *a poem*.

On page 19 of *The Excursion* (reproduced overleaf in full) something happens that causes Thelwall to make no less than four attempts at deciding on the music of a single line. The passage deals with the education of the Wanderer and his earliest inclination to a peripatetic life. The same 'kindly spirit who impels / The Savoyard to quit his native rocks....'

did | now im |pel
His | restless | mind | ┑   to look a | broad with | hope

𝄽♩ | ♩ ♩ | ♩ | 𝄾| ♪ ♩. ♪ | ♩|𝄽♩ | ♩ |

o   B   o   B   o B o   B   o   B

The prosodic matter at issue is the weight to be given to 'Mind' and 'Hope' and the quantification of the caesura so as to isolate 'Mind' for attention while not rupturing the syntactic integrity of 'impel / His restless mind to look abroad with hope'.

The bottom line of my transcription shows, in the inexpressive marking of Attridge-style scansion, how Wordsworth's line unproblematically 'realises' the so-called 'metrical set' of a pentameter. In between the verse and this crude scansion is the full attempt Thelwall makes at scoring this line musically (there are four attempts altogether at the mid-line phrase 'mind // to '). This expressive notation makes the first three syllables equivalent in duration as crotchets (although the 'rest' of restless carries the poise, it will not be longer in quantity) and gives 'mind' precisely twice the length of these (a

19

In the adjoining Village; but the Youth,
Who of this service made a short essay,
Found that the wanderings of his thought were then
A misery to him; that he must resign
A task he was unable to perform.

That stern yet kindly spirit, Who constrains
The Savoyard to quit his naked rocks,
The free-born Swiss to leave his narrow vales,
(Spirit attached to regions mountainous
Like their own stedfast clouds)—did now impel
His restless Mind to look abroad with hope.
—An irksome drudgery seems it to plod on,
Through dusty ways, in storm, from door to door,
A vagrant Merchant bent beneath his load!!
Yet do such Travellers find their own delight;
And their hard service, deemed debasing now,
Gained merited respect in simpler times;
When Squire, and Priest, and they who round them dwelt
In rustic sequestration, all, dependant
Upon the PEDLAR's toil—supplied their wants,
Or pleased their fancies, with the wares he brought.
Not ignorant was the Youth that still no few

minim); there is then a pause as we anticipate *what* the restless mind is to be impelled to do; the three syllables of 'to look a' are marked with their musical weight – none is heavy, because the beat in this cadence is realised by the rest, but 'look', being phonetically irreducible, gets a dotted crotchet whereas 'to' and 'a' are accorded quavers; 'broad' and 'hope' are long; and after 'abroad' there is another rest, shorter than the first (a semiquaver rest). These pauses are essential to the movement the reader's mind is required to make, if it is actively engaged (as Wordsworth requires it to be) in anticipating the movement of thought. Q: 'What will the restless mind do?' A: 'Look abroad'. Q: 'How will it do it?' A: 'With hope'. Anyone who wants the five 'beats' supposed to be necessary to a pentameter, can have them in the three minims, plus the cadentially prominent syllables 'rest' and 'look'. What Thelwall's notation does *not* do, as Joshua Steele's would, is also mark the three long syllables accentually on an implied musical stave (see pp 184–5 above). Had he done so I would surmise that 'mind' and 'broad' would be rising, because anticipatory, while 'hope' would be falling—not, of course, because it is a line ending—but because it is a syntactic close.

From this niggling rhythmic crux I turn to a far deeper topos shared by the man writing these lines, and the man scanning them; that of bereavement. Wordsworth's most explicit tribute to Thelwall as a writer of blank verse relates to Paternal Tears, Thelwall's effusions for his lost child Maria, and this tribute is of course the source of my essay title. Writing to Haydon in 1817 Wordsworth said of these effusions that they were in 'a harmonious blank verse, a metre that he wrote well, for he had a good ear'. They had 'great merit' Wordsworth said, except that because of their harrowing subject matter and inconsolability 'one cannot read them but with much more pain than pleasure' (*MY* 2, 361).

Wordsworth, presumably, felt that 'Surprised by Joy', his sonnet to Catherine, and the later six-line epitaph to Thomas, 'Six months to six years added', and perhaps 'Maternal Grief' (his first poetic explorations of the loss of children other than in the Lucy and Matthew poems) escaped this deficiency. In 'Maternal Grief', whose titular allusion to

Thelwall is unmistakeable, Wordsworth faces both the loss of two children in 1812, and the pain of witnessing Mary's disabling grief:

> In my soul
> Is present and perpetually abides
> A shadow, never, never to be displaced,
> By the returning substance, seen or touched,
> Seen by mine eyes, or clasped in my embrace.
> ('Maternal Grief' first paragraph)

Long before publishing 'Maternal Grief', however, Wordsworth recreated the lines as an expression of the multiple bereavement suffered by the Solitary, a character who is quite clearly a joint projection of both Wordsworth and Thelwall, and whose role (as a case needing therapeutic handling by other characters) is (equally clearly) modelled on that of the melancholic in Thelwall's *Peripatetic*. What we witness, therefore, in Thelwall's marking up of Book Three is the engagement of a man who cannot but know that he is reading a fictional blend of his own and the poet's experience—as sometime Jacobins, as fathers, and as husbands. The Solitary—despite Wordsworth's screen-nomination of Joseph Fawcett as his model when talking to Miss Fenwick—is Wordsworth, is Thelwall, is both.

'You', the Solitary exclaims dramatically to the Wanderer, introducing the topic of his bereavement, 'never saw, your eyes did never look, / On the bright form of her whom once I loved. / Her silver voice was heard upon the earth, / A sound unknown to you. Else, honoured Friend / Your heart a borne a pitiable share / Of what I suffered…': and in the drama of the poem, it is implied (the Solitary cannot know this but the reader can hardly miss it) 'you would not have spoken as slightingly and as maliciously as you did in Book 2 of my marriage, its motives and its meaning'.

The heart of Book Three, however, is the passage dealing with the loss of the Solitary's children and the struggle of the parents to cope: There is a huge tick to the left of the line (half way down the page) and the passage is sidelined to the bottom of the of the *following* page. The emotive force is patent, from the invocation of the 'dark seat of fatal power' to the shared experience of 'longing to pursue' the lost

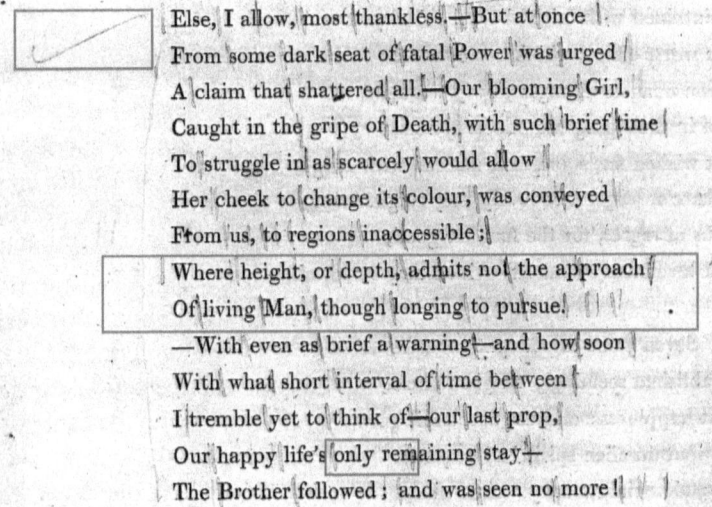

Else, I allow, most thankless.—But at once
From some dark seat of fatal Power was urged
A claim that shattered all.—Our blooming Girl,
Caught in the gripe of Death, with such brief time
To struggle in as scarcely would allow
Her cheek to change its colour, was conveyed
From us, to regions inaccessible ;
Where height, or depth, admits not the approach
Of living Man, though longing to pursue.
—With even as brief a warning—and how soon
With what short interval of time between
I tremble yet to think of—our last prop,
Our happy life's only remaining stay—
The Brother followed ; and was seen no more !

child. Note, more technically, how Thelwall's scoring of the poem indirectly acknowledges Wordsworth's insistence that the ending of line cannot be 'indifferent'; in Thelwall's system a silent beat initiates the next cadence. Note also that each line has a minimum of six cadences, often 8 and occasionally 9 – those above six are usually supplied by rhetorical rests occupying an entire cadence. In 3: 651-2

|Where |height|, ⁊or[1] |depth|, |ad|mits not| the ap|proach|
Of |living |Man|, |though |longing |to pur|sue.|||||

I would construe a rest after 'height', though in this case a stressed 'or' is rhetorically possible. Thelwall devotes a cadence to the first full stop in the second line, with its starkly Eurydicean theme, and four full-bar rests after the (already prolonged) 'pursue'. Wordsworth of course is writing to a theory of composition that pays no heed, mathematically, to pauses required in reading, whereas Thelwall is marking not the abstract shape of the line, but cadences required by 'the passion of the verse'.

Wordsworth's own punctuational breaks, even before Thelwall adds his rhetorical ones, depart provocatively from the rules laid

---

1   I have interpolated a rest, but in this case a stressed 'or' is rhetorically possible.

down by such as Bysshe and Blair. Edward Bysshe insists that a line of pentameter breaks in the middle, whether the poet will this or not; and Hugh Blair is equally insistent that if this break does not occur after the 4th, 5th 6th or in extremis, the 7th syllable, it is not poetry. On these rules, seven of these fourteen lines are not poetry. Brennan O'Donnell produced a remarkable tabulation in his book *The Passion of Metre* (102) showing that even in *An Evening Walk* and *Descriptive Sketches*, Wordsworth has three to four times more pauses after the first or second syllable than Pope, Goldsmith or Coleridge; four times as many after the eight or ninth; and twice as many lines with double pauses. These are conservative estimates: O'Donnell only counts pauses required by the punctuation, so that something like 'Once man entirely free, alone and wild' has only one pause, whereas a likely *realisation* has pauses after the second, sixth and possibly eighth syllables. In the sonnet size chunk quoted above, the breaks required by punctuation occur in the first line (Book 3, line 645) at syllables 1+4+7. The passage has two breaks after two syllables, and three after the 7th plus of course the pronounced pauses at some line endings. In fourteen lines we have one triple break, one double (not counting those with both a medial break and a heavy end stop) and only one repetition of break position from one line to the next. Admittedly, there are no breaks after the 8th syllable, but things are about to get worse: there are three of those on the next page of the poem, and one at the 9th.

'Calm as a frozen lake', the next page begins (Book 3: 659 ff), in an image of irremediable grief, and the page is sidelined from start to finish, with a triple exclamation mark (barely visible in photocopy) against the bitterly controlled lines, 'The eminence on which her spirit stood / Mine was unable to attain'. Taking the whole passage from 645 to 678, Wordsworth's truculent use of breaks in the first, second, eighth and ninth positions is reminiscent of Thelwall's own poetry at its most disruptive rather than his drawing room mode of later years, and—it seems to me—there is an unmistakeable *harmony* arising out of these vigorous combinations. And Thelwall, with his passionate admiration of irregular harmonies in 'our divine Milton' responds generously to such effects in Wordsworth's peripatetic poem.

> Calm as a frozen Lake when ruthless Winds
> Blow fiercely, agitating earth and sky,
> The Mother now remained; as if in her,
> Who, to the lowest region of the soul,
> Had been erewhile unsettled and disturbed,
> This second visitation had no power
> To shake; but only to bind up and seal
> And to establish thankfulness of heart
> In Heaven's determinations, ever just.
> The eminence on which her spirit stood,
> Mine was unable to attain. Immense
> The space that severed us! But, as the sight
> Communicates with heaven's etherial orbs
> Incalculably distant; so, I felt
> That consolation may descend from far;
> (And that is intercourse, and union, too,)
> While, overcome with speechless gratitude,
> And with a holier love inspired, I looked
> On her—at once superior to my woes

In the first superb image of emotional paralysis Thelwall marks the cadences as follows:

Calm as a | frozen | Lake | ⅂ | when | ruthless |Winds

This first line is a perfect iambic pentameter with a reversal (or trochaic substitution) at the start and a full bar rest at the obvious point for a caesura. In lines 669 and 678, interpolating the rests required by Thelwall's bars we arrive at these plausible intensifications:

Mine | ⅂ was un| able || ⅂ to at|tain|.|| ⅂ Im|mense|

   ...

And | Partner | ⅂ of my | loss|.—| O ⅂ | heavy | change!

In line 669 he implies a triple division of the line, with the major pause after the period to collect force for the second syllable of im-mense which forms a cadence in itself. And in line 678 a cadence-length caesura (required by Wordsworth's em-rule) is followed by emphatic poise on 'O' (itself a full cadence, beginning heavy and ending light), 'Heavy' and 'change!'. Even, that is to say, where the marking of cadences appear to convey rather little information, it can signify that in Mr Thelwall's ear, variety of musical effect, if not une-qualled, is indeed—compared to 18th century and indeed early 19th century norms—very, very remarkable.

Such passages perhaps explain why Thelwall generously ruptured the tone of his satirical *Musalogia* to pay tribute to Wordsworth's music as 'of awful aspiration born / That communes with the hidden sense / Of nature's vast magnificence' (Derby MS, 746–7):

> Draws shapes from sounds, & voice from looks,
> And seraph thoughts from murmuring brooks;
> From silent rock & roaring fall
> Extracts a spirit musical,
> Or from the rack, or glowing sky,
> Inhales creative harmony. (MS.

Many further illustrations could be adduced, of how Thelwall's practice attends to the full auditory manifestation of the move-ments of the mind, but I close with a few lines from one of the Wanderer's eloquent harangues; from page 388 of *The Excursion* (the opening of Book 9):

> Wha|te'er| e|xists |hath |properties |that |spread|
> Be|yond it|self, |com|municating |good,
> A |simple |blessing, |or with |evil |mixed ; |
> 4 Spirit that |knows no |insulated |spot. |
> No |chasm, |no |solitude |;| from |link to |link|
> It |circulates, the |Soul of |all the |Worlds. | | |
> 3 |This is the |freedom of the |Universe| ; |

The Wanderer's best speeches are often sidelined in Thelwall's copy, with apparently (though not unambiguously) commendatory crosses and exclamation marks against them, as indeed do the magnificent lines on this page about how 'we live by hope / And by desire ... / And so we live, or else we have no life'. But I include this passage simply for its numbers in the margin. From time to time, as here, there are lines which Thelwall marks as having only three or four cadences. Does he do so because he knows that human nature cannot keep his own iron rule one moment (Steele's iron rule that a line of blank verse *must* have from 6 to 8 cadences); or because he thinks Wordsworth has erred? Is it dawning on him that a system devised primarily for the heroic line of the couplet tradition (with its pre-scribed hemistich balances) has to be relaxed for blank verse? Or is it simply that, as he says in the *Introductory Essay on Poetic Rhythmus*, the tune of a poet of genius will be unique and will create its own rules to which even a practised ear will take time to adjust?

There is reason to think that a man with a 'good ear' for writing blank verse may be trustworthy, too, in the matter of hearing it. Thelwall's auditory interpretation would no doubt strike a modern ear as overly theatrical in many passages, as in that dramatic rising cadence on the second page of the poem:

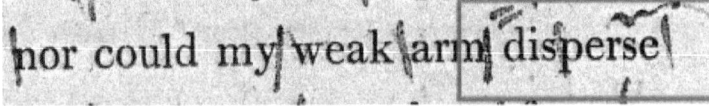

But his exemplary persistence in hearing *The Excursion*—and he does persist, with surprisingly few signs of exasperation, even with clotted syntax and awkward parentheses which seem to have been composed without much consideration for their sayability—suggests that Thelwall concurred with Keats and with Crabb Robinson: *The Excursion* is, whatever we belated readers may suppose, one of the glories of the age.

Felicity James

Writing *Female Biography*: Mary Hays and the life-writing of religious Dissent

One of the suggestions for the 2011 Wordsworth Summer Conference was the reminder that this is the bicentenary year of the publication of *Sense and Sensibility*. It seems particularly appropriate, therefore, to return to some bold, innovative, and experimental writing about the lives of women, by an author who is much less celebrated outside academia than Austen, but who may have helped shape her work: Mary Hays (1759–1843). *Sense and Sensibility* has striking parallels with Hays's exploration of thwarted sympathy, *Memoirs of Emma Courtney* (1796), which similarly takes as its subject female affection, and the ways in which emotional response might be evoked and directed. Hays is best known for this frank, provocative portrait of female desire—Emma Courtney is a woman who, like Austen's Marianne, does not hide her feelings, but who is denied a happy ending. The novel makes a powerful plea for emotional directness, but ends in disappointment and frustration, the more poignant because its details are drawn from Hays's autobiography, and her abortive love affair with William Frend, Coleridge's Cambridge tutor, Dissenter and philosopher. I will look briefly at this novel, but, following its lead, I will also draw some details from Hays's own life, in particular, her remarkable collection of love-letters—which amount to her first extended piece of life-writing. I will then turn to the biographical and autobiographical strategies of her six-volume work of 1803, *Female Biography or, Memoirs of Illustrious and Celebrated Women, of All Ages and Countries*, a largely forgotten work now, but a collection which deserves to be widely known. It is a bold and experimental piece of work—

a landmark publication in women's life-writing. Inventive and lively, it narrates the lives of 288 women, from Abbassa to Zenobia, including subjects as varied as Catherine II of Russia and Catherine Macaulay Graham. Mistresses, novelists, queens, Revolutionaries, Roman matrons, courtesans, intellectuals and Dissenters all take their place in Hays's biography, rubbing up against one another in a fertile cross-period jumble thanks to her alphabetised, non-chronological layout. Alongside the excellent reflections on *The Prelude* offered at the Wordsworth Summer Conference, this essay is an attempt to discuss a range of contemporaneous life-writing experiments: the growth, if you like, of a *woman's* mind.[1]

Mary Hays was born in 1759, in Southwark, to a family of Rational Dissenters, worshippers at a Particular Baptist Chapel. When she narrated her life-story subsequently, the main features of her early life were the death of her father in 1774, and, in the late 1770s, the frustration of her love for another Dissenter, John Eccles, who lived across the street from her—in fact the two could see into one another's windows. Their plans for marriage faced opposition from their families, due to Eccles' limited prospects, and they therefore sustained a long correspondence. Their frequent secret meetings were assisted by a code they had of leaving books against the window, and by messages carried by her younger sister. Permission to marry came too late, since Eccles died in 1780: Hays, distraught, ploughed her energies into her intellectual life. She was mentored by a Dissenting clergyman, Robert Robinson, who introduced her to the intellectual circle around Hackney New College—she began by venturing into theological debate, and then, through this, to the nature of women's rights. A close friend of Mary Wollstonecraft, she herself wrote *Appeal to the Men of Great Britain in Behalf of Women* in 1798, and was widely attacked as a radical Dissenter, controversialist, and advocate of women's rights. 'My pen has been taken up in the cause, and for the benefit of my own sex,' she writes in her introduction to

---

1   This paper is drawn from research undertaken for an essay to be published in *Women's Life Writing, 1700–1850: Gender, Genre, Authorship*, ed. Daniel Cook and Amy Culley (forthcoming, Palgrave: 2012). My thanks to the editors for allowing me to reprint my work here, and for the useful feedback from participants at the Wordsworth Summer Conference 2011.

Female Biography (1803).[1]

Hays begins her exploration of the female 'cause' by taking herself and her own feelings as her first subject. The first sustained piece of life-writing Hays undertook was the binding together of the letters she had exchanged with Eccles, in two morocco-bound volumes which were passed down through the family. These were eventually edited for publication in 1925 by her descendant Anne Wedd, a very common pattern among Dissenting families, who—as in the case of the Aikins or the Scotts—are often keen family memorialists.[2] The letters form a moving account of a late eighteenth-century love affair, filtered through the literature of sensibility and the culture of Rational Dissent. What is still more striking is their organisation and editing into a coherent volume by Hays. Eccles seems to have encouraged the construction of the letters into narrative form, commenting in November 1779 that he has been reading through the correspondence: 'We have now a pretty good collection; sufficient to make two volumes'.[3] The way in which Hays packages and presents these two volumes after Eccles's death shows a very clear awareness of her intended audience and the ways in which her story might be read.

The collection is destined for 'the perusal of my most dear, and intimate Friends, (who have been witnesses to most of the scenes of my unhappy fate)'.[4] Yet despite this sympathetic audience, she feels the need to defend her work. These friends 'may on perusing my letters with the cool, unprejudiced eye of reason, find many expressions exceptionable'; Hays counters this by arguing that she is deliberately contradicting 'the affected prudery, and insincerity which is generally

---

1   Mary Hays, *Female Biography; or, Memoirs of Illustrious and Celebrated Women, of All Ages and Countries*, 6 vols. (London: R. Phillips, 1803), I. iii.
2   Gina Luria Walker, in a feat of detective work, traced the letters to one of Wedd's friends in the 1970s, and the archive was purchased for the Pforzheimer collection; the second volume has disappeared, but Marilyn Brooks has now published the remaining Hays letters in *The Correspondence (1779–1843) of Mary Hays, British Novelist*, ed. Marilyn L. Brooks (Lewiston, Queenston and Lampeter: Edwin Mellen Press, 2004), hereafter Brooks, *Correspondence*. See also Luria Walker, 'Mary Hays's Love Letters', *Keats Shelley Journal* LI (2002): 94–115.
3   Brooks, *Correspondence*, 182.
4   Brooks, *Correspondence*, 34.

instilled into our sex'.[1] These most private of letters have become a public statement of intent about the ways in which female behaviour is formed. Within the collection, we see an awareness of the ways in which Hays's behaviour might be narrated to and observed by others; this is not simply a straightforward exchange between two lovers, but includes letters to third parties, such as Mrs Collier, a widow and friend of Hays, who facilitated her meetings with Eccles and allowed her access to her library. Here she tells Mrs Collier about her engagement, in language derived from the novels of sensibility she had borrowed from her friend and shared with Eccles:

> "What have been my engagements" – you ask my dear Madam. – Sighs – tears – and the extreme of wretchedness! – my fate is now I believe determined! one interview was allowed us! – a parting one! – last night he came. – Good God, what a scene! – he held me in his arms – sobs stopt his voice – he trembled – changed hot and cold alternately – then broke from me – walked about the room, and lifted up his eyes to heaven in a speechless agony! – What could I do? I was softened beyond expression – I endevered to console him – promised never to be the wife of any other – pressed his hand to my heart – my lips to his forehead. – He was insensible – stupefied – tears, heart rending sighs were all the answer he could make – he looked up to me with a countenance in which distress, love and gratitude were strongly painted! – the scene was too much for me – I fell back in my chair and gave vent to a torrent of tears – [2]

The passage throbs with sensibility, in all its breathless dashes, sobs, tears, sighs, trembling. It affords an early glimpse of the techniques Hays would use in her novel writing, since it is an artfully constructed narrative, from the moment of Mrs Collier's direct speech onwards, to ensure readerly participation and sympathy with the plight of the first-person heroine. Hays represents herself as overcome, sinking into a 'torrent of tears'. Yet at the same time, she is a keen observer, alert to the problems involved in *representing* feeling, exposing what

---

1   Brooks, *Correspondence*, 32.
2   Brooks, *Correspondence*, 39–40. Spelling and punctuation from her transcription.

Jerome McGann, commenting on the sensibility of Helen Maria Williams' sonnets, terms 'the necessary emptiness of the verbal response'.[1] Eccles is 'speechless', and 'tears, heart rending sighs were all the answer he could make'; Hays is 'softened beyond expression'. This is familiar from the novels the pair continually reference in their letters—Henry Mackenzie's *Man of Feeling*; Samuel Richardson's *Clarissa*; Frances Brooke's *The History of Emily Montague*—and it is no surprise that the love affair was facilitated by their code of leaving a book against the window, since both frame their stories through the literature of sensibility. Yet this is not to discount Hays's sincerity, but, rather, to point up the ways in which she puts the conventions of sensibility to work on her own life story, thinking about the ways in which an episode might become 'a scene', and how life-writing might overlap with fiction.

This interest in the role of emotion is drawn not simply from the literature of sensibility, but also from the language of religious Dissent. Indeed, Hays's early interest in the importance of emotional response might be set alongside Anna Letitia Barbauld's 1775 essay *Thoughts on the Devotional Taste, and on Sects and Establishments*. This is a plea for the importance of the aesthetic and affective in religious worship, as opposed to what Barbauld sees as dry and disputatious over-intellectualisation. Instead, the central place of 'sentiment and feeling' in devotion is emphasised: devotion is located, Barbauld writes, in 'the imagination and the passions, and it has its source in that relish for the sublime, the vast, and the beautiful, by which we taste the charms of poetry and other compositions that address our finer feelings'.[2] Barbauld is striving to articulate her own feelings in relation to Rational Dissent—although her version of religious devotion would be strongly refuted by Joseph Priestley, who, perhaps feeling his own disputatiousness was being criticised, responded to this passage with offence 'at your comparing devotion to the passion of love'.[3] Both Barbauld and Hays are interested in the ways in which

1   Jerome J. McGann, *The Poetics of Sensibility: a Revolution in Literary Style* (Oxford: Oxford University Press, 1998), 140.

2   William McCarthy and Elizabeth Kraft (eds.), *Anna Letitia Barbauld: Selected Poetry and Prose* (Peterborough, ON: Broadview Press, 2002), 211.

3   See Joseph Priestley, letter to Barbauld, Dec. 20 1775, in *Theological and*

the emotions of the individual might be evoked and directed; they are also positioning themselves as female counter-voices to male traditions of Dissent.

Hays's interest in the workings of emotion should not, therefore, be seen simply as an efflorescence of sensibility, but also as a deep-seated interest in the wider significance of the emotional life of an individual, and the serious importance of 'the imagination and the passions', integral to her identity as a Dissenter. For if Hays casts herself in relation to Eccles as a heroine of sensibility, she also, simultaneously, portrays herself as a woman of Rational Dissent, reasoning, defining, and seeking knowledge, with 'a thousand cases to put to you – I love to hear your definitions – I promise myself improvement as well as pleasure from them'. Eccles will be her 'guardian and adviser', and they will construct a relationship centred around exploration of the truth, a truth which, moreover, rests in sympathetic feeling: 'my thoughts, my heart shall be laid open to you'.[1] Once again, emotional connection—drawn both from sensibility and Dissent—is central to the way in which she constructs her own life-narrative.

Indeed, her facility at creating this sort of connection would later be noted by her mentor, the preacher and opponent of the slave trade Robert Robinson (1735–1790), who responds to Hays's first letter to him detailing some of her religious dilemmas: 'Short as the narration you give of yourself is, it is a miniature portrait of a lady in danger and distress, the work of an exquisite artist calculated to touch the heart'.[2] Robinson would have been well placed to understand Hays's desire to 'touch the heart'. He dated his religious sympathies to hearing George Whitefield preach; he had himself been a Methodist

---

Miscellaneous Works, ed. John Towill Rutt, 15 vols (1831–32), I. i. 280. In thinking through the potential parallels between Barbauld and Hays, we might also recall Lucy Aikin's barbed comment that Barbauld's attraction to her husband was caused by an excess of sensibility under the 'baleful influence' of too much Rousseau, and was 'the illusion of a romantic fancy, not of a tender heart': see William McCarthy, *Anna Letitia Barbauld: Voice of the Enlightenment* (Baltimore: The Johns Hopkins University Press, 2008), 135.

1   Brooks, *Correspondence*, 48.
2   Robert Robinson to Hays, 11 January 1783, quoted by Luria Walker, *The Idea of Being Free: A Mary Hays Reader* (Peterborough, ON: Broadview Editions, 2006), 99.

preacher, and kept a confessional diary, before becoming a Baptist minister.[1] By the end of his life, his religious affiliations were harder to pin down, but his main principle was the hatred of 'dominion over conscience', and he encouraged a questioning, probing approach to religious belief.[2] This made him particularly attractive as a correspondent for Hays, whose Dissent was similarly fluid and difficult to categorise exactly, and in whom he saw 'a wise and virtuous mind ben[t] upon the acquisition of truth'.[3] Robinson was deeply concerned with the education of women. As Joseph Priestley writes in his funeral sermon for Robinson, 'Getting over a vulgar and debasing prejudice (that women, being designed for domestic cares, should be taught nothing beyond them)', Robinson taught his daughters classical and modern languages, and had them 'instructed by others in mathematics and philosophy'.[4] This is reflected in the tone of equality Robinson adopts with Hays, repeatedly urging her towards 'free inquiry', and telling her 'you are not my pupil, but my friend'.[5]

The effect of Robinson's teaching is clear in Hays's subsequent works. After his death, Hays began to participate in a larger circle of Rational Dissenters around Hackney New College, including Priestley, and to publish her own writing. As 'Eusebia' she responded to Gilbert Wakefield's *An Enquiry into the Expediency and Propriety of Public or Social Worship* (1791) with a widely praised pamphlet on the benefits of social worship. Central to her argument here is the power of sympathy, which she sees as the great benefit of public worship: 'a very little acquaintance with human nature, must convince us that our feelings are sympathetic, benevolent affections

---

1   See George Dyer, *Memoirs of the life and writings of Robert Robinson* (London: G. G. and J. Robinson, 1796) for details of his early Methodism and a description of youthful 'diaries and love letters' which, writes the Unitarian Dyer, 'prove Robert to have been a warm enthusiast of the most innocent description' (22). The connections with Hays are reinforced, since Dyer's biography draws upon her correspondence with Robinson.
2   Luria Walker, *The Idea of Being Free*, 111.
3   Luria Walker, *The Idea of Being Free*, 100.
4   Joseph Priestley, *Reflections on Death. A sermon, on occasion of the death of the Rev. Robert Robinson, of Cambridge, delivered at the new meeting in Birmingham, June 13 1790* (Birmingham: 1790), 23.
5   Luria Walker, *The Idea of Being Free*, 100.

are reflected back from all hearts to the mind that cherishes them'.[1]
Hays followed this up with a volume of *Letters and Essays, Moral,
and Miscellaneous*, addressed to a female audience and dealing with
issues of women's behaviour and education. The volume is a way of
writing herself into wider Dissenting debate and a public statement of
identity—but like her private correspondence it returns to the importance of sympathetic connection as a way both of understanding the
lives of others, and of expanding the minds of women. This appeal to
sympathy is realised in terms both of form and style: firstly through
the social circle she creates for the volume itself, which is dedicated
to the Unitarian minister John Disney, and, in the 'Preface', mentions
her 'reverence and esteem' for Mary Wollstonecraft, with whom
Hays had become acquainted in 1792 through George Dyer. This
impression of affectionate collaboration with a larger community is
reinforced by the inclusion of work by Hays's younger sister, and
by Hays's use of quotation and allusion. Commenting on arguments
against female education, for example, she quotes from Priestley's
funeral sermon on Robinson, slightly altering his words:

> With the excellent Dr. Priestley, I repeat "this is a sordid and
> debasing prejudice," of the fallacy of which I have been con-
> vinced both from experience and observation. Numberless
> women have I known, whose studies (incapable of the "epicur-
> ism of reason and religion") have been confined to Mrs. Glasse's
> Art of Cookery... [2]

Through quotation and allusion—the 'epicurism of reason and religion' is borrowed from Lavater, translated by Fuseli[3]—Hays recre-
ates a circle of intellectual Dissent in her work. As in her love-letters,
these Dissenting affiliations are intertwined with her reading of sensibility, and quotations from her favourite novels such as *Clarissa*,
which she says she read 'repeatedly in very early life, and ever found

1   Mary Hays, *Cursory remarks on An enquiry into the expediency and propri-
    ety of public or social worship: inscribed to Gilbert Wakefield, B. A.*, 2nd edition
    (London: T. Knott, 1792), 27.
2   Mary Hays, *Letters and Essays, Moral, and Miscellaneous* (London: T. Knott,
    1793), 27.
3   Johann Casper Lavater, *Aphorisms on Man*, trans. J. H. Fuseli (London:
    Bensley, for J. Johnson, 1789), 125.

my mind more pure, more chastened, more elevated after the perusal of it', because of its capacity to arouse sympathy.[1] Again, Hays is fascinated by the power of texts to create emotional connection, and the uses to which this might be put. As a way of building on and further developing this capacity for sympathy in women readers, she suggests the reading of biographies, from the *Life of Petrarch*, in Susanna Dobson's translation, to Voltaire's *History of Charles XII of Sweden* (1731) and Gilbert Stuart's *The History of Scotland* (1782), because of its portrait 'of the unfortunate Mary, Queen of Scots'. Such works, she says, 'at once excite our sympathy, engage our affections, and awaken our curiosity'—just as Hays herself would do with her own portrait of Mary in *Female Biography*.[2]

This takes on a special aspect in her novel of 1796, *Emma Courtney*, when she incorporates aspects of autobiography. Where *Letters and Essays* shape themselves against older mentors, Robinson and Priestley, *Memoirs of Emma Courtney* is informed by Hays's discussions with William Godwin and the Unitarian mathematician William Frend, on whom the main male characters are based. Godwin, as the philosopher Mr Francis, offers advice to Emma; the frustratingly elusive character Augustus Harley is in part a portrait of Frend, and Hays's own inconclusive affections for him. But both Harley and Francis remain shadowy figures, since the main focus of the novel is the emotional life of Emma herself, a character constantly in search of sympathetic connection, and doomed never to achieve it. This is, above all, the history of an individual, shaped by education and circumstance—a character not of '*ideal perfection*', but of 'a human being', who is 'liable to the mistakes and weaknesses of our fragile nature'.[3] Hays's presentation of Emma's history, moreover, irresistibly recalls Robert Robinson's quest for truth and free inquiry, 'free thinking'. Robinson had taught his children to 'set out on a mathematical principle, that is, Take nothing for granted': Hays, true Dissenting protégée, similarly maintains that 'every prin-

---

1   Hays, *Letters and essays,* 95.
2   Hays, *Letters and essays,* 97.
3   Mary Hays, 'Preface', *The Memoirs of Emma Courtney,* ed. Eleanor Ty (Oxford: Oxford University Press, 1996), 4.

ciple must be doubted, before it will be examined and proved'.[1] In *Memoirs of Emma Courtney*, we see Emma investigating and doubting her own actions—'I interrogated myself again and again'[2]—and realise that this is a double movement, since through Emma's interrogation of her actions Hays examines her own life, critically analysing her own valorisation of sympathy and her reading of sensibility.

Yet this emotional analysis is, for Hays, inseparable from intellectual debate. The novel also responds to and deconstructs the ideas of Godwin, who had succeeded Robinson as mentor. In 'Of History and Romance', Godwin maintains that he would be better employed 'studying one man, than in perusing the abridgment of Universal History in sixty volumes'; similarly, Emma is engaged in the study of the 'human heart', in which the reader is invited to participate.[3] But Hays also uses Emma to counter Godwin's arguments, making the case for the personal affections which Godwin's *Political Justice* might seem to deny—a case which draws its power from the basis of Emma's experience in Hays's own life. Indeed, *Memoirs of Emma Courtney*, as Tilottama Rajan suggests, 'draws upon personal experience as part of its rhetoric', and we should be alert to the complexity of this practice. Rajan reads Hays's novel as 'part of a larger (post)romantic intergenre' of 'autonarration', a self-consciously fictionalised form of life-writing which overlaps with but differs from autobiography, used in varying ways by Rousseau, Wordsworth, Coleridge and Wollstonecraft. Hays's 'autonarration', Rajan argues, is 'a way of putting the finality of the text under erasure, by suggesting that what it "does" or where it ends is limited by its genesis in the life of a conflicted historical subject'.[4] By writing her own expe-

---

1   Luria Walker, *The Idea of Being Free*, 110; Hays, *Emma Courtney*, 3–4.
2   Hays, *Emma Courtney*, 37.
3   William Godwin, 'Essay of History and Romance', in *The Political and Philosophical Writings of William Godwin*, ed. Mark Philp, 7 vols. (London: Pickering and Chatto, 1993), V: *Educational and Literary Writings*, ed. Pamela Clemit, 290–301 (294); Hays, *Emma Courtney*, 102–3.
4   Tilottama Rajan, 'Autonarration and Genotext in Mary Hays' "Memoirs of Emma Courtney"', *Studies in Romanticism*, 32.2 (1993):149–176 (149–50). See also Georgina Green's very interesting re-reading of the subject, 'Fiction and Autobiography in Mary Hays's *Memoirs of Emma Courtney* (1796)', *Literature Compass* 4.3 (2007): 709–720.

riences into the novel, Hays demonstrates that, like Emma, she is a product of 'the irresistible power of circumstances, modifying and controuling our characters'—so, too, she invites us to recognise, are we as readers.[1]

In *Female Biography*, as in other pieces of life-writing such as her obituary of Mary Wollstonecraft, Hays returns to this concept of 'the irresistible power of circumstances', showing the different pressures exerted on women's lives, and different models of female behaviour. It begins with a reminder that this is a piece of writing for the *cause* of women, and that the best way to appeal to women is through the affections, the power of feeling called out through sympathetic biography. While attentive to cultural and historical difference, Hays's narratives suggest that the power of sympathy can work across such boundaries, enabling the reader to appreciate the particular circumstances of the individual, and indeed to break down the 'finality' of history; reading about the circumstances of earlier women might help the sex to advance 'in the grand scale of rational and social existence'. As Miriam L. Wallace suggests, *Female Biography* might be seen 'both as a direct intervention in the formation of female selves through active reading, and as constituting a shared identity across national and historical boundaries through a collective vision of "women"'.[2]

This shared identity is based, firstly, on the creation of sympathy for the individual woman subject in *Female Biography*. In *Letters and Essays*, Hays had praised Gilbert Stuart's *The History of Scotland* (1782), and suggested that its portrait of Mary, Queen of Scots, would 'excite our sympathy, engage our affections', and encourage the involvement of the female reader.[3] In *Female Biography*, Hays creates an opportunity to engage the reader's sympathy for the same subject. Over a long entry—almost three hundred pages at the start of the fifth volume, drawn partly from Stuart, and also from works by William Robertson, John Whitaker and David Hume—Hays vividly

---

1   Hays, *Emma Courtney*, 10.
2   Miriam L. Wallace, 'Writing Lives and Gendering History in Mary Hays's *Female Biography* (1803)', in *Romantic Autobiography in England*, ed. Eugene Stelzig (Farnham: Ashgate, 2010), 63–78 (65).
3   Hays, *Letters and essays*, 97.

characterises the queen through her susceptibility to emotion. Hays portrays Mary yearning for her beloved France, straining for a last glimpse of its shore on the boat to England, and then sympathetically narrates her growing love for Darnley: 'Led captive by her senses and her imagination, the heart of Mary became insensibly enthralled'.[1] A lengthy postscript explains that Hays has 'studiously avoided' any judgement on Mary herself, instead laying out arguments on both sides of the debate, so that the reader is 'left to form his own conclusions on the evidence presented to him': 'cold must be the heart,' she nevertheless concludes, 'that sympathises not with the woes of the lovely and unfortunate Mary'.[2] In *Female Biography*, Hays does not make moral judgements, interested instead, as in *Memoirs of Emma Courtney*, in the emotional trajectory of her characters in their historical contexts, and in evoking the response of the reader.

Like *Memoirs of Emma Courtney, Female Biography* also incorporates autobiographical elements, and the entry for Susanna Perwich (1636-1661) is a fine example of the ways in which we might see Hays's biographical strategies working on several different levels. The entry demonstrates the range both of her subjects—from monarchs to obscure Dissenters—and of her sources. What little we know about Perwich comes from a 1661 work by her brother-in-law John Batchiler, an extended obituary and memorialisation, *The virgins pattern, in the exemplary life and lamented death of Mrs. Susanna Perwich.* This 'exemplary life', which recounts the various talents and virtues of Perwich, is lent special weight by its authorship, so that it becomes both a family memorialisation, commemorating her talents, and recording her death bed testimony, and also a kind of ideal Dissenting life. John Batchiler [sometimes spelt Bachiler or

---

1   Hays, *Female Biography*, V. 22; 55.
2   Hays, *Female Biography*, V. 278; 286. Hays's portrayal of the emotional lives of monarchs would find an echo in Lucy Aikin's popular court histories, *Memoirs of the Court of Queen Elizabeth* (1818), *Memoirs of the Court of James the First* (1822), and *Memoirs of the Court of Charles the First* (1833) which similarly seek to combine the intellectual and the affective. Although Aikin did not approve of Hays, both women draw upon a shared Dissenting tradition; see Michelle Levy, 'The different genius of woman': Lucy Aikin's Historiography', *Religious Dissent and the Aikin-Barbauld Circle, 1740–1860*, ed. Felicity James and Ian Inkster (Cambridge: Cambridge University Press, 2011).

Batchelor] was an ejected clergyman, commemorated in Edmund Calamy's *Nonconformist Memorial*; prior to 1660, he had been both a parliamentary chaplain, and one of the twelve licensers of works of divinity, known for his progressive and tolerant views. In his imprimatur to John Goodwin's *Twelve Considerable Cautions* (1646) he explains these views, suggesting that his role in 'this discussing and Truth-searching age' is to 'suffer fair-playe on all sides' and to uphold liberty through a permissive attitude to the press. Recent criticism has seen him as occupying an important place in public discussion, emphasising, 'the pacific and conciliatory tendency of civilised, open debate'.[1]

After being ejected from the church, Batchiler worked at the school run in the house of his father-in-law, Robert Perwich, in Hackney; Susanna Perwich, a pupil at the school, must have been his sister-in-law. The 'life' of Perwich also functions as an advertisement for this school. Indeed, it is a defence of such education for women in general, 'there having been alwayes some as virtuous and religious young Gentlewomen brought up there, as in any Private Family whatsoever'.[2] This is supported by the way in which Batchiler describes Perwich's academic and artistic accomplishments as running alongside her domestic prowess, and connecting with her religious devotion. His biography revels in her exceptional intellectual achievements—she was reading at a very young age, and was a particularly talented viola player, who at the age of fourteen outshone all other pupils at the school. Yet she is also skilled in '*curious* Works at the *needle*', and an excellent dancer, housewife and cook.[3]

However, for Batchiler, the most important strand of Perwich's biography is her religious devotion, developed following a disappointment in love:

> About *four* years since, being *disappointed* in the enjoyment of her desires in a *Match* then propounded to her, by the *sudden*

---

1   Randy Robertson, *Censorship and Conflict in Seventeenth-century England: The Subtle Art of Division* (Pennsylvania: Penn State Press, 2009), 107.

2   John Batchiler, *The Virgins Pattern: in the exemplary life, and lamented death of Mrs. Susanna Perwich, daughter of Mr. Robert Perwich* (London: 1661), 'Dedicatory Epistle'.

3   Batchiler, *Virgins Pattern*, 7.

death of the party that had *gained* her affection, she *wisely* considered with herself, what the *meaning* of this so *sad* a providence should be; and at last, after many *Prayers* and *tears* to
God, that he would bless this *unexpected* stroke to her, and some
way make her a *gainer* by it, her heart began to be *much broken*
and *melted* towards God, not so much for this temporal loss
(which she often said might have proved a *snare* to her) as at the
sight and *sense* of *sin* ...[1]

Batchiler goes on to narrate approvingly how Perwich's new found
religious sense came to dominate her life, as she read and meditated
incessantly, praying and using key Dissenting texts, amongst them
Richard Baxter, and the Puritan ministers William Spurstowe and
Francis Roberts. Perwich eventually turns away from her music and
dancing, the better to achieve religious insight, and dies in a state of
grace.

   We can immediately see why Hays might have been attracted to
her—here is an earlier talented woman, with strong religious affiliations, similarly finding a new vocation for herself after the death of
a lover. The text comes with an impeccable Dissenting lineage, since
Batchiler followed the same ideals of truth-seeking and open debate
to which Hays would subscribe over one hundred years later; indeed,
Perwich herself is characterised as seeking '*satisfaction* by putting
questions'.[2] Hays follows Batchiler's text very closely; it probably
came to her through the Dissenting circles of Hackney, who held the
ejected ministers of the 1660s in high esteem. Edmund Calamy's
Nonconformist Memorial was something of a cult text amongst
them, to which they often turned at times of persecution. Theophilus
Lindsey, for instance, when he seceded from the Anglican church
in 1774 to found Essex Street Chapel, the first avowedly Unitarian
chapel, repeatedly records reading Calamy's biographies to sustain
him in the attempt; Hays worshipped at Essex Street, and Lindsey
writes in support of her volume of *Letters and Essays*. The inclusion
of Susanna Perwich in *Female Biography* continues a larger tradition which kept the early history of Dissenting characters and Puritan

---

1   Batchiler, *Virgins Pattern*, 9.
2   Batchiler, *Virgins Pattern*, 20.

conscience alive even in the later eighteenth century.[1] Looking back to Batchiler's text is therefore an act of Dissenting identity, paying homage both to author and subject, and writing them into a new context. Hays is often read as embattled Revolutionary, and her work placed in the context of the 1790s: her revival of Batchiler's pamphlet and presentation of his work alongside the biographies of women such as Mme. Roland allows us to see her radicalism as belonging to a larger tradition that was inflected by persistent anxieties over toleration.

Yet on the other hand, Hays presents a version of Perwich's story which is filtered through autobiography and feminist consciousness, and which can be sharply critical of Batchiler's narrative. A good example of her rewriting comes in her description of Perwich's thwarted love story:

> She suffered an early disappointment in her affections, from the death of a young man to whom she was tenderly attached, and to whom she was about to have been united. This misfortune seized on her spirits, while grief and sensibility prepared her mind for the reception of ardent devotional impressions. Her education and habits had been pious, and her heart, disappointed in its object, yielded itself to that sublime and flattering enthusiasm so congenial to fervent and susceptible tempers.[2]

The overlaps with Hays's own situation are irresistible, the more so because she increases the drama in Batchiler's narrative; he has 'a match propounded to her', Hays has 'to whom she was about to have been united', inviting comparison with the tragedy of Eccles' death. Just as in *Emma Courtney*, Hays presents an alternative narrative for her own life, and explores different approaches to grief. Whereas Batchiler had presented Perwich's withdrawal into religion as a manifestation of her grace, and Perwich herself as an exemplary pattern, in Hays's account, this becomes a story of female talent lost. Perwich

---

1   See John Seed's excellent discussion *Dissenting Histories: Religious Division and the Politics of Memory in Eighteenth-century England* (Edinburgh: Edinburgh University Press, 2008) for a detailed analysis of Calamy, and of Dissenting historiography more broadly.
2   Hays, *Female Biography*, VI. 52.

is shown 'neglecting those elegant and liberal pursuits' of music and dancing, as her religion becomes dangerously imbued with 'the fanatic character of the times'; her enthusiastic embrace of 'calvinistic notions' meant that 'she tortured her pure and innocent mind with fancied sins, doubts, and omissions'.[1]

Like Batchiler, Hays details the books Perwich read, but the reading here takes on a dangerously obsessive character, performed 'with the greatest avidity'.[2] This emphasis on 'avidity' connected to the perusing of books is a key theme in *Emma Courtney*: in the aftermath of Mr. Melmoth's death, for instance, Emma, shut off from 'my wonted amusements', turns to reading: 'my avidity for books daily increased' and she 'devoured [...] ten to fourteen novels in a week'. When a fellow schoolmate procures her romances and adventurous tales, she peruses them 'with inconceivable avidity'.[3] The repetition of the word shows that Susanna Perwich is being cast in an Emma-mould: her 'grief and sensibility' paving the way for an avid, enthusiastic, ultimately misguided receptivity to literature. Hays paints a tragic portrait of her growing fanaticism: 'all the energy of her character was directed against her own happiness'.[4] The biography becomes a condemnation of a 'morose and cruel system' of religion, which deforms female character, and a subversion of the 'exemplary life' of Batchiler's title: the saintly woman of an earlier age is revealed as cramped, repressed, and fatally thwarted.[5]

The Perwich biography is also an act of 'autonarration': a version of Hays's own life narrative, and a vindication of her personal life choices. It is a justification of her own version of Rational Dissent: a religion which relies not on '*religious cant*', as she explains to her niece, but on 'your understanding and your heart – the offspring of love, not of fear'.[6] This approach has its roots in Robinson's rejection of 'dominion over conscience', and shows Hays urging a progressive, late eighteenth-century version of Dissent which, even as it pays

---

1   Hays, *Female Biography*, VI. 53.
2   Hays, *Female Biography*, VI. 53.
3   Hays, *Emma Courtney*, 18; 20.
4   Hays, *Female Biography*, VI. 54.
5   Hays, *Female Biography*, VI. 54.
6   Luria Walker, *The Idea of Being Free*, 309.

homage to its forebears, critiques them. She brings to this a feminist consciousness, keenly alert to the ways in which women's emotional lives might be circumscribed, and their very life-narratives shaped by history. She performs an act of sympathetic recovery on Perwich, rejecting her pious solitude and instead, retrospectively placing her in a larger community of talented women. The biography functions as a vindication, too, of Hays's own move into the public sphere following the death of Eccles: Perwich had denied her talents, but Hays is determined to develop hers. Indeed, Hays's will expresses 'the humble hope that I may not have lived wholly in vain, or 'folded in a napkin' the talent entrusted to me'.[1] *Female Biography*, as a whole, is the expression of that talent, and the manifesto for other women's freedom to express theirs, too.

The afterlives of *Female Biography* are numerous, if not yet fully understood. We might note that a copy was in the library of Jane Austen's sister-in-law at Godmersham.[2] Might Austen herself, with her attention to the pressure of circumstance on the lives of women, and her detailed analysis of emotional connection, have been a sympathetic reader? Certainly, *Female Biography* might have been the perfect offering for Catherine Morland, yawning over history which presents merely 'the quarrels of popes and kings, with wars or pestilences, in every page; the men all so good for nothing, and hardly any women at all'.[3] And, returning to the idea with which I began, *Sense and Sensibility* shows a similar interest in the nature and responses of female desire, and the ways in which women's lives might be shaped and described.

Female Biography also reaches into the Victorian era: to take one example, it was read by Elizabeth Gaskell, whom Hays knew, and to whom she gave a letter by Mary Wollstonecraft. Gaskell notes on the letter, now in the Pforzheimer collection, 'this letter written by Mrs.

---

1   Luria Walker, *The Idea of Being Free*, 309.

2   See Luria Walker, 'Pride, Prejudice, Patriarchy: Jane Austen reads Mary Hays', Fellows' Lecture, Chawton House Library 2010 [accessed 14/01/2011]. <http://www.soton.ac.uk/scecs/newsandevents/2010/11_03_walker.shtml>

3   Jane Austen, *Northanger Abbey; Lady Susan; The Watsons; Sanditon*, ed. James Kinsley, John Davie, Claudia L. Johnson (Oxford: Oxford University Press, 2003), 79.

Wolstonecraft authoress of the Rights of Woman and addressed to Miss Hays authoress of The Lives of Illustrious Women was given me by Miss Hays'.[1] Even though the title of *Female Biography* is misquoted, Hays is remembered primarily as biographer. When Gaskell writes her sympathetic *Life of Charlotte Brontë* (1857), which draws both on Gaskell's own affection and friendship, and on Brontë's own correspondence, repeated verbatim in the biography, is she reflecting the immediacy and boldness of Hays' biographical and autobiographical practice?

The full story of Hays's influence is yet to be told, but she deserves an important place in a study of life-writing in the period. Using different genres—love-letters, novels, essays and obituaries, as well as more traditional forms of biography—Hays self-consciously investigated the ways in which female lives, including her own, could be written. Her work, which cuts across genres and brings public and private together in startling ways, and which challenges the boundaries between autobiography, fiction, and history, expands our sense of what constitutes life-writing in the period. I hope we might come to set it alongside the work of more canonical Romantic and Victorian authors and open up more discussion on the capacious genre of life-writing.

---

1   Luria Walker, *Growth of a Woman's Mind*, 248.

Wordsworth from Humanities-Ebooks

The Cornell Wordsworth: a Supplement, edited by Jared Curtis ††

The Fenwick Notes of William Wordsworth, edited by Jared Curtis, revised and corrected †

The Poems of William Wordsworth: Collected Reading Texts from the Cornell Wordsworth, edited by Jared Curtis, *3 volumes* †

The Prose Works of William Wordsworth, Volume 1, edited by W. J. B. Owen and Jane Worthington Smyser †

Wordsworth's Convention of Cintra, a Bicentennial Critical Edition, as edited by W. J. B Owen, with essays by Simon Bainbridge, David Bromwich, Richard Gravil, Timothy Michael, Patrick Vincent †

Wordsworth's Political Writings, edited by W. J. B. Owen and Jane Worthington Smyser. †

Other Literary Titles

John Beer, *Coleridge the Visionary*

John Beer, *Blake's Humanism*

Richard Gravil, *Wordsworth and Helen Maria Williams; or, the Perils of Sensibility* †

Richard Gravil and Molly Lefebure, eds, *The Coleridge Connection: Essays for Thomas McFarland*

Simon Hull, ed., *The British Periodical Text, 1796–1832*

W. J. B. Owen, *Understanding The Prelude*

Pamela Perkins, ed., *Francis Jeffrey: Unpublished Tours.*†

Keith Sagar, *D. H. Lawrence: Poet* †

Laura Vivanco, *For Love and Money: the Literary Art of the Harlequin Mills & Boon Romance*

Irene Wiltshire, ed. *Collected Letters of Elizabeth Gaskell's Daughters* [in preparation]

† Also available in paperback, †† in hardback
http://www.humanities-ebooks.co.uk
all available to libraries from MyiLibrary.com, EBSCO and Ebrary